Str8 B8

K.C. WELLS

This is a work of fiction. Names, characters, places, and incidents either are the product of the author's imagination or are used fictitiously, and any resemblance to actual persons, living or dead, business establishments, events, or locales is entirely coincidental.

Str8 B8
Copyright © 2023 by K.C. Wells
Photo: Wander Aguiar
Model: Travis S
Cover Art by Meredith Russell
Edited by Sue Laybourn
ISBN: 978-1-915861-71-9

Warning
This book contains material that is intended for a mature, adult audience. It contains graphic language, explicit sexual content, and adult situations.

CHAPTER ONE

May

It didn't matter how many times Tom Ryder went through his accounts—the situation did not improve with each new viewing. If anything, the queasiness intensified, and he came out in a cold sweat.

Going under seemed like more and more of a certainty rather than a possibility.

He wasn't the kind of man to complain that life wasn't fair, but damn it, right then life *wasn't* fair. It wasn't as if he was one of those fly-by-night cowboys, the ones who showed up, looked at a job, sucked air through their teeth, then gave an eye-watering quote that would require the sacrifice of someone's firstborn to pay for it. And *then* they did a half-arsed job that often required fixing, usually by someone like Tom, because the original cowboy had long gone.

Probably sunning his fat arse on a beach in Spain.

Tom was good at what he did. Once he'd gotten his qualifications, it had taken him ten years to build his business up to the point where he was happy with it. Ten years of getting the word out, customer referrals, business cards pinned to noticeboards in supermarkets, cafés, libraries... Hell, he'd even tried flyers shoved through letterboxes, although in hindsight that might have worked better if he'd paid someone to do it, rather than doing it all on his laptop and printer. Technology had never been his strong point, but along the way he'd acquired new skills, priced his services ethically...

In the end, none of that mattered, not when the competition waded in with their vans—plural—emblazoned with bright lettering, their adverts on the huge digital screen facing the most popular supermarket, where *everyone* could see it, their uniforms with the business name and logo stitched across their backs…

The present situation had begun as a trickle. A year ago, a new building firm set up shop a stone's throw from him in Ewell. They were slick, they had a team of workmen, and it seemed every time Tom went to give someone a quote for a job, a few days later there'd be an apologetic call. *'Sorry, but we've decided to go with someone else.'*

Yeah, it didn't take a genius to work out who that someone was, not when Tom drove past their house in his solitary white van, and spied two vans from the competition, parked outside.

Bastards.

Tom didn't get calls complaining about his results, not when he ensured his work was of a consistently high standard. Word-of-mouth, positive referrals… these were *gold*. Except that gold seemed to have been mined out.

So much for customer loyalty.

And then another firm had started business in Epsom, even bigger than the one currently digging the ground out from under him.

More fucking bastards.

He'd tried spreading his net wider, but that achieved little in the way of results. New businesses seemed to be springing up like weeds, which did little to ease his concerns.

Tom was never one to give in, but fighting to keep his head above water grew so fucking *tiring*. Things had got so bad, work became as scarce as rocking horse droppings, as his granddad was fond of saying, much to his grandma's chagrin.

Yeah, it was official. Tom Ryder was pissed off, worn out, and about to go down for the count.

He knew that was probably the reason for the most recent invite to dinner with his ex, Deb, and her partner Sharon.

on each plate. Deb dealt with the garlic bread that filled the tiny room with its glorious aroma. They moved around each other, navigating the small space with practiced accuracy.

They were such a contrast: Deb was almost as tall as him, with long brown hair and hazel eyes hidden behind gold-rimmed glasses, while Sharon was shorter, with more curves, her tousled blonde hair perpetually trying to get into her eyes.

Deb glanced at him. "What are you staring at?"

"I'm imagining you with a bump." It wasn't true, but better than saying *I'm enjoying seeing you so happy*. Not that he and Deb had been miserable as a couple, but marriage had put a strain on what had been a marvellous friendship, something neither of them had anticipated. When it became clear—to both of them—that things had been much better before they'd put a ring on it, they decided to ditch the rings and go back to being friends.

Best decision ever. Tom had got his best friend back, and Deb had found her soul mate.

Her face glowed. "I was in H&M last week. So many cool things to wear. I didn't buy anything though. That felt as though I'd be tempting fate." She carried the dish of garlic bread into the dining room, Sharon following with two plates.

Tom had been on tenterhooks ever since she'd finished the second cycle of IVF, waiting for the call to tell him he was going to be a… whatever. It had to be the oddest relationship, but Deb and Sharon had become part of his life, and it stood to reason their child would be part of it too.

The conversation lapsed for about ten minutes while they ate, Tom and Sharon both making appreciative noises. His hunger assuaged, Tom helped himself to more wine. The knot of tension curling and writhing in his belly as he'd walked from the station had slowly dissipated, and a calm stole over him, a comforting warmth fuelled by good food, good wine, and even better company.

"I thought of you last week," he admitted to Deb.

She tilted her head in that quirky, bird-like way he'd loved since they were teenagers. "Good thought or bad thought?"

"Good. They were showing *Lord of the Rings* on TV."

Deb laughed. "Which one?"

"*The Two Towers*."

She grimaced. "That one was so much darker."

Tom couldn't resist. "Maybe, but that didn't stop you from being glued to the screen every time Éowyn was on it." He grinned. "Maybe that should've been a clue. We were both lusting after the same woman."

Sharon stared at Deb. "Oh, *now* I get it. That explains why every time I suggest putting on a film, it ends up being *Lord of the Rings*."

"I was *not* lusting after Éowyn," Deb protested. Tom didn't break eye contact, and she heaved a sigh. "I was more into Arwen."

He burst out laughing, and pretty soon Deb joined him.

Sharon shook her head. "I know I've said it before, but anyone seeing you two together must ask themselves why the hell you got divorced." Her eyes twinkled. "Not that I'm complaining, you understand. Tom's loss was definitely my gain."

"We always got along," Deb confessed. "We were best friends all through the latter end of secondary school. It was getting married that really screwed things up."

"Yeah. We were much better as friends," Tom admitted. "At least we didn't screw things up completely by having kids. I think that would've made things worse." He gazed at them warmly. "You two will make great parents." He placed his hand over his heart with a dramatic sigh. "Not that I'm offended you didn't ask me to donate my sperm. I'm sure Gavin's is just as good." He grinned. "Maybe."

Deb chuckled. "It's better this way. Gavin's the closest we can get to Sharon—I mean, they must share a *few* genes, right, being twins?" She stroked her chin. "Although…"

Sharon's eyes flashed. "Do *not* say that again."

Deb blinked, the picture of innocence, except Tom knew better. "Say what?"

Sharon narrowed her gaze. "You *know* what."

Tom looked from Sharon to Deb, then back to Sharon again. "What am I missing here?"

"Deb thinks our future offspring will end up somewhere on the LGBTQ+ spectrum, having a gay father."

Deb nodded. "Trust me, one day they'll prove there's a gay gene." She glanced at Tom. "Want to tell us why you were such a grump the other day when Shaz called? What was getting you down?"

It was on the tip of his tongue to tell her Sharon had imagined it, that everything in the garden was rosy, but then he reconsidered.

Deb saw through him like no one else did.

He went with a shrug. "Same thing that always gets me down." He drank a little more wine. "This is really good."

"Tom."

The entreaty in her voice made his chest tighten. "I don't want to talk about it, okay?"

Her face fell. "Is the money situation really that bad?"

Another shrug. "It's been better." He wasn't about to tell them how close to the wire things had gotten lately. All it took was a couple of customers taking their time paying him, and a few jobs falling through—well, more than a few—and suddenly Tom was contemplating eating nothing but beans on toast for a while.

Like a year.

"We're struggling too," Sharon said in a low voice.

"Shaz!" Deb glared at her.

"Well, we *are*," Sharon fired back with wide eyes.

"What's going on?" Tom didn't want to think of them in dire straits.

"Work's cut my hours—again. And Deb's tried God

knows *how* many times for that promotion, and her arsehole of a boss always says the same thing: 'Not if you're going to go off on maternity leave, then come crying to me when you need time off because you can't get a child minder, the brat is sick, or any of the hundred other excuses I'm sure you'll come out with,'" she mimicked in a high, squeaky voice.

Tom gazed at Deb in horror. "Okay, two things. One— why haven't you ever told me this?"

"Probably for the same reason you don't let on about how bad business really is—I don't want to worry you." She frowned. "What's the second thing?"

"What he's doing is downright illegal, so either sue the arse off him, or quit and get a better job." It made Tom's blood boil when he thought of Deb having to suffer working under—yeah, Sharon had nailed it—an arsehole.

"I've no proof he's said any of that." Deb's voice sounded strained. "It would be his word against mine. And getting another job right now is a bit risky. Not when it costs almost five grand for IVF."

Sharon got up and stood behind Deb's chair, her hands on Deb's shoulders, rubbing them with a gentle motion. "But we won't *need* any more money for IVF because it's going to work this time. Never mind about third time lucky—round two is going to deliver the goods." She kissed the top of Deb's head. "Right?"

Deb took Sharon's hand and brought it to her lips, kissing her fingers. "That's my Shaz. Talk it into existence."

Thank God they found each other. Sharon was Deb's rock, the fortress she retreated to when the world gave her shit.

Tom needed a rock of his own right then.

He cleared the dishes from the table. "Want me to do the washing up?"

"No," Deb told him emphatically. "That's what the dishwasher is for. You know, the one you magically found space for in our minuscule kitchen? You don't have to stay, not if you're up early tomorrow." Another bird-like tilt. "Have you got a job on at the moment?"

"No. Going to make some calls in the morning. I might get lucky."

In the meantime, he was going to avoid stepping on the cracks in the pavement, going anywhere near a mirror—for fear of breaking one—putting shoes on the table, walking under ladders, and if a black cat showed even a sign of wanting to cross his path, he'd coax it with kitty treats to make sure it never wanted to leave him.

I need all the good luck I can get.

The chances of coming across a four-leafed clover on the way home were pretty slim, however.

Tom's phone vibrated in the back pocket of his jeans, and he removed it to peer at the screen.

"Is it work?" Sharon demanded. "Buckingham Palace needs renovating, and they say you're the right man for the job?"

He laughed. "No such luck. Andy wants to meet me for a pint and a game of darts." He frowned as he read the text. "I'm not going to the Stranglers though."

"The what? I don't know of any pub called that," Sharon remarked.

"That isn't its real name. The couple who used to own it? Someone strangled the husband in the pub. The police questioned the wife at the time." His thumbs flew over the screen. "It's got a decent enough dartboard, but there's one outside in the beer garden at the Barley Mow. Much better. Got a good vibe too."

Deb snorted. "As long as you know you'll be the one who pays for the pints. Andy hasn't changed. He was mean when we were in high school. I swear he keeps a padlock on his wallet."

"I haven't seen him for a while. And one pint won't hurt." One pint was probably all he could afford at today's pub prices. Anyone thinking of buying a pint needed to take out a second mortgage.

Okay, so it wasn't *that* bad, but bad enough that he'd stopped drinking in his local boozer.

"I remember how you and Andy used to spend most of Friday night at the pub." Deb regarded him with obvious concern. "Don't stay until last orders, okay? Besides, you've got a train to catch."

"I won't stay that long. And even if I did, it's not as if I have to be up early to go to work in the morning, is it?" Tom did his best not to let even a hint of bitterness creep into his voice. He said good night to them and hugged them. "Thanks for dinner. The company was pretty good too. Call me as soon as… what happens anyway when you do a pregnancy test? Is it a blue line for a boy, pink line for a girl?"

Deb laughed. "Neither. One line means I'm not pregnant, and two lines is—"

"Break out the non-alcoholic champagne," he concluded.

They walked him to the door and stood there waving at him as he headed back toward the main road.

He hoped round two would deliver the goods. They needed some good news right then.

I could do with some too.

CHAPTER TWO

The Barley Mow wasn't all that far from Deb's place, and it was a pleasant evening for a stroll. Getting home was a matter of one stop by train from Epsom to Ewell, and the night was still young.

He wasn't planning on downing several pints with Andy, however. Deb had nailed it—Andy kept a tight hold on his money—and Tom couldn't afford to spend cash he didn't have on alcohol that would probably make him feel worse.

Except he'd passed Worse as soon as he reached the end of Adelphi Road and was now well on his way to The Pit of Despair.

Dinner with Deb and Sharon had been wonderful as ever. It was only the change of direction in their conversation that had spoiled his enjoyment. He didn't want to think about work. It was far too depressing.

And it was too late for that. A familiar queasiness stole over him, the same queasiness that swelled into existence every time thoughts of his dire financial situation surged into his head and swamped everything else.

Call him. Tell him you've changed your mind. Tell him you'll meet him another time.

Andy would understand. Andy was in the same boat, after all.

Tom was beginning to feel everyone he knew was sinking into quicksand, dragged down by the clutching claws of debt and worry that curled around the ankles, digging their talons into flesh, determined to pull their victim under.

Maybe going for a drink with Andy in his present frame of mind was not conducive to a pleasant evening. But Andy was usually good for a laugh, and God knew Tom needed that at the moment, even if lately Andy's repertoire was limited to sending amusing reels and memes.

That was okay by Tom. If fact, it was a definite improvement. Andy's taste in jokes veered into dangerous territory at times, and the last thing Tom wanted was for one of the pub's clients to overhear Andy's latest humorous—and undoubtedly inflammatory—offering, and take exception to it.

It wouldn't be the first time.

As he drew closer to the pub, he decided to push aside all maudlin thoughts, pull himself together, paste on a smile, and fake it until it was time to go home.

Tom could manage that much.

The wooden tables outside the pub were all occupied, the pub's patrons sitting beneath red parasols, chatting loudly, while from inside came the sound of live music.

Great. I won't be able to hear myself think.

He pushed open the door and the noise level rose instantly. The bar resonated to the sound of the band taking up the far end of the space. There was a drum kit, a couple of guitars, a keyboard, and a bald middle-aged guy wailing into a mic.

Okay, that was unfair. The guy could sing, thank goodness. And the songs were pretty decent too. A lot of people stood around listening, some of them joining in. More congregated at the bar, their voices loud as they struggled to be heard above the music. Every table was occupied, every inch of space filled.

Conversation was *not* going to be an option.

Andy raised his hand as Tom neared the wood-panelled bar. "Over here, mate. I've got you a pint," he yelled above the strains of 'Wonderwall'.

Tom eased his way through the crowd of drinkers to where Andy stood at the end of the bar. Sure enough, a pint of pale amber liquid awaited him.

"I may faint, except there isn't room for that in here," he hollered.

Andy's brow furrowed. "What does that mean?"

He grinned. "You bought a round."

"Bastard." Andy gave him two fingers. "Wanna go outside? Can't think straight with all that racket going on."

The woman standing next to him jerked her head in his direction and glared. "My husband happens to be the lead singer." She pushed the words through gritted teeth.

Tom sized up the situation and did the first thing he could think of. He grabbed Andy's arm and gave her an apologetic glance. "Some people just have no taste in music, do they?" he said to her as he propelled Andy toward the rear of the pub where it opened out onto the beer garden.

Once they were outside, Andy stared at him open-mouthed. "What was that all about?"

"My good deed for the day. I was getting you out of there before someone decided to rearrange your face with their fist."

He snorted. "I'm not scared of *her*."

"No? Then how about the huge guy to her left who was pushing back his sleeves? The one with hands like shovels?"

Andy swallowed. "Good call, mate." He scanned the garden, then pointed to a table all the way at the rear. "That'll do."

"I thought we were playing darts." The two guys at the board had just finished their game.

"That was a ruse to get you here," Andy said as he strode over the stone flags to their table. Most of the other tables were occupied, and he waved to a couple of people as he and Tom wove their way through.

Tom sat with his back to the dark, brown-stained fence, looking toward the rear of the pub. The band's rendition of a James Taylor number was muted, but still audible.

He took a long drink from his glass before speaking. "If

you need a loan, forget it. I'm skint."

Andy gave him a knowing nod. "That's exactly why I asked you to meet me."

"Ah, so it was a pity pint? Fair enough. That tastes just as good as the normal variety."

Andy leaned forward in a conspiratorial manner. "How would you," he began in a whisper, "like to earn seven hundred and fifty quid?"

Tom blinked. "Doing what?" Andy glanced around in a furtive manner, and Tom had to laugh. "For God's sake, you're acting like some secret agent."

"I'm being careful, that's all. This isn't something you'd want getting out, if you know what I mean."

"No, I *don't* know what you mean because you haven't actually told me anything, but I wish you'd just come right out with it." The touch of exasperation in his voice made Tom take a deep breath and force himself to be calm. "Okay. Seven hundred and fifty quid for doing what, exactly?"

Andy leaned even closer. "Porn."

What the fuck?

Tom widened his eyes. "Seriously?"

Andy gave another slow nod. "Yeah, I'm being serious. There's a guy I know. He's just setting up a new 'adult studio'." He hooked his fingers in the air. "They're not even online yet. He wants to build up a stack of videos before he launches the site."

"What makes you think I'd be remotely interested in doing porn?"

Andy glared. "Keep your voice down, mate. *You* might think we're living in more liberal times, but that ain't the case. There are some really weird people around at the moment."

Tom forced himself not to smirk. "You don't say."

"And you'll fucking *love* the name of the site."

"I dread to think."

Andy grinned. "*Hard Hats.*"

wouldn't it?"

Andy had him there, and he fucking *knew* it, the little shit.

Tom downed the rest of his pint. "Thanks for the drink." He stood.

"You're not going?"

"Why would I stay? To buy drinks I can't afford? You keep telling me how much I need the money. So I'm going home to consider the proposal—if that's okay with you." He wasn't, of course, but he had no desire to continue the conversation.

Of all the hare-brained ideas Andy had come out with over the years, this one took the cake.

Andy stood too. "All bullshit aside, I really *was* trying to help you. And I'm not sharing this with just anyone, okay? You're the only one."

Tom's annoyance abated. "I get it. Thanks. I won't deny the money would come in handy, but I'm not sure I'm so deep in shit that I'd consider fucking on camera to help me climb out of it."

"All I'm saying is… you've got the…er… tools, and you've got the talent."

Tom glared at him. "You're talking about my dick again, aren't you? Give it a rest, for Christ's sake."

Andy flushed. "What—you never heard of penis envy? When I was sixteen, all I wanted for Christmas was *your* cock." He froze. "Wait—that didn't come out right—what I meant was—"

Tom chuckled. "Stop digging that hole, Andy. See you around."

Before Andy could get another word out, Tom walked with a brisk stride to the side gate that led onto the street. He hurried along the street, calculating if he could make the next train to Ewell.

And definitely *not* thinking about doing porn.

Except thinking about porn was a vast improvement on thinking about money—or the lack of it—so maybe it wasn't such a bad alternative after all.

Tom came out of the kitchen, carrying a mug of decaf tea. He placed it on the coffee table, then flopped into his armchair. Beyond the patio door, the sky showed dark between the white strips of the blinds, the hum of traffic a constant soundtrack. He picked up the TV remote and hit the standby button. There was nothing on worth watching anyway. He'd taken a look at Netflix but nothing appealed to him there either. Besides, he was considering cancelling his subscription. He wasn't paying out much, but as Tesco was fond of proclaiming in every advert they ran, *Every Little Helps.*

An early night was on the cards. He could lie in bed and try not to think about... well, everything.

His gaze alighted on his laptop on the couch.

I wonder.

It wouldn't do any harm to take a look, right?

A wank before bed would also help him sleep.

Tom grabbed the laptop, opened it, and switched it on. He pulled up a search engine and typed in *Hard Hats.* Andy hadn't lied about that, then—the site didn't exist.

Yet.

On impulse, he opened Porn Hub, and typed in Construction. What he got was a screen full of videos. He clicked on the first one. A construction worker was shagging the young woman who was employing him to lay her patio—and her too, by the look of it.

God, the acting is really shit.

Tom laughed out loud. "Since when did anyone nominate porn stars for acting awards?"

He clicked on another. A guy up a ladder fixing a light was approached by a young woman who unzipped him and sucked him off.

Has no one ever heard of Health & Safety?

In yet another, a horny housewife was gangbanged by four guys in orange reflective jackets and hard hats. Judging by the cries pouring from her, she was enjoying every second of it. Come to think of it, the guys were having a good time as well, passing her around and getting into all kinds of positions.

There were *tons* of similar videos.

So why create another site?

Stupid question. Of *course* the world needed more porn.

There was no end to the situations those well-endowed construction workers found themselves in, and Tom found himself automatically sizing up the competition. He could compete with any one of those guys in terms of equipment and body shape—except for the guys whose muscles had muscles. They had to *live* in a gym, for God's sake.

He watched one video to its conclusion, then another, and another. When he'd seen enough, he shut the laptop down and drank his—by now—lukewarm tea. Maybe the lack of caffeine was scrambling his brain cells, because he couldn't believe he was even *contemplating* acting on Andy's proposal.

What if I go to someone's house, and they look at me and say 'Wait—haven't I seen you in a porno?'

He wouldn't know where to look.

Are things really that bad?

That had to rate as the stupidest fucking question of the century. Yes, they were that bad. They had to be, or else why would he be sitting there, seriously thinking about baring all on camera?

On impulse, he got up from his chair and went into the

second bedroom that served as his office. He pulled the folder containing his bank statements from the shelf, opened it, and stared at the last few sheets. Then he opened his diary, and his heart sank to see so few entries.

Something occurred to him. He went back to the bank statements.

Aw shit.

The next payment on the van was due any day now. It had seemed like a good idea the previous year to change his old, dilapidated van for a newer, slightly less dilapidated version, and the payments had seemed reasonable at the time.

Except that was when he had a steady income coming in.

Now? One payment could take him into the red.

Andy's suggestion didn't seem so preposterous anymore. In fact, it was looking more viable by the minute. There had to be worse ways of earning money, right? When it came down to it, all he'd have to do was take his clothes off, do a hell of a lot of touching and kissing, and fuck them into the mattress.

Couch.

Back lawn.

Sun lounger.

Whatever.

I could do that.

Seven hundred and fifty quid to get his cock out? *Why not?*

By the time he turned out all the lights and went upstairs to bed, he'd come to a decision.

Fine. I'll do it.

And if he was lucky, his dreams would be filled with nubile women bucking as he thrust into them, their voices hoarse as they faked an orgasm.

That was *way* better than the alternative.

CHAPTER THREE

Denny Bailey stepped out of the shower and grabbed his towel from the rail. He jumped when someone rapped on the door. "Gimme a minute, for God's sake. I'm still dripping."

"I need to take a leak, Meena's in the other bathroom, and Lisa's in the downstairs loo," Chris hollered. "Come on, I'm desperate."

Denny unlocked the door. "Get your arse in here."

Chris hurried into the room, and Denny closed the door. He towelled himself dry, chuckling at Chris's heartfelt sigh of relief behind him as he emptied his bladder.

Chris flushed, then washed his hands. "God, I needed that." He glanced at Denny in the mirror. "You got a class this morning?"

"Nope. Going to the studio." He was going to take a shower there too, but that was work. That was more involved. Besides, he'd rather douche without his housemates around.

Chris snorted. "You mean they actually shoot porn in a studio? Not in a poky little flat with the curtains drawn, containing nothing but a bed?"

He laughed. "Yes, it's a real studio, you dick." It wasn't all that big, occupying a single building on an industrial estate. No sign outside to point to what took place inside, and Ari had ensured all the walls were soundproofed.

"So what are you today then? Or is it just a turn-up-and-fuck shoot?"

Denny arched his eyebrows. "You know, you take a lot of interest in my porn career. Something you want to try yourself? I could always put in a good word for you." He grinned. "Not that I have a clue what kind of… equipment you're playing with."

Blatant lie, but he didn't want Chris feeling uncomfortable. There were way too many straight guys out there who believed all gay guys were after their precious arse.

The only straight guys Denny dallied with were the ones who wanted the cash and didn't mind what they had to do to earn it.

Chris blinked. "What? Me do porn? Not bloody likely. I'm shy."

Denny burst into laughter. "So that *isn't* you streaking across the landing when you know the girls aren't around?" He wrapped the towel around his hips. "And for your information, I haven't had a shoot for weeks." One glance at his latest bank statement had been all he'd needed before he called Ari to ask if there were any scenes he could do.

Thank God for Ari.

There was barely a trickle of funds from his OnlyFans account, but what did he expect when he hadn't uploaded anything new for months?

He could rectify that after the shoot. He'd wear his new mesh briefs and put on a show for the camera.

The only downside was that he couldn't make all that much noise in the house, not without attracting too much attention. He was well-versed, however, in the art of silent masturbation, and what he couldn't say with words, he got across with—hopefully—smoking looks at the camera, and a fuck-load of rubbing and stroking.

"I envy you," Chris blurted out.

Okay, that was unexpected. Chris drove for a limo company, and he got to chauffeur some top-drawer clients to and from the theatre, expensive restaurants, Heathrow…

"Why would you envy me?"

"Because from where I'm standing, it looks as if you've

got your shit together. You're doing your master's, you love doing porn… You've got it made."

Denny could have told him appearances were deceptive. What Chris said was true enough, but there was a hole in Denny's life—a man-shaped hole—and one of these days Denny would find the man who slotted right into it.

Now, if said man walked into the studio, that would make things a lot easier.

Yeah. That only happened in films or books.

Denny patted Chris's arm. "I'm not there yet."

One day, though. Preferably *after* he'd got his postgrad degree.

Denny pushed open the main door to the studio. Carol was at the desk, and she glanced up at him with a smile. "Hey there. It's been a while."

"Am I okay to go through?"

She nodded. "You're the last to arrive. Fran is with the new guy, going through his paperwork, and Ari's setting up. No one else around today."

That meant he had the showers all to himself.

Denny hurried to the locker room. On the way, he passed the green room. He tried to peek at his screen partner, but the door was shut, and all he got was the rumble of a deep voice.

Denny couldn't wait to see who he was filming with.

He knew he had plenty of time to shower and prep. The bag slung over his shoulder contained an assortment of dildos and butt plugs in various sizes, so he'd be ready for whatever awaited him.

I hope he's big enough to make me feel every inch.

Once he was clean inside and out, he got into his jeans and a plain blue T-shirt, then went to the set, which was nothing more than a couch with drawn curtains behind it. The lights were on, revealing every nook and cranny.

Ari was there, checking the cameras. He smiled when he saw Denny.

"I was starting to worry." They hugged.

"Sorry. The train broke down and I had to wait for the next one." Ari's full, dense beard tickled him. Denny pulled back and peered closer at Ari's neck. "Ooh, you've got another tat. Nice." It looked like the King of Hearts from a playing card, except blood dripped from his eyes and spattered his crown.

"Which only goes to show how long it's been since you were here. This was done ages ago. You've obviously been studying way too hard."

Denny rolled his eyes. "That's because they don't hand out master's degrees in Management and Finance just for writing your name on the exam paper."

"How long do you have left to go?"

"Only until August. That's if I ever finish my dissertation." His Upper Second-Class Honours degree in Business and Marketing seemed like a walk in the park compared to his present course of study, but he knew it would be worth it in the end.

Then all I'll need is for someone to give me a job. A good job.

Denny had seen the career paths of past graduates, and he didn't intend stacking bookshelves in Waterstones or working the counter at McDonald's for a living. Except he knew what the job market was like.

He'd take whatever he could get, as long as it put money in his pocket. And if it didn't pay enough?

There was always porn.

"Not too busy to wank on camera though." Ari's eyes glittered. "I've been watching."

"Then you haven't been watching all that closely, because there's been nothing new for months."

Ari widened his eyes. "Then get your finger out." He chuckled.

That was one thing Denny loved about working with Ari. He didn't give a toss about Denny's OnlyFans stuff.

"Who've we got coming in today? The green room door was closed so I couldn't take a peek."

Ari beamed. "You are going to *love* me."

Denny smiled. "Yeah?" That boded well. After at least four years of working together, Ari knew his taste in guys.

"Oh yeah. Tall hunk. He's a builder. With tattoos." Ari grinned. "And he's got a big dick."

Denny's day was improving by the second. "Okay, now you've got me drooling. So what is he? Straight, gay, bi...?"

Ari wagged a finger. "What does Uncle Ari say about labels? But if you really wanna know, he's straight." He pointed toward the door. "Fran says if *you* don't wanna fuck him, she will."

Denny snorted. "Tell her, Hands off, bitch, he's all mine."

Ari gestured to the couch. "Ready to do the usual shit before he comes in?"

"Sure." He sat, leaning back against the cushions, awaiting the round of questions he'd answered so many times before.

Ari stood behind the camera facing the couch. "Still using the same name?" When Denny nodded, he rolled his eyes. "Really? I thought you'd have grown out of it by now." Denny simply stared at him, grinning. "Fine. And what's your occupation today?"

"Given the circumstances, how about... electrician?"

"That works."

"About the brief you sent him... does he really think you're putting together a new site about construction guys?"

Ari stared. "Who says I'm not? I think it's a fabulous idea. It'll go great with the priests and choir boys, scout leaders, twinks, counsellors, security guards..."

Denny laughed. "I think you've got every gay fantasy catered for."

Ari grinned. "Oh God no. I keep coming up with new ideas every day." He gave Denny a firm stare. "Okay, work time." He turned the camera on. "And today we have with us our old friend, Luke Thighwalker. Welcome back, Luke."

Denny smiled. "Hi. It's good to be here."

"For any new viewers out there, tell us your age."

"I'm twenty-five."

"Single, in a relationship, playing the field?"

Denny gave a half smile. "Single." He was getting tired of giving the same answer.

"And remind me what you do for a living."

"I'm an electrician."

Ari cackled. "Well, you're clearly good at your job because you turn *me* on." Denny responded with a chuckle. "So Luke, what's your ideal guy like?"

"I prefer men who are taller than me, but apart from that, I'm easy." He grinned. "Except that's not quite true. I like 'em big."

"Let's not be coy here. Are we talking cock?"

"We most definitely are." Denny was an old hand at this kind of banter.

"What is it about big dicks that does it for you?"

Denny smiled. "They hit all the right buttons."

Ari glanced at his crotch. "But *you're* not all that small. Does he have to be bigger than you, the same size, a bit smaller?"

He shrugged. "Like I said, I'm easy."

"Well, the good news is, the guy doing his paperwork as we speak? He's got a big dick."

Denny grinned. "Bring him on."

"Just a reminder. He's come here expecting to do a straight scene, so don't forget to play along, okay?"

"I know the drill." Denny chuckled. "And I'm looking

forward to being drilled too."

Ari laughed. "I'll go fetch him." He turned the camera off, then nodded to Denny's crotch where his dick was already tenting his jeans. "Don't appear *too* eager?"

Denny laughed. He'd been looking forward to this all week.

Five minutes elapsed before Ari returned with Denny's prospective co-star, and Denny did his best not to react when the guy walked in.

Oh my.

It was as if the Porn Gods had gazed down from on high and decided to make all Denny's wishes come true at once. The guy was tall, with dark hair and blue eyes, Denny's favourite combination. One glance at his beard, and Denny was imagining it scraping through his crack, over his hole. The guy was built, and either he spent a lot of time in a gym, or he had a very physical job.

Denny didn't care which. He was too busy trying not to let his twitching cock attract attention.

Tattoos too. Fuck. Denny wanted to trace over them with his tongue.

The guy didn't seem fazed by Denny being there, so he figured Ari had already clued him in that it was a threesome scene. He gave Denny a polite nod.

Ari gestured for the guy to sit. "This is Luke. He'll be in the scene too."

Denny raised his hand. "Hi. And what do I call you?"

"Gavin." They shook, and Denny tried not to smile. *How very British, shaking hands before performing a porn scene.*

Ari went behind the camera. "I'm gonna turn this on, and then we'll do a little interview, like I told you. Okay so far?"

Gavin nodded.

"Okay, and now we have Gavin. Welcome, Gavin."

Gavin gave a nervous smile.

"So Gavin, tell us a bit about yourself. How old are you?"

"Thirty-five."

Denny stared at Ari. Even his *age* was perfect.

Ari grinned back at him, then gave his full attention to Gavin. "And what do you do for a living?"

"I'm a builder."

Denny didn't know if that was a lie for the camera or the truth, but he could believe it, looking at the guy.

"And what decided you to try your hand at porn?"

Gavin didn't answer right away, but that was par for the course. A lot of the guys Denny filmed with had been ashamed to say what had brought them there was money, pure and simple. That had been one of Denny's initial reasons—that, and the fact that he loved to fuck, and getting paid for it was his version of the perfect job.

"To be honest, I'm short on cash at the moment. Bills to pay, food… you know how it is."

Gavin went up in Denny's estimation. *Good for you.*

Ari nodded. "I've been hearing that a lot lately. Luke here is doing this to pay off all those student loans, right?"

Denny nodded.

"Okay, Gavin, what turns you on in a girl? What's your favourite type?"

Gavin shrugged. "I like all kinds of girls, really. And I suppose what turns me on is… a really nice bum."

Denny grinned. "Oh, me too." He didn't miss Ari biting back his laughter.

"As you might have guessed by Luke here, we're going to be shooting a threesome. Is that okay? Have you done one before?"

"No, I haven't, but I'm up for it."

Ari beamed. "Good man. And seeing as you like bums, the girl who's gonna do the scene with you? She *loves* taking two guys at once. What about it? Are you up for a little DP action?"

Gavin bit his lip, and Denny fought the urge to adjust his

hard-on. "I've never really thought about it, but yeah, I'm game."

"It works best when the guys have a similar dick size." Ari smiled. "And Luke here is a big guy." He straightened. "Okay, before I go out there and bring in our actress, there's something I need to explain. We shoot a lot of porn, and one of the things we see a lot of is guys who have trouble getting hard." Ari shrugged. "It happens, all right? They get in here with all these lights, the cameras are rolling... So what we like to do is a kind of test."

Gavin blinked. "Test?"

Ari pointed to the TV on the wall. "As you can see, we've got a porno playing. So you're both gonna get naked, sit on the couch, and jerk off. We know from experience that if you can get hard with no girl in here, you'll be fine once we get started with the scene." He gestured to Denny. "Luke has filmed with us plenty of times. We know he has no trouble getting hard. Isn't that right, Luke?"

Denny grinned.

"You okay with that, Gavin?"

"I suppose."

"Then get naked, get hard, and ignore the cameras."

Denny stood, and Gavin followed his lead. Denny didn't look at him as he kicked off his trainers, stripped off his T-shirt, unbuttoned his jeans, shoved them down to his ankles, then stepped out of them, leaving only his white briefs that did little to hide his burgeoning erection. Gavin hesitated when he got as far as his black boxers, and Denny took pity on him.

He sat on the couch, leaving his briefs in place. His gaze locked on the TV, Denny eased his hand under the white cotton and stroked his dick. When the couch dipped, he flickered a glance and saw Gavin doing the same.

Much better. Some guys needed easing into a scene, and Ari wouldn't mind, not if it loosened Gavin up a bit. Neither of them said much, but Denny was used to that. It had to be a bit of a culture shock, wanking next to a complete stranger.

When Denny's cock poked above the elasticated waistband, he figured it was time for it to put in an appearance. He pushed the fabric lower, hooking it under his balls, and continued working the shaft.

Gavin took the hint, shoving his boxers over his hips, revealing a long thick dick that made Denny's hole tighten in anticipation.

So far so good.

Denny removed his own underwear, tossing them onto the pile of clothing. He kept his gaze focused on the screen.

He could almost hear the thought in Gavin's head. *Fuck it.*

Gavin pushed his boxers all the way down, removed them altogether, then placed them on his heap of clothing. His cock was hard, and like Denny, he used both hands to tug on it.

Ari hadn't lied—Gavin was a big boy.

Ari whistled. "You work out a lot, don't you, Gavin?"

"Not really. I suppose it's the job. It keeps me fit."

Ari lowered his gaze. "You're already getting excited about this, aren't you?"

Denny grinned. "Looks that way." He gave his own stiff dick a vigorous tug.

"Wow." Ari's grin matched his. "I know one actress who's going to be very happy. I'll go get her." He left the camera running then walked out of the room, closing the door behind him.

They sat on the couch, Gavin stroking his cock, his eyes glued on the TV screen.

"Have you seen this girl?"

Denny hated lying, but he had a part to play. "Yeah. She's hot. She's also got a fabulous arse."

"What about costumes? Aren't we doing this in costumes?"

Shit. This was one guy who remembered the brief.

"Ari'll bring those with him. After all, we'll have to get dressed again to shoot the scene."

Maybe this was also one guy who might bolt when he heard what Ari had in store. It had been known to happen.

Please take the bait. Please take the bait. Please take the bait.

Tom was trying not to stare at Luke's dick because that felt weird, but he couldn't help it. Luke had a long, slim cock, pink and firm.

It was then the thought struck him.

When Ari said this girl liked DP, he did mean she'd take one of them vaginally and the other anally, right? Because the alternative was his dick getting up close and personal with Luke's, and he wasn't sure how he felt about that.

He *couldn't* think about that.

Second thoughts had surfaced as soon as he'd entered the studio, and he'd been so close to telling the nice receptionist he'd made a mistake. Then he recalled what had brought him there, and he quashed his nerves.

It'll be fine.

If he told himself that enough times, he'd do what Deb was always saying—talk it into existence. Taking his clothes off had been the tipping point, and he'd managed that, right? And there he was, sitting next to a guy he was trying his damnedest not to look at, harder than he'd been in a long time.

In his defence, the porn had a lot to do with that, coupled with the illicitness of the situation.

Tom pointed to the screen. "She's pretty hot too." Anything rather than keep staring at Luke's cock.

"Yeah, she is."

"Ari said you've done this before?" Small talk when both of them were naked and tugging on their shafts had to be the most bizarre experience ever.

"Lots of times, yeah. First time surprised the hell out of me."

"Why?"

Luke shrugged. "I thought it would be a case of cameras get rolling, we fuck, and then the cameras stop. But it's not like that. It's more of a stop-start-stop-start kinda thing. Ari will give directions, we'll change positions, he'll film us from different angles... Then he'll edit out all the chat and the spare bits."

Tom hadn't given much thought to the process. "You're right. That's not what I expected at all." For the first time he took a good look at his co-star. He estimated Luke to be in his mid-twenties, with closely cropped brown hair and a tidy, short beard. His brown eyes twinkled, the studio lights reflecting in them. It was a nice face, but when Luke smiled, it was transformed into a handsome face.

Luke must break a lot of hearts.

His chest was smooth, and Tom had to wonder if it was that way by design, or if Luke was naturally free from hair.

Then the door opened, and Tom's heartbeat went into overdrive.

Here we go.

Ari came into the room—alone.

Uh-oh.

He gave them an apologetic glance. "Okay, guys, I've got some bad news. The girl hasn't shown up. My assistant has been calling her all morning but got no answer. We tried her agent too, but he couldn't reach her either. So she's a no-show. I've called round a few other agents, but no one's available."

Tom gaped. "So that's it?" He wasn't sure if he was disappointed or relieved.

"Not exactly. There *is* another option. You know how

much I said I'd pay you for this?" Tom nodded. "Well... What if I told you I could double it?"

Tom arched his eyebrows. "You've got my attention."

"The thing is, it would involve you doing something a little... different."

"And what would that be?"

Ari looked him in the eye. "You two have sex with each other."

CHAPTER FOUR

In the silence that followed, Tom was aware of his quickening heartbeat, his breathing that sounded way too loud…

Fuck.

Then he realized Ari was speaking. "Sorry. I missed that."

"I was saying, we shoot all kinds of porn here—girls with girls, guys with guys, threesomes, orgies…"

Tom's imagination did a tumble down the rabbit hole at that last one.

"How open-minded are you?" The question was directed at both of them.

Luke shrugged. "I'd be up for it."

Tom's breathing hitched. *Oh God.* "I… I've never done anything like that on camera." As soon as he said the words, he flinched.

The cat wasn't all the way out of the bag, but it had definitely stuck its head out and was having a damn good look around.

Ari's gaze homed in on him with all the speed of a missile. "But you *have* experimented in the past?"

The lie fell from his lips without a second's hesitation. "No, never."

Ari continued to stare at him, and Tom knew his cheeks had to be flushed because he could feel the heat rising in his face. He swallowed hard, positive that sweat was popping out on his brow.

Tom couldn't lie for shit.

His conscience pricked, he cleared his throat. "Well…"

Ari's eyes sparkled. "Aha."

"It wasn't much," Tom blurted out. "A little fooling around when I was in secondary school."

"Who didn't do that?" Luke murmured.

The confirmation that he hadn't been the only one to let his intense curiosity get the better of him eased the tension across Tom's shoulders, and he unclenched a little.

"What form did this experimentation take?" Ari gave him an encouraging smile. He held up his hands. "This is a no-judgement zone, okay? I mean, what is it we do here?"

Fair point.

Tom had the feeling he wasn't about to reveal something Ari hadn't heard before, probably more times than Tom could imagine. "Me and another boy wanked together, and…" His stomach tightened.

Ari chuckled. "Oh, those happy, happy school days." He tilted his head to one side, that sparkle still evident. "Did you get to touch his cock?"

Fuck.

"Yeah."

He could hear Andy in his head. *'And the rest.'* At least it was out. Now all he had to do was fuck, and all the discomfort and embarrassment would be over. He could go home with a wad of cash in his pocket and forget the experience had ever taken place.

Except Ari wasn't done. "With your hand—or your mouth?"

Fuck.

"He… He put his mouth on me." And that had been the extent of it.

Ari's nod told him he'd heard it all before. "Well, this would be full-on sex."

Tom's hole clenched.

Ari peered at Luke. "Would you be willing to get fucked?"

Tom held his breath. *What if he says no,* he *wants to be the one doing the fucking?*

Was that a line Tom was prepared to cross?

"Fine by me." Luke gave Tom a sideways glance. "He's hot."

Okay, Tom hadn't expected *that*. He fought the urge to push out a relieved sigh.

Luke lowered his gaze to Tom's shaft, which had wilted a little. "Although that looks as if it'll need a *lot* of lube."

Tom veered between embarrassment and pride.

He'd always been curious about anal, but the opportunity had never presented itself. And now it was being offered, he'd be a fool to refuse.

His cock seemed to like the idea—it was sitting up and taking notice again.

"So that's a yes?" Ari was smirking.

"Wait… don't we need costumes?" Tom wasn't ready to capitulate yet.

"Not if we're doing a scene like this. This is different. It would end up on a different site."

Of course it would—a *gay* sex site.

It was *make your mind up* time. The dynamics might have changed, but his financial situation hadn't.

Despite his churning stomach, Tom managed a smile. "Yeah, I'll do it."

Ari beamed. "Okay, then why don't you two start off by working each other's dicks?"

Crunch time.

Tom sat still, his heart hammering, and then his breathing caught when Luke wrapped his hand around Tom's cock.

Oh fuck. It had been a while. The first time in eighteen years, in fact.

He reached over and curled his fingers around Luke's dick. It was warm to the touch and silky soft. A familiar tingle of excitement thrummed through him, coupled with that same sense of illicitness he'd felt all those years ago, only, it had grown, blossoming into something adult, something way more sensual, sexier than his and Andy's frantic fumblings.

He resisted the temptation to push up through the warm funnel of Luke's hand, and focused his attention on the TV screen, where the guy was going down on the girl. The sound had been muted, but her open mouth hinted at constant noise pouring from her lips.

Now and then he snuck a glance at Luke's shaft, noting how stiff it had become.

Tom had to admit, it felt amazing. Luke worked his dick, sliding up and down, settling into a rhythm, and Tom fell into sync with him, both of them breathing a little faster. Ari said nothing but watched them, changing the angle of the camera now and then, and Tom knew he was doing a close-up of their busy hands.

This is okay. He breathed a little easier.

"Hand jobs feel great, but you know what feels even better?" Ari asked them.

Tom knew the answer to that one. "A mouth."

Andy's mouth had been *much* better than his awkward hand job.

"Would you let Luke blow you?"

What idiot would say no to that? "Sure."

"Stand up," Luke instructed. He knelt on the floor, at right angles to the camera.

Tom got to his feet, facing him, his cock jutting out, pointing right at Luke's lips. Luke stared at it for a moment, then leaned in and licked along its length from root to head.

Jesus…

Tom knew he was trembling and did his best to rein in the tumult of emotions bubbling inside him. Luke gazed up at him as he took the head into his mouth, and that glance almost unravelled Tom on the spot. Luke didn't break eye contact as he worked Tom's shaft with one hand while sucking and licking the head.

When he swallowed Tom to the root, his nose buried in Tom's pubes, Tom couldn't suppress the shudder that coursed through him.

"Oh my God. I never found a girl who could do that."

Luke pulled free, his face red, and grinned. "Do you like it?"

"Yeah." Another shiver trickled through him.

Luke took him deep again, but this time he cupped Tom's buttock, squeezing it. He pulled free again, glanced at Tom's long, rock-hard cock, and smiled. "Yeah, you do." He kept his gaze fixed on Tom as he lapped up the pre-cum that had emerged from the slit. Tom laid his hands on Luke's silken head, and exerted a slight pressure, Luke's head bobbing as he slid his mouth up and down Tom's length. Ari lowered the camera to Luke's head height, and Luke stared into the lens as he gave Tom's dick a hard suck.

"Okay, Gavin?"

Tom stilled, turning his head to look at Ari. Luke paused too, his lips glistening with saliva.

Ari gestured to Luke. "He's doing such a great job, I think it's only fair you reciprocate, don't you?"

Fuck.

He'd known it was coming. That didn't mean he was ready for it.

Tom sat on the couch, and Luke stood, still at right angles to the camera. Tom tugged on his own dick with one hand, the other wrapped around Luke's slim cock. Luke cupped Tom's nape, and Tom leaned forward to give the head a cautious lick.

"Just like that," Luke whispered. Emboldened, Tom sucked on the flared head, and Luke groaned. "Oh yeah. Fuck."

That was all the encouragement Tom required.

He licked the shaft the way Luke had done and was rewarded with a soft whimper. He couldn't manage Luke's feat, succeeding in taking about half of him into his mouth, but Luke wasn't complaining. On the contrary, he gave a little thrust of his hips, guiding Tom's head with his hand, his breathing shallow.

"Your mouth feels so good," he murmured.

Tom hadn't expected Luke's dick to feel as good as it did, but Luke's appreciative noises and full body shivers spurred him on, his own cock so hard it ached. Determined to give as good as he got, Tom took Luke a little deeper, then coughed and spluttered when his dick went a bit too far.

Ari chuckled. "This might be a good point to take a breather. You did really well."

"Fuck yeah. You did fantastic." Luke cupped Tom's chin, tilting his head up, and gave him a bright smile. "I mean it. That was great." He stretched out his hand toward the table where the bottle of lube sat, and grabbed two bottles of water. "Here." He held one out to Tom.

"Good idea," Ari remarked. "Why don't you stand up for a sec? We'll take a short break."

Tom got up off the couch, unscrewed the cap, and drank half the bottle's contents, while Luke did the same. The cool water was exactly what he needed.

Luke glanced at his crotch. "Wow. That's gonna be a stretch."

Ari chuckled. "You two could have a sword fight, looking at you."

Tom frowned. "A what?"

Luke laughed and moved in a little, swinging his dick so that it collided with Tom's with a meaty *smack*.

"Have you ever heard the term frottage?"

Before Tom had the chance to ask what that was, Luke grinned. "I have." He wrapped his hand around both shafts and gave them a gentle squeeze, then slid his hand along both.

Holy fuck, that felt better than Tom would have believed.

"You two are virtually the same size," Ari commented, focusing the camera on their cocks, both of them pushing toward the other, the friction delicious. Luke brought the head of Tom's dick to his own, rubbing them together, and Tom couldn't keep still.

Then Luke let go, shifted a bit closer, and their upright cocks went into battle, rolling over each other, Luke's shaft hard and warm against his own. Luke's hand was on his neck as he stared into Tom's eyes and closed the gap between them, his breathing heavy and harsh. Tom's heartbeat quickened when he realised Luke's intent, and he pulled back.

Fucking a guy? Fine.

Kissing him? That was something else.

Luke didn't react to his abrupt recoil, but grabbed their dicks once more, rubbing them, squeezing them together.

"Luke, why don't you kneel on the couch, and show Gavin what he gets to play with?"

Ari's timing was perfect.

Luke turned and wiggled his arse, reaching back to spread his cheeks. "I think I can take all of you."

Tom couldn't help himself. He stroked the firm globes, rubbing the edge of his hand through Luke's crack, noting the crevice's warmth. Then Luke knelt on the couch, gripping the arm, one foot on the floor.

It didn't matter that Tom had taken a test prior to the shoot, as requested.

It didn't matter that Ari had confirmed the status of all the participants.

The only thing that registered in his head was that he was about to slide his bare cock into another man's arse.

Luke grabbed a bottle of lube and poured some into his hand. He rubbed it over his hole.

Tom got the message. He took the bottle Luke held out to him and slicked up his cock. "Don't I need to… to prep you?"

"You're good," Luke assured him. He pulled his cheeks apart. "Now put it in me."

Tom knelt on the couch, mimicking Luke's stance. He aimed the head of his dick at Luke's hole, feeling the warmth of him. Slowly, hesitantly, he pushed, gasping as the head breached the ring of muscle. He froze at the sound of Luke's laboured breaths.

"Is that okay?"

Luke bowed his head. "You're big. And that's not a complaint, by the way." He turned his head to gaze at Tom. "Keep going, only, do it slow."

Tom inched his way inside Luke's body. "Fuck, it's so tight," he whispered as warm flesh surrounded his dick.

"Feels good," Luke told him.

No, it felt *too* fucking good.

Tom grabbed Luke's waist and held on tight as he moved in and out, keeping the motion leisurely, mesmerised by the sight of his glistening shaft penetrating Luke, the sounds Luke made when Tom filled him to the hilt, the way he turned to look at Tom, nodding, his eyes wide, his mouth open, his arm jerking as he worked his dick unseen.

Luke reached back and grabbed Tom's hand. "Fuck me on my back?"

Tom gave a grateful nod. He was perilously close, and he didn't want it to end. He withdrew, and Luke lay on the couch on his back, his legs spread wide. Tom shifted closer, guided his dick into position, and slowly filled him again, holding onto Luke's raised leg, anchoring himself.

"Oh yeah, that's it." Luke wrapped his hand around his cock, tugging it, his body shaking as he picked up speed. "Feels really good."

The tightness of Luke's body propelled Tom toward the finish line, and then it got tighter still, imprisoning his shaft in heat.

Luke moaned, and an arc of cum shot through the air, landing on his chest and neck. Tom couldn't tear his gaze away, lost between the exquisite sensation of his dick wedged in Luke's body, and the sight of creamy cum decorating his skin.

Too much.

He pulled free, his shivers multiplying. "Gonna come."

Luke was upright in a heartbeat. He took Tom's still rigid dick in his mouth, burying it in his throat, and that was it, Tom shot harder than he'd ever done. He shuddered through his orgasm, his cum leaking from Luke's mouth, Luke staring at him with shining eyes as he licked and sucked the head clean.

All too soon it was over. Ari turned off the camera, and Luke got off the couch.

Tom was once again not sure if he was relieved or disappointed.

"Go grab a shower, then come back here in just a towel, and we'll finish the shoot."

He blinked. "We're not done?"

Ari shook his head. "I like to do a little Q&A at the end, if that's okay."

Tom didn't have a clue if it was okay or not—he was still reeling from the experience.

It wasn't what he'd expected when he'd walked into the studio.

It wasn't even close to how he thought it would be when he knew what was going to happen.

No, it was…

Mind-blowing.

Tom sat on the couch next to Luke. He knew his dick was poking out from beneath the small towel they'd given him, but after what he'd just done, he was way past being shy.

Ari got behind the camera again.

"So Gavin, tell me a little more about your experiences in secondary school. Was it just jerking off? A bit of dick-sucking?"

"I got my dick sucked, but I never sucked one before today."

Ari's eyes twinkled. "Confession time. Have you ever tried to suck your own cock?"

Luke burst out laughing. "Hasn't every man tried that?"

Tom chuckled. "Pretty sure they have. And I did manage to get maybe an inch into my mouth once."

Ari cackled. "There. You *have* sucked a dick before today."

"Technically, yes, but I don't think it counted." His heartbeat was back to normal, but his anxiety level was climbing. All he wanted was to get out of there.

I fucked a guy. I fucked a guy.

"So here's the million pound question." Ari locked gazes with him. "Would you do it again?"

Fuck.

He went with noncommittal. "Maybe?"

Ari smiled. "And would you do it for money again? Or just because you liked it?"

What shocked Tom was he didn't know how to answer that one.

Ari turned the camera off. "And we're done."

That was all the impetus Tom needed. "I have to go."

Ari nodded as though he'd expected that response. "Sure. Stop at the reception desk. Carol will have your money waiting for you. And if you ever decide to do this again, I'd be delighted to accommodate you. Both of you."

Tom wasn't listening. He grabbed his clothes and left the room, heading for the locker room next to the showers. He hoped Luke wouldn't get the same idea, because Tom didn't feel he could indulge in small talk, not after he'd been balls-deep in Luke's arse.

Luke's incredibly tight, warm arse.

No. No. No. He couldn't think like that.

It was over.

Job done.

Never to be repeated.

By the time he reached reception, he'd calmed down a little. The lady behind the desk—Carol?—handed him an envelope. She was a middle-aged woman—no, older than that—with grey hair, glasses and a great smile.

Why didn't I notice her on the way in?

Stupid question. He'd been a bit preoccupied. He wouldn't have noticed her if she'd danced naked on the desk, wearing a feather boa.

Okay, *not* a direction he wanted to go in.

"Did it go okay, hon?" Her Cockney accent pinpointed her origins with great accuracy.

Tom wasn't sure how to answer that. "Yeah." It was all he could manage right then.

"Well, I hope you enjoyed it. That's what counts."

It was a surreal conversation to be having with a little old lady in a porn studio.

She bit her lip. "Not what you were expectin', I know." Her gaze was sympathetic. "These things 'appen. But you know what you need to remember? Like Ari always says, don't get hung up on labels."

He blinked. "He says that?"

The skin around her eyes crinkled and she beamed. "Didn't you get the speech? He always tells new guys the same thing. You're adults, an' if it feels good, an' you're not hurtin' anyone, then what's wrong with enjoyin' life's experiences?" She made a clicking noise with her tongue. "You take my grandson. He can't make his mind up. One week he could be datin' a girl, the next week it's a boy…Every time I mention it, he rolls his eyes an' says 'Grandma, life's too short.'"

Tom took a deep breath. Carol's comment struck him to

the core. He *had* been thinking about labels, about how he'd feel if anyone he knew saw this video.

How he'd excuse what he'd done.

Carol had nailed it—Tom *had* enjoyed it. He just wasn't sure he wanted to admit it out loud.

To anyone.

CHAPTER FIVE

Tom closed the front door and stood in his long hall, staring ahead to the open door that led to his conservatory. All the way home, he hadn't been able to shake the experience from his mind.

Can't believe I agreed to it.

Except the reason for that was in his jacket pocket, and because of it, there would be no beans on toast that evening. Tom liked baked beans as much as the next man, but it was possible to have too much of a good thing.

Even more so where beans were concerned.

He removed his jacket, walked into the kitchen, and filled the kettle.

I still can't believe it.

He supposed the novelty of the situation would wear off eventually. The cash would provide a buffer until the jobs started coming with greater frequency.

They better had. Tom couldn't last much longer if they stayed at the present almost non-existent level.

He grabbed a mug and dropped a tea bag into it. While he waited for the kettle to boil, he opened the fridge, then regretted it. Nothing in there but a half-full two-litre container of milk, some butter spread, a lump of cheese that was going green, a box of eggs, and a plastic tray containing two rashers of bacon, brown and curling at the edges.

Maybe it *was* time to do a little shopping.

When the kettle beeped, he poured the hot water into the mug, stirring it with a teaspoon, his hands on autopilot. He closed his eyes, and what came to mind was a warm, wet mouth on his dick, a tight hole sucking him in deeper, Luke's noises filling the air… He gripped the edge of the worktop, hips moving as he recalled driving his cock all the way home, his fingers digging into Luke's calf, his hand on Luke's quivering belly, torn between the sight of Luke's hand tugging frantically on his shaft and the sight of his own dick sliding in and out, slick and fast, gathering momentum.

Tom opened his eyes, shivering.

Fuck.

He told himself the intense recollections had nothing to do with him fucking a guy, and *everything* to do with the fact that he hadn't had sex in way too long. So long, that he couldn't even remember when that was. He knew one thing for certain, however—he wanted a word or two with Andy.

Actually, several words.

What he needed right then was a little normalcy. Anything to push the afternoon from his mind.

Tom grabbed the pad of yellow post-It notes and a pen, and began composing a shopping list, picturing the aisles in his local Lidl supermarket. He considered splashing out and buying a couple of decent ready meals for a change. Then he remembered Saturday nights when he and Deb were still married. Their occasional treat had been crispy roast duck from M&S. It worked out cheaper than going to a Chinese restaurant to eat it, and Tom had been a dab hand at getting every sliver of duck off the bones.

When was the last time I did that? A quarter duck meant six pancakes, and compared to his recent fare of beans on toast, that sounded like a banquet. M&S was located in the Ashley Centre in Epsom, not that far away.

Once he'd started on that road, it wasn't long before he thought about other M&S dishes, ones he'd avoided for what seemed a lifetime because he couldn't afford them: moussaka, chicken korma, and so many other meals that made his mouth water just *thinking* about them.

A few ready meals wouldn't break the bank, right? I could do the bulk of the grocery shopping at Lidl, same as always, but then I could treat myself to something nice and tasty from M&S.

God knows he'd gone above and beyond to be able to afford them.

His phone buzzed, and he saw it was an unknown number.

It had better not be someone selling me something, or telling me my computer is about to fail, or some other bullshit like that.

He clicked on Answer, and was relieved when it was a potential customer, inquiring about a quote for a kitchen refurb. He scribbled down the details and arranged a time the next day to drive over and assess the work required. As he finished the call, Tom smiled.

Maybe he'd finally turned the corner.

Maybe things were looking up at last.

God, he hoped so. He never wanted to be in the position where he considered doing another porn shoot.

Except it hadn't been *that* bad, had it? Really?

I thought you didn't want to think about it.

Tom could be honest with himself.

It hadn't been bad at all. In fact, he had a feeling that when night came and he lay in his bed, the memory of coming inside that tight arse would probably bring him off again.

I've been alone too long, that's what it is.

A steady girlfriend, and sex on a regular basis would soon put paid to the thoughts colliding in his head right then.

Tom wandered through the racks of shirts, sweaters, and pants. They were the kind of clothes that reminded him of his dad, stuff Tom wouldn't be caught dead wearing, but hey, each to his own, right? In one hand he clutched a plastic bag containing seven meals. He intended putting most of them in the freezer, eking them out for as long as he could.

And speaking of food, he was starving. No wonder—he hadn't eaten since breakfast, and he'd expelled a lot of energy.

And there you go, thinking about it again.

Then he came to a dead stop. Andy stood a few feet away, pulling out woollen cardigans and checking the labels.

Talk about timing…

Tom didn't wait for him to turn and see him. He marched over to Andy and grabbed his shoulder. "That's not your colour, you know."

Andy gave a start, his hand pressed against his chest. "Christ, you nearly gave me a heart attack." He arched his eyebrows. "You don't usually shop in here, do you?"

"I'm treating myself." Tom thought fast. "Why don't you join me for a coffee in the café upstairs?"

Andy gave a polite smile. "Thanks, but I don't really have the time. I was on my—"

"Let me put it another way." Tom stared at him. "Come upstairs now and have a coffee with me, because we need to talk." He paused. "I don't have to say what about, do I?"

Andy widened his eyes. "Oh, *right.* Yeah. You know what? I *could* do with a coffee right now."

"I thought that might be the case." Tom pointed toward the lift. "After you."

He followed Andy through the store, his heartbeat quickening. He'd had time to think about what had happened that afternoon, to go over what Andy had said, and he'd reached a conclusion.

Something about the whole shoot had felt… off, and he

wanted to know if Andy had been through the same experience. Part of Tom said surely not. He'd have mentioned it.

Because why the fuck would he keep quiet about something like that?

Tom pointed to a table in the corner, away from most of the café's customers. "Grab a seat. I'll get the coffees." He walked to the counter and ordered the drinks, his mind slipping into overdrive.

How do I start this?

He figured he'd play it by ear.

By the time he got to their table, Andy was leaning back in his chair, relaxed.

"What's this all about, Tom?"

Tom pulled out a chair and sat. He tore open a packet of sugar and dumped its contents into the dark brown steaming liquid, not looking at Andy, deliberating how best to broach the subject.

"Tom? You're worrying me." He paused. "Is this... is this about my suggestion?"

And there was his opening.

Tom raised his chin and smiled. "Yes, it is, but I'd like to talk about *your* experience first, if that's all right."

"My experience?" Andy straightened in his chair. "I'm not sure what you mean."

"You did mention you'd done a shoot too, right?"

"Yeah, that's right."

"Was it just the once?"

"Yeah. Once was enough to be honest."

Tom had gotten the impression during their last conversation that Andy was more a regular performer than a one-off, but he could have been mistaken.

Tom nodded. "So... you told me it was hot. You said your co-star was hot too. Actually, it's your co-star that I want to discuss."

"Oh?"

Tom cocked his head. "Was there something you forgot to mention about them?"

"Such as?"

"Oh, I don't know," Tom said with a nonchalant air before looking Andy in the eye. "Maybe the fact that he was a guy?"

Andy's mouth fell open.

Bingo.

Tom stirred his coffee. "You see, I've been thinking about how carefully you worded your description of the event. The fact that you didn't use a single pronoun to describe them. Actually, there was no description at all, but that would've given the game away, wouldn't it?"

Andy took a drink from his mug, wincing at the heat. "So you did go there after all."

"Yup."

He took a deep breath. "Look, if I'd said it was guys, would you have gone? And I thought you'd be up for it. Wouldn't be the first time, right?"

Tom glanced at the occupied tables, then leaned in. "At the risk of repeating myself, firstly, that was a long time ago," he said in a low voice. "Secondly, I don't think giving each other hand jobs and you giving me the occasional blow job is on the same level as fucking another guy in the arse, do you?"

Andy blinked. "Did… did you do that?"

"We're not talking about me, we're talking about what you said to me. The 'picture' you painted," he air-quoted.

"But it *was* good money, right?" Andy remonstrated.

Tom couldn't deny that. He sat back in his chair. "Did they pull the same stunt on you? Get you there to shoot a threesome, then tell you there was no girl?"

Andy nodded. "Yeah. That's pretty much how they work. There are loads of gay porn sites out there where that happens. They basically bait straight guys."

And I took the bait.

Then he thought about Luke.

"So the guy I was… filming with… he *knew* what was going to happen?"

"Yeah. He would've been part of the setup."

Damn, Luke had fooled him. What an act.

"I see. So he was probably gay?"

Another nod. "Since I did my shoot, I've found lots of similar videos. The straight guy either fucks the gay one, or occasionally he gets fucked—if he's amenable." He peered at Tom. "So… how did it go with you? Did you—"

Tom snorted. "Do you really think I'm gonna sit here and tell you all about it?" A thought occurred to him. "Did they pay you to bring in *other* straight guys? Was that why you told me about it? They've got some kind of a deal going where you get paid for every guy you send their way?"

Andy widened his eyes. "God, no. Honestly, Tom, I only told you because I knew what a hole you're in."

Unlike Luke, Tom had known Andy for years, and he didn't think him capable of that good an act.

At least, Tom hoped so, because he didn't like the alternative.

"I'm trying my hardest here to believe you."

Andy gave him a pained look. "Come on, don't be like that."

"Like what? You hooked me with the idea of money I badly needed. You neglected to tell me what the real setup was. I walked into that studio expecting a very different outcome."

Andy sighed. "Look at it this way. You got paid a chunk of cash that'll come in very useful. You don't have to think about it ever again. And you need never *do* it again—unless you want to, of course."

"Would *you?*"

He gaped. "Jesus, no. Are you kidding? Why would I want

to do that? I'm fucking straight." He cowered as some of the customers stared in their direction.

Tom reined in his annoyance. Yes, Andy had deceived him, but Tom had been the one to take the bait, hadn't he?

I have no one to blame but myself.

"Thanks for the chat. It was… illuminating." He pushed back his chair and stood. "But the next time you have a scheme to make me some money? Keep it to yourself." He leaned in. "And for the last time, you do not *ever* mention what we did in secondary school. Have you got that?"

And before Andy could splutter out a half-arsed apology—again—or make a joke of it, Tom walked out of the café.

I can't be too pissed at him. I didn't have to do it.

He headed for the car park, got into his van, and sat there, his hands on the steering wheel.

Andy was right about one thing. He didn't need to do it again.

Unless you want to.

Nope.

Nope.

Nope.

Wasn't gonna happen.

CHAPTER SIX

Tom put his notepad away in the pocket of his jacket. "I think I've got everything I need, Mrs. Delaney. I'll be in touch with a quote."

She showed him to the door. "I have several building firms who are providing us with quotes. Once I have them all, I'll let everyone know. Thank you for your time."

Tom stepped outside, and the door closed behind him before he'd even taken two steps.

One hour. One hour of talking, nodding, smiling, offering suggestions, and she hadn't once offered him a cup of tea. It was always the way. The more affluent the neighbourhood, the less likely the customer was to offer refreshment. And Wimbledon was fairly affluent. One glance at Mrs. Delaney's historic double-fronted, six-bedroom house overlooking Wimbledon Common had told him plenty.

Why would she choose a one-man band like me, when she could have her pick of the bright and shiny firms operating in the area?

As soon as the thought slipped into his head, he sighed. Tom wasn't by habit a negative kinda guy. His run of bad luck was clearly getting to him.

I need cheering up. He had no jobs planned for the rest of the day. His accounts were up to date, and they made for miserable reading.

Tom climbed into his van and sat there without turning the key, his mind going over everything he'd seen. Mrs. Delaney's kitchen was in dire need of some TLC: at some point in the past, it had been a show kitchen, but that had to have been at least forty years ago. It was woefully short of electrical sockets, the worktops needed replacing, the tiling was…

The less said about the tiling, the better.

Tom would go home, work out his quote, and email it to her, but he wasn't going to hold his breath.

Was it only yesterday that I thought I'd turned a corner?

The newfound optimism he'd experienced after Mrs. Delaney's call had dwindled. The reassuring wad of cash in his pocket had already shrunk from its original girth. And in moments when all was quiet, what stole into his head were recollections of the studio shoot, robbed a little of their intensity but still powerful, still capable of making his breathing quicken, his stomach clench…

His dick twitch.

His late-night wank had sent him to sleep, same as it always did, but he'd awoken in the middle of the night and lain there in the semidarkness, trying to shut out the memories.

Except they weren't bad memories, just a reminder of how desperate he'd become.

He drove away from Mrs. Delaney's house with its walled garden and annex, and turned onto Coombe Lane. On the right, he spotted a wooden signpost standing on the pavement, nestled between Boots the Chemist and Wimbledon Dental Care: Three Apes Coffee. The black silhouette of an ape was painted above the lettering.

Coffee. Now *there* was an idea. And maybe he'd find something else to cheer him up.

Something sweet.

He scanned the road ahead for any sign of a car park, and grinned when one came into view.

Perfect.

Tom pulled into it, found a space, turned off the engine, and got out to inspect the Pay and Display notice. Then he strolled back along the lane until he reached the coffee shop.

Two wooden benches sat outside, occupied by a group of

walkers, drinking and chatting. Tom peered through the glass door. It seemed like a decent enough place: the walls were white, giving it a clean appearance, and the tables and chairs were made from birch or ash or some other pale wood. It wasn't that busy either, and the smell wafting from the vent above the door was nothing short of heaven.

Even better—he spied a glass counter filled with pastries and other delicious-looking goodies.

And then he froze.

Sitting in the corner, hunched over a laptop, was a familiar figure.

Well, well, well.

That did it. Tom was going in.

Denny did a save before he picked up his latte. His laptop had had a hissy fit the previous week, and he thought he'd lost almost three thousand words of his dissertation.

That had been enough to give him palpitations. Thankfully, Robin had worked his usual miracle, restoring Denny's precious words to their correct file, before issuing him with the same old warning. 'For God's sake, get yourself a laptop that isn't powered by steam.'

Denny huffed. Easy for him to say. Robin's salary was three times the size of the other housemates' earnings combined.

He'd tipped up his cup before he realised it was empty. *Damn.*

"So what do you do when you're not tricking straight guys?"

Denny jumped. He recognised that deep voice. He raised his chin to find Gavin standing in front of him, dressed in jeans, a blue shirt, and a denim jacket, a pen poking up from the breast pocket.

The most disconcerting thing?

He wasn't smiling.

Shit.

Denny went with ignorance. "Excuse me? What are you talking about?" He put his cup down.

Gavin leaned forward, his palms flat on the table, his face hovering above Denny's laptop, his cheeks flushed. "Don't bother lying. I know all about it. A friend of mine filmed with you guys too and got the same treatment. He was the one who gave me the idea of coming to you in the first place."

Denny knew from experience that this kind of thing happened every now and then. A guy did the deed, got paid for it, then had second thoughts, and went back to voice his regrets and embarrassment, usually at the top of his indignant voice.

Except Denny had never been in the firing line before, and he didn't like it.

He forced himself to stay calm, to keep breathing evenly. "Will you please sit down?" No one was glancing in their direction—yet—and Denny didn't want to attract any unwelcome attention, not in his favourite coffee shop-cum-workspace.

Gavin didn't budge, and Denny's heart sank.

This is not *going to be easy.*

He went with the first thing he could think of. "Do you like lattes?"

Gavin blinked. "What?"

"It's a simple question. Do you like lattes?"

"Yes, but—"

Denny caught Anna's attention. "Anna, can I have two lattes over here, please? Plus, an almond croissant, and—"

"A blueberry and oat crumble slice too. I know." She

grinned. "Sure thing, Denny. I'll be right over."

"Denny, huh?" Gavin straightened, then arched his eyebrows. "So your name isn't Luke?"

Denny bit his lip. "Seeing as I used the name Luke Thighwalker, no—thank God." He peered at him. "Is Gavin *your* real name?" He thought it unlikely.

No one used their real name.

He flushed. "No. It's Tom."

Denny gestured to the empty chair facing him. "Then Tom, please… sit down. There's a latte on its way. Trust me, the coffee is great, and so are the pastries."

Tom still hadn't moved.

Denny let out a sigh. "I promise, I'll answer all your questions, but you're making me really nervous right now."

That seemed to do the trick. Tom pulled the chair out and sat, hands clasped on the table.

"You must come here a lot," he remarked. When Denny frowned, Tom gave a quick shrug. "They know your name. *And* your favourite dessert."

Okay, Tom was observant.

He glanced at their surroundings. "Seems like a nice place."

"It is. And you're right. I *do* come here a lot." Denny liked everything about it, from the pots of ivy on high shelves, their foliage trailing, to the little pots containing a cactus on every table, the wonderful smell of coffee, sugar, spice, right down to the Pride flag in the corner of the window.

It was a safe space.

"Do you live in Wimbledon?"

"About fifteen minutes' walk from here. I share a house with four other people."

"Then why come here to work?"

Denny grinned. "I like to people-watch. Plus, I get to eat

the sweet stuff. One of my housemates is always lecturing me about eating healthily. I figure what she doesn't see won't hurt her. The coffee is a major selling point too."

"Interesting name," Tom commented. "Three Apes, I mean." He shifted on his chair.

At least he wasn't looking daggers at Denny anymore.

"The place is run by three siblings. Anna over there has a degree in Zoology and a master's in Primate Conservation, hence the name."

And speaking of Anna…

She came out from behind the counter, carrying two plates. After placing them on the table, she smiled. "And now I'll bring your coffees." Her gaze flickered to Tom, then back to Denny. "New friend?" Her eyes twinkled.

"Not exactly." Denny waited until she'd retreated to the counter before pointing to the plates. "Have whichever one you want. They're both equally delicious." When Tom reached for the almond croissant, Denny blurted out, "Not that one!"

Tom froze. "But you said…"

Denny smiled. "Gotcha."

It took a second or two, but finally Tom cracked a smile.

Anna returned with the cups, then withdrew.

"Okay, we've got our coffee. Can we talk now?" Tom shifted closer, scraping his chair legs across the wooden floor.

"Fine." Denny had a question of his own. "Who was your friend? The one who told you about the studio."

"His name's Andy, only he probably didn't use his real name either. I got the impression it was a recent thing."

"Then I wouldn't know him. That was the first shoot I'd done for a while." He cocked his head. "Did he get an invite back?"

Tom's brow furrowed. "I don't know. He said he wouldn't do it again."

Denny hid a smile. That implied a lot. Ari didn't ask

everyone back. In fact, some guys he couldn't get rid of fast enough. Maybe this Andy was one of those.

"You don't *really* go by the name Luke Thighwalker, do you?"

Denny laughed. "Why not? It's memorable."

"Oh, it's certainly that. So you don't do... porn full-time?"

Denny smiled. "What Ari said about paying off student loans? That was true. Only, I'm still a student." He closed the laptop. "But not for much longer. I'm working on my dissertation for my master's."

"In what?"

"Management and Finance."

"So you've already got a degree?"

Denny nodded. "Business and Marketing."

Tom blinked. "You've obviously got brains. Which makes me wonder why on earth you're doing porn."

Denny leaned back. "You said you were a builder. Was that something you made up, or is it the truth?"

"It's true."

"I assume you've got qualifications."

Tom set his jaw. "Of course."

Denny gave another nod. "So it looks as though I'm not the only one around here with brains. And yet you were doing porn too."

Tom sipped his coffee. He smiled. "You were right. This is great."

Denny knew evasion when he saw it.

He studied Tom. "You were telling the truth about your reasons for doing the shoot, weren't you? Money worries?" When Tom's face tightened once more, Denny sighed. "I can't tell you how many guys do what you did for exactly the same reason, but I can assure you, it's a lot. And there is nothing wrong with doing porn. Even if I didn't need the money, I'd probably still do it." Tom's breathing caught, and Denny smiled.

"Didn't expect that, did you? I like sex, pure and simple."

Tom bit off the corner of his croissant.

He couldn't put his finger on it, but Denny felt certain there was more to come.

He leaned forward. "What it boils down to is, we see sex from two different perspectives."

"What do you mean?"

"I don't know you, but I'd be willing to bet you only take a woman to bed when you're in a relationship with her. Probably a relationship that you're hoping will develop into something more than casual. Am I right?"

Tom stared at him. "Yeah."

"So it's more than sex—emotions come into it too. But for me? I do my best to keep a lid on my emotions. It's just sex. I get to meet some gorgeous guys, we have fun, we get paid, we go home. End of story."

"*Can* you do that? Keep your emotions out of it, I mean?" Denny could hear the genuine interest in Tom's voice.

"Most of the time, yeah."

"Most?"

Denny shrugged. "We all have stories we could tell, right?"

Except he did *not* want to tell his.

He took a long drink from his cup, then put it down. "Look, I'm sorry you're pissed off that we did a number on you."

"*Yesterday* I was pissed off, after I talked with Andy. I thought I'd got past that—until I looked through that window and saw you. But you know what? The more I think about it, the more I realise it was my choice. I could've said no," Tom reasoned. "But I didn't. I'm a big boy. I'll live with it."

"But this is where I add that I'm not sorry I got to shoot with you." Denny grinned. "Pun intended."

Tom spluttered coffee over the tabletop.

Denny grabbed a couple of napkins and wiped up after him. "And I'd do it again, in a heartbeat." He didn't believe in hiding his feelings. "Would *you* do it again?"

"Ari already asked me back, remember? You were there at the time. I'll tell you the same thing I told him—I'll think about it." Then his shoulders sagged. "But I don't think that's likely. I... I'm not like you."

Denny took a stab in the dark. "You still think about the scene, don't you?"

Tom swallowed.

"It's okay if you do. I just hope you're not remembering it and cursing yourself because it was an awful experience."

Tom's chest heaved. "I don't remember it as being awful."

Another statement that rang with truth.

On impulse, Denny opened the notepad next to his laptop and scribbled a couple of lines on it. He tore the sheet off and held it out to Tom. "Here."

Tom took it. "What's this?"

"My number. In case you change your mind."

"I'm never going to do that again." Tom's tone was gentle but firm.

Denny held his hands up. "Hey, never say never."

"Besides, Ari already gave me his number."

"And now you've got mine. In case you lose his." Except that wasn't why Denny had given it, and he knew it.

Supposing this is the last chance I get to see this guy?

His heartbeat quickened. "By the way... I loved doing that scene with you."

Tom flushed. "Flattery will get you nowhere."

Denny shook his head. "Not flattery—sincerity. You were hot as fuck." He smiled. "Which I believe I said at the time."

A tide of deeper red climbed Tom's neck, spreading over his cheeks.

Denny smiled. "And you're also my type, so that made everything absolutely perfect. You walked into that room, and I swear, I was drooling."

He cleared his throat. "What did I just say about flattery?"

"This is me being sincere again. You have *no* idea how hard I was willing you to take the bait." He bit his lip. "Actually? You remember how hard I was when we stripped?"

Tom coughed, and croissant crumbs coated the table. "I'm trying not to think about it." He brushed them into a napkin with the edge of his hand.

"Well—*think* about it. Because that was all for you."

Tom gaped at him. "Do you *always* say what comes into your head?"

"Yeah. Except when I'm around my parents. You wouldn't recognise me then."

"I only came in here because I recognised you."

"But hopefully, you're in a better mood than you were then."

Tom finished his latte and wiped his hands on a napkin. "Yeah, I am."

"Good. Then we can part on good terms." Denny held out his hand. "It was good to see you again—Tom." He smiled. "I have to ask. Why did you choose the name Gavin? Is it your middle name?"

"No, it's the name of a friend's twin brother. He happens to be gay."

Denny couldn't suppress his grin. "Well, what do you know about that?" He glanced at the closed laptop with a heavy sigh. "But now I have to get on."

Tom rose. "Then I'll leave you to it."

Denny pointed to the piece of paper he'd left on the table. "You've forgotten something."

Another flush. Tom picked it up, folded it, and placed it in his jacket pocket. "What do I owe you for the coffee and croissant?"

"Nothing. It was my treat."

Tom gave a single nod, then turned and headed for the

door.

Denny watched him go, trying hard not to stare at Tom's arse encased in tight jeans, and failing miserably.

He won't do it again, will he? Damn.

CHAPTER SEVEN

As soon as Denny opened the front door, he heard Robin's cry of exasperation.

"Oh you bloody pain in the arse!"

He dropped his laptop bag at the foot of the stairs and hurried into the kitchen. "What's wrong?" The pungent aroma of garlic filled the air.

Robin turned to look at him. "The sodding induction hob, that's what's wrong. I'm standing here, pressing and pressing, but the bloody thing won't come on."

"I *told* you what to do." Lisa went over to the panel on the wall and flipped the red switch up then down again. "Try it now."

"That doesn't work," Robin whined. "I've tried that before. It just—"

The hob beeped into action, its icons glowing red against the black surface.

"You contrary bastard," Robin groused at it. He glanced at Chris. "Add that to the list, will you?"

Chris nodded and went to the whiteboard they kept on the wall, a black pen dangling from it on a string. It was their Things-Ken-Needs-To-See-To list, and judging by the length of it, Ken was long overdue for dealing with it. He wasn't a bad landlord, just a busy one, with properties all over London.

Too many, if he couldn't take care of all of them, but that was Denny's private opinion.

Lisa gave Denny a warm smile. "Did you get a lot done?"

"Yeah." Well, he had—right up to the point when Tom had walked in.

It had been difficult to get his focus back after that.

Lisa peered at his jacket.

"What are you looking for?"

Her eyes sparkled. "Evidence. I have to admit, you're good. Not a single croissant crumb." His mouth fell open, and she laughed. "Did you think I didn't know? I'm fond of their lemon and rhubarb cake myself. Not too sweet." She came over and squeezed his shoulder. "Even midwives need a pick-me-up now and then."

Denny reminded himself often how lucky he'd been to spot the card on the noticeboard in college. His last accommodation had been very different, not to mention uncomfortable, although that had been more mental than physical. The meeting with the others had been primarily to vet him, but it had worked both ways—he'd liked what he'd seen. Almost a year now, and Denny had no plans to move out once his studies were completed. He was the only student in the house, and they were great at giving him space when he needed to get his head down and do some work.

Chris reached into the fridge and brought out a can of beer. "Here you go. You look as if you need one. You've got time before dinner."

Denny took it. "Thanks." He'd forgotten it was Housemates Night. Once a week, one of them cooked for everyone, and they caught up with the news and gossip. The latter was where Chris excelled. How he learned all the things he did, Denny had no idea. The rest of the time, they fed themselves.

"Did someone mention the state of the front wall, the last time they spoke to Ken?" Robin asked, stirring something in a saucepan. "It's looking decidedly dodgy. One push and it'll topple like… like…" He grinned. "Like a ton of bricks." Groans greeted his joke.

"I told him last week. Again." Meena rolled her eyes. "I think the only thing that'll force his hand would be if our posh neighbours complained he was bringing down the tone of the neighbourhood."

Denny sniffed. "What's for dinner?"

Robin snorted. "It's me cooking. Do you have to ask?"

Everyone said "Spag Bol" at the same time, then burst out laughing.

"I made it this afternoon. Left it to stew a little. It all adds to the flavour."

Denny took a swig from his can. "I thought we bought you a cookery book for Christmas."

"You did. I haven't read it yet." He glanced at Meena. "Get the garlic bread out of the oven, there's a love. This is done."

She grabbed the oven glove, then peered at the hob. "Is that small saucepan for me?"

"Yup, that's the veggie version. Lisa, drain the spaghetti?"

"Will do."

It wasn't long before they were all seated around the table. The room had originally been a sitting room, but they used it as their dining room as it was closest to the kitchen. Robin's spaghetti Bolognese was as delicious as ever, and the garlic bread vanished from its plate within minutes.

"Brought any new lives into the world today?" Robin inquired.

Lisa smiled. "Yes, as a matter of fact. A little boy. Although we weren't sure he'd make it. It was touch and go for a while this morning."

"Did you never want kids of your own?"

She blinked at Meena's question.

Denny held his breath. It was something he knew the others had wondered about, but up till then, no one had brought the subject up. They tended not to ask about each other's personal lives: if someone wanted to volunteer such information, that was fine. Chris was never one to keep quiet about his latest conquests, but everyone else kept such things close to their chest.

"You don't have to answer that, you know," Denny said in

a quiet voice.

Lisa gave him a grateful smile. "It's okay, really." She gazed at the others. "Yes, I wanted children, but it wasn't to be. So I did the next best thing—I deliver other people's children. I love what I do, especially on days like today."

"Why particularly today?" Chris asked. "Because it was a difficult birth?"

She shook her head. "Because one of the parents was trans. He'd put off having a hysterectomy because he badly wanted to have a child first. You should have seen them when they got to hold the baby for the first time." Her eyes glistened. "It was so beautiful."

Denny took her hand in his and gave it a squeeze. "I'm glad they got you as their midwife."

"I'm sorry." Meena's face contorted. "I shouldn't have asked."

"Like I said, it's okay."

"Just because everyone here knows the ins and outs of a cat's arse when it comes to what *I* do, doesn't mean we have to know *everything*." Denny grinned.

Robin almost choked on his spaghetti. "The ins and outs of a—where do you get these from?"

"It was something my grandma used to say when I was little."

Robin gaped. "Your grandma? Wow. I'd have loved to meet *her*. She sounds as if she was a fun person to be around."

"She is," Denny corrected. "She lives in a retirement home now. I can only hope her fellow occupants are as lively as she is." He sighed. "I haven't been to visit her in so long."

He needed to put that right, and soon. God knew how long she had left.

Chris cleared his throat. "On an entirely different note, what were you today—student or porn star?"

Denny laughed out loud. "I wouldn't call me a star, exactly.

And I was working on the dissertation. Then things got a little... hairy." He told them about Tom's debut the previous day, and his entrance into the coffee shop.

Meena frowned. "I don't blame him for being annoyed. You tricked him."

Robin widened his eyes. "Now wait a minute. He didn't *have* to say yes, did he?"

"That was actually what he said to me this afternoon. I think he'd calmed down a lot by then." Denny wished Tom had stayed a little longer, but he had work to do, and presumably so did Tom.

"Can I ask something here? About your... job, I mean."

Denny chuckled. "Since when are you this polite? Come on, Chris. Say what's on your mind."

"Does anyone *ever* say no?"

Denny smiled. "Yeah, it happens. Not often though."

"And when it does, it's a waste of studio time, and no one gets paid?"

He bit his lip. "Not exactly. Ari makes a few calls, and he gets someone in who's done porn before, to play the straight guy."

Lisa's jaw dropped. "Seriously?"

Denny nodded. "I've seen guys walk in there whose faces—and other bits—I recognised immediately. That's the toughest part—having to keep a straight face when they look at the camera and say they're only into women."

The times he'd had to overcome an attack of the giggle-snorts...

"Robin's right though," he added. "It's their choice."

Lisa cocked her head. "Do you think he'll do it again?"

Denny chuckled. "We have some really interesting conversations around this table, don't we? Last week we were discussing whether aliens are among us. Before that, it was tattoos."

"You didn't answer the question." When Denny said

nothing, Chris grinned. "Ah… you *wish* he'd do it again. Did he get your engine running, Denny?"

Denny wiped his lips with his napkin. "You know what? I'm sorry I ever told you lot what I do."

Robin smiled. "No, you're not. Because we all know, and we don't give a shit. That's why you love us."

Wasn't *that* the God's honest truth? They'd become his family and had proved on countless occasions how much more supportive they were than his own flesh and blood.

With one exception.

Denny was going to take a hard look at his diary and try his damnedest to squeeze in a visit to Grandma sometime soon.

"You did like him, though, didn't you?" Meena's voice was soft.

Denny leaned back in his chair. "I didn't get to spend enough time with him to know if I liked him or not."

Except that was a lie, and he knew it.

"Was he good-looking?" Robin asked.

Hell yes.

"His body? Sure. Not a damn thing wrong with that. As for what lies between his ears? I probably won't get the chance to find out."

More's the pity.

He helped clear the table, then Robin suggested congregating in the living room to watch TV or a DVD. Denny made his excuses and went upstairs to his room. He wanted to work a little more to make up for the time he'd lost.

Not that it had been a complete waste of time. He'd gotten to see Tom again, hadn't he? And he'd been just as hot with his clothes on.

Denny sat at his desk and fired up the laptop. The day hadn't been a total bust, and he'd completed one section he'd always known was going to break his balls. Okay, it needed honing, but that was par for the course.

His phone buzzed, and Denny glanced at the screen. It was Ari.

Need some work?

It was a tempting thought. *Maybe?* The money always came in handy.

When his phone rang, he knew exactly what Ari was going to say.

"You have this knack of calling me when I'm at my weakest."

Ari chuckled. "I'm sitting here with the diary. I could really use you next week. You up for an orgy?"

"How many guys? And how down and dirty is it going to be?" He'd done this a few times. He also knew those type of shoots took much longer to film, and he wasn't sure he could spare that amount of time.

On the other hand, the money involved...

"Seven guys—eight, if you say yes. And it's a no-holds-barred kinda scene. DP, fisting, gangbang..." Ari paused. "I was hoping you'd be the power bottom."

"Give me a sec." Denny opened the spreadsheet where he kept track of his word total and different sections. Such a shoot would require a day.

He could spare a day.

"Okay, I'm in. Anything I need to know?"

Ari snorted. "Yeah. Prep your hole. You're gonna be on the receiving end of some very big dicks. And you'll be taking two at once, a few times." Another pause. "You remember Ty, right? Those big hands of his?"

"Oh Christ, is he the one doing the fisting?" Denny wouldn't be walking straight for a week.

"Yup. So find the biggest dildo you've got. Do you still have Gargantua?"

Denny chuckled. It was the nickname he'd given his longest and thickest toy. Ari had joked it resembled more of a traffic cone than a dildo. "Yeah, still got it."

"Good. Then put it to good use. I've been editing the stuff we shot yesterday, by the way."

"Tom's scene?"

There was silence for a moment. "I didn't tell you his name. How'd you find that out?"

Denny coughed. "He… er… he turned up at the coffee shop where I was working on the laptop this afternoon."

"Everything okay?" Denny didn't miss the note of concern.

"It's all good. At least, it was by the time he left."

Another pause. "I don't suppose he mentioned whether he was up for—"

"Forget it. He's not interested."

"Pity."

Denny let out a rough chuckle. "Funny. That was my reaction too."

Oh well. You win some, you lose some.

He didn't know what caused the brief flare of lucidity that followed, but he was grateful for it. "Wait a minute…"

"What's up?"

Denny thought about how to frame his misgivings. *I'm studying for a business masters, for God's sake.* Maybe doing gangbang, fisting, and DP scenes wasn't such a good idea. Sure, it would pay well, but… what if it got out later on? He could imagine his future employer not looking kindly on discovering Denny's porn past.

"You know what? I appreciate the thought, I really do, but… maybe you could find someone else to be your power bottom."

"Seriously?"

The more Denny considered the proposal, the more he liked it.

"Yeah. I can think of half a dozen guys off the top of my head who'd be up for it."

"Like who?"

"Who was that screamer? Remember him?"

Ari chuckled. "He's the reason we got the soundproofing done in the first place."

"And what about that guy who talks all the way through his scenes?"

Another chuckle. "Oh yeah, I remember him. The only way we got him to shut up was to stick a dick in his mouth, and he still tried to keep on yapping. Great little bottom though."

"Then there's that other guy…. The one you have to remind to douche every time. You always get a lot of engagement when he does a scene."

"Oh, *I* know who you mean. Yeah, you're right."

"And as for the fisting part… what about the Smurf?"

"The who?"

"*You* know, that really skinny small guy? The one who can take a guy up to the elbow. The one who goes blue from all the poppers?"

"Ohhhh, *that* guy. Yeah, okay. But why not you? I thought you'd be up for it."

"And I would be—if I wasn't thinking about the future."

Silence. Ari coughed. "Isn't that sort of closing the barn door after the horse has bolted? You've already done a ton of kinky shit. That doesn't go away, you know. It's still out there, somewhere. The Internet has a *long* memory."

"Yeah, I know, but I just don't want to take any chances. What if I do this scene, and this is the one that attracts the wrong kind of attention? I don't wanna push my luck, Ari."

"Gotcha. And it's a fair point. But you're still okay to do scenes for me?"

"Sure." Denny just thought fisting and gangbangs might be a little hard for a boss to swallow—*if* they ever got to his or her attention.

"Then I'll leave you to get back to your studying, Einstein."

Denny laughed. "Thanks for thinking of me." He finished the call, then leaned back in his chair.

Besides, what would Tom think if he ever saw me in scenes like that?

He stilled. Why should he even care what the guy thought? Denny would probably never see him again. And since when had Tom's opinion become so important?

For the life of him, he couldn't find the answer to that one.

CHAPTER EIGHT

Tom put his tools away in the van and pulled the sliding door shut. It hadn't been a big job—repairing a hole in someone's ceiling where they'd put their foot through it—but at least it was something.

Now all I need is about twenty more such jobs, and I might get things back on an even keel.

His phone vibrated in his pocket. It was a text from Sharon. *Where are you?*

Epsom. Why?

Can you stop by?

His heartbeat quickened, and a trickle of excitement shivered its way through him. Then he went cold when the next message arrived.

Bring flowers. She needs something to make her smile. We both do.

His heart sank. *Aw fuck.*

Yeah, that.

Tom did a quick assessment of his surroundings. Flowerwise wasn't that far away, and they'd done a great bouquet for Deb's thirtieth birthday a few years ago.

On my way. Put the kettle on.

Ten minutes later, he drove the van into the space outside their house, picked up the bunch of pink roses, lilies, and other assorted flowers from the passenger seat, and got out. Sharon opened the door, her eyes puffy and red.

"Thanks for coming over so fast." She stared at the bouquet. "Oh, she loves pink." Then she sighed. "But of course you know that. Come on in."

He stepped into the living room to find Deb curled up on

the couch, a box of tissues next to her on the seat cushion, and a wad of tissue clutched in her hand. She turned her head as he approached, and her reddened eyes widened.

"They're lovely. You shouldn't have."

He leaned over to kiss the top of her head.

Sharon took the flowers from him. "I'll put these in water." She disappeared into the kitchen.

Tom perched on the couch next to Deb. "I'm so sorry."

Deb shrugged. "It happens, right?" Her voice cracked. "I took the test first thing this morning. I hadn't been feeling well all day yesterday, and I'd told myself that was because... it had worked. So there I was, peeing on a stick—"

Tom covered his ears. "Too much information," he sang at the top of his voice.

She whacked him on the arm. "We were married, remember? You've heard far worse things. Done them too." But she seemed to be a little brighter, which was the result he'd been after.

"Okay. You peed on a stick."

"I really thought it was going to be positive. I'd got my hopes up, hadn't I? And then when it wasn't..." She gulped, swiping her cheeks with her hand.

"How long before you can try again?" He was trying to stay positive for their sakes.

"She has to wait four to six weeks at least," Sharon called out from the kitchen. "Then another two weeks after they transfer the embryo." He caught a loud sniff and understood why Sharon had done a vanishing act so fast.

Tom held his arm wide, and Deb cuddled up to him. He stroked her long hair, pushing it away from her face. "Do they know why it didn't work?"

She sighed. "They said it all comes down to the embryo quality. It must have been flawed in some way. It looked good in the lab, but maybe it had defects that meant it didn't take."

Sharon appeared in the doorway. "I keep telling her, there's a twenty-five to thirty-two percent success rate of giving birth after IVF for women her age. She can do this." Her gaze narrowed. "And if I wasn't diabetic, *I'd* be the one having the kids."

Deb gave her a compassionate glance. "We're in this together, right?"

Sharon smiled. "Right." She went back into the kitchen.

"So you *will* try again?"

Deb nodded. "Yeah, once we've saved up enough. That might take a while. But there's a limit to how many times they'll let me try with my own eggs before they suggest using someone else's. If we have to go down that route, I may be asking you for a donation after all, because no way am I going to ask Gavin again."

Sharon walked in carrying the glass vase full of flowers. She set it down on the coffee table, and Deb sniffed.

"They smell wonderful. But I mean it. You shouldn't have." She wiped her glistening eyes once more.

He gave her another light kiss. "You're worth it."

"Can you stay for dinner?" Sharon asked. "Neither of us feel like cooking, so it'll be pizza, I'm afraid."

"Yeah, I can stay." It felt like the least he could do. "Want me to go fetch it?"

"No, Domino's will deliver."

"Well, then let me pay for it." Tom forced a smile. "You need to save your pennies, remember?"

Deb blinked. "First flowers, now pizza... Did you find a ton of change down the back of the couch or something?"

"I've been working, that's all." He wasn't about to share what that work had entailed.

Her face brightened. "Oh, I'm so glad. I was getting worried."

Tom gave her a squeeze. "Okay, no worrying allowed. Not about me, at any rate. You've got enough to occupy you."

He could spend a few hours with them. Anything to see

Deb smile again.

Tom flicked through the pages of his diary. In the week since he'd gone to the studio, he'd had two jobs. Mrs. Delaney had called to say thanks but no thanks. And there was little else in the pipeline, or on the horizon if it came to that.

Not that he was thinking about work. His mind was elsewhere.

He hadn't known why it had been Deb trying to get pregnant rather than Sharon. Once he'd got home, he'd looked up pregnancy and diabetes. After reading the post, he understood a hell of a lot more.

Yeah, that idea was a non-starter.

He wanted them to be able to use Deb's eggs because it meant so much to them, but even if there was a limit to how many times they could do that, it didn't matter if they couldn't afford it. Deb's mum was *not* sympathetic. She made noises about fostering and adoption, and in the end, it had driven a wedge between them.

Tom was there for them because they wanted it so badly, and he'd give all the support he could manage.

I wish I could help in a more practical way.

Except Tom was pretty much in the same boat, and the way things were shaping up, it wasn't looking hopeful.

If anything, the future seemed as bleak as it had prior to his shoot.

A thought came to him, a quiet voice somewhere at the back of his mind.

What about another *porn shoot? That would make a dent in the IVF bill.*

He dismissed it.

Except it wouldn't go away.

Hey, it's an option, right? Ari asked, didn't he? They paid you like they promised. And it wasn't a distasteful experience, was it?

Quite the opposite.

The more he thought about it, the more convinced he became it was the only way to go. He knew Deb and Sharon wouldn't be keen to take his money, not that he'd tell them where it came from.

Some things were *not* for sharing.

Once he'd made the decision, he knew he had to strike while the iron was hot.

Or more aptly, before he changed his mind.

He grabbed his jacket and rummaged through the pockets to find the card Andy had given him. He emptied the contents onto the coffee table, and soon spied it. Then he went to the fridge, removed a can of beer, pulled the tab, and took a long drink.

A little Dutch courage was called for.

He wasn't sure why he was so nervous. He'd already done it once, so why be concerned about a second time? Except he knew why.

I don't want to get a taste for it.

This is a once-only deal, okay?

Only, that was what he'd said the last time too.

By the time he'd finished the can, he had a pleasant buzz going on. He sat in the armchair and dialled Ari's number.

"Hello?"

Tom launched into the speech he'd been rehearsing over and over in his head.

"Look, I'm sorry to be calling you so late, but I've been thinking…"

There was a pause. "Tom? Tom Ryder? Is that you?"

Tom rolled his eyes. Yeah, it might have been a good idea to give his name at the start. He blamed it on the beer.

"Yeah, it's me. I was calling to… to take you up on your idea. *You* know… of me filming with you again."

"Aw, that's great." Tom could hear the smile in his voice. "Same rate of pay as last time? That okay?"

"That's fine." Actually, it was more than fine.

"But *this* time…"

Tom's heart went into panic mode. "What?" His imagination ran riot as he wondered what Ari was going to ask of him.

"I think I might get you to wear a costume. Maybe a builder…"

He pushed out a sigh of relief. "I could do that." Then he chuckled. "I wonder what gave you that idea?"

Ari laughed. "Don't bother bringing your own gear—we have plenty."

"So you really *are* putting together a site called *Hard Hats*?" That hadn't been a total lie to get him to the studio?

"God, yes. One question, though. Are you okay to top again?"

It took him a second. "Top? Oh. Oh, yeah. That's fine."

If anything, it was a load off his mind.

"Great. It'll probably be a different co-star this time."

Tom's stomach clenched, and his breathing hitched. It took him a moment to analyse his physical reaction to Ari's words.

He was disappointed it wasn't going to be Denny.

"Tom? You still there?"

"Yeah, still here. So… when would you want me at the studio?"

Ari suggested a date and time, and Tom made a note of it. A little small talk followed before he finished the call.

There. It's done.

There was an empty feeling in the pit of his stomach that had nothing to do with hunger. His mouth was dry. His heart pounded.

What the hell have I got to be nervous about? I've already done this once.

His gaze alighted on the heap of paper, receipts, and scraps he'd removed from his pocket. A folded piece of paper caught his eye, and he grabbed it, unfolding it and staring at the scribble.

Denny's number...

On impulse, he dialled it, his heart still hammering.

"Hello?"

He took a deep breath. "Hey... this is Tom Ryder. You know, the guy you—"

"I remember. What can I do for you?" He came across as polite.

Tom had no clue why he was calling him in the first place.

"I... I'm going to do another shoot."

"Oh." There was a pause. "What happened to 'never again'?" There was a hint of amusement in his voice.

Yeah, Tom got that part. "Okay, okay. Circumstances change, all right?"

"Sure. And if it's what you want, then great. But... I still don't understand why you're calling *me*?"

A very good question.

Christ, his heart was thumping. "Well... I was wondering... could you do me a favour?"

"That would depend on the favour."

"Ari said he has a different guy for me to film with, but... would *you* be there too, please?"

Say yes. Please say yes.

Tom didn't know why it should be so important, only that it was.

"Really? But... why?"

He sucked air into his lungs. "As a sort of... moral support?"

Denny laughed, but it didn't sound mean. "I'm not sure if porn and morals mix."

"It's just that… I filmed with you last time… and I felt comfortable with you… and then we met and talked…"

He was making a real mess of this. *Denny must think I'm a total idiot.*

Finally, Denny spoke. "Sure. I can be there to hold your hand. Only, you won't need it. You'll be great."

He breathed easier, the tightness around his chest dissipating. "Thanks. I really appreciate this."

There was silence for a moment. "Tom?"

"Yeah?"

"Don't you think it would be a good idea to let me know when the shoot is? What time?" That amused tone was back.

Tom gave a nervous laugh. "Yeah, good thinking." He read aloud from the note he'd scribbled.

"Okay, I'll put it on my calendar. See you then."

"Denny?" he blurted out.

"Yes?"

Another calming breath. "Thanks."

Denny chuckled. "That's twice now you've thanked me. It's okay, honest." He hung up.

Tom scraped his hand back through his hair, raking his nails over his scalp.

Why the hell did I ask him to be there?

He didn't have a fucking clue, but he was damn glad he'd done it.

CHAPTER NINE

Tom gazed at the racks of clothes. There were so many of them. It was like being in a fancy dress shop.

"Do you use all these?" He walked over to one rack, at the end of which hung a priest's outfit, the dog collar pinned to it. And now that he looked closely, there were a few such outfits, not to mention several white cassocks.

Ari chuckled. "You'd be surprised."

"And guys *like* that?"

Ari snorted. "They lap it up." His eyes glittered. "Well, they do when they've finished."

"That was bad, even for you, Ari." A young man walked into the costume room, dressed in jeans and a tee. He was slightly built, with short, neat brown hair.

Tom blinked. He looked as if he still went to secondary school.

Ari gave the guy a hug. "What is it with you? Is it Botox, a painting in the attic, what?"

The young man laughed. "I'll take that as a compliment." His gaze drifted up and down Tom's body. "Is this my screen partner? Ohh, nice."

Tom flushed. He'd come from the shower, and the towel wrapped around his hips wasn't large.

He felt naked, and this guy wasn't helping, especially when he lowered his eyes to take a good look at Tom's crotch.

Nothing to see there, mate.

A phrase from a film came to mind. 'As limp as a bone fish.' Not that Tom had any idea what a bone fish was, but it seemed kinda apt.

And where is Denny? So far there was no sign of him, and there'd been no text either. Tom hoped to God he hadn't changed his mind. Ever since he'd woken up that morning, his stomach had been tight, his appetite non-existent. It had occurred to him to call it off, but the thought of Deb and Sharon's faces when he handed over the money overrode that idea.

I'm doing it for them.

Tom knew his nerves would dissipate once he got into it—that had happened last time, right?—he just had to get past that initial bout of 'What the hell am I doing?'

"Gavin, this is Jake." Ari had confirmed Tom still wanted to go by that name on set.

Tom gave Jake a polite nod. "Which costume will you be wearing?"

Jake grinned. "You're looking at it."

Tom cast his mind back to the brief Ari had emailed him. He hadn't really paid it a lot of attention.

"Jake's parents have gone out for the day, leaving him home with the builder who's working on their kitchen," Ari explained. "Jake will make the first move, you'll both flirt a little, he blows you, you blow him, and you end up fucking him on the kitchen table. The set's all ready." Ari pointed to another rack containing nothing but overalls. "There'll be something your size. The tool belts are on the table in the corner." Ari's phone buzzed, and he removed it from his pocket and peered at the screen. He scowled. "Damn. I have to take this. Sort yourself out with some overalls, and when I get back, we can make a start." He hurried from the room.

Tom went over to the rack and rifled through the hangers. Anything was better than standing there while Jake ate him up with his eyes. He selected a dark blue overall with a zip up the front.

Easy access, I suppose.

He frowned. "I left my underwear in the locker room."

"You won't need it," Jake told him.

"Really?"

Jake flashed him another grin. "It'll look better this way. Just think of your dick poking against the overalls."

"Have you done many videos?"

Jake sounded so confident, so self-assured.

"Sure. I've been in the adult industry for five years. I tend to get typecast a lot, though." He gestured to his face. "I blame this."

How old was he when he started—twelve? Unease bloomed in Tom's belly. *This can't be legal.*

"'Adult industry'?" The words felt incongruous when spoken by someone with Jake's boyish appearance.

"Most people tend to call it that. I think it sounds better than porn, don't you think?" Jake arched his eyebrows. "Shouldn't you be getting into your costume?"

What you really mean is, lose the towel. Tom wasn't *that* naive. Then he reasoned Jake was going to see it all at some point. He turned his back to Jake, slipped off the towel, and quickly stepped into the overalls, careful not to catch his pubes in the zipper. It was a snug fit.

"Maybe I should've chosen something a bit bigger," he mused.

Jake chuckled. "God no. You look great in that. Besides, it shows off your bum." His eyes twinkled. "And it's such a nice bum too."

"You leave his bum out of it." Denny stood in the doorway, holding a cup of coffee, a bag slung over his shoulder. "It's where no man has gone before."

Relief flooded through Tom. "There you are."

Denny smiled. "As requested. The moral support has arrived."

Jake's eyes lit up. "Hey. Haven't seen you for a while. Still studying?"

Denny laughed. "Oh yeah. Not for much longer though."

"So you're going to get a job after? Or are you going to start another degree, and become a lifelong student?"

Denny snorted. "God no. I want money in my pocket, no more early morning lectures, and no more moronic conversations with eighteen-year-olds who keep asking what I'm still doing at uni at my age." He grinned and wrinkled his nose. "They don't call undergrads the Great Unwashed for no reason."

Jake laughed. "Well, if you're here to support Gavin, I'll let you two talk." He wandered away from them, fished his phone out of his jeans pocket, leaned against a table, and scrolled.

"And that's the last we'll hear from him until Ari yells Action," Denny murmured as he drew close to Tom. "I think he's surgically attached to his phone." He glanced at Tom, and his eyes widened. He pressed his hand to his chest. "Be still my beating heart. Look at *you*. Is this how you dress when you're working?"

Tom laughed. "Not exactly. My overalls have a little more room for manoeuvre in them." Denny's obvious appreciation went some way to fuelling Tom's confidence. He inclined his head toward Jake, still engrossed with whatever was on his phone screen. "Should he even be doing this? He looks as if he's still a teenager."

Denny chuckled. "He's twenty-three. And he gets that a lot." Tom expelled a long breath, and Denny studied him. "Did you think you'd got caught up in child pornography or something?" Amusement danced in his chocolate-brown eyes.

"Something like that, yeah." He sighed. "How was I to know? I only met Ari the once."

Denny closed the gap between them. "Then here's what you need to know. He runs a tight ship. No test results? You use condoms. No one underage. If you turn up with an STI, you're sent home. And if he gets so much as a whiff that you'd be a danger to his actors, you're outta here, and you'd better believe he'll spread the word."

"'Danger'? What kind of danger?"

Denny bit his lip. "There was one incident, a while back. A newbie. He did his scene, then had a major attack of the guilts afterwards. He beat up his screen partner in the locker room."

"That's awful." Then Tom recalled Denny's cautious greeting in the café. "You were worried about what *I'd* do, weren't you? At Three Apes? You thought maybe I'd had regrets too."

"The thought did occur to me, yeah."

Ari bustled into the room and came to a dead stop when he saw Denny. "What are you doing here? You're not filming today."

Denny straightened. "I'm here in an advisory capacity. I've come to support… Gavin, in whatever way he needs. At his request, I might add."

It didn't seem to bother Ari in the slightest. "Fine. You know the drill. Just keep behind the camera." He stroked his beard. "And offer him any tips you think are useful."

"Have you done one of these before?" Jake inquired, dragging his attention away from his phone as they followed Ari and Denny out of the costume room and into another that was clearly the set. Kitchen cabinets stood around, half finished, wiring hung from walls, and the place had a real feel to it. Cameras had been set up on three sides, and a mobile camera sat on the kitchen table. Lights flooded the room.

"This is my second." Tom envied Jake his calm, his self-assurance. Then he glanced down and realised part of Jake's confidence might stem from the fact that for someone of his size, he was rather well-endowed.

Not to mention hard.

Tom's erection, meanwhile, was still MIA.

"I might have a problem," he muttered, pointing towards his crotch.

Everyone looked, and Tom's face heated.

"You managed great last time." Ari didn't appear concerned. "Don't worry, it happens. I can give you a pill. You'll have a raging boner in no time."

Tom was *not* going to take a fucking pill. If he couldn't get hard under his own steam, he wasn't doing it, and that was final.

"I'm not happy about that," he murmured. He knew from Ari's furrowed brow that he'd just created a problem.

Tom felt as if he were walking the ridge of a precipice, and it wouldn't take much for him to turn around and head back.

Don't they pay people to be guinea pigs in tests for new drugs?

Except Andy had nailed it. Getting paid to fuck on camera had to be one of the sweetest ways to earn cash.

All he had to do was find his nerve again. That was MIA too.

"Hey, Ari?" Denny piped up. "We could always do it the old-fashioned way."

Ari grinned. "You up for that?"

Denny's eyes gleamed. "Sure."

"Okay, go for it."

Before Tom could ask what on earth they were talking about, Denny walked over to him, knelt in front of him, reached up—and lowered his zipper all the way to his pubes, his dick flopping out.

Tom gaped at him. "What are you—oh my *God*." Denny's warm, wet mouth took him deep, and Tom instinctively placed his hands on Denny's head, hips rolling, thrusting his dick into heaven.

"Fuck." Jake chuckled. "It looks as though he's good at that."

"He is," Tom confirmed, then groaned, his cock filling as Denny's head bobbed. Then Denny's tongue and hands came into play. He sucked on Tom's balls while he slid his hand up and down his now slick shaft. It didn't take long before it was standing to attention.

Denny pulled free with a grin. "Been a while since I was a fluffer. Brings back happy memories." He stood, tugged Tom's zipper to his neck, then moved to the rear of the set behind the cameras where he perched on a stool.

Ari cackled. "I might have to employ you to do that full-time." He smiled. "Okay, boys, let's do this."

They spent a few minutes working on the dialogue, with Denny chipping in now and then with suggestions. Once they had it down, Ari got behind the camera and they were off, with Jake wandering onto the set with a glass of water for the hunky builder.

It was a little corny, but Tom soon got into the swing of it, and it wasn't long before his overalls were pushed down to his waist and Jake was on his knees, sucking him off with great enthusiasm, not to mention a lot of skill.

Yeah, Tom wasn't seeing a downside to this at all.

As Denny had said the last time, it was stop-start-stop-start the whole way through. The toughest thing to remember was getting the angles right: Ari wanted him to fuck Jake in such a way that the camera got to see everything, and that meant angling his body in a manner that didn't feel natural.

Then there were his hands. They always seemed to be in the wrong place. It took him a while to remember not to block the camera's view.

Andy had got one thing wrong.

Shooting porn was *not* easy. In fact, there were moments when it didn't even feel sexy.

Penetrating Jake's tight arse felt as good as it had done to fuck Denny, however, although it was a bit disconcerting when Ari stood next to him while he thrust into Jake's hole, the camera focusing on his slick bare cock sliding in and out. Then Jake lay on his back on the table, knees pulled up to his chest, and Tom slammed into him, each thrust punctuated by Jake's moans and whimpers, while Ari shot the penetration from beneath them.

No wonder Denny had said this could take hours.

They took a short break every time they changed position, and Tom gulped down the bottled water Ari had provided.

Denny came over to him in one of the breaks. "You're doing great."

"Really?" It felt so awkward compared to his first scene.

"Really," Denny assured him. "You're a natural. I wouldn't say it otherwise."

"You certainly know what to do with that cock," Jake remarked from across the room where he leaned against a kitchen cabinet, his phone back in his hand. "You keep hitting my sweet spot. Much more of that, and I'm gonna come way too soon."

"Denny? You got a minute?" Ari beckoned him toward the rear of the set.

"Not Luke anymore?" Tom commented, smiling.

"Not much point. We all know each other here." Denny strolled over to where Ari stood, and Ari whispered in his ear. Denny's grin widened and he nodded vigorously.

Now what's that all about?

Ari cleared his throat. "Gavin? How would you like to earn more money for this scene?"

Tom gave him a blank stare. "Doing what?"

Ari pointed to Denny. "We get Denny in as the electrician. He wanders in and catches you and Jake in the act. Then he asks if he can join in."

Oh God.

"A threesome?"

Jake grinned. "I'd be up for that."

Ari laughed. "Hold your horses. You're still only getting Gavin's dick in your arse. Gavin gets more money because he'd be pulling double duty."

Double duty?

"What does that mean?" But even as he asked the question, an idea trickled into his head, and he had a feeling he knew what was coming.

He just wasn't sure how he felt about it.

Ari folded his arms. "You fuck Jake—and Denny fucks

you."

Yup, there it was.

Tom gave a hard swallow. "But I've never—"

"Don't worry about it," Denny interjected. "I'd prep you first. Taking a dick is easy once you're all loosened up."

"Says the porn star who's probably taken quite a few," Tom flung back at him, his heartbeat racing, the blood rushing through his ears.

"Don't forget the more money part," Ari added.

Denny gave Ari a hard stare. "If Gavin doesn't want to do it, he doesn't have to. That's not what he came here to do, after all." He glanced at Tom. "Okay? It's your decision. You say no and that's it, you finish the scene the way you started it, with just you and Jake."

"Denny's right," Ari said with a resigned air. "It's up to you."

Tom swallowed again. "How much more money are we talking about?"

Ari stilled. "Another seven hundred."

That would make a serious dent in Deb and Sharon's next IVF bill.

"Make it a grand, and he might consider it," Denny butted in, winking at Tom.

A grand? Tom jerked his head in Ari's direction. He felt as though he was in the middle of a bidding war.

Ari shrugged. "Fine. An extra grand."

Denny beamed. "*Much* better."

Tom gave him a grateful smile. Then his heartbeat went into overdrive.

Don't even think about it—say yes.

"I'll do it," he blurted out. "But..." He caught Denny's gaze. "Only if *you* prep me." He shivered. "Where no man has gone before, remember? Well, if anyone's going there first, it's gonna be you."

Denny didn't break eye contact. "I can do that."

Ari walked toward them. "Then we'll break for a little longer—unless you wanna prep him on camera?"

Denny shook his head, much to Tom's relief. "Nope, I'll do it off camera." He picked his bag up from the floor and crooked his finger. "You come with me." He glanced at Jake. "And you? Keep playing with yourself."

Tom ignored Jake's chuckle.

What occupied his thoughts was what was about to go into his virgin arse.

CHAPTER TEN

Tom followed Denny from the room, along the hallway, and into the room where he'd done the paperwork the last time. It was sparsely furnished with a table, two chairs, and a large green velvet couch.

"This'll do." Denny closed the door. "A little privacy. Is that okay?"

"More than okay," Tom assured him. His heart was still thumping.

"Okay, serious question. Do I need to send you to the toilet to clean yourself out?"

Tom shook his head, his face hot. "Already did that." He hadn't wanted to run the risk of anything… unexpected happening on set.

"Good man." Denny put his bag on the table and opened it. "I think we might need a little help." He took out a dildo, long but not too thick. "Perfect." Then he removed a bottle of lube and some wet wipes.

"Do you always carry all this around with you?" Tom had to ask, despite his nervous state.

Denny chuckled. "Let's just say I know how Ari's mind works. It pays to be prepared for any eventuality." He pointed to the couch. "Kneel on there, facing the back, and pull your overalls down to your knees. In fact, take 'em off."

Tom did as instructed. He knelt on the couch, his knees sinking into the cushions, conscious of his nudity.

Denny's seen it all before.

"Oops. Hang on a minute." Denny rummaged in his bag and pulled out a small hand towel. He went behind the couch and hung it so it covered the seat cushions in front of Tom. "If you get pre-cum on this couch, Ari'll kill me."

"You're expecting pre-cum?"

Denny's eyes sparkled. "With what I have planned for your hole? You bet." He moved to stand behind Tom. "Now spread your legs."

Tom slid his knees wider, and then gasped when cool hands pulled his cheeks apart. "You could've warmed them first, or at least warned me."

"Sorry. Push your arse toward me." Tom complied. Denny stroked his back. "You know what? You've got a pretty hole."

"Not a compliment I'm familiar wi—" He shuddered when a warm tongue licked over his pucker. "C-Christ."

It was as if he'd stuck his finger into an electric socket, the shockwaves of pleasure ricocheting throughout his body.

"Never been rimmed before?"

"Never." Then Denny's tongue was back, lapping his hole, probing it, sending multiple shivers through him that collided, spreading out like ripples on a pond. "Fuck."

"Oh, I think you like this," Denny murmured.

Tom twisted around to glare at him. "Don't you dare stop." He wanted to reach back, push Denny's face into his crack, and hold him there.

He didn't want the exquisite sensual torture to end.

"Eyes front."

Tom resumed his position. Denny worked his tongue deeper, and Tom let out a low moan. It felt amazing. But then Denny slipped into a higher gear, humming against his hole, sucking on it, his tongue flicking around the rim, driving Tom's desire into a rising spiral of need. He buried his face in the towel, its fibres grazing his cheeks, muffling the constant stream of noise bursting from his lips.

He caught a *snap*, and a cool, slick finger pressed slowly into his body. Tom tensed, and Denny came to a dead stop.

He rubbed Tom's back. "Breathe, okay? It's easier if you relax."

Tom took a couple of deep breaths, willing himself to relax. Denny waited a minute or two before continuing, and Tom had to admit, his finger entered more easily. More minutes went by, the initial burn he'd experienced faded, and in its place was a pleasant sensation that built slowly, until he was pushing back with his hips, chasing it.

"Another finger, okay?"

Tom did his best not to tense up again, keeping his breathing steady as Denny added a second finger alongside the first. "We... we're not taking too long, are we?"

Denny chuckled. "It takes as long as it takes. I guarantee you, as we speak, Jake is on his phone watching porn, and Ari is on *his* phone, making calls, setting up shoots. Remember what I said? Making porn is *not* a quick process." Another gentle rub on his back. "You okay?"

Tom nodded, digging his fingers into the back of the couch. "It feels... good."

"Ready to try the dildo?"

"Ready as I'll ever be." Tom held his breath as Denny removed his fingers. "Will your dick feel pretty similar?"

"I chose this one because it's roughly the same size. But my cock will feel *way* better than the dildo. The real thing always does." Something cool and blunt met his hole. "Breathe."

Tom inhaled, exhaled, inhaled, and caught his breath as the head popped through. He held himself still as Denny slowly filled him with the silicone toy.

"That feels huge," he said with a groan.

"It will until you loosen up," Denny said with a confidence Tom appreciated. "Now relax and go with it."

Tom gripped the seat cushions and took long, deep breaths while Denny slid the dildo in and out of his body. It wasn't long before it started to feel good.

Then it felt *really* good.

If Denny's right and the real thing feels even better...

Tom couldn't wait to discover if Denny was telling the truth.

When the sensual penetration came to a halt, he realised it was show time.

Denny swiped a wet wipe over Tom's hole, then wrapped the dildo into a towel, stuffing it into his bag. "I'll take care of that when I get home. Now, overalls back on. You've got a scene to finish, and I need to find a suitable costume."

It was looking like a day of firsts. His first threesome loomed next, but Tom was shocked to realise he wasn't nervous, not after Denny had taken such good care of him.

Bring it on.

Tom had seen a few threesomes online, usually two guys and a girl, and he'd wondered how such a scene would work between three guys.

Three dicks, three mouths, three holes?

He had to admit, it was hot. Once Denny made his entrance, it took mere minutes before his hard dick was in Jake's mouth, Jake's cock in his, while Tom fucked Jake as before. The sounds the two men made as they 69'd filled the air, and when Jake declared he was getting close, Ari called for a break, and moved Denny into position behind Tom.

"I'll take it slow at first, all right?" Denny reassured him.

Tom nodded, his heart hammering. He guided his dick to Jake's hole and drove all the way home, then stilled as Denny pressed the slick head of his cock to Tom's pucker. There was slight pressure, and then Denny was inside him, warm and thick, stretching him in a way the dildo hadn't.

Denny's hand on his shoulder was yet more of the reassurance Tom craved.

"Fuck, you're tight," Denny moaned, and Tom wasn't sure if that was for real or an act for the cameras.

Jake groaned beneath him. "Oh yeah. Fuck him into me."

Dear God, the friction was exquisite.

Tom held Jake's ankles, spreading his legs wide as he shuttled back and forth, thrusting into Jake, impaling himself on Denny's shaft, the momentum increasing along with the hoarse cries that escaped from all of them.

He was right. It does *feel better.*

"It's like you're jacking off my cock with your hole," Denny said with a groan.

Jake's arse had got tighter, the sounds were slicker and more erotic, and suddenly it felt *too* good. Tom realised how close he was to shooting his load. "Gonna come," he murmured, striving to hold back the orgasm that was hurtling toward him, lighting up every nerve ending, sending electricity jolting through him.

"Fuck yeah, come in me," Jake ground out, meeting Tom's thrusts while Denny sped up, driving his cock deep.

And when he came, pulsing warmth into Jake's tight arse, it felt amazing—until Denny groaned and gripped Tom's waist. Moments later, he felt a throbbing inside him, accompanied by a slow heat that made him cry out from the pleasure of it all.

A pleasure he had never expected.

Then he realised Ari was giving whispered instructions.

"Gavin, pull out of Jake, slowly."

Tom eased himself out of Jake's arse, Denny's shaft still wedged inside his own. He watched as his cum trickled from Jake's hole, then caught Ari gesticulating for him to slide his shaft back in, pushing the creamy spunk deep into Jake's body, Ari capturing it on camera.

Then Ari shifted, Denny extricated himself from Tom's arse, and Tom felt that trickle for himself. Denny's warm head penetrated him once more.

And now I know how that looks.

Jake's body tightened around Tom's dick, and his cock pulsed onto his belly, creamy white against his tanned skin.

Denny moved slowly inside him, a gentle rocking that felt like the perfect end.

"Cut."

That one word wrought a dramatic change. The three men separated, and Tom was left feeling empty. Jake was off the table in a heartbeat. "That was great." He scanned the room, then launched himself across it, grabbing a towel from a pile. He wiped away all traces of cum. "Shower time," he said with a grin as he made a dash for the door.

Denny laughed. "It's always like a Le Mans start when we finish shooting. Jake treats it like a race. Who'll get to the shower first."

Tom's heartbeat hadn't started its climbdown to its normal rhythm. Endorphins flooded his body, which still shook from the force of his orgasm.

Don't Denny and Jake feel that too?

Ari put down his camera. "That was fantastic. Tom, the camera loves you. You're a natural."

That got another laugh from Denny. "And *that* is Ari-speak for 'I want you back.'"

Ari raised his hands. "Hey, I'm just telling it like it is. That scene will look amazing when it goes out."

"And when will that be?" Not that Tom had any inclination to watch it. That would feel weird.

"*Hard Hats* launches in about four weeks, and I should think this will be one of the first to be shown." Ari's eyes twinkled. "I could send you the link when it releases."

"You know what? I… I don't need to see it."

Ari gave a rough chuckle. "I get that a lot." He glanced at Denny. "Thanks for stepping up. That was a fabulous threesome. You can play electrician again some time."

"Fine by me. Just remember—"

"I know, I know, nothing too kinky." Ari began removing the cameras from the tripods. "Okay, enough talking. I've got editing to do. Thanks again, Tom. Carol will have your money— that includes the extra, by the way. I already messaged her."

"Thank you."

Ari exited the room, leaving him alone with Denny. Now that it was over, the awkwardness from before returned with a vengeance.

I need to get out of here. His mind was reeling.

He forced a smile. "Thanks for showing up. And… *you know*…"

Denny's smiled seemed a lot more relaxed than the one Tom felt certain was pasted on his face. "You're welcome. Any time." He cocked his head. "You okay?"

Tom snorted. "I'll tell you tomorrow. Maybe my first dick could've been a bit smaller."

Denny grinned. "But you took it like a champ. You were great, by the way. Ari was *so* pleased." He picked up his clothing from the floor where he'd dropped it. "Well…. Two scenes under your belt. Think you could do it again? Ari's right—you're a natural." Tom opened his mouth and Denny laughed before he could utter a word. "I know—you'll think about it."

What Tom needed right that minute was to *talk* about it.

"Have you got time for a coffee?"

CHAPTER ELEVEN

Denny glanced at Tom seated at the corner table of Three Apes.

He looks like a skittish colt.

Tom was fidgeting, shuffling his feet under the table, tapping out a nervous rhythm on the wooden surface with a teaspoon, and darting glances at the other customers. He'd been quiet all the way from the studio, and Denny hadn't broken the silence. For all he knew, Tom was one of those people who liked to concentrate on their driving, with no interruptions. Denny's dad was like that, and Denny had learned from an early age not to talk when his dad was behind the wheel.

But it was more than skittishness or an inability to sit still. Tom seemed... baffled.

What is going on?

It couldn't be the scene. Tom had aced that. Ari had already sent Denny a text, asking if he could talk Tom into doing more.

No, it couldn't be the scene—could it?

Denny thanked Anna, then carried the tray with the two lattes and the croissants over to where Tom sat.

"I figured we've earned a treat." He pulled out the empty chair facing Tom and sat, grabbing a packet of sugar and dropping it in front of him. Tom jerked his head up, and Denny shrugged. "I remember you take sugar."

Tom tore it open and dumped the contents into his cup. He stirred the coffee in an absentminded kind of way. Denny said nothing for a moment, studying him, trying to fathom what on earth was happening inside his head.

There was only one way to find out.

"What's up?" When Tom stared at him, blinking, Denny gave him an encouraging smile. "You asked if I wanted a coffee. I got the idea you felt like talking, only, you haven't said a word since we left the studio, except to ask if I wanted to come here."

"How do you do it?" Tom blurted out.

Denny arched his eyebrows. "Do what?" He leaned forward and lowered his voice. "You mean porn?"

Tom shook his head. "When we... when we got to the end, I felt the same way I always feel after sex. You know, your heart's pumping, your skin tingles, you've got these little tremors running through your body..."

Denny smiled. "Sounds exactly how I feel too."

"Yeah, but then you sort of... switched off. It's as if you flipped something inside you and..." He sighed. "I can't describe it. Jake headed for the shower as though he'd just been for a walk, you were laughing and joking with Ari..."

"And all you wanted to do was lie down for a while and enjoy the sensations," Denny guessed. He chuckled. "Most of the time, I can do what I did today. You're right. I flick a switch, and it's back to reality. But... it doesn't *always* work that way."

"What do you mean?"

Denny leaned back. "There *have* been occasions where the cameras stopped rolling, but me and my screen partner, we just carried on fucking. The director and the camera guys left us to it."

"Seriously?"

He laughed. "Hey, if it feels good, why stop?" Denny cocked his head. "Today *was* okay, wasn't it? It didn't feel too weird?"

Tom bit his lip, and Denny fought the urge to adjust his dick.

"I never thought I'd do anything like this."

"Porn? Or fuck a guy?"

"Both?" Tom sipped his latte.

"You seemed to enjoy it. And it wasn't as if you were a total novice, right? I mean, you fooled around in secondary school."

Tom stared into his coffee. "You don't get it. Despite my… experiences back then, I'm only into women." He smiled. "And so is my ex-wife."

Denny blinked. "You were married?"

"For eight years."

"Then you're bi?"

Tom smiled. "What's this talk Ari gives about labels? Apparently I missed it. And if I *am* bi, I'm only just discovering it. Not that I'm completely sold on the idea." He paused. "Can I ask you something?"

"Ask away." Denny was relieved Tom was opening up—and relaxing—a little.

"What did Ari mean when he said 'nothing too kinky'?"

"Oh. That." Denny bit into his croissant.

"Yeah, that."

He swallowed. "The thing is, in the past, I've done a few videos that were a bit more… adventurous than what we shot today." He didn't want to overshare—Tom was skittish enough.

Tom chuckled. "Being the filling in a Jake-and-Denny sandwich was pretty adventurous from where *I* was standing."

Denny laughed. "Fair point. But Ari was talking about gangbang scenes, fisting…" He peered at Tom. "You know about fisting, right? I mean, the term is fairly self-explanatory."

Tom flushed. "I did a little research before today. And yeah, I saw a few fisting scenes. Looked kinda… intense, not to mention painful."

Denny shook his head. "Not if it's done right, and that means nice and slow, with a whole lotta lube. And to be honest? A fisting scene for the camera, and one done in private? There's a vast world of difference between them."

"What do you mean?"

Denny thought best about how to describe it. "It requires a deep level of trust, a connection, communication… If you're with someone and you share all that?" He whooshed out a breath. "Then it can blow your fucking mind."

"And has it ever blown yours?"

"Just the once." He'd had to talk Adam into it, through it, every step of the way. And when Denny had come, shaking like a leaf, he'd looked at Adam, and—

No. he wasn't going to let Adam intrude. He'd lost that right.

"There was something else I wanted to ask you about."

Denny managed a wry chuckle. "We've already discussed fisting. I don't think you can top that."

"It was just… Well… I got to thinking about the two scenes I did. Today's… well, there was a lot of touching, it even got a little rough at times… but there was no kissing. And yet…"

Denny gazed at him with interest. "And yet what?"

"I… well… when we did our first scene, I sort of had the feeling that… you wanted to kiss me when you were… *you* know… with your hand around…" He did a hand gesture.

Denny thought his embarrassment was adorable.

"But I didn't. Do you want to know why?" Tom nodded. "Because I had a feeling too. Intuition told me you weren't comfortable with that, so I backed off. So did you."

"And today?"

"I gave Jake a signal before you got started. No kissing." Denny shrugged. "It happens. Some straight men aren't happy kissing a guy. And a scene doesn't have to include kissing."

Not that he hadn't thought about it.

"Thank you for that. And also for… negotiating my bonus payment."

Denny laughed. "I was glad to help. I'll be honest, you surprised me."

Tom frowned. "How did I do that?"

"I never thought you'd be back for more. I got the impression it was a one-time deal."

Tom took a bite from his croissant. He swallowed. "And it would have been, but like I said, circumstances change."

"Is money that tight?"

Tom let out a sigh. "Ordinarily, I wouldn't share personal stuff with a complete stranger, but you're not that, not anymore."

Warmth barrelled through him. "Thanks for that."

"I… my business is facing a lot of stiff local competition, and I'm finding it tougher to get work, that's all." He held his hands up. "I'm good at what I do, so it really galls me when potential customers go for flashier businesses with far less rigorous standards than mine."

"Now I understand why you came back. If your financial situation is dire, you need all the help you can get."

Tom blinked. "Oh, but I wasn't doing it for me." When Denny gave him an inquiring glance, he smiled. "I was doing it for my ex and her partner."

Something stirred in his memory. "Did you say your ex-wife is into women?"

"Yeah. Her partner's called Sharon. They're trying for a baby. They've already gone through two rounds of IVF."

"And you want to help them pay for another."

The more Denny learned about Tom, the more he liked him.

Tom nodded.

"Is that why you divorced? Because she's a lesbian?"

"Not exactly." Tom drank more of his latte. "We married right out of secondary school. I was still learning my trade. Deb was training to be an accountant." He smiled. "She's the smart one."

Denny frowned. "Hey, we've already had this conversation. It takes brains to be a builder. I know. My uncle was in the trade. He had to pass a load of exams, just like you did."

Another nod.

"Okay then. Don't denigrate yourself, what you've achieved." The words came out more firmly than he'd intended.

"Yes, sir." Tom's eyes twinkled.

"Tell me about Deb. What happened?"

Tom gave a shrug. "We married at nineteen. We were divorced by our late twenties. That's it."

Denny wasn't buying it. "There has to be more to it than that." Then he reconsidered. "You know what? It's none of my business."

"It's okay. Hell, I've got this far, I might as well finish the story."

"What went wrong?" Denny asked in a softer voice.

"We met during the last two years of secondary school, when Deb's family moved into the area. From the beginning, we were inseparable. The best of friends. We loved spending time together, we had similar interests…"

"Didn't I read an article recently that said marrying your best friend makes for a stable foundation for a marriage?"

Tom chuckled. "I think I read that too."

"So what went wrong?"

He clasped his hands on the table. "I've asked myself that same question. We got married because one night, we ended up in bed, and suddenly everyone was telling us marriage was the next logical step. And we thought maybe they're right. Maybe we can take our existing great relationship, make it permanent, and then that too would be great."

"I'm guessing things didn't work out that way."

Tom sighed. "It took a few years before reality set in. We were *way* too similar to be together all the time. The change in dynamic spoiled what we had, and we realised we'd been much happier as inseparable best friends. And then children entered the equation." Another sigh. "Deb wanted kids so badly, but I wasn't fussed about them. We stuck it out a few more years. She didn't stop wanting to be a mum. I never started wanting to be a dad. And in the end that was the dealbreaker. We came to the conclusion that remaining married would destroy our friendship, so we decided to split up before we reached the point of no return."

"That sounds like it was a sensible idea." Denny knew a few couples who'd stuck it out way longer than they should have done, until things got acrimonious, even caustic, and the resulting breakups had been bitter and painful.

"Once we'd divorced, it took us a year or two to regain what we'd had before. And in the meantime, Deb met Sharon."

"Was she into girls when you were in high school?"

Tom shook his head. "Nor when we were married. I think it was something she came to realise gradually. Sharon…" He smiled. "Sharon is amazing. You want to know something funny? I lost my best friend when I got married, but after the divorce, I found I had two best friends."

"Really?"

Tom chuckled. "Andy thinks I'm weird. Deb and Sharon have me over for dinner once a month. Sharon says we still sound like we're an old married couple, but to my ears, we sound like we always did, and that makes me happy."

"You haven't found someone else?"

Tom shook his head. "I haven't had the time. Oh, I went on a few dates, but that was right after the divorce, and they didn't last long. Then I poured all my efforts into building the business. Romance? What's that?" He peered at Denny. "What about you?"

"What about me?"

"Are you single? Except I can't imagine a boyfriend being happy having a porn star for a partner, knowing you're off having sex with other guys."

Denny huffed. "A lot of gay men out there would agree with you. And I've dated a few of them. They think it's hot at first, but then the green-eyed monster digs its claws in, and suddenly they go from 'No, of *course* you can carry on with your career' to 'It's the career or me.'" He finished his latte. "Somewhere out there is an exceptional man who'll accept that porn is work like everything else, a job I can do, then leave it on the doorstep when I get home."

"I take it you haven't met him yet. Mr. Exceptional, I mean." Tom tilted his head to one side. "Are you looking for him?"

Denny smiled. "Nope. If it's meant to be, he'll find me."

"Has no one come close to stealing your heart?" Tom asked in a teasing tone.

Denny's stomach clenched. "No one," he lied. He glanced at his phone. "And delightful though this conversation is, I can hear my laptop calling me from here."

Another lie. He'd got plenty done before he came to the shoot, but he didn't want to continue in the same vein.

We've both bared our souls enough for one day.

"Then I guess this is goodbye." Tom stuck out his hand. "Thank you again. For everything."

Shit.

Denny shook it. "You know, you still have my number. If you ever need to talk, I'm a good listener." He gestured to the coffee shop. "My office keeps reasonable hours."

Tom chuckled. "I might take you up on that, if I'm ever passing by." He stood. "I'd better be going too. I need to make some calls."

"I hope all goes well with Deb and Sharon's IVF."

Tom's face lit up. "Yeah, me too."

"Let me know?"

It was only then Denny realised how desperately he was striving to hold onto the fragile friendship blossoming between them.

"Sure, I can do that." Tom smiled once more, then turned and walked out of the coffee shop.

But not out of my life. Not completely.

By hook or by crook, Denny was going to see to that.

Chapter Twelve

June

Denny opened his eyes. "Wha was that?" He blinked groggily. Something had jarred him from his doze on the couch.

A very loud something.

He glanced at the clock over the fireplace. It was past eleven-thirty. Then he caught noise from outside. Loud voices. Come to think of it, a *lot* of loud voices.

"Denny!" Robin hurried into the room.

"Okay, so I fell asleep. I blame the film." Not to mention the couch. It sort of sucked him in and cocooned him in comfort. Saturday night was DVD night, and it had held his attention for the first hour. Then a day of concentrating on his dissertation had taken its toll, and he'd slipped into a doze that had effortlessly developed into sleep.

"Didn't you hear that?" Robin was frowning. "Some drunken idiot just ploughed his car into the front wall."

That woke him up fast. He was off the couch in a heartbeat. "What?" He dashed from the room in his bare feet and went to the open front door. The street was full of their neighbours, some of them with torches, the beams bouncing around.

"Call the police!"

"Call an ambulance!"

The torch beams picked out a Ford Fiesta that had mounted the pavement and was now sitting in the middle of what had been the front garden wall. Its bonnet was crumpled, its headlights smashed. Only the gatepost was left standing: the rest of the bricks lay on the lawn, along with the driver. Lisa was checking him over.

Chris came over to where Denny stood. "He says he swerved to avoid a cat." He rolled his eyes. "I think it was more to do with how much booze he's had. He stinks of beer." He held up the notepad that usually sat next to the phone. "I've taken down his number."

"I've called the police," Meena told them as she approached. "Stupid drunk."

"Is he okay?" Denny called out to Lisa, peering at what he could see of the driver in the light from the streetlamps. The guy looked middle-aged, and even at that distance Denny could hear the slurring in his speech.

She nodded. "The airbag didn't inflate though, and he took a wallop on the head. He'll have a bump, that's for sure. No other injuries." She helped him to his feet.

"'M fine," the guy said, weaving.

"All that booze probably made him numb to the pain," Robin muttered. Then his eyes widened. "Hey, stop him, one of you."

Denny jerked his head in time to see the driver stumbling over to the car and getting behind the wheel.

"Surely that thing can't be safe to drive, and he's even less safe to drive it. Besides, he can't leave. The police'll want to talk to him." A crowd of neighbours had gathered in front of the house, and Denny could see a lot of phones recording the incident.

"We can't force him to stay put," Chris groused. "We'll have enough footage, plus his registration number, for the police. And if he has *another* crash and kills himself? His own stupid fault."

"Yeah, I'm sure that'll be a great comfort to his family," Lisa remarked, glaring at Chris.

By now the Fiesta was moving backwards, its rear narrowly missing a parked car, its front end a mess. There was the clanging of metal, so Denny guessed *something* was hanging off somewhere.

Denny watched the drunken arsehole drive off. "Ken is going to be pissed," he said gloomily. "At least it wasn't one of us."

Lisa walked toward them. "Well, we can call him in the morning. It's too late now." She glanced back into the street. "I hope he's all right."

Denny gave her arm a squeeze. "You tried to help him, that's the main thing." The effects of adrenaline had dissipated, and he was craving his bed.

"What about the police?" Robin demanded. "Shouldn't we stay up till they've been?"

Chris snorted. "You think they'll turn up tonight? Aw, how cute is that?" Another eye-roll. "I looked up average police response times. If there's an immediate threat to life or property? Fifteen minutes, so that one's out. A serious threat? One and a half hours, so *that's* out. Non-urgent? Bingo. More than eleven hours, and it could be as high as forty-eight." He waved his hand. "Go to bed, guys. If we're lucky, they'll have paid us a visit before Monday morning."

They trudged back into the house, and Robin closed, locked, and bolted the front door.

"Anyone want some hot chocolate?" Meena asked. "And there's a thriller on TV if you feel like staying up."

Denny shook his head. "Chris had the right idea. I'm going to bed." He'd had enough drama for one night.

Ken Loomis was doing an awful lot of tut-tutting, and Denny was starting to worry.

"This isn't going to be added to our rent, is it?" he asked as Ken surveyed the mess of rubble that had crashed in a wave over the front lawn.

"Lord no. It was nothing to do with any of you lot. The lady across the street came out as I arrived, to show me the video she'd recorded. Have the police been yet?"

Denny laughed. "It's only been ten hours."

"Yeah, what was I thinking? You know, I reported a burglary once, in one of my houses. Took 'em three days to turn up, and *then* they told me they'd probably never catch the guys. What do we pay our taxes for?" Ken slapped Denny on the arm. "Look who I'm talking to—the student." He grinned. "You wait. You have all this to come." He gazed at the wrecked wall again and pursed his lips. "God, he made a right mess of it. Oh well. *And* it was on my list of repairs. I'd better find myself a builder. That'll probably cost me an arm and a leg."

Lightbulb.

"I might be able to help you there." Denny fished his phone from the front pocket of his jeans and scrolled until he came to Tom's number. He copied it, then sent it in an email to Ken. "This guy's really good." Okay, he had no idea if that was true, but based on what Tom had said, it seemed likely.

Ken peered at his phone. "Does he have a name?" he teased.

"Tom."

"Tom what?"

It was only then Denny realised he didn't have a clue. "I don't know."

"Oh, mystery man, huh?" Ken narrowed his gaze. "He's not a cowboy, is he? I mean, he's not dodgy."

"No, no, not at all. Why don't you call him? That way, you can decide for yourself." Tom needed the money, Denny knew that much.

"I'll think about it." Ken gave the collapsed wall one last

glance before heading for the door. "Okay, while I'm here, I suppose I'd better check out your list." His eyes twinkled. "It must've grown since my last visit."

Denny followed him indoors.

He was going to keep his fingers crossed. There seemed little point in telling Tom what he'd done, not if it didn't come off.

Please, let it happen.

Tom needed a break.

Even with the house number, Tom had no trouble spotting the address. Someone had made a real mess of the front wall. He parked the van and got out. It was a pleasant suburban street in Wimbledon, two rows of semi-detached houses, complete with garages and short driveways. The house in question was done in red brick on the ground floor, the pale grey door with its circular window set between a square bay and a white-doored garage. The first floor was rendered white, with three windows: a round bay, a tiny window with a triangle of red brick beneath the sill, and a square one above the garage. A dark-tiled porch ran along the front of the house, curved elegantly around the upper bay window and supported by posts sunk into brick pedestals on either side of the garage.

A well-built house. The same could *not* be said about the front garden wall.

"Mr. Ryder?" A middle-aged man in a brown leather jacket and black jeans walked toward him, his hand outstretched. "I'm Ken Loomis. We spoke on the phone." They shook, then Mr. Loomis indicated the heap of bricks. "As you can see, it needs rebuilding completely." In his other hand he clutched a plastic wallet.

Tom glanced along its length. It wasn't a long wall: most of the house's frontage was taken up by the gravel in front of the garage and the concrete-slabbed path that led to the front door. "I can do that, Mr. Loomis. It'll look just like the original. Better, even." He shook his head. It needed to be wider. It wouldn't be a big job, but Tom wasn't about to complain.

Work was work.

"Ah, but what if I don't want it like that?"

Tom arched his eyebrows. "What did you have in mind?" He reached into his pocket for his notepad and pen.

"I'd like it higher, maybe with iron railings. Something more upmarket. Maybe curved? And I'd want you to get it done ASAP."

Tom nodded. "Okay, two things about that. To build it higher than it is now would require planning permission, and that could take weeks. I'm sorry, but I'm not one of those people who build first and ask for retro planning permission after."

"Glad to hear it." Mr. Loomis smiled and held out the plastic wallet. "This is planning permission for a higher wall. I applied for it a couple of months ago, when I was first alerted to the state of the wall. I figured why repair it when I could have it rebuilt and looking better than before." He cocked his head. "What's the second thing?"

"The footings will need to come out. What you have here won't support a higher wall. Plus, I'd like it to be about eight inches wide, rather than the four inches you have here."

Mr. Loomis nodded. "Then they come out."

Tom went to his gallery and scrolled. "I was thinking of something like this." He showed Mr. Loomis the photo. "A straight wall, to mirror the lower square bay. And I'd set arch top railings into it, to mirror that curve around the upper bay."

Mr. Loomis smiled. "I like that."

"And if you're going for a more upmarket feel, you might consider railings like this." He scrolled again, then held out his phone. Each black wrought iron post was topped with a fleur-de-lys, and in the centre the metal divided into four strands that curved to form a basket.

Mr. Loomis beamed. "Perfect. Can you fit me in?"

Tom blinked. "I haven't given you a quote yet."

He waved his hand. "That's okay. I've already spoken to some of your previous clients. Thanks for the references, by the way. They all spoke very highly of your work." He gave Tom a frank stare. "So when could you start?"

Tom wanted to laugh with relief. "Tomorrow?"

"Excellent. Buy what you need in the way of materials, then bill me for them right away. No reason why you should be out of pocket. You can invoice me for the labour when it's done." He smiled. "I have several properties all over London, and I deal with a lot of tradesmen. This is how I do things."

"You have no complaints from me. Thank you, Mr. Loomis." Then he remembered. "I'm curious, though. You said on the phone I'd been recommended. Can I ask by whom?"

"One of my tenants." His eyes twinkled. "He couldn't remember your surname, but he said you were good."

Tom had no clue who that might be, but as Loomis had stated he owned a lot of properties, it could be one of Tom's previous customers.

Whoever it was, he owed them.

He scanned the driveway. "Will I be okay to use the driveway for tools and such?"

Another nod. "One of the tenants has a car—she's a midwife. I'll let her know to park it on the street."

"One more thing. I'll have to hire a mini skip for the rubble. Are they okay to leave that on the driveway too?"

Mr. Loomis's brow furrowed. "For how long?"

"A day. If I start on it first thing, I could have it all cleared by the evening."

Mr. Loomis pursed his lips. "Okay. Will you be able to dig for the new footings by hand?"

Tom shook his head. "I'll hire a mini digger too. Once the footings are in, I'll leave them for a week to harden, then I'll come back and build the wall. It shouldn't be a long job. It'll actually take more time to clear the old wall than it will to build the new one."

Mr. Loomis expelled a breath. "It sounds to me as if you've thought of everything."

"Then I'll make some calls to order the ready-mix concrete, I'll—"

"You don't mix your own concrete?"

Tom smiled. "Well, I *could*, but it would take longer. Getting a load of concrete here ready to pour might work out more expensive than buying the materials, but you have to factor in the labour. And that always costs more than the materials. This is the most cost-effective way—and it cuts your bill down."

Mr. Loomis smiled. "Sounds good to me."

"I'll sort out a skip and a digger, and I'll be here first thing in the morning to start work."

"Not before eight o'clock?" Mr. Loomis glanced up and down the street. "I don't want to be swamped with complaints about noise from drills or whatever tools you'll be using."

Tom assured him he'd only work between eight a.m. and six p.m. They shook once more.

"Thanks for coming out on a Sunday afternoon. I appreciate it." Loomis headed back to his BMW, and Tom went to the van for a tape measure.

Things were looking up.

Monday morning, Tom pulled up outside the house. He switched off the engine and grabbed his SDS from the back of the van. He'd made sure all his tools were fully charged the night before. The skip was due to be delivered by ten, and the mini digger by three that afternoon. He'd brought along his earbuds so he wouldn't be working in silence, and his earplugs for when he used the power tools.

The only thing he had left to arrange was where to take a leak. If the tenants weren't happy about him trudging through the house, leaving a trail of cement dust, there was always the recourse of the bottle he kept in the van for such emergencies.

The front door opened, and a woman came out, wearing a dark blue nurse's uniform with white trim. She smiled when she saw him.

"Hi, I'm Lisa. You must be the builder."

"Guilty as charged." He returned her smile. "You must be the midwife."

She chuckled. "What gave it away?" She pointed to the garage door. "It's unlocked. If you go through it to the rear door, you'll find a toilet. That way you won't need to go through the house. The kettle's on and someone will be out with a mug of coffee shortly. And one of us went to the local shop yesterday for a packet of chocolate biscuits. He said coffee and biscuits at regular intervals were vital if we wanted a good job doing." She grinned. "His uncle is a builder too, so I guess he knows about these things." Then she walked briskly to her car, got in, and drove off.

Thank God. Wimbledon wasn't going to be as bad as he'd anticipated.

The first task was to take down the wall. After assessing its width—it was only a single skin of brick—he decided to go first with the old-fashioned method of taking a sledgehammer to it. By the time the skip arrived, he'd have a load of rubble ready to toss into it.

Tom went to work, wondering what had happened to the promised coffee and biscuits. He attacked the brick pillar at the end of the wall with gusto, smiling in satisfaction when it toppled to the ground.

"Never mind studying—I think I'll bring out a garden chair and sit and watch *you* all day."

Tom froze at the sound of that familiar voice. He straightened, turned around, and there was Denny, grinning, a cup in one hand, a ramekin containing three Kit Kats in the other.

Tom burst out laughing. "You know, when Lisa mentioned one of the tenants having an uncle in the trade, it rang a bell. Now I know why—you mentioned him last week." Then it clicked. "You were the one who recommended me to your landlord."

That earned him another grin. "Yup."

"Thanks for that."

"You're welcome." Dimples appeared in Denny's cheeks.

Tom stared at the house. "So this is where you live."

Denny nodded. He pointed to the window above the garage. "That's mine." He set the mug and ramekin on the pillar next to the front door. "I'll leave these here for you. I didn't mean to interrupt."

"I hope the noise doesn't bother you, if you're working."

Denny waved a hand. "I can always work at the dining table if it does. That's at the back of the house." He cocked his head. "When do you plan on taking your lunch break?"

Tom raised his eyebrows. "Why do you ask?"

"Oh, I thought I might join you. There's a door next to the downstairs toilet that leads into the garden. No one would mind if you brought dust out there, and it's such a nice day."

Tom chuckled. "You've thought of everything, haven't you? I usually stop around twelve-thirty."

"What have you brought for lunch?"

"Sandwiches and fruit."

Denny held his hand out. "Give me the sandwiches. I'll put them in the fridge for you."

Tom was still chuckling as he walked to the van to fetch them. "I don't usually get this sort of treatment."

"You do when you work at my house." Denny flushed. "Well, Ken's house." He joined Tom and took the blue plastic lunch box. "Don't let your coffee go cold. You take one sugar, right?"

"Right." Tom was feeling ridiculously happy.

Denny's eyes sparkled. "Now... back to work."

Tom laughed. "Yes, sir." He watched Denny walk back to the front door, hips swinging a little.

I wonder if that was for my benefit? Tom wouldn't put it past him. He'd seen Denny in action, flirting up a storm as a horny electrician.

It was shaping up to be a very good day.

CHAPTER THIRTEEN

So much for spending the day on the dissertation.

Denny figured he'd spent most of the morning staring out of his bedroom window, watching every swing of that sledgehammer, especially when the outside temperature climbed, and Tom removed his T-shirt.

Oh yeah.

Dissertation well and truly forgotten.

Be honest. You stayed home to work today because you knew he was coming.

Ken had called the previous evening to inform them he'd found a builder. Denny had done his best not to punch the air when Ken thanked him for the recommendation.

He peered out of the window again, trying not to make it too obvious. Then a truck pulled up, backed onto the driveway, and a mechanical arm lowered a bright yellow skip onto the gravel. Once the truck had driven off, Tom began picking up bricks in his gloved hands and tossing them into it. Denny smiled as Tom rolled his hips fluidly to whatever music was playing in his ears, his body moving in sinuous motion, the muscles in his back and arms rippling when he launched each handful of rubble into the skip.

Oh baby, look at you.

Okay, so he was drooling over a straight guy. Tom didn't need to know that, right? He'd seemed so pleased when he realised Denny had put a good word in for him.

Not as pleased as Denny was with the sexy but unexpected entertainment. Thank God everyone had gone to work. No one around to catch him watching Tom with his tongue hanging out.

Okay, he wasn't *that* bad. At least he'd kept his hands out of his jeans.

He wasn't sure he could resist the impulse for much longer, however.

Another peek, only this time, it coincided with Tom glancing up to his window, and he beat a hasty retreat. Not too hasty—there was long enough to register Tom's grin.

Busted.

Denny forced himself to go back to the dissertation. It seemed like a thousand years since he'd begun working on it, but the end was in sight. *As long as it does what it's supposed to and gains me some interest.*

He wasn't going to hold his breath. He knew what it was like out there in the real world.

A short while later, he caught Tom's shout, and opened the window.

"Something wrong?"

Tom grinned up at him, tapping the huge plastic watch on his wrist. "It's lunchtime."

Denny jerked his head to where his phone lay on the desk. *Already?* "I'll meet you in the garden." He did a save, closed the laptop, and thudded out of the room and down the stairs. By the time he'd grabbed the box of sushi he'd treated himself to, and Tom's lunch box, he heard the door open at the back of the garage. "I'll be right out," he hollered. "What do you want to drink? There's tea, coffee, juice, water… There's even coke if you're really desperate."

"Water, please. In a pint glass if you have one."

Denny resisted the urge to snort. They had an entire cabinet full of glasses of all descriptions.

He brought the food outside, and found Tom standing on the patio, gazing at the garden. It was a pleasant space, but there wasn't a whole lot going on: a lawn stretched toward the rear fence, and hedges marked the boundaries with the houses on either side. The patio was done in alternating slabs of pink and sandstone, furnished with a long rectangular table and eight chairs. Trees grew from the long beds framing the lawn, and a shed sat in the bottom right-hand corner.

"This is nice." Tom chuckled. "It's also a carbon copy of my garden, except I have fewer trees, a huge hedge at the end, and there's only a wooden bench on the patio, next to the shed. I keep meaning to do something with it, apart from use it as somewhere to hang my laundry out to dry."

Denny gestured to the chairs. "Please, have a seat." He placed the food on the table.

Tom glanced doubtfully at the green seat cushions. "I don't know about that." Then he smiled. "Hang on. I'll be right back." And before Denny could get one more word out, he'd disappeared through the back door.

Denny followed, going into the kitchen to fetch the water. When he returned to the patio, Tom had spread a colorful towel over one of the seat pads.

"I keep one in the van for just such emergencies." He sat at the table, glancing at the box of sushi. "I've never tried that. Isn't it raw fish?"

"It can be." Denny took a seat and opened the box. "I like these. They're California rolls. They've got avocado and crab in the middle. And that's salmon. And these rolls have a bit more of a kick to them." He took out the small black paper box and poured the soy sauce into it, then tore open the packet of wasabi.

"What's that?"

"It's a kind of Japanese horseradish. It gives the fish a little heat. Why don't you try one of the California rolls? They taste great." Denny smiled. "You never know. You might like it." He squeezed the wasabi into the sauce, then stirred it with the end of a chopstick.

Tom bit his lip. "I don't know."

Denny picked one up with the chopsticks provided and

held it out to him. "Try it with or without the soy sauce."

Tom studied it for a moment, then took a bite. Grains of rice dropped onto the table, falling through the spaces in the lattice top. "It disintegrated."

"Yeah, that can happen." Denny tried not to laugh.

Tom finished the morsel, then nodded. "Hey, that's not bad." He opened his lunch box. "But I think I'll stick with my ham and cheese sandwiches. Far less mess involved."

They ate in silence for about ten minutes, and Denny relished the warm sunlight on his face and arms. *Summer at last.* The winter had been particularly vicious, and he'd yearned for the day when he could lie in the garden, soaking up the rays, listening to music through his earbuds.

He sat back in his chair. "How much more can you do today?"

Tom took a long drink of water before replying. "I need to finish breaking up the concrete by three. That's when the digger arrives. I hope to have the new footings dug out before I leave. Then tomorrow, I'll be back to lay concrete." His eyes sparkled. "So expect a delivery tomorrow morning. A truck full of ready-mix cement."

Denny blinked. "All that for one wall? I thought you'd just need a bag of cement."

"Concrete is usually made up of one part cement, two parts aggregate, and three parts sand. The aggregate is stuff like gravel, crushed stone, recycled concrete… It helps to make concrete mixes more compact. And it means you use less cement and water. It also makes the concrete stronger. And buying it ready-mixed saves time." Tom grinned. "If you're not working on your dissertation tomorrow, you could lend me a hand."

"Doing what?"

He laughed. "I'm joking."

Conversation dried up for a few minutes, but Denny wasn't about to break the pleasant silence just for the sake of it.

Peace and quiet in that place were a rare commodity.

"You do know this feels a little... weird, don't you?" Tom murmured.

"'Weird'?" Denny straightened in his chair. "In what way?"

"Okay, maybe that's the wrong word." Tom stroked his beard. "Awkward. That's a better description."

"Why do you feel awkward? All we're doing is sitting in a garden eating our lunch."

Tom chuckled. "The awkwardness has nothing to do with the surroundings or the activity, and everything to do with the fact you've seen me..." He clammed up.

Denny tried not to smile. "Naked?"

"As Andy would say, 'And the rest.'" A flush inched its way from beneath the neckline of the T-shirt Tom had put back on—*damn*—and reached his face. "Seeing you is... I mean, it's not awkward all the time, it's just..." He cleared his throat. "Now and again, I look at you, and..."

"And you think about the shoot," Denny surmised. "So it's only *slightly* awkward? It'll pass. I mean, it's not as if you're sitting there picturing me without my clothes on, right?"

Tom exploded into a bout of coughing. "Er, no," he exclaimed. Then he stiffened. "Why did you say that? *You're* not..."

"Fuck yeah, I am. Like I said, you're hot." Denny laughed. When Tom stared at him, he laughed even harder. "Oh, come on. You're talking to a gay man. What did you expect?"

Tom gave a mollified smile. "Can't stop you thinking, I suppose." Then his face brightened. "I could always keep my shirt on for the rest of the afternoon, so that I don't give you any more... ideas."

Denny gaped at him in mock anger. "Don't. You. Dare."

Seconds later, they were laughing again, and he felt a little lighter.

Tom leaned back. "So... this dissertation you're working

on… does it have a catchy title?"

Denny laughed. "Oh, totally." He cleared his throat. "'A comparative study on how the macro and micro perspective of leadership provide insight into effective leadership characteristics required to sustain competitiveness on a continuous basis in the United Kingdom.'"

Tom widened his eyes. "Whoa. That sounds like it's a lot of work. It also sounds like you're very intelligent. You must be, to be doing a master's. Your parents must be so proud of you."

Denny's good mood crumbled like the cement taking up space in the skip. "Yeah, you'd think so, wouldn't you? I mean, any *normal* parents would be, right?"

Tom sat very still. "Why do I get the feeling I've just put my foot in it?"

He could change the subject.

He could say he didn't want to discuss it.

In the end, he did neither.

Denny expelled a long breath. "They think education is a waste of time."

Tom frowned. "What?"

He nodded. "Neither of them studied past secondary school. They've both worked since they were sixteen. And they say it's never done *them* any harm, not having qualifications."

"They don't support you?"

"Nope. And that's figuratively *and* financially." Denny took another drink from his glass. "When I was at school, most of the kids I hung around with dreaded the end of year report. Mine? Straight As. Every teacher said the same thing. 'Dennis has the potential to go far.'"

Tom bit back a smile. "'Dennis'"?

He rolled his eyes. "Why'd you think I call myself Denny? I mean, do I *look* like a Dennis?"

"Absolutely not," Tom intoned in a solemn voice, but there was an attractive twinkle in his eyes. "Back to what you were saying."

"When I was eleven, every kid in school had to sit a load of tests. It wasn't until later that I realised they were testing for our IQ."

"And what *is* your IQ?"

Denny shrugged. "I don't know. My parents were informed of it, but they said I didn't need to know, because it wasn't going to affect my life. I could've taken an IQ test—you just send off for them from MENSA—but I never got around to it. Anyhow, I got into an argument with them when it came time to choose my A-levels. Dad wanted me to work with him, in his company."

"What kind of company?"

"Office supplies."

Tom stared at him. "I'm sorry, but…" He shook his head. "No. I might not have known you all that long, but it's obvious to me anyone who's tackling a dissertation like yours would be wasted in a job like that." He cocked his head. "You got to do your A-levels though, didn't you?"

"Yeah, but they weren't happy about it. They were even unhappier when I told them I wanted to go to university." His stomach roiled at the memory of those bitter arguments.

"So what changed their minds?"

Denny huffed. "Nothing did. My Grandma weighed into the battle at that point, and said it was my life, not theirs, and they should be proud of me. So…" He met Tom's gaze. "I applied for uni, got in at my first choice, and then applied for a loan—well, the first of a few loans—to pay for it. Except it wasn't just for my studies—it was for food, clothing, and everything else I'd need." He smiled. "Grandma helped a little, but then she had to go into a retirement home, and that ate up all her money. My parents were pissed off, but there wasn't much
they could do about it." He gave another shrug. "I've been taking care of myself ever since."

"*Now* I get why you're doing porn. How did you get into it? And when?"

"I was nineteen. I'd met this guy called Jon, in my first year of uni." He grinned. "We were fucking like we'd invented it, every chance we got. Then Jon suggested doing porn. I didn't see a single thing wrong with that. We both went along to a studio, and that was the start." He gave a wry smile. "Okay, the start of my porn career—the end of me and Jon. I did shoots all through my degree course."

"You must have done well," Tom remarked.

Denny snorted. "I walked away with an Upper Second Class Honours, when it could easily have been a First."

"What happened?"

No. Denny was *not* going to talk about it.

"Let's just say I got a little... distracted at the time. Anyway, I pissed off my parents even more when I announced I was going to do a master's." He shook his head. "I got the impression they thought I was doing it to spite them." He finished his water. "So I started my postgrad course and knuckled down. No more distractions for me. I did fewer shoots, only resorting to them when I needed the money. Kink pays better, but I can't risk it. That comes under the heading of something-I-wouldn't-want-to-suddenly-surface-later-in life. Especially if I'm working for a prestigious firm who would probably *not* take kindly to discovering a video of one of their employees with someone's arm in his arse up to the elbow."

Tom blinked, then burst out laughing. "Okay, that was an image I didn't need." He gave Denny a thoughtful glance. "What distracted you? Was it the porn?"

"Not exactly." Denny shifted on his chair. "I'm sorry, but I really don't want to talk about this, okay?"

A flush crept over Tom's cheeks, and his ears turned red. "I'm the one who should be sorry. I had no right to pry." He picked up his pear and bit into it, juice trickling down his chin. He pulled a tissue from his pocket and mopped it up. "Sorry. It's a really ripe one."

Denny smiled. "That's fine. It could've been worse." When Tom gave him an inquiring glance, he grinned. "You could've been eating a mango, and the only way to eat one of *those* and not get juice on you, is to eat it in the bath, stark naked."

Tom burst into more laughter, and the sound melted Denny's unease away.

"Thanks for telling me about you and your parents. It makes a change, I suppose."

"What do you mean?"

"Well, it was higher education that drove a wedge between you, not the fact you were gay." Tom froze. "They didn't reject you for that reason too, did they?"

Denny snorted again. "They don't give a shit that I'm gay. Sometimes it's hard to believe we're related."

"Have you got any brothers or sisters?"

"One of each."

"And none of them know about the porn."

Denny shuddered. "Fuck no. Not that I care who else knows about it—apart from the aforementioned future boss, of course." He gestured towards the house. "All my housemates know."

"Really?"

Denny nodded. "And you know what? They're cool with it. But my family... They already see me as a disappointment. Learning about the porn would only confirm it."

Tom pointed to the house. "How long have you lived here?"

"Almost a year."

"I think you said you share with four other people. I met one of them this morning. Lisa?"

Denny smiled. "Yeah, she's great. Then there's Chris, Robin, and Meena."

"Do you all get along?"

"Better than I did when I was in university accommodation." Denny didn't want to talk about himself anymore, not when the conversation had already veered perilously close to a precipice. "Do you have any funny stories about stuff that's happened to you on some of your jobs?"

Tom chuckled. "Only a couple. There was that time I was working in a guy's back yard, building a house, and it was pouring down. My boots were covered in mud. Anyway, worst timing ever—I needed the bathroom. So I asked if it was okay to use the one in the house. The owner frowned, then said fine, but he'd have to put down newspaper first. I looked him in the eye and told him I was already toilet-trained." His lips twitched.

Denny groaned. "Seriously?"

Tom laughed. "You think *that's* bad? But it's true. My mate Andy has a ton of builders' jokes. I think he collects them, just to make me roll my eyes."

"Tell me some of them."

Tom guffawed. "You have no idea what you're asking."

"Hey, you can't back out now. Tell me."

"Okay then." Tom folded his arms. "Why did the plank of wood go to the bar? Because he wanted to get hammered before he got nailed."

Denny cackled. "Okay, I take your point."

"Oh no, you don't get out of it *that* easily. You started this, remember?" His eyes twinkled. "I had this great joke about construction, but I still need to work on it."

Another groan rolled out of him. "Okay, that's bad."

"What music do builders listen to? The Carpenters."

"Stop!" Denny begged. "Mercy."

"Or what about the one with the three nuns?"

Denny widened his eyes. "Oh Lord."

"There's this builder, working in a monastery, rebuilding part of the wall. Anyway, he slips in the mud—"

"*Another* mud-related joke?" Denny rolled his eyes.

"Let me finish, okay?" Tom said with a mock glare. "So he goes to the head monk, and asks if he can shower off all the mud. The monk tells him their shower is broken, but he can use the one next door in the nunnery. Only, he has to be quick. None of the nuns have ever seen a naked man before."

Denny coughed. "Oh my God, where are you going with this?"

Tom ignored him. "He climbs into the shower, and just as he finishes, he hears some nuns come into the bathroom. So he grabs a bar of soap in each hand, and freezes as if he's a statue. In walk three nuns, and they spot him right away. 'Oh,' says the first. 'Look. Someone's delivered a new statue.' She peers closely at him. 'What's that?' Then she pulls on his cock, and he drops one of the bars of soap. 'It's a soap dispenser,' she announces, delighted.

"'I want a go,' says the second nun. She gives the guy's dick a good tug too, and he drops the second bar. 'My turn,' says the third nun. She grabs his cock and pulls it. Nothing. Pulls it again. Nothing. So she sets to tugging on it, getting faster and faster. Then she smiles. 'Ah. I got *liquid* soap this time.'"

Denny roared with laughter, and Tom beamed.

"I did a job for a gay guy once." Tom shook his head. "I'll never forget it."

"Why? What happened? And how did you know he was gay?"

"There's a story to this." Tom smiled. "My dad used to watch these dreadful films that got made about fifty years ago. The *Confessions* series. Really cheesy films. Like *Confessions of a Window Cleaner.* The cleaner ends up in all sorts of compromising positions involving sex, and then the woman's husband comes home unexpectedly."

"Not my kind of film," Denny remarked.

"Mine neither, but…" He flushed again.

Denny's mouth fell open. "That happened to you?"

Tom's eyes widened. "God no. I've never had sex with a client." He coughed. "But it *was* offered once or twice."

Denny grinned. "Oh really? Tell me more."

"I was building a granny flat in a garden for this guy's mum. The house was plenty big enough, but he said he didn't feel comfortable having her in his home. I wondered about that—then his husband came home, and I got it. But then *I* was the one who got uncomfortable."

Denny frowned. "You didn't mind working for a gay couple, did you?" It didn't seem likely, given that his ex was a lesbian.

"Not at all. Everyone's entitled to live their life their way, but... well, one of them propositioned me."

"Oh?"

"They had this swimming pool, and every day while I was working out there, he'd swim in it. In the nude. He sunbathed in the nude. Walked around the house in the nude." Tom shrugged. "That was okay. No skin off *my* nose if he was a nudist, right? I mean, I'd done a job once at a naturist club." He cleared his throat. "Except there was one major difference. The guys at the club didn't have a permanent hard-on—this guy did." Another cough. "Anyhow, I got the message—he was interested. Only, I wasn't. And I felt really uneasy about it. Not because he was doing his best to get me into bed, but because he seemed okay with cheating on his husband. Then one day said husband came home early. Judging by his expression, he was surprised to find his other half with no clothes on. Less than a minute later, he was naked too—and suddenly there were *two* guys with boners."

Denny chuckled. "That could've been your first gay threesome right there."

Tom gaped at him. "I was sure my face was about to catch fire, it was that hot. It was like how people talk about the eyes in portraits following you around the room. Everywhere I looked, there was a dick pointing at me."

Denny laughed and laughed until he was doubled over with it, clutching his aching stomach.

Then Tom started laughing too. "I suppose looking back, it *was* funny." He straightened. "But you know what? It's time for both of us to go back to work. I've got more concrete to break up and dig out—and *you* need to work in the dining room."

Denny blinked. "Why do you say that?"

Tom grinned. "Because maybe then you won't be distracted by the sight of me." His eyes sparkled. "Who knows, you might actually get some work done, instead of spending your time peeping through the curtains and trying not to get caught in the act." He aimed a hard stare at him. "I do *not* want to be held responsible for your dissertation not getting finished on time."

Denny sighed. "All right, all right. I'll work downstairs." He gave a playful pout. "Spoilsport." He got to his feet, picked up the two empty glasses and the sushi box, and trudged toward the back door.

"I'll say goodbye before I leave, okay?" Tom followed him, clutching his towel.

Denny smiled. "Yeah, that would be nice." He glanced at the garden. "We could do this again tomorrow, if you like."

Tom's smile lit up his eyes. "I'd like that."

If Denny had his way, they'd do it every day that Tom spent at the house.

Once it's done, he'll be gone again.

Unless Denny could come up with *another* reason to keep him coming back.

CHAPTER FOURTEEN

Tom finished his coffee and glanced at his phone. It was nine-thirty, but he wasn't in a hurry. The girl from Express Concrete had texted him to say the lorry would be there by ten-thirty. The trench was ready, and he had several lengths of rebar in the van. The footings would be laid by lunchtime, then that would be him done until the following week.

Pity.

He'd enjoyed his lunch with Denny. It made a pleasant change from sitting in the van, listening to the radio while he ate. They'd covered a lot of ground in their conversation, and once he'd gotten over his initial feelings of awkwardness, Tom had relaxed.

He's a smart guy. The title of Denny's dissertation alone made Tom's head spin. But the more they talked, the easier it became. *He didn't have to ask me to have lunch with him.* It had been a sweet gesture.

And speaking of sweet…

Tom had an idea. He'd have to leave right away, but the thought of Denny's face when he turned up was worth missing a few more minutes at home and another cup of coffee.

Tom pulled up outside the house and switched off the engine. There was no sign yet of the concrete lorry. The orange cones he'd left in place in the road the previous day were still there. He got out from behind the wheel and slid the side door open to begin removing the rebar.

"Can I help?" Denny stood at the front door.

Tom shook his head. "I've got this. But if there's a coffee going, I wouldn't say no. You might want to have these with it." He grabbed the bag from the dashboard and waved it aloft.

Denny widened his eyes. "You've been to Three Apes." He ran along the path and skidded to a halt in front of Tom, who handed him the bag. Denny opened it and grinned. "Almond croissants, and blueberry and oat crumbles slices. Oh wow."

His obvious delight sent warmth trickling through Tom. "It's to say thanks for yesterday."

Denny frowned. "What did I do to earn this?"

"Invited me to have lunch in your garden, that's what. By the way, we might not get to do that again after all. I should be finished before lunch."

"Do you have another job to go to after that?"

Tom shook his head.

Denny smiled. "Then stay and have your lunch with me." He traced a cross over his heart with his finger. "I promise to work my arse off until then. That way, it'll be a reward."

"But I didn't bring any lunch with me, because I knew I'd be out of here by then."

That smile morphed into a grin. "There's leftover lasagne if you're interested. Enough for two."

Tom groaned. "*Now* you've gone and done it."

"Done what?"

"Tempted me with my favourite meal."

Denny laughed. "Then it's settled. We'll both work our arses off to earn it." A rumble came from farther long the street, and he turned his head in its direction. "Don't look now, but I think your concrete has arrived."

Sure enough, the white lorry with its slowly rotating drum drew closer. Tom removed the cones, and it came to a stop in front of the house.

Denny ran toward the front door. "I'll put the coffee on," he yelled back.

Tom waited for the chute to swing into position, and soon concrete was pumping through the pipe and into the trench.

The prospect of more time spent with Denny had Tom smiling. *Looks as if I've got a new friend.*

One that was the result of a very different experience.

Tom scraped the last vestiges of lasagne from the plate with his fork, then sat back with a sigh. "That was delicious."

"Thanks for the compliment."

He blinked. "*You* made that?"

Denny nodded. "It was my turn last night."

"Turn?"

"We have a system. One night a week, one of us cooks for everyone. We tend to stick to old favourites, and this was something I've cooked plenty of times before."

"I'd say you've perfected the recipe then." Then he became conscious of being stared at. "Do I have tomato sauce on my nose or something?"

Denny shifted his chair closer to the patio table, his elbows on its patterned top, his fingers laced, chin resting on them. "I wanted to ask you something, but…"

"But what?" Denny's hesitance intrigued him.

"I don't want to make you feel awkward—again."

Tom smiled. "Ask whatever it is you want to know."

"It was about what you told Ari that first shoot. You mentioned secondary school."

A tingling sensation swept up the back of Tom's neck and across his face. "Oh. That."

Denny's expression tightened. "I *have* made you feel awkward, haven't I?"

"It's okay. It's just something I don't talk about. I try not to even *think* about it, if I'm honest."

Denny's brow furrowed. "But why? All you did was jerk off with a guy and let him suck your dick."

Tom gave a short chuckle. "You say 'all' like it was nothing out of the ordinary. But… it was a big deal at the time. For me, at any rate."

"But *why* was it such a big deal? You were a teenage boy coping with raging hormones and insatiable curiosity. And I meant what I said. We've all been there, me included."

"Okay, then here's a question for you. When *you* did it… did you know you were gay at the time?"

Denny pursed his lips. "I guess I did." His breathing caught. "Wait a minute. I think I know where you're going with this." He tilted his head to one side. "You felt bad about it because you enjoyed it." Tom stared at him, and Denny nodded. "I'm right, aren't I?" He smiled. "But it's *okay* to enjoy it, really. Someone's hand on your cock? Someone sucking you off? Best. Feeling. Ever." His eyes twinkled. "Okay, maybe they run a close second to having my dick in someone's arse or vice versa, but I'm biased."

Tom was trying not to smile and failing miserably.

"Remember at the shoot when you told Ari you hadn't done anything like that on camera?"

Tom wasn't likely to forget it.

"Well, I had the feeling at the time that you hadn't intended letting that slip out, but you were nervous, and your tongue kinda ran away with you."

Despite his churning stomach, Tom chuckled. "You're really good at this. I think you're studying for the wrong job. You should analyse people for a living." The light-hearted words were nothing but a smokescreen, and he knew it, because *damn*, Denny had nailed him.

"I meet a lot of people. I pick up on things." Denny's cheeks pinked. "And I did Psychology A-Level. Does it show?"

"A bit, perhaps?"

Denny peered at him. "Want to know what I've picked up about you?"

Tom had a feeling Denny was going to tell him regardless. "I'm all ears."

Denny sat back. "I think you've tried to shove the memory of all the stuff you and—Andy, was that his name?—Andy got up to someplace deep, but you know what? The truth always comes out when we're angry or nervous, when we're not totally in control of our emotions." He looked Tom in the eye. "Something keeps telling you that you ought to feel bad about you two did, but all that does is cause internal conflict, because..." He paused. "You never felt that way about it, not really."

Tom's heartbeat stuttered. "What you said about anger... When Andy reminded me of... of what we'd done, I was pissed off. But the more I think about it, the more I realise what bugged me most wasn't being reminded of what I did... it was remembering that... I liked it."

He'd said it. He'd *finally* said it.

"You've felt torn, haven't you?" Denny's eyes were warm. "Shame, self-loathing, and underneath it all, the knowledge that *damn* it, it felt good." He smiled. "So here's the million pound question. The shoots... did they feel good too?"

He could hear Carol's words in his head.

'Don't get hung up on labels...If it feels good, an' you're not hurtin' anyone, then what's wrong with enjoyin' life's experiences?'

Tom took a deep breath. "Yeah, they did."

Denny beamed. "Now doesn't that feel better?"

Fuck, it did. It really did.

A sudden lightness overcame him, and he twitched his shoulders, almost as if he felt the weight lifting from them, melting into nothingness.

"You know what this means?" Denny covered Tom's hand with his. "You get to haul yourself out of that hole you've dug, brush yourself down, and move on. You can get past all the self-recrimination, the self-doubt." He grinned. "Repeat after me. 'It's okay to have sex with a guy because it feels good.'"

Tom laughed, relief flooding through him. "I'm not sure I'm ready to say that out loud quite yet."

What surprised him?

How good Denny's hand felt curved around his.

"As long as you're thinking it, that's okay. And something else I should say at this point." Denny's cheeks dimpled. "You don't have to take everything I just said as gospel, okay? Because I am well aware I can come across as patronising sometimes." He chuckled and inclined his head toward the house. "God knows how many times this lot have told me that. So please, feel free to tell me to take my layman's analysis and shove it where the sun doesn't shine."

He still had hold of Tom's hand, and there wasn't a thing wrong with that.

"Well, I wasn't going to say it, but yeah, a little patronising," Tom said in a teasing tone. Denny blinked, and he laughed. "Kidding. You were pretty accurate, actually. I'm impressed." Denny released his hand, and Tom expelled a breath. He drank what was left of his water, and gazed at the garden, watching the gentle breeze ruffle the leaves of the slim birch trees.

"What does the rest of your day look like?"

And just like that, Tom knew that part of their conversation was over.

Back to normal life.

"I'm going to go home and find more work."

"Before you go, would you do something for me?"

Tom arched his eyebrows. "That would depend on what you wanted doing." He was quickly learning that he had no idea what Denny would do next.

It was refreshing.

"Come into the house, would you? I want you to take a look at the kitchen."

"Sure." He followed Denny into the house, then took a right into the kitchen. One glance told him Denny's purpose in bringing him inside. "Oh boy. This has seen better days." The cabinet doors needed their hinges adjusting, every surface was cluttered with appliances, and it was obviously short on cupboard space.

"My point exactly. We've been telling Ken it needs an upgrade for *ages*. So here's my idea. Once you've finished the wall—and knocked his socks off with how amazing it is—we go to work on him to get you in to redo the kitchen." He glanced at Tom. "You can *do* kitchen renovations, can't you?"

Tom chuckled. "I've lost count of how many I've done." He gave Denny a fond look. "This is good of you."

"Hey, you need the work, we need a new kitchen, and Ken gets to employ someone who knows what he's doing. That sounds like a win-win situation to me."

"Okay, put the idea to him, by all means, but don't force him if he doesn't want to go down that route."

"When will you be back to finish the wall?"

"Next Monday ought to do it. The concrete should have gone off by then. I'll have the bricks and railings delivered." He gave Denny a stern glance. "And now I need to go so *you* can get some work done."

"I've had a good day so far." Denny's face lit up. "Are you doing anything tonight?"

"Apart from putting my feet up and watching TV? No."

"Well… would you meet me for a drink? And maybe a bite to eat?"

Tom stilled. "Seriously?"

"Why not? It'd be fun."

It was on the tip of his tongue to come out with an excuse, but he stopped himself. *Why not indeed?* Denny was fun to be with, wasn't he? And what harm would it do to have a drink and a meal?

"Did you have a place in mind? Somewhere in Wimbledon, maybe?"

Denny smiled. "Actually, I was thinking more of meeting up in Soho."

Okay, he hadn't expected *that*. "Not a place I'm familiar with. Except by reputation."

Denny smiled. "Trust me. There's this great restaurant/bar on Old Compton Street, and it's got a wonderful atmosphere. Plus, there are tables at the back if we want to talk." His eyes sparkled. "As an added bonus, the eye candy is pretty good too. Except that's more for me than for you." He batted his eyelashes. "Please? Say yes? Pretty please? I need saving from the meagre offerings in the fridge, and I don't want to go shopping until the weekend. So you'd be doing me a favour."

Tom held his hands up. "Fine, I'll meet you there." It was half an hour into London by train from Ewell, and the last train home wasn't until past eleven-thirty. Not that he intended staying out *that* late, not on a weekday. "Will jeans be okay?"

Denny laughed. "Of course. I'll text you the address. Shall we say seven o'clock?"

"That works."

When was the last time I did this?

Maybe this was what he needed—a night of good food, a little alcohol, and a lot of conversation.

Chapter Fifteen

Tom got off the tube at Piccadilly Circus and strolled along Shaftesbury Ave. The pavements were crowded with theatregoers, all hurrying to get their seats before the curtain went up. Tom couldn't remember the last time he'd been to the theatre. It had to have been years since he'd watched a play.

I wouldn't go on my own, and it's not something either Deb or Sharon is into. He wondered about asking Denny along, then dismissed it. *He'd be more into musicals.* That wasn't Tom's cup of tea. Then he berated himself for such a stereotypical thought.

All the time he'd spent getting ready, his mind had been on the go.

It's just a drink and a bite to eat, that's all.

Then why did he feel so… quivery? As if all his muscles were in a state of constant twitch. He hadn't chosen anything special to wear, just a shirt and jeans, and his brown leather jacket. And it wasn't as if he'd be out all night.

Now all he had to do was get his body to calm the fuck down.

He turned left onto Dean Street, and when he reached Old Compton Street, he paused to check Denny's text. Balans was to the left on the other side of the street. Tom glanced in that direction and smiled when he caught sight of a familiar figure.

Denny leaned against the wall between Balans and what looked like a handbag shop, his hands stuffed into the pockets of his denim jacket worn over a black tee, his long legs encased in skinny jeans. Sunglasses hid his eyes, but when he turned in Tom's direction, he grinned and removed them, then waved.

Tom breathed a little easier.

It's just a drink and a bite to eat.
With Denny.

That last thought made him smile, but what inexplicably came to mind was Denny's hand on his.

Denny led Tom into the loud interior, and Max was there in a heartbeat, beaming.

"Where have you been? Haven't seen you for ages." They hugged.

"It's called being a student." Denny nodded toward the rear. "Have you got a table back there?"

Max grinned. "For you, honey, anything." He picked up two menu cards. "Follow me."

Denny tried not to laugh as Max sashayed his way between the bar and the booths. The restaurant was full of its usual patrons—a lot of gay men in twos, fours, or more, mixed groups, and women in twos or fours. The music wasn't obtrusive, and the servers darted all over the place, delivering cocktails or food that smelled heavenly.

Denny hadn't eaten since breakfast, and he figured the noise from his growling stomach would probably drown the sound of the music.

Max led them to a table in the far right corner, then deposited the menus on the table. "You want some water?"

"Yes please."

Max dimpled a smile, then headed back towards the bar.

Tom glanced at their surroundings as he removed his jacket and hung it over the back of his chair. "I see what you mean. This place has a good feel to it."

Denny loved the artwork. It was an eclectic mix of portraits and semi-nudes that really gave the restaurant atmosphere.

Tom picked up the menu and perused the drinks, but Danny snatched it from his hands.

"Do you trust me?"

Tom blinked. "I don't think I've known you long enough to answer that question."

Denny nodded in approval. "Good answer. Okay, next question. Do you like passion fruit?" When Tom said yes, Denny signalled to Max who was hovering at the cutlery station. He hurried over to them, bringing two glasses and a bottle of water.

"What can I get you to drink?"

"Two porn star martinis, please."

Max grinned. "Coming right up." He snorted. "As if I didn't know." He went back to the bar.

Tom chuckled. "Seriously?"

Denny widened his eyes. "Hey, it's not just a gay thing, you know. You can get a porn star martini in *soooo* many places. Hell, I once bought a pitcher of porn star martini at a Wetherspoons." He shuddered. "Never again."

"That bad?"

"Enough for me to know the only two places I can get a really good porn star is here, or Freedom."

"I've heard of that place."

"Lots of celebs like to hang out and dance there." He grinned. "If you're into celebs."

"Not really."

That was one more tick on Denny's list of things to like about Tom Ryder.

Max was back with their cocktails. He placed the four glasses on the table. "Will you be eating?"

"Yes, but we haven't got that far yet," Denny told him.

"Then enjoy your drinks, and I'll be back later." Another

swish of his hips, and he was gone.

Tom chuckled. "He's a character."

"He's a sweetheart. He's worked here ever since I first came to Balans." Denny smiled. "He could win an Olympic medal in flirting." Tom gazed at the two glasses in front of him. "You really haven't had one of these before?" When Tom shook his head, Denny picked up his own shot glass of prosecco and poured it into the orange-coloured cocktail. Tom copied him. Denny raised his glass. "To your first ever porn star martini. Trust me, it won't be your last."

Tom sipped cautiously, and then his eyes lit up. "Oh wow."

Denny chuckled. "Another convert." Then he gasped as Tom knocked it back. "Hey, steady on there. It might *taste* like Fanta, but it isn't."

Tom licked his lips, and Denny forced himself not to think of where he badly wanted those lips to go. "I'm not usually one for cocktails. I'm more a pints kinda guy."

"No pints tonight." Denny bit back a smile. "Let's get you another, but *only* if we order some food to go with it."

He had to wonder what a tipsy Tom was like.

Denny would guess at fucking adorable.

The burgers had been delicious, and Tom was feeling mellow after his second martini. Too mellow, because when Max reappeared, he ordered two more.

Denny's eyes twinkled. "What have I created?"

"We had food with them," Tom protested.

"And that cancels out the alcohol?"

Tom ignored the teasing remark. He was relaxed, pleasantly full, and the cocktails made him feel chilled and at ease.

Denny leaned back in his chair. "So..."

Tom arched his eyebrows. "So?" He was starting to get a feel for Denny.

Something was coming.

"Can we talk about you for a sec?"

"What do you want to know?" Tom thought they'd already covered pretty much every topic.

"I've been thinking about you, and—"

"Don't you have better, more important things to think about? Like... oh, I don't know... a certain dissertation?"

Denny gave him a mock glare. "I *am* allowed to think of things outside of my degree, you know. If I didn't, it'd drive me up the wall."

Tom waved a hand. "Go on, ask away." Mellowness flowed through his veins like honey, slow-moving and delicious.

"You said there have been very few girlfriends since the divorce."

"What's your point?"

Denny shrugged. "It could have been a sign."

"Of what?

Denny smiled. "Your subconscious acknowledging you're into women *and* men."

Tom shook his head. "Not buying it." He wasn't convinced about the whole bisexual argument.

Denny leaned forward. "Doing gay porn felt good. You said as much."

"Yeah, but I put that down to several factors."

"Such as?"

"The length of time I went... without. Something I saw once on a video..." He grinned. "'A hole is a hole,' I think they said."

Denny chuckled. "Can't say I agree with that. The only

holes *I've* ever got up close and personal with were male." He cocked his head. "So you don't find men attractive?"

"I never said that." Tom clammed up as Max reappeared with the drinks. He thanked him, then watched him walk away from the table.

Except that wasn't really walking, it was as though he was moving to the rhythm of music Tom couldn't hear.

"What about him?"

Tom jerked his head back in Denny's direction. "Hmm?"

Denny pointed to a guy seated a few tables from them. "What about him? Do you find *him* attractive?"

Tom pursed his lips. "Too short."

Denny laughed. "Ooh, picky. What about him then?" He indicated another diner.

Tom let out a snort. "He looks as if he's twelve."

"You said that about Jake," Denny reminded him.

Tom thought it was time to turn the tables. "Never mind about me, what about you? What do *you* look for in a man?"

Denny leaned back, arms folded. "Maybe... someone who can engage me in a really good conversation." His eyes twinkled. "You know, like the kind *we* have. Someone who's understanding. Considerate."

"Interesting."

Denny arched his eyebrows. "What do you mean?"

"You didn't come up with the things I was expecting."

"And what were they?"

Tom counted off on his fingers. "Sexy, good in bed..."

Denny sighed. "Sex isn't everything. And if I meet someone who wants to be in it for the long haul, there will come a day—not *too* soon, hopefully—when what happens outside the bedroom matters more than what happens in it."

"But for now?"

Denny rolled his eyes. "Okay, you got me. Sexy is pretty high on my list." They laughed.

"Can I ask you something about porn?"

Denny chuckled. "You mean we still have stuff to talk about?"

"What was your first scene like? I think you said it was with your boyfriend."

"My first scene had everything—a fuck-load of dirty talk, kink, passion… And I wasn't nervous. Actually, it was more a wow-look-what-*I've*-found feeling."

"How you are on camera when you're having sex, and when it's *not* on camera… is it much different?"

Denny smiled. "The only difference is the stuff shot in the studio is scripted, and Ari is *really* into his choreography."

Tom laughed. "Yeah, I noticed that." He took a drink from his glass, studying Denny's relaxed features. "You keep coming back. To porn, I mean. You must like it."

"I like the people, to be honest. Sure, I get to work with some really hot guys." He looked Tom in the eyes, and heat crawled over Tom's neck and face. "But the people who work in the industry—Ari, the cameramen, Carol… they're some of the most understanding people you'll ever meet."

Tom smiled at the memory of Carol. "She wasn't what I expected."

"There's a story behind how she came to be working at the studio."

He took another sip. "Can you share it?"

Denny drank half his cocktail in one gulp. "I don't know how this came about—and I haven't delved into it—but Carol used to follow a gay porn star on social media. She commented on all his posts, she went to porn award shows to support him—"

"They have awards for *porn?*"

"That's a story for another time. Anyway, he was going through a bad patch, and we lost track of him for a while. Turned out he'd committed suicide."

Tom's stomach clenched. "Oh no." He reached for

Denny's hand and squeezed it.

Denny blinked, then gave him a grateful glance. "We don't know what was going on for it to get to that point, but it cut Carol pretty deep. She felt as if she could've done more to support him, be there for him."

Denny's slim fingers in his felt good, but then Max gazed at them with interest, and Tom relinquished his hold.

Denny continued talking as if he hadn't noticed Tom's abrupt retreat. "And then she cornered Ari at one of the awards parties. She told him she'd retired from her job, she was sitting at home twiddling her thumbs because the kids had all flown the nest, her husband was never home, and she wanted something to do." Denny shrugged. "Maybe she reminded Ari of someone, because he gave her the job of receptionist. Except she's way more than that. She's like a mother to some of the guys who shoot there. I get the feeling that was what Ari employed her to be." Tom finished his cocktail, and Denny laughed. "You really like those, huh?"

"What's not to like? It's just fruit juice, right?" He grinned. "In fact, I think I could go for another."

"And I think I might have to put a limit on the number of porn stars you have." Denny sighed and gestured to Max. "Round four, please."

Max guffawed. "I've known you to have five in one night. You're not even warmed up yet."

By the time he'd drunk his fourth cocktail, Tom had to admit he'd passed the muzzy stage. Thinking clearly wasn't so easy, for one thing. Then he remembered something he'd been meaning to ask.

He leaned in close, beckoning to Denny to do the same, and their faces met almost at the middle of the table.

Close enough to kiss.

Where the hell did that come from?

And why did he keep staring at Denny's lips?

With an effort, he forced himself to remember his question.

"You know that second scene I did? When you… got me ready?"

Denny nodded.

"Well, something I wanted to ask. The firs' scene we did, how come *you* didn't need preppin'?"

Hey, look at me, not slurring one little bit.

Denny tapped the side of his nose. "That was because I'd prepped after my shower. Same as you, with a dildo. Plus, I was already lubed up." He smirked. "Thank God. You are *not* small in that department."

Tom narrowed his gaze. "So the goal was always for me to end up in your arse?"

Denny grinned. "Yup. It usually works out that way nine times out of ten."

"And the tenth time?"

He shrugged. "Occasionally we get a guy who's curious enough to want to know how it feels to get fucked. And now and then we get a flip flop scene."

"A… flip flop?"

Denny's eyes sparkled. "Both of us end up getting fucked."

"You like those kinda scenes?"

Denny's grin was answer enough.

As soon as the fifth round arrived, Tom knew he'd reached his limit. In fact, he'd probably passed it at some point between rounds three and four.

"I think I'm gonna go home," he announced. "You don't have to. Stay here if you want. You never know, you might get lucky."

Denny laughed. "No, I think I'm done too. Want me to walk you to the Tube?"

Tom waved his hand through the air. "Gonna call an Uber." He didn't fancy negotiating the streets of London on a

Saturday night with that much alcohol in his system.

"Where's home?"

"Ewell."

Denny smiled. "Wimbledon's on the way. Can I share an Uber, and you can drop me off first?"

Tom got his phone out and clicked on the app. It took him a while to fathom it out, and in the end, Denny helped, but at last they'd split the bill and were standing on the corner of Dean Street, waiting for a black Volvo.

Tom wasn't so drunk that he missed all the gay couples strolling along the street holding hands. "That's nice," he murmured.

"What is?"

"Holding hands. Can't tell you the last time I did that."

Denny chuckled. "About ten minutes ago." When Tom gave him an inquiring glance, he grinned. "You were holding mine, remember?"

The Volvo pulled up beside them, and they piled into the back seat. Denny confirmed the addresses, and Tom leaned back against the headrest. "'M sitting still and yet the world is spinning."

"No shit. Me too." Denny touched his knee. "You had a good time tonight?"

"Yeah," he said with a smile. "Good food, fabulous drinks… great company."

Denny's hand moved from his knee to his thigh, and Tom wasn't complaining. "Ditto." Denny left it there as the car sped toward Wimbledon, and Tom had no complaints.

A comfortable silence fell, and Tom closed his eyes.

Denny squeezed his thigh, his fingers inching closer to Tom's crotch, stilling when Tom opened his eyes. He glanced at Denny's hand, then at his face. Whatever he'd meant to say died in his throat when he met Denny's gaze, the light from the passing headlights catching in his eyes, making them shine.

Denny was staring at him.

Tom's pulse raced. "Have I got somethin' on my face?" It was a struggle to keep his voice even.

Denny shook his head. "No. Just a sexy pair of lips." He leaned in closer, and Tom's breathing hitched. Denny rubbed his thumb over Tom's bearded jaw, then shifted to his neck, stroking him there, his eyes still focused on Tom's.

Closer.

Closer.

The world was still spinning, only now it was for a different reason, and Tom didn't want to fight this anymore.

He reached for Denny, sinking his fingers into layers of soft hair, and drew Denny to him, brushing his lips over Denny's, tasting that last porn star martini on his breath.

Then Denny's lips locked onto his, and they collided, his body warm against Tom's, his hands still on Tom's neck, holding him there while Tom moaned quietly into the kiss, sweeping his tongue between Denny's parted lips, tasting him.

Denny broke the kiss and nuzzled his neck, sucking hard on the skin, and Tom's cock got in on the act, hard behind his zipper as he slid his hand under Denny's open jacket, flicking his nipple that pushed against the cotton, stiff and proud.

Tom couldn't get enough of him.

He buried his face in Denny's neck, breathing him in, kissing and sucking the skin smelling of soap and Denny.

Then he realised the car had stopped moving.

The driver coughed. "Oy. Romeo and Romeo. One of you is getting out here, remember?"

They sprang apart, and Denny planted a swift kiss on Tom's lips before he stumbled out of the Uber and closed the door.

Tom twisted in his seat to stare at him through the rear window as they pulled away.

What the fuck was that?

CHAPTER SIXTEEN

Tom opened his eyes and the light seared his eyeballs.

Okay, that was an exaggeration.

Maybe.

At some point in the night, someone had surgically removed his tongue and replaced it with a suede tie, or at least that was how it felt. He glanced over at the alarm clock.

Eight o'clock? He hadn't heard the alarm go off. Then he peered closer, squinting at the dial with bleary eyes.

That might be because you didn't set it.

He threw back the duvet, planted his feet on the rug, and rose to his feet, a little unsteady.

Just how much did I have to drink last night? Vague recollections of several rounds of cocktails filtered through his aching head. *Oh God. I hope I didn't do something embarrassing.* He wasn't a big drinker. Deb used to say he could get drunk from merely sniffing a glass of wine, but that was one of her jokes. He wasn't *that* bad.

He padded out of the bedroom and along the hall to the bathroom, scratching his balls. He needed a drink of water, but the first order of the day was to empty his bladder. Once he'd relieved himself, he washed his hands in cold water because it took fucking *forever* for it to get warm, dried them, and then summoned up enough courage to peek at his reflection.

Oh dear Lord.

He hadn't done something embarrassing the previous night—he'd done something *mega* embarrassing, by the look of it.

There was a love bite on his neck.

The dam burst, and memories flooded in.

Denny. In the Uber.

He couldn't recollect who had kissed who at that moment—*let's not be coy here. We snogged*—but he remembered his hands on Denny's chest, his face…

The taste of him.

Holy fucking shit.

Tom flipped the shower on, then sat on the closed toilet while the steam built up inside the glass enclosure.

I am never drinking ever again.

He stepped into the shower and stood there, doing his best not to think about him and Denny in a lip lock, but now that the floodgates had opened fully, there was no stopping the assault on his memory. It didn't matter that he'd fucked Denny previously—that was just penetration. In Tom's mind, illogical or not, kissing was a different matter altogether.

Kissing was… intimate.

More than that, kissing Denny had felt bloody good.

God, his head was a mess.

By the time he'd made himself a cup of strong coffee, the situation hadn't improved. It was almost as if his brain didn't want him to forget the experience, releasing more and more images, more sensations…

He made himself some toast, but it was like eating a piece of insulation board. He glanced at his phone. No texts from Denny.

I could message him.

And say what?

Fucked if he knew.

The only thing Tom was sure about was that looking Denny in the eye the following week might prove awkward as hell.

He spent the morning cleaning the inside of his van. He took everything out, vacuumed the interior, then put everything back in its proper place. He knew why he'd chosen to carry out such a mundane task—it was mindless.

It kept him occupied.

As lunchtime approached and he experienced the first pangs of hunger, an idea came to him. He pulled his phone from his pocket and composed a brief text.

How long do you get for lunch?

Deb's reply was swift. *An hour, but I usually eat at my desk. Why?*

Can we meet?

1.00 outside the office? There's a coffee shop across the road.

See you there.

Tom breathed easier. A dose of Deb's clear thinking was what he needed.

He just wasn't sure what he was going to say to her—or how much he was willing to give away.

Tom arrived at the accountancy firm about ten minutes early. He paced up and down the road, gazing in shop windows, doing his best to distract himself.

It wasn't working.

It was just a kiss, for God's sake.

Then why did he feel as if he'd been turned upside down and inside out?

"Are you *trying* to wear a groove into the pavement?"

He turned to find Deb standing behind him, looking smart in a dress suit. "You look nice."

She smiled. "I had a meeting with a new client. First impressions and all that." She gestured to the other side of the road. "The coffee shop's this way. They do sandwiches, and I can recommend the chicken salad." Her eyes twinkled. "The pastries are pretty good too."

That made him smile. "You know me far too well."

They crossed the road and went around the corner. The coffee shop appeared inviting, although a bit busy, but Deb found them a table. "I'll get lunch. Do you want coffee or tea?"

That queasy feeling in his gut hadn't abated all morning. "Do they have peppermint tea?" He'd read something once about how it settled the stomach, and his could sure do with settling right then.

She arched her eyebrows, then nodded before heading to the counter.

Tom removed his jacket and sat, facing the street. Outside, passers-by walked, all locked into their own little worlds.

Tom's world had been rocked to its core, and he wasn't sure why.

Deb rejoined him, taking the chair facing his. She placed her tray on the table. The tea smelled wonderful, and the sandwich looked like it wasn't made out of Celotex, thank goodness. He might even be able to enjoy it.

Maybe.

She smiled. "Look, I'm okay, really. Sure, not getting pregnant knocked me for a loop, but there'll be another time. You don't need to worry about me."

Worrying about her? Tom's chest tightened. "Okay, *now* I feel like a total shit."

Her brow furrowed. "What do you mean?"

"I didn't ask how you were doing. My head is too full of… other stuff."

Yeah, like himself.

Tom felt like a total selfish bastard.

Deb did the eyebrow arching thing again. "What, exactly?" She frowned. "Come to think of it… are you all right? You look… rough."

"I've been better. But before you get overwhelmed with sympathy, it's self-inflicted. I… I went out for a drink last night."

She bit her lip. "And how many pints did you put away with Andy?"

If I'd been with him, I wouldn't be in this state.

There wouldn't be a love bite on his neck, for one thing.

"I wasn't with Andy, and..." He looked her in the eye. "You used to like cocktails, remember?"

Deb blinked. "Er, yeah. Can't tell you the last time I had one, but yeah."

"How come you never told me how lethal they are?"

She stared at him for a moment, then burst into laughter. "Well, that depends on how many of them you drink." She tilted her head. "How many was it—and what exactly were you drinking?"

"Five porn star martinis. I think."

Deb widened her eyes. "Whoa. I don't have to ask how *your* head is doing right now." Another frown. "Who were you drinking porn star martinis with?"

"A... a friend." His stomach roiled, and he wasn't sure if that was due to the hangover or his feelings of regret.

Why did I kiss him? He had a vague memory of Denny initiating the kiss, but Tom knew for certain he'd reciprocated. Not only that, he'd wanted to kiss Denny earlier, hadn't he?

Then he realised Deb was far too quiet.

In fact, she was staring at him.

"What's wrong?" Tom feigned innocence.

Another spike of her neatly sculpted eyebrows. "I was going to ask you the same question." She leaned forward. "Why did you want to meet me for lunch? *Is* there something wrong?" Her voice was low, her eyes filled with concern.

Tom had to tell *someone.*

"Actually? There *was* something I wanted to talk to you about. I..." He took a deep breath. "I *might* have made out with a guy last night."

"'Might have'?" Her eyes sparkled.

"Okay, fine. I snogged him in the back of an Uber."

Deb studied him in silence. Another tilt of her head. "Was it good?"

Tom gaped. "*That's* what you're going with? And I don't remember."

*Liar liar...*His pants weren't merely on fire, they'd been reduced to ashes.

Then Deb reached out and pulled down the scarf he'd tied around his neck with a gentle hand.

"What are you doing?"

She bit her lip. "Since when do you wear scarves? In *June?*" Her gaze fell on his neck, and heat bloomed in his cheeks. "Oh my." She eased the scarf back into its original position, then picked up her cup and took a drink. "Do you want my advice?"

"Does that mean you have some?"

She smiled. "Sure. Do it again—but *next* time, make sure you're sober." Her lips twitched. "And make sure he eats something. That way, he won't be tempted to take a bite out of you."

The foundations of Tom's world were rocking again. "You don't seem shocked."

Deb shrugged. "That's because I'm not."

"So I tell you I was snogging a guy in the back of an Uber, and you think that's okay?"

"Hey, some people don't work it out right away. When we were in secondary school, I didn't know I was into girls. Even when we were married. Then I met Sharon, and *bam*, I knew." Her smile grew warm. "You were the only guy I ever slept with."

Tom's brain defaulted to the nearest implication. "So it's *my* fault you're a lesbian? I turned you off men?"

She chuckled. "No, sweetheart, but maybe it's just another part of why we broke up. We both know we should've stayed best friends, and as it turned out, I was more into women than men." She looked him in the eye. "But enough about me. If you're only just finding out now that you might like men, then I say better late than never." She gave him a speculative glance. "Are you going to see this guy again?"

"Only if there's no alcohol involved," he joked. "And… It's not like that."

"I take it this is the *friend* you shared several cocktails with?" He nodded. "You *sure* there's nothing else you want to tell me?"

His heartbeat quickened. "Why do you say that?"

"Because I know you. And right now I *know* you're hiding something."

Tom swallowed. "I wouldn't know where to start."

"Then I'm not going to push. But you're all right?"

"I'm fine," he assured her. Or at least he would be soon enough. "Confused but fine."

She nodded toward his sandwich. "Eat. You'll feel better."

He took a bite, thankful that the bread didn't taste like sandpaper.

"Are you sure about the tea? Maybe coffee would be better?"

"Trust me, right now tea is the best thing."

Deb leaned back, studying him once more. "So what *is* the issue here? Is it 'shock horror, I kissed a guy' or more a case of 'shock horror, I kissed a guy and I liked it?' A guy you might be attracted to?"

"'Attracted'?"

She smiled. "It's not as uncommon as you might think. Why, only this morning I read an article on this very subject."

"What subject?"

"The upshot was, a surprising number of straight people admit being attracted to the same sex."

"And what counts as a surprising number?" Tom wasn't a great believer in statistics. *How does the saying go? 'There are lies, damned lies, and statistics.'*

Deb removed her phone from her bag and scrolled. "I bookmarked it." She gave a triumphant smile. "Thirty-one percent of het women, thirteen percent of het men."

It didn't seem all that big a number to Tom.

"Wait a minute. Hold the phone." Deb rolled her eyes. "The survey was conducted in Spain."

"Why should that make any difference?" Tom's head was spinning.

"Because it's a very different culture over there. A lot more pressure on men to conform to society." She put her phone away. "Okay, enough. The way I see it, this all boils down to two things. One—did you like it?" Her eyes met his. "And be honest."

"I thought you said you weren't going to push." He stared hard at her.

"I changed my mind. It's a woman's prerogative, apparently. And answer the question."

Did *I like it?* How did he feel about it, several hours after the deed?

"Maybe? Like I said, I'm really confused about it."

Another lie. The more he thought about his lips brushing against Denny's, the feel of that taut little nipple stiffening even more beneath Tom's fingertip, the moan Denny fed him when Tom used his tongue…

Okay, he'd liked it. He'd *really* liked it.

"What's the second thing?"

She didn't break eye contact. "Do you want to do it again?"

Tom didn't know how to answer that.

Deb sighed. "Eat your sandwich. Drink your tea. And let's talk about something different. Have you had any work since I last saw you?"

He nodded, then told her about the wall he was rebuilding, and how there might be another job coming up at the same location. He didn't mention Denny. And with each bite, he felt a little less queasy, a little more his old self.

Except… Am I sure I want to go back to being my old self?

One night of cocktails, and his life had veered off in a totally new direction.

But where does it lead to?

CHAPTER SEVENTEEN

I fucked it up, didn't I?

Denny hadn't planned on kissing Tom, but once he'd gotten the idea in his head, it wouldn't budge. All it had taken was one glance in the back of an Uber, and Denny had made his move, unable to resist the lure of that mouth.

Kissing Tom had been… delicious. Sensual. Hot as fuck. In fact, every bit as hot as he'd imagined.

That doesn't make it right.

Even if Tom had returned the kiss. No, not just returned it—*amplified* it. He hadn't imagined Tom's quiet moan, had he?

Denny knew better than to think everything had somehow changed with that one kiss. The skittish colt he'd perceived in Tom was only hiding just below the surface, and it wouldn't take much to make him bolt.

And I don't want *him to bolt.* Denny liked Tom. It wasn't just his looks, it was the whole package. Tom was a genuinely nice guy, and Denny could quite willingly spend a lot of time around him.

What bothered Denny most was his motivation for kissing Tom.

Don't go there. Just… don't. Because you don't want to go through that again, do you?

Hell no.

He had to admit it. With one kiss he might have messed everything up.

One kiss that was four days *ago.* Four days, and not a word from Tom.

But why would he get in touch? There was no reason to do so.

No reason for Denny to do likewise either.

He closed his laptop with a sigh. The words were dancing on the page anyway. He couldn't concentrate. In fact, his concentration had been for shit since that night.

Get your act together. He had a meeting with his tutor Monday morning, to check on his progress. Time was running out, not that Denny was in a panic about that. He knew how he worked. A bit of added pressure always helped to push him toward a goal—hell, he was always a last-minute kinda guy—although he really had tried to buck that particular trend with his postgrad studies.

At least I won't be around when Tom comes back to finish the job.

He wasn't sure if that was a good thing or not.

Tom tossed the remote onto the seat cushion beside him.

Sunday night, and there was nothing worth watching on TV. Mr. Loomis had called to check if he would be at the house the following day. He also said there was something he'd like to discuss.

Tom had a feeling that would be about the kitchen, assuming Denny had put in a good word.

The intervening days since cocktails at Balans had been quiet. No work, which only meant more time to think, and that was the last thing Tom wanted to do. Building a wall would at least keep him focused on something else apart from what was going on in his head. And if he were to renovate that kitchen, that would be a step in the right direction.

The noise from the TV drowned out his thoughts. It was supposed to be a comedy, but Tom hadn't laughed out loud once. He grabbed the remote and switched it off. The sudden quiet was a shock to the system, and his babbling thoughts filled the void.

What if Denny's home tomorrow?
How do I look him in the eye?
What do I say to him?

He'd been the one to bring up the subject of kissing, hadn't he? And he hadn't beat Denny off with a stick when they'd kissed. Far from it.

Tom walked into the bathroom to brush his teeth before bed. The bruising on his neck was fading fast, but each time he saw it in the mirror, the sight took him back to that trip, plunging him into a vat of memories.

Denny's hand on his thigh. God, he'd forgotten about that. His fingers within touching distance of Tom's cock.

No—his hard-on. Because he *had* been hard, hadn't he?

Denny's warm body against his, the smell of him filling Tom's nostrils, the last remnants of their cocktails on his breath and skin.

Denny's fucking *moan*.

Then Tom stilled.

He'd been the one to moan, not Denny.

He stared at his reflection, his toothbrush forgotten. "Just be fucking *honest* about it," he shouted at himself. He gripped the cool porcelain, his heart hammering.

Say it out loud.

Say *it*.

He shivered.

"I fucked a guy. I kissed him. I liked it. I… I want to do it again."

And the rest.

Tom took a deep breath. "I'm attracted to Denny," he whispered.

Louder.

A hard swallow. "I'm attracted to Denny. And I don't know what to do about it."

A giddiness stole over him, and his legs felt wobbly. He

bowed his head so as not to see what lay in his own eyes.

He had no clue what he was going to do when he came face to face with Denny.

He would have to wing it.

Nine o'clock Monday morning, Tom pulled up outside the house. A pallet of bricks sat on the driveway, along with the wrought iron railings, encased in cardboard. He'd received a text from the builders' merchants to say they'd been delivered at eight-thirty.

Must be a good neighbourhood. Tom could name certain districts where the supplies would have been snatched within minutes of delivery. Then he gazed at his surroundings and smiled to see all the curtains twitching.

How many pairs of eyes are on me right this minute?

He glanced up at Denny's window, but there was no sign of him.

Forget about Denny. You have work to do.

Tom opened his van and proceeded to take out his tools, including his cement mixer. Once he'd set everything up, he scanned the exterior of the house, searching for an outside tap. He remembered seeing one inside the garage, but when he tried it, the door was locked.

That made it official. No one was home.

The thought didn't bring the relief he'd anticipated.

"Can I help you?" An elderly man in a grey cardigan peered at him over the fence from the house next door.

"I was looking for a tap." He pointed to the hose he'd removed from the van. "I need water for the cement."

The man held his hand out. "Give it here. As long as you don't plan on washing that van while you're at it." He arched his thin eyebrows. "I *am* on a water meter, you know."

Tom assured him he wouldn't need that much.

For the rest of the morning, he built the new wall, using headers and stretchers to bond the two skins of brick together. He got into his routine—butter each brick surface with cement, lay the next brick on top, tap it, level it, scrape off the excess, grab another brick… He paused at ten-thirty to drink coffee from his flask, then it was back to work. When he needed to pee, there was the bottle, and when lunchtime came around, he sat in his van and ate his sandwiches, listening to the radio.

Still no one around.

At four o'clock, he finished setting in the railings, embedding them in the cement-packed ridge between the two skins of brick. He'd just packed all his tools away when Mr. Loomis arrived. He beamed as he walked towards Tom.

"Oh, that looks wonderful. You were right about using the arch top railings."

"It'll take a while for the cement to go off, so you'll need to be careful. Don't go knocking into the wall."

Mr. Loomis nodded. "I'll make sure they all know."

From the corner of his eye, Tom caught movement. Denny walked up to the front door, glancing in Tom's direction.

Fuck.

Tom gave him a polite nod, keeping a professional air about him. Denny stilled for a moment, then returned the nod before disappearing into the house.

Fuck.

Fuck.

Fuck.

Then he realized Mr. Loomis was speaking.

"So, is that it? Job done?"

Tom shook his head. "I'll need to come back when

everything's hardened to apply the grout and make it neat. But I'm done for now."

"Well, before you go, there was something else I wanted to discuss." Mr. Loomis gestured to the house. "Could we step inside? It's easier if I show you."

Tom glanced at his boots and overalls spattered with blobs of cement. "I don't think that's a good idea."

Mr. Loomis lowered his gaze. "Oh. I see. Okay then. Could we arrange to meet next week? There's another job I'd like to discuss with you."

"That sounds fine. I'll call you, and we can arrange a time." Tom made sure his hand was clean before they shook. When Mr. Loomis made no move to leave, Tom realised he had no excuse to go into the house. "Well, I'd better be off then. I'll email you the invoice for the labour."

He walked toward the van, resisting the urge to look up once more at Denny's window.

Tom was getting tired of being torn between relief and disappointment.

He walked through the front door and kicked off his boots, leaving them on the mat. The shower was calling him, and he shucked out of his overalls. The hot water washed away all traces of the job, and by the time he emerged from the bathroom, hair still damp, a towel wrapped around him, he felt human again.

Not to mention awkward as fuck.

I should've said something.

Except that hadn't been an option, not with Mr. Loomis present.

I should've sent a text before now.

Procrastination was a bastard.

I've put it off long enough.

He grabbed his phone and composed a quick text.

Got a sec?

When no reply was forthcoming, his stomach clenched. *I knew I should have said something to him today. Too late now.*

His phone pinged. *Hey there, str8 guy.*

Relief swamped him. *About that… Who kissed who?*

A grinning emoji popped up. *rme*

Tom frowned. *What does that mean?*

Rolling my eyes. And I kissed you. [grin] You kissed me back. I have proof. [grin]

An image popped onto his screen. Denny had taken a selfie in his bathroom mirror, revealing a love bite on his neck. And yeah, he *was* grinning.

OMG.

It's kk.

Tom blinked. *kk?*

That means it's okay or cool. Another grin. *u don't do textspeak, do u? This is all n2u, rite?*

Tom hazarded a guess at what that meant. *Yeah.* Thirty-five years old, and he suddenly felt ancient.

I was gonna call u. Sorry we didn't get the chance 2tlk earlier. And the love bite is kk bc I'm not doing any scenes this week. wrud this w/e? Sat nite?

Tom was getting a crash course in textspeak, but he was catching on fast. *Nothing so far. Why?*

was gonna invite u2 my place 4 dinner. I can cook btw. But you know that already.

Tom considered the idea for all of three seconds. *kk*

Denny replied with a smiling face with heart-eyes emoji.

He grinned. *Look at me, learning a new language.*

Better than that—everything seemed to be okay between

him and Denny.

Thank God for that.

Denny stepped into the quiet house and closed the door. He lugged the shopping bags into the kitchen and dumped them on the table. He'd found everything on his list, although he'd had to hunt around for one of the items.

I hope he likes this.

He couldn't shake the feeling he should have stuck with the old tried-and-tested lasagne, but Tom had already eaten that, and Denny *always* made it, so it was time for a change. The recipe didn't look all that difficult, and he hoped the bottle of wine he'd chosen would complement it.

He hoped.

Why the fuck am I so nervous? It's just dinner.

Except it was more than that. He needed to know things were okay, that he hadn't spoiled everything. Tom's texts had gone a long way to settling his doubts, sure, but…

I don't want to lose him as a friend.

Not that Tom could ever be more than that, no matter how many times Denny's fantasies strayed in that direction.

Been there, done that, got my fingers burned, and my heart broken.

Never again.

Chris strolled into the kitchen. "Thought I heard you." He peered into one of the bags. "Ooh, what are we having?"

Denny gave him a hard stare. "*We* aren't having anything. I'm cooking dinner for a guest tomorrow night. *You* said you'd be out. All night. Meena's gone to see her family, Lisa is staying over at a girlfriend's place, and Robin is away for the weekend. So I thought I'd have the place to myself." He speared Chris with a mock glare. "I will, won't I?"

Chris chuckled. "Relax. I'm pulling your leg. And yes, I'm going out. Me and the lads from work are going to a club. I hope to be dancing until the wee small hours." His eyes sparkled. "Doesn't take three guesses to know what *you'll* be doing till the wee small hours, does it?"

Denny couldn't blame Chris for coming out with the suggestion. It was all *he'd* thought of since Tom agreed to come to dinner.

He'd had an idea that could prove beneficial to both of them.

Now all he had to do was work out how to put it to Tom in such a way that Tom didn't run a mile.

CHAPTER EIGHTEEN

Tom glanced at the front wall. He was happy with the end result, especially if it brought him more work. Only, he wasn't sure if that would be because of his skills, or because Denny had put the idea into Mr. Loomis's head.

Either way, a job was not to be sniffed at.

He walked up to the door and knocked, one hand clutching the plastic bag containing a bottle of wine. He had no clue what they would be eating, so he'd played it safe with a rosé.

So much for saying never again. Except wine was different, wasn't it? And he could have one glass with his meal. He'd even come by train so he could have one drink.

The door opened and Denny stood there in bare feet, jeans, and a tank top that revealed more flesh than Tom had expected. "I suppose it makes a change to be coming in via the front door."

Tom inhaled. "Something smells good." There was a whiff of garlic, onions, tomatoes…

Denny chuckled. "Well, that's a good start. Come in."

Tom stepped into the bright hallway with its white walls, and cream curtain on a rail above the door, tied back. Beige carpet covered the floor and staircase, and a pretty patterned rug done in blue and red ran the length of the hallway. He waited until Denny had closed the door before proffering the bag.

"A good guest never turns up emptyhanded, my gran used to say."

Denny smiled. "My grandma says the same thing." He peered into the bag. "Ooh, nice. I'll put it in the fridge. Now you get to choose which wine we have with dinner."

Tom stared at him in mock horror. "You didn't mention anything about me having to make a *decision*."

Denny laughed. "You can hang your jacket on one of the hooks by the door." He turned and went into the kitchen.

Tom removed his jacket. From somewhere came the faint strains of music. "What can I hear?"

"No idea," Denny called out from the kitchen. "It's something I found on YouTube. It's called Chillout Lounge. It's supposed to be relaxing background music that you can listen to while you're studying, working, even sleeping."

Tom had to admit it sounded good. "And what can I smell?" He wandered into the kitchen and came to a dead stop. "Are you always such a tidy cook?" The worktops were devoid of clutter and there wasn't a bowl or a kitchen utensil in sight.

Denny let out a snort. "Usually? No. My housemates say the kitchen looks as if a bomb's detonated in there when I've finished preparing a meal. I got all the cooking out of the way hours ago. And as for what you can smell, we're having chicken parmesan with homemade marinara sauce, green beans, and cauliflower mash, followed by mocha trifle."

Tom stilled. "I've never heard of that."

"You cut trifle sponge fingers in half, stand them upright in a glass dish, and wedge them in there. Then you pour strong black coffee over them and let it soak in. When it's cooled, you spoon chocolate dessert onto that, and finally add a layer of whipped cream. I normally grate dark chocolate onto the top."

Tom had to resist the urge to drool. "When do we eat?"

Denny chuckled. "Whenever you like. It's all ready." He pointed to the right. "The dining room is thataway. Go sit, and I'll bring the food."

"Is it just us?"

Denny's smile sent a trickle of warmth through him. "Yeah, we've got the house to ourselves."

Tom ignored the empty, fluttery feeling in his stomach.

I'm just hungry, that's all.

He went into the dining room and stopped at the sight. Two sparkling wine glasses stood on a snow-white tablecloth. A tea light burned in a little glass jar in the centre of the table. The cutlery gleamed, and the blood-red napkins stood out against the white.

"You've gone to a lot of trouble," he said at last.

Denny appeared behind him, carrying two plates in oven glove-covered hands. "I wanted to apologise for last week."

Tom frowned. "What on earth have you got to apologise for?"

"Kissing you the way I did. I kinda cornered you, didn't I? I mean, you couldn't exactly escape from a moving car, right?" Denny set the plates down on the table mats, then turned to face him. "And... I should have asked first. I didn't give you a choice. Coming from someone who works in the adult industry, I should know better. Consent matters." His face flushed.

The tight vines that had been twisting their way around Tom's guts for the past week, loosened their grip. "I think you could take the fact that I kissed you back as consent, don't you?"

"Maybe, but I still shouldn't have done it in the first place." Denny pulled out a chair for him. "Now sit, please, before it gets cold. I'll ditch these gloves." He chuckled. "It might be a bit easier to eat without them."

Tom did as he was told, his heart light for the first time that week.

Things were going to be okay.

Tom pushed his bowl away from him with a contented sigh. "Okay, I need to write down the recipe for mocha trifle." Sharon would love that. "My compliments to the chef. Every mouthful was delicious."

Denny's smile lit up his face. "Thank you. That was a new recipe for me, so I'm glad it worked out."

Tom let his mouth fall open. "I was a guinea pig?"

Denny's laughter only relaxed him more. The evening was shaping up to be better than he'd hoped.

"So how much did you get done on the dissertation this week?"

Denny's cheeks pinked. "Let's just say I got closer to the finish line."

Tom cocked his head. "What distracted you this time?"

The way Denny stared at him with wide eyes was almost comical. "Who told?"

He laughed. "You did, remember?"

Denny twisted his napkin in his hands. "To be honest, I was thinking about you."

"*I* distracted you?" Tom didn't like that. "But I wasn't even here."

"You didn't need to be. I felt so guilty about—"

Tom held his hand up. "Stop that, okay? It takes two to tango, so they say. Well, we were both... tangoing." He sighed. "And if it makes you feel better, I was thinking about it too. I wanted to say something on Monday, but Mr. Loomis was kinda hovering, and..."

"He does that a lot," Denny admitted. "And I do get it. You were there to do a job, not talk to me."

"Then let's change the subject." Tom leaned back in his chair. "How big is this place? Do you all get a bedroom each?"

Denny nodded. "We share the living room, this room, the kitchen, and the two bathrooms. Except the girls come off better than the guys. Lisa and Meena share one bathroom, and the three guys another." He pushed his chair back. "Want a tour? It'll be fast, because I'm not showing you their rooms." He snorted. "Trust me, you wouldn't want to see Chris's, at least not without a map, a trail of breadcrumbs, and a minesweeper."

Tom liked the living room with its brick fireplace, big, squashy couches, and thick warm-coloured rug. He liked the patio doors in the dining room opening out onto the garden. He imagined that could be pleasant on summer evenings.

Denny led him up the staircase with its sharp left turn, and at the top of the stairs he pointed to the right. "Those are Lisa's and Meena's rooms, and that's their bathroom in the middle." He indicated the door behind him. "That's our bathroom, except there's no bath—the girls got that—and it's tiny. Robin is the one who keeps the mess in check. Which usually amounts to a lot of yelling at me and Chris to squeegee the shower screen." He grinned. "He'll make someone a wonderful husband." Then he pointed to the corner room. "And that's mine. Want to see?"

"Sure."

Denny went to the door, and Tom was surprised to see a cable looped around the handle and through a hook screwed into the door frame, its ends secured in a padlock.

"That looks like a bike lock," he observed.

"That's because it is." Denny fished a key from his pocket and unlocked it. He opened the door, and Tom went inside. It was a squarish room with pale green walls, and floral curtains at the window. To the left were fitted wardrobes, and a wide bed stood against the external wall. A shelf ran the width of the bed, covered in books, and a desk sat under the window.

What drew his attention, however, were the three tripods standing around the bed, each one with a camera attached. Several ring lights were set up around the perimeter, with one attached to the wall via a suction cup.

"There's a lot of hardware in here," Tom mused.

"There's a ghost in the house," Denny said with a smile.

"I'm trying to capture it on video."

Tom rolled his eyes. "Do I look *that* stupid?"

Denny let out a sigh. "Okay, I don't just do porn with the studio. I have an OnlyFans account." He gave Tom an inquiring glance.

Tom chuckled. "Yes, I know what that is. Do you film just yourself, or are there other guys?"

Denny gave a shrug. "Usually it's just me wanking or using toys. You wouldn't believe how many of my subscribers get off on watching me make myself come with a dildo or a prostate massager."

"Do you have many? Subscribers, I mean."

Denny grinned. "Enough that I can earn more with OnlyFans than I can with the studio."

"Do you keep the door locked to protect all this stuff?"

Denny shook his head. "I secure the door because I don't want the others finding out what I do in here. They're fine about me doing porn—I don't think they'd take so kindly to me filming it in here. And I'm certain Ken wouldn't be happy." His face tightened. "I'm not happy about it either, if it comes to that. It would be different if I had my own place, but I can't afford it, not yet. So I have to be careful. I shoot content when I'm the only one in the house, for one thing. I wouldn't want them to hear something and wonder what I was doing in here. Especially if someone asks to film with me."

Tom wasn't sure why, but Denny's confession and consideration towards his housemates endeared him all the more.

"How does that work?"

"Filming with someone else, you mean? We both have an OnlyFans account. We shoot as much footage as we can, then we edit it into two versions. We each upload one. That way, we have different content, and we both get paid." Denny's eyes sparkled. "*You* could do it."

"Do what?"

"Set yourself up with an account, get a camera, a couple of lights…"

Tom blinked. "Film myself jacking off? Who'd want to watch me?"

"The same guys who are going to watch you fuck me and Jake in Ari's videos. Once they go live, you'll have any number of subscribers. And if you think about it, that makes good financial sense."

Tom folded his arms. "Oh yeah, Mr. Management and Finance? How so?"

Denny counted off. "You shoot video one time with Ari, he pays you once, right? But if you upload your *own* stuff, the money keeps coming in, the more subscribers you get. Shoot it once—get paid for it many times over."

He had to admit, Denny made a lot of sense.

"Plus, if you did set up an account, you could film with me, and we'd share the footage."

Everything ground to a halt.

"Film—with you?"

What came to mind was the tight heat of Denny's body wrapped around Tom's cock, the jiggle of his arse cheeks as Tom had slammed into him, the contrast of cream spunk on tanned skin, the noises he'd made when he came…

His dick reacted, and he covered it with his hands.

And Denny noticed. For a second there, his gaze alighted on Tom's crotch before he raised his head, his eyes shining.

Breathing suddenly required effort.

Denny nodded. "Think of the benefits. No obtrusive cameras, Ari zooming in on your dick. No awkward angles. No stop-start. We just shoot as much as we want, then edit it. Plus, we'd be working for ourselves rather than someone else."

Tom strove to keep drawing air into his lungs.

He wasn't considering this—was he?

"Does Ari know you do this?"

Denny nodded. "Which means I bring in more subscribers to his channel."

Tom tried to think lucidly for a moment.

The only reason Denny wants me to do an OnlyFans video with him is because it'll earn him more money than he'd get for a solo one.

Yeah, that made sense.

Denny touched his back, and Tom almost leaped out of his skin, he was so lost in his own thoughts.

"You don't have to. It was only a suggestion. Plus, you might prefer to find someone else to—"

Tom's heartbeat raced. "No. Only with you."

Denny smiled. "I'm flattered." He gestured to the bed. "We could even shoot some footage tonight."

Tom's heart thumped. "Now?"

CHAPTER NINETEEN

Denny grinned. "Why not? Everyone's away for the night. No one to listen in. You could relax and get into it."

Tom vacillated between *why not?* and *Oh my God,* except the line between the two opposing states kept blurring. "I don't know…" His heart hammered, his stomach churned.

It's not as if it's the first time, right?

At least I know what to expect.

The sound of harsh, erratic breathing filled the air, and he realised it came from him.

"Hey." Denny's voice was soft. "Breathe, Tom. It was only a suggestion." His hand was gentle on Tom's upper arm.

Tom forced himself to calm down and look at the situation with a degree of perspective. It wasn't the idea of having sex on camera that was giving him heart palpitations, he knew that.

It was the prospect of doing it with Denny.

That first time, it had been sex with a stranger. He'd been hesitant, but in the end, he'd let himself go, and it had ended better than he'd hoped.

This time would be different.

This would be with a man he'd already admitted being attracted to, in an act he'd thought about nonstop since their first meeting—an act he wanted to experience again.

And why would *I be doing it again? Do I need the money that badly?*

Stupidest question of the decade. Of *course* he needed the money.

Tom grabbed hold of his resolve with both hands. "Let's do it."

To his surprise, Denny didn't react with his habitual smile, but studied Tom for a moment. "Wait here." Then he dashed from the room, and Tom heard him thumping down the stairs.

Now what?

A minute later he heard footsteps again, only this time more measured. Denny walked back into the room, a shot glass in each hand, both filled with a slightly opaque liquid.

"What are these?"

"Kamikaze shots. Vodka, triple sec, and lime juice." Denny's eyes twinkled. "For Dutch courage—if you need it. And we don't have to film anything if you don't want to. I mean it. I won't turn the cameras on until you give the word."

Tom forced a chuckle. "It'll take you a minute to get them all running. I think you've covered every angle."

"Except one." Denny pointed to the ceiling. "I always wanted to film from above." He stared. "Hey, maybe I could tape my phone—"

Tom covered Denny's mouth with his hand. "No. I think you've got enough." Denny's laughter tickled his palm. He removed his hand, glanced at the shot glass, then knocked it back. He licked his lips. "Tastes great. Goes down really easily too." Andy's choice of shots always set his throat on fire.

Denny waggled his eyebrows. "Yeah, it does, but it's a dangerous combo."

Tom handed him the empty glass and Denny placed them on the bedside table.

He cleared his throat. "So… how does this work? I mean, do we work it all out ahead of time?"

Denny chuckled. "All we'll do beforehand is discuss a few positions. Then we just roll with it." He looked Tom in the eye. "You okay with kissing?" He grinned. "I tend to do a lot of that."

Tom suppressed a shiver. "Yeah, that's okay."

More than okay.

"You've watched porn, so you know it can get kinda noisy. Some of that is for the cameras, all right? But here's what *I* think. If you want to make a noise, then make it, because that's what *I'll* be doing."

"Do… do you ever fake it? For the cameras?" If that was the case, how would Tom know he was doing it right?

Denny stilled. "I don't need to fake it. If I'm naked with a hot guy, and he's hitting all the right spots, then what comes out of my mouth is going to be the genuine article. So my advice is… Keep it real. If you want to talk dirty, then do it. You won't hear any complaints from me."

The tightness around his chest loosened, only Tom wasn't sure if that was as a result of Denny's assurances or the alcohol. "Okay. You mentioned positions."

Denny nodded. "I thought we'd keep it simple. Missionary, doggy, maybe you standing beside the bed with my arse hanging out over it… I could ride you…" He smiled. "My favourite position is on my side, getting fucked from behind." He squeezed Tom's arm. "Just go with it. Do whatever feels good, feels natural." He cupped Tom's cheek. "At the end of the day, it's not a stage production, it's two guys having sex, and enjoying it."

Tom didn't think enjoying it would prove to be difficult.

His main concern was the possibility he'd enjoy it too much.

"One thing, though. Be aware of the cameras. Some guys like a side view, so they get to watch the dick slide in. Others like the rear view. They get to see two holes that way. And when it comes to blow jobs, it's all about the neck and throat."

Tom gave him an inquiring glance. "Huh?"

Denny smiled. "If you were standing, and I was lying on my back on the bed, you sliding into my throat, there'd be a great view of my neck as you go deep. Plus, you get to stroke it while you fuck my mouth. And if you think the blow job is going on for too long, that's probably a sign you should keep doing it." He grinned. "Trust me, a blow job scene can *never* be too long."

"So… should I just follow your lead?"

Denny shook his head. "Far from it. They're going to expect you to be the more dominant of us. So feel free to manhandle me, be a little rough. I can take it." He cocked his head to one side. "You've never rimmed anyone before, have you?"

Tom shook his head, his pulse racing.

"Want to try? Think of it as prepping my hole. It'll open me right up for your cock."

Oh fuck.

Denny's eyes sparkled. "And before you ask, I took a shower right before you arrived. You'll probably be able to smell my grapefruit bodywash back there. I used enough of it."

Tom narrowed his gaze. "You had this planned, didn't you?"

Denny gave him an innocent glance. "Maybe?" Tom started laughing, and Denny smiled. "I like it when you laugh. So you don't feel as if I've manipulated you, backed you into a corner?"

Tom had to smile at that. "Far from it. Do we take our clothes off before we start?"

"No, keep them on." He tilted his head. "Got it all straight in your head?"

Tom laughed once more. "Not sure 'straight' is entirely apt, but yeah."

"Ready to do this?"

He sucked in a deep breath. "Ready when you are."

Denny went around the room, turning the cameras on, and Tom waited for him beside the bed. Denny walked up to him, smiling.

"Hey, gorgeous." His voice was low and sensual, and it made Tom feel wanted.

He followed his instincts, drew Denny into his arms, and kissed him, his hands on Denny's back and waist, feeling the heat of him through the tank top, the warm, bare skin so smooth beneath his fingertips. Another kiss, and Denny looped his arms around Tom, the tiniest noise escaping as he opened for him, his fingers grazing Tom's neck.

Tom could have stood like that for years. Nothing else mattered but the feel of Denny's body pressed against his, Denny's soft lips that opened for him, his hand curling around Tom's nape, his warm, musky scent infiltrating Tom's nostrils...

The tremor that rippled through him.

Tom tilted Denny's chin up with his fingers. "You're shaking."

Denny swallowed. "I'm thinking about what's to come." Another kiss, slow and tender. Their foreheads touched, and Denny let out a sigh. "This is good."

Tom couldn't agree more.

He recalled Denny's instructions about being dominant. He turned Denny as if they were dancing, joined at the hip, stomach, chest, thigh, then shuffled him backwards toward the bed, their lips in a constant connection.

"You need to be on the bed," he murmured as he took a breath.

Denny sat, and Tom went with him, bending low, unwilling to break the kiss. Tom cradled Denny's head in his hand, and lowered him onto the mattress, going with him, sucking on Denny's upper lip, exploring him with his tongue. Tom's thigh was wedged between Denny's spread legs, and he moaned to feel hardness there.

"That's because of you," Denny said in a low voice. He locked gazes with Tom.

Fuck.

It could have been just a line, something to say for the cameras, but the heat in Denny's eyes...

How could he fake that?

Tom gazed at the tank top where Denny's nipples pushed

against the soft cotton. "I want to see."

Denny's pupils dilated, and Tom got the impression he'd said the right thing. Denny pulled the fabric of his tank top aside, revealing his nipple. Tom kissed Denny on the lips, then laid a trail of kisses to the bronze pebbled flesh with its proud, hard nub, and flicked it with his tongue.

Denny's soft moan as Tom sucked on it sent the blood rushing south, and on impulse, he deliberately pushed against Denny's crotch, rolling his hips, grinding...

Denny closed his eyes, and Tom couldn't resist the siren call of those lips. He covered Denny with his body, rocking against his rigid dick, kissing him, exploring him with his tongue.

I can't get enough of him.

"Want to see you too," Denny murmured into their kiss.

Tom stood, his fingers working their way down the buttons of his shirt in a tantalising ballet of fingers and thumbs, his senses telling him slow was good.

Slow was *definitely* good.

Once the shirt was in a heap on the carpet, he lifted Denny into a sitting position and tugged his tank top over his head. "Move back a bit," he murmured.

Denny shifted backwards, and Tom gave him a playful push before unfastening Denny's jeans, his erection popping free, tenting his briefs. Tom grasped the hems of his jeans and tugged, chuckling.

"They're so tight. How do you even get into these things?"

Denny grinned. "They're designed to be tight. And it's called practice." Tom threw them to the floor, then brushed his fingers over the waistband of his briefs. Denny covered Tom's hand with his. "Leave them on."

Tom nodded, trying not to stare at the cotton moulded around Denny's long shaft.

Denny pressed his foot to Tom's chest, and Tom took it in both hands, kissing the toes on impulse. Denny's shudder told him he'd done the right thing yet again, so he repeated it. He kissed along Denny's calf, tiny, sweet, nibbling kisses, then past his knee, up his thigh, until at last he rubbed his nose over Denny's bulge.

Oh fuck, how he smells… It was a musky, earthy scent, and Tom buried his nose in the warm cleft between thigh and groin, breathing him in.

Denny whimpered. "You've been taking lessons on the quiet, haven't you?"

Tom wasn't about to tell him where his new-found knowledge came from.

Gay porn was proving hard to resist.

"Don't take them off," Denny pleaded. "Kiss it."

Tom did as he was told, planting a line of kisses along its length. A damp spot formed at the head, and he didn't want to wait a second longer. He pulled the briefs over Denny's hips, and Denny's solid cock rose to greet him.

"He remembers you," Denny teased. Then he arched his back when Tom took the head into his mouth and swirled his tongue around it. "*Fuck*, you're a fast learner."

Tom hollowed his cheeks as he sucked, watching Denny while he did so, loving the shivers that multiplied when their gazes locked. Denny reared up, grabbed Tom's head, and pulled him into a brutal kiss. He dropped back onto the mattress and Tom resumed, only this time, Denny held his head steady while he gave small thrusts of his hips, pushing up into Tom's mouth.

"Love your mouth on me." Denny's breathless appreciation was music to Tom's ears. Then Denny let go of him. "But I'd love the feel of you in my mouth even more."

Tom didn't need a second invitation.

He removed his jeans, climbed onto the bed, and Denny lay at right angles to him, his head at Tom's groin. Denny wrapped his hand around the base of Tom's rock-hard cock. "You're so big."

Before Tom could respond, Denny took him in deep, until

Tom's dick bumped against the back of Denny's throat. He lay there, hips rolling, chasing the sensations, hard as steel, his hand on Denny's back. Tom got to his knees, feeding Denny his cock, thrusting deeper and faster, watching Denny's face redden, his eyes water.

Then he remembered what the viewers would want to see.

"Lie on your back," he ground out. "I want to fuck your mouth."

Oh dear God, the brown of Denny's irises was almost totally obliterated by black. He scrambled to flop onto his back, his head hanging over the edge, his hand curled around his own cock. Tom clambered off the mattress and stood at Denny's head, legs wide. He aimed his dick at those wet lips, nudged the head inside, then rocked, dipping into Denny's warm, tight throat.

Oh my God.

Tom watched, mesmerised, as his thick cock distended Denny's throat, watched Denny's cheeks fill with every stroke of Tom's shaft. Tom planted his hands on Denny's chest, pushing on it, hips snapping as he plunged deep, before shifting to an almost jackhammer action as he fucked Denny's mouth again and again, his hand on Denny's throat.

Feeling his dick in there was the hottest thing ever.

He pulled free and bent to kiss Denny, an upside-down kiss that should have felt awkward but somehow worked, then resumed face-fucking him, picking up speed, his shaft slick with Denny's saliva until it dripped from the corners of his mouth, Denny's moan around his dick sending delicious vibrations through it. Conscious of the camera behind him, Tom planted one foot on the mattress and drove his cock deep, grunting as he thrust.

"If I keep this up, I'm gonna come down your throat."

Denny gave a strangled cry, and Tom pulled free. Denny moved lithely, turning until his arse was where his head had been, his knees wide. The motion spread his cheeks a little, revealing that same pucker Tom had slid into a few weeks ago.

Denny twisted to peer at him, his arse tilted higher, and Tom smiled. "I think your hole is crying out for my tongue." He knelt on the rug, grabbed the warm globes in both hands, and pulled them apart, stretching Denny's hole, opening him a little.

Do it. You know you want to.

He lowered his head and licked the rim of muscle.

Denny whimpered. "Oh fuck."

Tom did it again, only this time he pushed his tongue into Denny's hole.

Denny's warm, tight hole.

Fuck. He could get to like this.

Tom anchored himself, his hands under Denny's body, holding onto his arse while he fucked Denny's hole with his tongue.

"Please," Denny gasped.

Tom broke off from his sensual assault. "What do you need?"

"Rub your beard over my hole?"

He grinned, then buried his face in Denny's crack, sliding his beard slowly over Denny's pucker.

Denny shivered. "Oh fuck, again."

Tom repeated the move until Denny was rolling his hips, gaining momentum. He slid his hand between his body and the sheet, shifting the position of his dick until it lay between his legs, poking towards Tom, pre-cum leaking from it.

Tom chuckled. "Is that a hint?" He licked from the head all the way along the underside of Denny's shaft, dragging his tongue over Denny's sac, over his taint, until he was once more at Denny's hole.

"Fuck, do that again." Denny's voice cracked.

Harsh breathing filled the air as Tom licked and sucked, his own moans of pleasure mingling with Denny's. He kissed the firm flesh of Denny's arse, kissed his pucker, and with each slow lap of his tongue over Denny's hole, Denny's writhing increased, his whimpers intensifying.

The same whimpers that went straight to Tom's dick.

"I need to fuck you." His voice had a rough edge to it. "Sit up."

Denny responded without hesitation, turning his head in a request Tom couldn't deny. Their lips met, and Denny hooked his arm around to cup the back of Tom's head while they kissed.

"You ready for me?" Tom asked as they parted.

Denny's response was to point to the bottle of lube on the bedside table. Tom grabbed it, slicked up his cock, then held the bottle above Denny's crease and squeezed out a trickle of clear viscous liquid. Denny arched his back and shivered as Tom rubbed the head of his dick through his crack, sliding it over Denny's hole.

Then he did it again, only faster.

Faster.

When Denny reached back to spread himself wide, Tom aimed his cock and sank into him, no hurry, just a slow, measured penetration, enjoying the sensation of Denny's body imprisoning his shaft. He held onto Denny's shoulder as he moved in and out. All he could hear was their shallow breaths and the wet sound of his dick inching its way into Denny's hole.

Only now he wasn't inching—he was driving his cock home.

Tom planted his foot on the bed once more, pressed one hand to Denny's arse, and rocked in and out, admiring the visuals: the curve of Denny's arched back; the way his narrow waist tapered into slim hips; and the dimples just above his arse cheeks, calling out to be kissed.

He gave Denny a rough shove, and Denny's chest hit the mattress, his moans multiplying when Tom grabbed the back of his neck and held him to the bed.

Christ, he needed to get deeper.

"Shift forward a bit," he demanded.

Denny obeyed, and Tom climbed onto the bed, straddling Denny's arse. With both hands gripping Denny's waist, Tom thrust all the way home, unable to tear his gaze away from the sight, watching that tight hole suck him in. Denny grabbed fistfuls of the sheets, turning his head to the side to gaze at Tom, open-mouthed, a litany of moans and whimpers falling from his lips.

"Your hole feels amazing," Tom murmured, hips rolling faster, his fingers digging into Denny's sides. With his knees spread wide, he knew the camera behind him was getting a great view of his cock spearing Denny's hole, and the thought made him speed up a little until his body was slamming into Denny's, a sharp *smack* of flesh against flesh.

Tingles shot up and down his spine, and he pulled free of Denny's body. "Get on your side." Anything to delay the orgasm he knew was imminent.

Denny responded with obvious eagerness, and Tom spooned around him, holding Denny's upper leg aloft as he guided his cock back to where it needed to be. Tom slid deep with one fluid glide, and Denny moaned. Tom rocked faster, and when Denny dropped his leg, rolling fully onto his side, Tom grabbed his waist and drove his shaft deeper still.

Too close. Too close.

Tom slowed his thrusts and wrapped both arms around Denny, enfolding him, kissing his neck, his cheek, his shoulder. And suddenly they were rocking together, connected, in harmony, Denny craning his neck for a kiss. Tom picked up speed once more, slamming into him, each slap of their bodies punctuated by Denny's whimpers and sighs.

"Oh fuck."

"Don't stop."

"Yeah, just like that."

His words fuelled Tom's desire, propelling him closer to his climax. He gave Denny's ear lobe a gentle tug with his teeth, then grazed his neck, sucking there, kissing him again and again.

"Where do you want me to come?"

Oh God.

Denny didn't hesitate.

"Fuck. Come in me." He was so close.

Tom pulled out of him, and Denny rolled onto his back, bringing his legs up and wrapping them around Tom's waist. Tom aimed his dick and there he was once more, deep in Denny's arse, Denny's arms looped around his neck as they kissed.

Then Tom changed gear, and Denny grabbed onto the rails of his headboard as Tom drove into him, *slammed* into him, both of them breathing heavily, Denny's gasps synchronised with Tom's thrusts, his fingers curled around the metal posts, holding on for dear life. Tom propped himself up on his hands and fucked him with long, deep strokes, until Denny's toes curled and the only word to tumble from his lips was "fuck."

His arse was taking a pounding, and Denny loved every second of it.

He gazed at Tom, and the sight unravelled him. Tom's face was flushed, as was his chest, and Denny knew they were almost there.

"Fuck me," he pleaded. "Harder."

Tom buried his face in Denny's neck, his hips jerking, no grace in his movements but so much raw passion, no sounds except whispered words that made no sense, whimpers and soft cries filling his ears. Denny cupped Tom's nape, his other hand working his cock, tugging, blurring…

He shot, crying out from the sheer pleasure of his orgasm, feeling his warm release coat his stomach, followed by the tell-tale throb inside him. Tom's arms tightened around him, their bodies frozen in that one glorious moment, locked together, both of them breathless, covered in a sheen of sweat.

He clung to Tom, waiting out the mini shocks and trickles of electricity, conscious of his heartbeat slipping back into its normal rhythm, Tom's body still caged between his thighs. He should have told Tom to withdraw and shoot his load within sight of the cameras, but he'd wanted to feel the pulse of Tom's cock inside him.

Tom kissed him, first on the lips, then on his forehead, his breathing more even.

"That was… incredible." He eased out of Denny's body, then gazed at his hole. Denny bore down, pushing out his cum, and was rewarded by Tom's groan. "And that is so *hot.*"

That was also Denny's signal to move.

He got off the bed and turned all the cameras off. Tom appeared unsure of himself, and Denny didn't hesitate. He got back onto the bed and lay next to him, his head on Tom's damp chest.

"News flash. I like to cuddle after sex too."

Tom's arm around him was the perfect ending.

They lay in silence, the thud of Tom's heart lulling him into a doze.

"So… what happens now?"

Denny didn't want to be practical. He wanted to enjoy the sensation of thick cream running through his veins, the sated feeling that only ever came from really good sex.

He wanted to savour their connection, but that moment was slipping by, and he couldn't hold onto it.

Back to real life.

He suppressed his sigh. "Now I upload it to my laptop, play with it, and when I have two versions, I email one to you—providing you've got an account set up. Then you're in business."

Is that all this was to you—business?

The thought sent a trickle of alarm through him. *Fuck. No.* Business was all it *could* be.

Tom sat up, swung his legs off the bed, and reached down to pick his shirt up. "I should go."

Fuck.

"You don't have to," Denny blurted out.

Tom frowned, the picture of confusion.

Denny forced himself to sound calm. "Stay. The bed's big enough, and like I said, there's no one else here. It's just us." He looked Tom in the eye. "Do you *want* to go?"

Say no.

Say no.

Tom bit his lip. "Would I be okay to have a shower?"

"No." Denny gazed back at him with a solemn expression. Except he couldn't keep it up. He chuckled and rolled his eyes. "Of course you can." His stomach clenched. "Does that mean you'll stay?"

Tom cleared his throat. "You have to understand... I... I haven't shared a bed with anyone since the divorce." He gave a shrug. "So it feels a bit... weird."

Denny smiled. "Want me to make it feel less weird?"

"How?"

Denny held his hand out to Tom, and when Tom took it, he pulled him back onto the bed. "Come here."

Tom closed the gap between them, and Denny kissed him on the lips. "I don't move around much when I sleep, I don't snore—because trust me, in this house? Someone would tell me if I did—and I'll make you a cooked breakfast in the morning, because that's what I do every Sunday."

Tom smiled. "I'll stay."

Denny grinned. "It was the breakfast that swung it, right? Then let me find you a towel, and you can grab the first shower."

"You're on." Tom made a quick exit.

"Something I said?" Denny called out after him.

"I need to pee!"

Denny shook his head. He glanced at the bed and made the decision to change the sheets. Anything to keep his mind off his impulsive request.

I shouldn't have asked him to stay.

I should have let him leave.

I shouldn't be doing this.

He knew all that, and yet he felt powerless to stop himself.

The roller coaster was in motion, the seatbelts were locked, and there seemed to be no stopping this ride.

CHAPTER TWENTY

Tom opened his eyes, and for a moment he didn't have a clue where he was. Then he realised what was so different.

Someone was in his arms.

Denny faced towards the wardrobe, Tom's arm draped over him, his chest pressed to Denny's back.

When was the last time I woke up like this?

That was easy—never. Deb wasn't a snuggler, not at night at any rate. She used to say it made her feel claustrophobic, which was why there had always been no man's land between them, an invisible wall Tom didn't dare cross. He'd grown accustomed to it, although there were times he'd wondered what it would be like to curl up around a warm body, to be aware of them through the night, to wake with them cradled against him...

Now he had his answer.

It was bliss.

Not that he could recollect anything. Denny had switched the lamp off, Tom's head had hit the pillow, and that had been it— lights out.

So at some point in the night, he'd reached for Denny.

An enticing scent of cotton sheets and a bed-warmed body assaulted his nostrils, and Tom breathed it in. He lay still, unwilling to move in case his motion shattered the moment.

What is it that feels so good about this? Was it waking to find a warm body in his arms? Or was it more the fact that it was Denny?

"Morning." Denny stirred, rolled over, and two sleepy brown eyes met his. Denny's lazy smile was adorable.

"Good morning."

And just like that, everything changed.

I should go.

He shouldn't have stayed in the first place.

A faint crease marred Denny's smooth brow. "Are you okay?"

He could lie.

Except Tom was never a fan of lying. It always came back to bite the liar on the bum. He went with a half-truth.

"Like I said last night, I haven't done this in a long time."

Denny sat upright, more alert. "Hey. I promised you breakfast, didn't I?" He threw back the covers and stood, giving Tom the perfect view of his bare arse. He grabbed his jeans from where he'd dumped them over the back of his chair before they'd gone to sleep. He squirmed into them, ending up lying across the foot of the bed to tug them higher.

Despite his anxious state, Tom had to chuckle. "I didn't realise breakfast came with entertainment too."

Denny paused, eyebrows arched, then stuck his tongue out. "Just for that, I might steal one of your hash browns." He grinned. "Actually, I think that's worth a sausage." He sucked in his gut and pulled the zipper up. He peered at Tom. "Are you a coffee person or a tea person first thing in the morning?"

"Coffee. My brain needs that jolt of caffeine."

"Me too." Denny crawled over to where Tom lay, leaning over him. "Take your time. I'll see you downstairs when you're ready." Then he gave Tom a peck on the lips. "And after that, we can talk about setting up your account." Another grin before he launched himself off the bed and out of the door.

Tom listened to the dull *thud thud thud* of Denny's bare feet on the stairs.

Why did I agree to film with him?

That was simple. It had seemed like a good idea at the time.

An idea he was now regretting in the cold light of day.

Get out before you get in too deep.

Tom wasn't thinking about the porn. What filled his mind was how it had felt to wake holding Denny.

The bacon was sizzling under the grill, the sausages were done and encased in a little foil tent along with the mushrooms, and the hash browns were a lovely golden-brown colour in the oven. Coffee dripped into its glass pot.

That left the eggs.

Denny went to the foot of the stairs. "You have about one minute," he hollered. Then he went back to the kitchen. Moments later, he heard Tom coming down. "Coffee's done, help yourself," he said without turning round. He poured beaten egg into the frying pan, swirling it with a spatula to incorporate the melted butter.

Tom peered over his shoulder. "I usually do mine in the microwave."

Denny stared at him, holding up the spatula. "Any more comments about my cooking, and this will end up across your knuckles." He brandished the blue plastic implement. "I'm not afraid to use it."

Tom laughed. He grabbed a clean mug from the drainer, poured coffee into it, then scanned the worktops.

Denny pointed to the white canister. "Sugar and sweeteners are in there." He pushed the eggs around the pan, watching for any sign they'd passed the point of no return. "Make yourself useful. There are two plates warming under the grill pan. Turn the grill off and dish out the bacon, then turn the oven off and do the same with the hash browns. The sausages and mushrooms are in that foil."

That earned him another wry chuckle. "Yes, sir. I forgot how bossy you can be."

It wasn't long before they were seated at the dining table, the doors opened wide to let in both the fresh morning air and the sound of birdsong.

Okay, this is nice. Denny liked having Tom all to himself, and making breakfast for him had felt so… domesticated. He was starving, attacking his food with enthusiasm. Tom ate more sedately.

Denny glanced at him. "Is it okay?"

Tom smiled. "It's perfect."

"Oh. Then I think you'd better tell that to your face, because it seems to have missed the memo."

Tom put his fork down. "Do I really need an OnlyFans account?"

Denny blinked. He placed his cutlery on either side of his plate and reached for his coffee. "No, but the whole point of last night was so we could both—"

"I got that part," Tom interjected. "Could you just… I don't know… make a note of how much income it generates and… split it with me?"

Denny twisted in his seat to stare at him. "Why don't you want an account of your own?"

Tom took a drink. "It's okay for you. This is what you do, right? I mean, you've been doing porn for how many years? It's like a… career." Tom's lips pressed together, his nose wrinkling. "But it's never going to be that for me, all right? Fuck, it was supposed to be a one-off, and now I've made three gay porn videos. *Three. Gay porn.*" He swallowed. "I'm just not sure I want to go down that road."

Denny let out a sigh. "It's okay, I get it. This was a means to an end. Sure, I can split the proceeds with you." He cocked his head. "Maybe you'd prefer cash rather than PayPal? I was thinking you have your accounts to do. Might be a little awkward."

"Why don't you message me nearer the time, and we'll sort something out?"

Denny opened his mouth to say he could do that, when the front door opened.

"Morning! I smell bacon. Great. I hope there's some left for me. I danced my legs off last night, and I could eat a horse between two bread vans."

Tom stiffened.

"That's Chris, one of my housemates," Denny informed him. *Who has the worst timing in the history of bad timing.*

Chris came into the dining room, stopping short when he caught sight of Tom. "Well, good morning." His eyes twinkled. "Not interrupting anything, am I?"

"Only breakfast." Tom wiped his lips on his napkin. "And it's time I was out of here." He pushed his chair back, then met Denny's gaze. "Thanks again for dinner last night. And..." Another swallow. "I'll be in touch, okay?"

Something in Denny's gut told him he'd just been handed a big fat lie. "Sure." He made as if to rise, but Tom waved his hand.

"Stay put. Finish your breakfast. I'll see myself out." He gave Chris a polite nod. "Nice to meet you." And before Denny could perform introductions, he was gone. A moment later, the front door opened and closed.

Well, fuck.

Chris arched his eyebrows. "Something I said?"

No, I think it was something I said—and something we did.

"This wasn't on you," Denny said with a sigh. "He's... he's just not used to this yet."

Chris frowned. "Used to what?" He peered at Denny. "Are you okay? You seem kind of... I don't know... upset."

Disappointed was nearer the mark.

"Remember the guy I did the scene with? The straight guy I told you about?"

"Yeah." Denny pointed to where Tom had sat, and Chris's

eyes widened. "That was him?"

Denny nodded.

Chris gave a low whistle. "You have good taste in men, I'll say that for you. I mean, I'm straight, and even *I* think he's a hunk." He cackled. "*Now* I get why you wanted the place to yourself last night." He grinned. "Did you have a good night?"

I thought so—right up to the point where he got out of here as if he were on fire.

Tom closed the front door behind him. There'd been a knot in his belly all the way home, and a dullness in his chest.

I shouldn't have left like that.

He still had to go back and finish the wall. Plus, there was the meeting with Loomis that week. All of which was going to feel awkward as fuck after that swift exit.

Not to mention the previous night.

That glorious, sensual, hot as fuck night.

On the train back to Ewell, he'd done his best to switch his brain off, but the thoughts kept coming, an overwhelming torrent of flashbacks.

Denny's body writhing on Tom's dick.

The smell of him.

The exquisite tightness of Denny's throat around his cock.

And there was more, only, that had nothing to do with sex, and *everything* to do with the man Tom couldn't push from his mind.

Denny's laughter.

The light in his eyes.

The playful banter.

The way he'd felt in Tom's arms.

He said it though. It was business. A way to earn money.

Denny hadn't taken Tom to bed because he had the hots for him—he'd done it for cash—and Tom needed to hold onto that reality.

His phone vibrated, and he pulled it from his pocket. Unknown caller. His chest tightened. He'd hoped it would be—

His phone was ringing.

Tom clicked on Answer. "Hello, Tom Ryder."

"Hello. My name is Craig Holdness. I run a construction company in Epsom—"

"Holdness Holdings. I've seen your van around the place." Tom didn't think it was a large operation, but they *had* been responsible for him losing out on a couple of jobs in recent years. "What can I do for you, Mr. Holdness?"

"Are you busy this afternoon? I know it's the weekend, but I really need to talk to you. There's something I'd like to discuss that would be to our mutual advantage."

Tom glanced at his gleaming kitchen. The laundry was done, as was the weekly dusting and vacuuming. *What else am I going to do with my Sunday? Tidy the garden? Repaint the gnomes?*

Hell no. He *loathed* the fucking gnomes. He'd have gotten rid of them years ago, but they'd been Deb's, and she looked at them every time she visited.

He could imagine the sharp intake of breath and the hurt expression if she turned up and they were no longer there.

Besides, Mr. Holdness's call intrigued him.

"I can do that. Where do you want to meet?" He scribbled down the address. "What time?"

"Three o'clock?"

"Fine. I'll see you then." He hung up.

Tom stared at the notepad. At least it would take his mind off Denny.

Yeah, fat chance of that.

CHAPTER TWENTY-ONE

Tom got out of the van and crossed the street. Holdness Holdings amounted to a front yard covered in paving slabs. A truck sat on them, together with a caravan and another van with the company's branding on the side and rear door.

Their owner was clearly not the gardening type. The only evidence of greenery was the weeds forcing themselves up between the slabs. Holdness had a pretty good crop of those.

The front door opened, and a middle-aged man stood there in jeans and a plaid shirt. "You must be Tom."

He held out his hand. "Good to meet you, Mr. Holdness."

"Call me Craig. Come inside."

Tom followed him in, and the aroma of freshly brewed coffee assaulted his nostrils. He sniffed.

Craig chuckled. "A coffee man. That bodes well."

Tom was dying to know what this was about.

They went into the kitchen, a square room with cabinets and worktops on three sides, a small table in the centre with two chairs pushed under it. Craig gestured to one of them. "Take a seat. How do you like your coffee?"

"Black, please. Do you have any sweeteners?"

Craig laughed. He opened a cabinet, and Tom saw several boxes of them. "My wife's idea. She thinks I need to watch my figure at my age." He patted his belly.

Tom chuckled. "Which was why I started having them instead of sugar." He watched as Craig poured coffee into two fat mugs, then brought them to the table. He placed a small glass jar in the centre, and Tom helped himself to a packet of sweetener.

Craig sat facing Tom, hands on the table, fingers laced. "I

suppose you must be curious as to why I called."

"Just a little," Tom replied, with a polite smile.

"So here's the thing. I have a job that's due to start this week. It's an extension—two, actually, to the side and back of a property. The deadline for completion is one month, and that can't be budged."

"Okay." Tom sipped his coffee and smiled. "This is good."

"I usually work with another guy, Barry. It's just the two of us—I contract out when I need to—and that works well." His face contorted. "Well, it did until last week. Barry wasn't feeling so good, and I told him to get himself to the quack's and get checked out." His expression tightened. "It wasn't good news. He was diagnosed with late-stage lung cancer. They admitted him to the hospital right away and operated to remove most of one lung."

Tom's stomach clenched. "I'm sorry. Have you worked together long?"

"Since I started out in the business."

"Craig, I… why did you call me?"

"I wanted to pull out of this upcoming job, but it's complicated, and…" Craig sighed. "That's not quite true. I *don't* want to, not really. The side extension is for an elderly woman and her husband. She needs level access, and adapting her home would be difficult. Plus, they're at an age where they need to have people around them. Her son and daughter-in-law are paying for the extensions, and then they'll move into the main house with their family. She's being looked after in a local nursing home, but they need the beds, so—"

"Hence the deadline." Tom got the impression Craig was a good bloke.

"Now you see why I can't pull out. I've made so many calls the last few days, trying to find someone to take over from Barry." He gazed at Tom.

The penny dropped. "You're asking *me* to do it?"

Craig nodded. "One of the guys I called mentioned your

name. He said you were good at your job. So I started asking around." He smiled. "I like what I heard."

"There must be *tons* of builders out there who—"

"Oh, there are," Craig agreed. "And some of them scrape pretty close to being mediocre. I don't *do* mediocre, Tom. I only subcontract out to people who work to the same high standards I do." He leaned back. "Here's the deal. I know you're self-employed like me, so what I propose is that we work together, and each of us invoices the clients separately for our labour. That way, I won't be employing you. It'd just be for one month, and we'd have a lot to do in that time." Craig took another drink. "Of course, all of this is academic if you're rushed off your feet with work. If that's the case, say so. I'll understand."

Tom bit his lip. "I'm not exactly snowed under right now."

Craig stilled. "Really? Then what do you say?"

Tom drank a little more. A month of good, solid work.

"Sure, I'll work with you."

Craig's face lit up. "Thank you. I was starting to panic. The footings need to be dug out this week, but I've hired a guy with a mini digger. The concrete arrives Friday."

Tom laughed. "You don't mess around, do you?"

Craig smiled. "I'm not one of those builders who sits around on his backside all day, drinking coffee and looking at his phone. I like to get in early, do a full day's work, and then go home."

Tom couldn't help liking him. "I think we're going to get along just fine. When do you want me to start?"

"You can come with me to the property tomorrow. See what we're up against."

That worked for Tom. Then he remembered. "I have a garden wall to grout first thing. Last week's job."

Craig blinked. "Job? As in, singular?" His gaze grew thoughtful. "*Not exactly snowed under* sounds like a euphemism for—"

"An empty diary," Tom concluded. "So yes, I'd be

delighted to work with you."

A month of keeping busy. Exactly what he needed.

Wednesday evening, Tom left his muddy boots on the doormat, shucked off his clothing, and hit the shower. The mini digger had shown up on time that morning, but then it broke down after an hour, so he and Craig resorted to the old-fashioned way.

Dear God, he ached like a son of a bitch, but it was a good ache.

The hot water went a long way to relieving his twinges, and by the time he flipped off the jets, he felt almost human again. He pulled on a clean pair of sweats, shoved his phone into one of its deep pockets, and went into the kitchen. There was one can of beer in the fridge, and Tom swore he'd heard it calling to him all the way from Epsom. He grabbed it, padded barefoot into the living room, and flopped onto the couch.

Food could wait.

He removed his phone and hit Email. He'd only had time to glance at it once during their lunch break, and there'd been nothing of interest or urgency.

Then he saw it.

Denny Bailey. No subject, but an attachment.

Tom clicked on the email.

Hey. All done, so it's all yours. Call me if you need help setting up the account.

Denny.

Tom hadn't gotten as far as pulling up the OnlyFans website.

There'd been no sign of Denny two days ago when Tom had arrived to finish the job, and he'd been ashamed to realise his primary emotion was relief.

Maybe this is for the best.

Then why didn't it feel that way?

He could go through the rest of his life without ever feeling the need to shoot porn again, but the thought of not seeing Denny?

Talk about torn.

Loomis still wanted to discuss another job and had arranged a meeting at the house, but Tom now had obligations. He'd called to tell Loomis he'd be unavailable for a month, and if it was an urgent job, he'd be better off looking for someone else. He could've strung Loomis along, but that wasn't his style.

To his relief, Loomis had said the job would wait for him, and asked Tom to contact him when his present stint finished. Not meeting Loomis meant no opportunity to see Denny, not that it was certain he'd have been at the house anyway.

Denny hadn't been far from Tom's thoughts ever since shooting that scene. In fact, in the days since then, Tom had thought of little else. He'd got into bed each night, closed his eyes, and Denny was *right there*, Tom's tongue in his hole, Denny's whimpers filling his ears.

I'm not like him. Tom couldn't divorce his emotions from the act. Every moan that fell from Denny's lips, every quiver of his belly when Tom sucked his dick, every shudder rippling through him as Tom filled him to the hilt... All of it conspired to suck Tom in, drag him in, make him want to do it again, and again, and again...

Porn might have been out, but sex with Denny was something else.

That little paperclip on the screen called to him.

Download it. Watch it.

Tom didn't think that was such a good idea. He wasn't

even sure he was going to reply to Denny's email.

That's done. Leave it. Make a clean break.

Only one problem—he didn't want to.

One week later

It had been a tiring day. The house they were working on was covered in concrete blocks made to look like sandstone, and the clients wanted the side extension to match, blend in... That had meant removing every block from the back of the house with painstaking care, then chipping off the old mortar, in preparation for using them to cover the side wall of the extension, followed by the task of rendering the rear.

Tom didn't mind. He was getting used to working with Craig. They shared a similar sense of humour, the same outlook on life, and lunchtimes had become their time to discuss whatever was in the news that day.

Tom grinned. There had been some very lively discussions.

Once he'd showered, Tom went through his ritual of checking his phone. He'd kept it on mute all day: constant pinging pissed both him and Craig off.

Denny's name popped up, and just like that, Tom's gut roiled.

Hru?

He'd hazard a guess what that meant. *Fine. You okay?*

F9. And jsun, the dissertation is going gr8.

Tom reckoned he needed to take a degree course just to understand Denny's texts.

Ru f2t?

Tom's thumbs got busy. *Okay, you lost me with that one.*

LMAO. Are you free to talk?

No. He did *not* want to talk. *Sorry. Busy. I'll text l8r.* Despite his churning stomach, Tom grinned. *Hey, get me.*

Sure he was busy. He had dinner to cook and a TV to veg out in front of. All big important tasks. The thought tightened his chest.

Sorry 2 disturb u but ltns. There was a pause. *That means long time no see LOL.* Another pause. *It would be g2cu.*

Tom didn't need any help to decipher that one. Something turned over in his stomach. *Not right now ok? Really am busy.*

Yeah, busy feeling guilty as fuck.

Denny's reply took a few seconds to appear. *Nbd. Kit.* Then an emoji popped up, one with a winking eye and stuck out tongue. *That translates as no big deal. Keep in touch. Ttfn granddad.*

Tom burst out laughing. That little shit. *F9. Go play with your toys.* Two could play at that game.

What popped onto his screen a moment later was an image of Denny's bed, on which lay a bottle of lube, the longest, thickest dildo Tom had ever seen—which wasn't many, but *oh my God* the *size* of that thing—a string of black beads, and something made out of what resembled silicone, curved and alien-looking.

Denny's text pinged. *Toys. And now I'll go play with them. [grin]*

Tom couldn't resist. *What's that one on the right?*

Prostate massager. I might try it on u ootd.

The babel fish in Tom's head did its thing. *One of these days.* Oh fuck.

I'll let u go. An emoji winked into existence, blowing a kiss.

If there was one act from their night together that Tom recalled more than any other, it was Denny's kisses.

Nope. Nope. Not a good idea.

He was doing the right thing.

Wasn't he?

One week later

Thursday night, and Tom was already looking forward to the weekend. Thank God Craig only worked weekdays.

Maybe I should return Denny's calls. And his texts…Each time he ignored them, all it did was make him feel anxious. He knew the longer he let things go on like that, the more difficult it would become.

None of this is Denny's fault.

No, this was all on Tom.

He propped his feet up on the coffee table and aimed the remote. What he needed right then was some mindless action movie with a lot of bangs, crashes, chases… Anything so as not to *think*.

His phone burst into life, a loud klaxon that made his windows shake.

One of these days I really need to find a more subtle ring tone. He glanced at the screen and froze.

It was Denny.

He couldn't keep ignoring him forever.

Tom clicked on Answer. "Hi."

"Oh my God, you're alive."

He chuckled. "Sorry. I took on a big job and I'm about halfway through it."

"Sounds to me like you need a day off. Are you working this weekend?"

Say yes. Tell him you're busy.

Tom was getting sick and tired of lying.

"No, I'm not."

"Great. I am in *dire* need of a break, so let's do something."

"You got any ideas what?" *And does it involve a camera, lights, and lube?*

"Yup. A weekend by the sea."

That caught him on the hop. "Seriously?"

"Sure. Why not? I haven't done that in so long."

Tom thought fast. *Where do gay guys go?* "We'd be going to Brighton, I suppose." It stood to reason. Brighton Pride was huge, he recalled. It had to be a haven for gay men, right?

"Actually? I had someplace else in mind. We'll go to the Isle of Wight."

Tom frowned. "I'm not going all the way up there just for a weekend."

"'Up'—" Denny snorted. "That's the other one—the Isle of Man. The Isle of Wight is off the south coast." He cackled. "Geography wasn't your strongest subject in school, was it?"

Tom snorted. "Deb used to say I could get lost in a car park."

"What time do builders usually knock off work on a Friday? POETS and all that…"

"Three-ish, maybe four o'clock."

"Okay then. Tomorrow, finish as early as you can, go home, get changed, pack a bag, and meet me at Guildford station. It's easier that way. Why go up to Waterloo just to come down again? We can get the train to Portsmouth Harbour, and then the ferry. I'll find us a B&B. Somewhere with a sea view."

Tom had to smile. "Sounds as if you've been there before."

"Virtually every summer when I was a kid. Grandma lives over there in a retirement home—well, she does now, but she didn't then. I guess I've been thinking about her a lot lately. Haven't seen her for a while."

Warmth trickled through him. "And you want to visit her." That put Denny's suggestion in a whole new light.

"Yeah." He paused. "So say yes? Two nights in a B&B. You'd be back Sunday night on the last ferry. Please?"

How could he refuse such a heartfelt invitation?

"Fine. I'll text you when I'm on the train to Guildford."

"Great. Don't forget to pack your sunglasses. It's going to be a lovely weekend, and besides, the sun always shines over there." He chuckled. "Grandma used to say summer comes soonest in the south, and the Isle of Wight is about as far south as you can get."

They said goodbye and Tom hung up. He got off the couch and went into the kitchen in search of something for dinner, his mood vastly improved.

It was only as he opened a can of baked beans that the thought occurred to him. Denny had said he'd book them into a B&B.

He'd have booked one room, right?

CHAPTER TWENTY-TWO

As soon as they walked off the FastCat and strolled through the ferry terminal, Denny let the stress of study slip from him and allowed himself to relax. He remembered summer holidays as a child when he'd been in a frenzy of excitement leading up to the day of departure, but once his feet were back on solid ground, the familiar sights and sounds all around him, a calm always stole over him as he returned to his happy place.

Nothing changed, it seemed. The terminal certainly hadn't, although the catamaran was a newer model than the one he'd caught his last visit.

A visit that had been far too long ago.

"Where now?" Tom looked pretty relaxed too, his overnight bag slung over one shoulder, sunglasses tucked into the breast pocket of his denim jacket. When they'd met at Guildford, he'd seemed tired, and once they were on the way to Portsmouth, it had taken maybe a couple of minutes before he'd fallen asleep.

Denny had been fine with that. An hour or so's power nap meant Tom would be more alert by the time they reached the island.

What was really cute?

Tom had fallen asleep during the twenty-minute crossing too.

Denny pointed to the wide glass doors. "Through there. That's where we catch the train." He peered through the salt-encrusted windows, and grinned. "Hey, new trains."

Tom followed his glance and gaped. "New? That looks like an old Tube train."

Denny chuckled. "That's because it *is* an old Tube train.

And if you think *this* is old, you should've seen the ones they had running when I was little."

"How far does it go?" Tom gazed out at the long pier stretching toward Ryde.

"Not that far. There's only a small bit of track left between here and Shanklin. That's the end of the line. But there's a steam railway too. Again, not that long a track. All the carriages have been restored by volunteers." He smiled. "We used to go on it during the Steam Fair every August."

They walked along the platform and boarded the train, which chugged its rickety way along the track, heading towards the esplanade. Their carriage was filled with people: families with kids, couples of all ages, hikers, a couple of young men with bikes and backpacks, and a few commuters on their way home for the weekend.

Ryde lay before them, nestled between twin spires, rolling green hills in the distance, and pale golden sand as far as the eye could see off to the left. The four round Sea forts sat out in the Solent, accessible only by boat. Denny had expressed a desire to live in one as a child, and he'd learned not that long ago that one of them had been turned into a luxury hotel.

"Does the train always go this slow?" Tom inquired.

"Always. Any faster, and it would probably shake itself to bits."

"How old is this pier?" Tom murmured, a touch of anxiety in his voice.

"It doesn't feel very solid, does it?" Denny gave a wry chuckle. "I asked my dad that question once. He said it was a little older than Grandma. So when we got to her house, I asked her how old she was. When she found out why I was asking, she gave Dad such a slap. Then she told me it had been built in the early eighteen hundreds, and I suddenly got why she was so pissed off."

Tom leaned back against the seat. "It's a bumpy ride."

"It takes us along the coast, through Brading, Sandown,

Lake, until the line comes to a dead end at Shanklin." Denny smiled. "Names I haven't said for a while."

"Where is your grandma?"

"On the outskirts of Ventnor, in a place called St. Lawrence, toward the south of the island."

"Don't you think now would be a good idea to tell me where we're staying for the next two nights?"

Denny grinned. "Aw, I wanted it to be a surprise."

"Great. *Now* I'm worried."

He fought the urge to take Tom's hand in his and give it a squeeze. Denny had been buzzing with anticipation ever since Tom had agreed to come with him. The prospect of a weekend away with him, showing him places that had been so important to Denny growing up, had proved a huge distraction, and he'd gotten very little work done. He'd had to go through a lot of options before he found them a hotel with a vacancy, but then, it *was* summertime, when the island's population doubled in size.

The train trundled along, and Denny lost himself in the view. It was almost eight o'clock, and sunset would take place in maybe an hour's time. He imagined walking along the promenade, sitting on the sea wall, watching the last rays of the sun hitting the house high on the cliffs above them.

Sounds kinda romantic, don't you think? Watch your step there.

Sometimes his inner voice knew *exactly* what it was talking about.

The train pulled into Shanklin station, and everyone piled out. They walked through the tiny station to the car park, and Denny pointed to the left.

"Now we head that way."

They strolled down the hill, and Atherley Road gave way to Hope Road, a gradual incline that dipped toward the sea, lined with hotels and guest houses, some of which hadn't changed since he was a kid.

"Are we staying in one of these?"

"Nope." Denny smiled to himself, picturing Tom's face when he saw their destination. The road curved to the left, and suddenly a breeze off the Channel caught him full in the face, and his breathing hitched.

Tom peered over the wall that lined the twisty-turny road. "I don't want to worry you, but there are dinosaurs down there."

Denny stopped to take a look. "Oh wow." The last time he'd played mini golf on the sea front, it had comprised boring green felt courses with white-painted holes. Now, it was an intricate layout of sandstone-coloured paths, with model dinosaurs standing at various intervals. In the middle of the course, he spied a wall that resembled a long curved skeleton.

He grinned. "Now *that* is going on the list of things to do this weekend." He glanced at Tom. "Do you play?"

"I tried my hand at golf once—the proper kind."

Denny narrowed his gaze. "Hey, don't you trample on my memories. I used to be really good at mini golf."

Tom's eyes lit up. "Oh really? This might prove interesting."

Denny had a feeling he'd just set something in motion.

They followed the zigzag road down the steep hill to the promenade, where cars filled all the parking bays. Denny pointed farther along. "That's where we're going." Then he realised he was speaking to thin air.

He turned to find Tom standing by the sea wall, gazing out to sea.

"Look at that." A note of awe tinged his voice.

The sky was on fire, a canvas of golds, oranges and reds that reflected on the still surface of the water below. Cumulus clouds stretched far above their heads, a carpet of red.

"Wait until sunrise." The view would probably take Tom's breath away.

As they walked past the amusement arcade, a delicious aroma assaulted him. "Oh my God, I *love* that smell."

Tom inhaled deeply. "Fish and chips." He broke into a broad smile. "Fish and chips by the sea. Even better."

Denny chuckled. That was dinner sorted, at any rate.

After the arcade came the Shanklin Beach Hotel, and Tom gave him an expectant glance. "Here?"

"Nope." Denny was enjoying himself.

They passed the second of the promenade's two car parks, and Denny slowed. Tom glanced right and snorted. "As long as we're not staying *there*."

Denny came to a halt. "Hey, how did you guess? This is ours."

Tom stared at the wide frontage. "The Pink Beach Guest House?" His lips twitched. "I think you chose this on purpose."

Denny laughed. "It was the gayest place I could find." They mounted the steps to the front door hidden beneath a porch where patio chairs sat. There were more chairs on the front lawn, around tables covered by parasols.

They went inside, and Denny checked them in. When they reached the door of their room on the first floor, Tom stopped him with a hand to Denny's arm. "Are we sharing?"

Denny nodded. "It was the last room they had. But it does have a king-size bed." He cocked his head. "Is that okay?"

Tom smiled. "It's fine. It's not as if we haven't shared a bed before, right?"

They opened the door, and what greeted them was a view of the Channel reflecting the last rays of the setting sun.

Tom sat on the bed, giving an experimental bounce. "This is nice." Denny's stomach chose that moment to growl, and Tom chuckled. "Someone needs feeding." His own belly grumbled, and he flushed. "Two someones, by the sound of it."

Fifteen minutes later, they were sitting on a bench looking out to sea, each of them with a polystyrene box on their laps, filled with a generous portion of chips, which were covered with a large battered cod.

Denny glanced at Tom as he squeezed a sachet of mayonnaise into the lid. "Seriously? What's wrong with salt and vinegar?"

"I like mayo on my chips." He held out a sachet to Denny. "Want some?"

Denny shook his head. The fish was heavenly, hot and flaky, and the batter was just right. He gazed along the prom, where coloured summer lights decorated the lampposts.

Beautiful.

Tom took a moment from eating and heaved a sigh. "This was a good idea."

Denny smiled. "I have them occasionally." He had to agree though.

Tom leaned back. "Have you started looking for jobs yet?"

"Sure, I've looked. Haven't found anything yet." That wasn't true. He'd found a couple, but they hadn't filled him with enthusiasm. Denny breathed deeply. "I know there's no such thing as the perfect job. I mean, I'm looking at business management posts, and they're not exactly thrilling." He smiled. "Grandma told me something once about jobs. Let's see if I can remember it right." He frowned. "A job you like, but the pay is dreadful? That's a bad job. A job you don't like, but the pay is great? That's a bad job too. But a job you like, where the pay is great? Now *that's* a good job." He chuckled. "I expect she'll be happy to see me in any job."

"When are you going to visit her?"

"Tomorrow." He paused. "You don't have to come with me. I can deposit you in a café or something while I see her."

Tom bit his lip. "Would you mind if I came too? I'd like to meet her. She sounds like an amazing person."

"She is." Denny's stomach tightened. "Or she was. I haven't seen her in a long time, which is pretty crap when you consider she helped pay for my tuition at the start. We exchange cards, and she writes letters now and then."

He didn't know what he was going to find when he got there. Grandma had always had a mind like a meat cleaver, and he prayed the intervening years hadn't blunted its sharpness.

"So it's okay if I tag along?"

He smiled. "Sure. Just be prepared."

"For what?"

That was the problem. Denny didn't know.

He went with humour. "If I turn up there with a guy in tow, there's only one conclusion her mind will leap to, and you know what that is, right?"

Tom laughed. "Forewarned is forearmed." He peered at Denny's lap. "You finished?" When Denny nodded, he took the box from him and got up to walk over to the rubbish bin a few feet away. When he returned to the bench, he was yawning.

Denny laughed. "It's all that sea air. Fancy an early night?" Tom blinked, and Denny realised the implication. "I don't know about you, but I think I'll be asleep the second my head hits the pillow."

Tom opened his mouth to reply, but another yawn overtook him.

That was it. Bed was calling them.

They strolled back along the prom to the guest house, Denny's mind alert.

The most difficult part of the weekend loomed—sharing a bed with Tom, and keeping his hands off him. Tom hadn't signed up for that, and Denny wasn't about to make him feel uncomfortable.

Maybe a cool shower before bed would take the heat off, because God knew, the thought of lying next to Tom had Denny's temperature rising.

CHAPTER TWENTY-THREE

Tom opened his eyes and knew two things instantly.

It was a beautiful day, and his cock was like steel.

He snuck a glance at the other side of the bed. Denny was still asleep, his back uncovered, the duvet pushed down to below his waist, revealing the top of his crack and those cute little dimples above his arse cheeks.

Cute little dimples?

Denny is starting to rub off on me.

No sooner had the thought flitted through his mind, than Tom slid his hand beneath the white cotton boxers to curl his fingers around his solid dick. Rubbing off sounded like a great way to start the day, as long as he could accomplish it without waking Denny.

Then he reconsidered. Not a good idea, especially if Denny woke up. Shooting a video together was one thing—jerking off with a spectator was another.

He eased out of the bed and crept into the bathroom to relieve both his bladder and his morning wood. But by the time he'd brushed his teeth, his erection was back with a vengeance, and he knew he had to do something.

He returned to the bed to find Denny lying on his back, tugging on his cock. He glanced at Tom's crotch and smiled. "*Someone's* awake bright and early."

Why did I take my boxers off? There seemed little point hiding his turgid state. Tom moved his hand out of the way and his dick bobbed.

Denny's eyes twinkled. "How about we give each other a helping hand? Because I am *not* going down to breakfast like this."

It wouldn't hurt, right?

We've done it before, haven't we?

Tom recalled the feel of Denny's hand on him, and what little resistance he had left packed its bag and went.

He got back into bed, and Denny shifted closer. They reached for each other, and Tom sighed when Denny's fingers closed around his shaft. Tom's palm moulded around warm, stiff flesh, and he worked Denny's soft as silk length, his own hips in motion as he pushed his cock through the funnel of Denny's hand. Denny's breathing quickened, and Tom's was soon in sync with it.

"I want to try something," Denny murmured. "I think you'll like it."

And before Tom could get a word out, Denny let go of his dick and rolled on top of him. Instinctively, Tom wrapped his arms around Denny's nape and his legs around Denny's narrow waist, his heart racing.

Denny smiled. "That's better." He buried his head in Tom's neck, nuzzling him while he slid his hot, hard cock over Tom's.

Oh fuck, that feels good.

Better than that—it felt incredible.

Tom pushed out a sigh, and Denny stopped it with a kiss. Tom couldn't help but respond, scraping his fingers through the short layers of Denny's hair, deepening the kiss, feeding Denny a whimper when Denny circled his hips, grinding his dick against Tom's.

He couldn't keep still. He met Denny's thrusts, rocking up into him, clinging to his shoulders, his harsh breaths mingling with Denny's, each grind pushing him farther up the bed. Their foreheads touched and Denny's exhalations fanned Tom's face, both of them building up a sheen of perspiration in the warm room.

Then Denny's lips were on his neck once more as he ground faster, harder, and their thrusts grew so much slicker.

Denny shuddered through his orgasm, and the knowledge that he'd brought Denny to the edge pushed Tom over into his own climax. He dug his heels into Denny's arse, trying to stifle the cries of pleasure he felt sure would be heard by everyone in the guest house.

"Fuck, Tom," Denny whispered, his body damp with sweat in Tom's arms. He propped himself up on his elbows and leaned in to kiss him, a lingering, sweet kiss robbed of its previous intensity.

Tom didn't want to move, didn't want to disturb the blissful sensations flowing through him. He closed his eyes and breathed Denny in, his heartbeat shifting back into its normal rhythm.

Denny pushed Tom's hair off his face. "Now *that's* how to start the day with a bang." He grinned. "Last one in the shower buys lunch." Then he lurched off the bed, pelting across the floor to the bathroom.

"That's called taking advantage," Tom hollered after him.

Denny poked his head around the door. "Did I mention that I fight dirty?" He disappeared from view, and the sound of running water filled the air.

Tom grabbed a tissue from the box on the bedside table, and wiped up their cum. What lingered in his mind was not shooting his load—his *hands-free* load—but the sound of Denny's breathless utterance.

"Fuck, Tom."

There wasn't anything heavy about what they'd done. They were simply two men being practical. Two men dealing with a normal everyday occurrence.

Yeah right.

"You could always join me," Denny called out.

Tom was off the bed and heading to the bathroom before his inner voice had time to make him change his mind.

Tom couldn't remember the last time he'd been on a bus. He avoided them in general. Cramped conditions, too many people, having to stand…

The bus to Ventnor was a different experience.

They sat upstairs at the front, giving them the perfect view of the winding road snaking its way along the coast, the sea below, sunlight sparkling on the waves that rolled toward the shore. Hills rose on the right, covered in grass, trees, sheep, cows, and the occasional goat. Denny pointed out the village of Luccombe, and the tea rooms where his grandma used to take him.

Then the road dipped as they approached Ventnor, ending in another zigzag that led into the town. The bus came to a halt outside Boots, and they got off.

"Now we walk," Denny told him.

It was a wonderful morning for a leisurely stroll. Tom couldn't believe the number of palm trees he saw in front gardens, giving the place an almost Mediterranean feel. Denny took him along a narrow road where the land fell sharply on one side, and they stood and gazed at the Victorian-built houses clinging to the hillside.

Denny chuckled. "Only the Victorians would build on a landslip."

"Seriously?"

He nodded. "That's why now and then, the road collapses."

They passed a hotel, and Tom caught the sound of children's laughter and a lot of splashing behind its high wall. "It must have been great to come here as a child," he remarked.

"Some of the happiest days of my childhood were spent here." Then he pointed to a large gable-ended house on the opposite corner. "That's the retirement home."

It seemed a pleasant enough place, set back from the road, surrounded by trees. "Does she know you're coming?"

Denny nodded. "They told her last night when I called. The lady I spoke to said Grandma's talked a lot about me." His face tightened. "She also said Grandma's not been well."

"Nothing too serious, I hope." It was obvious Denny cared a great deal for her.

"She said not, but I'll know more when I see her." He gave a half smile. "Which will be any minute now."

"Then let's not waste any more time."

As they crossed the road, Tom sent up a prayer.

Don't take Denny's grandma just yet, okay? Give him more time with her.

He had a feeling losing her would devastate Denny.

"You're sure you're okay?"

Grandma gave him a mock glare. "When I find out who told you I'd been sick, I'll give them a good talking to. I am *fine*, okay? It was just a stomach bug. The older you get, the more often the plumbing breaks down." She stole a glance in Tom's direction. "He's a tall one. Good-looking though." Tom was strolling around the gardens, ostensibly checking out the plants and flowers.

Denny knew better. *He's giving me some space.*

"Grandma." Denny knew his warning tone would cut no ice with her.

She gave him an innocent look. "What? Am I not allowed to pay him a compliment?" Her eyes sparkled.

"He's a friend, all right?"

She let out a very unladylike snort. "Poppycock. I might be old, but I'm not daft."

He chuckled. "I don't know anyone who says that word like you do." When she gave him a puzzled glance, he smiled. "'Daft'. Makes you sound as if you're from up north."

"Silly boy. I *am* from up north. You can take the girl out of Manchester, but you can't take Manchester out of the girl."

"You don't miss it, do you?"

Grandma cackled. "Are you kidding? Why would I miss those grim streets when I have all this? No, moving here was the best thing I ever did. Besides, I couldn't have stayed, not once we lost your granddad. And it meant I was closer to your parents. Though why anyone would choose to work—*and* bring up children—in London is beyond me."

"Do they visit you much?"

"Probably about as often as you visit them, I should imagine," she said dryly. She speared him with a look. "Still no entente cordiale in sight?"

"Change the subject? Please?" All it did was create knots in his stomach.

She folded her hands in her lap. "Okay then. Are you almost ready to give up being a student?"

He laughed. "Almost." He glanced in Tom's direction.

"You know, you do a lot of that, considering he's just a friend."

Denny jerked his head toward her. "What?"

She frowned. "What did I tell you when you were little? A gentleman says *pardon*, not 'what'. And you heard every word, so don't come the innocent with me."

"He really is a friend," Denny insisted.

She stared at him. "Mm-hm."

"Grandma."

"Don't you 'Grandma' me. I don't doubt he's a friend, but I'm also fairly certain you'd like him to be more than that. Else, why bring him here to meet me?"

Denny shook his head. "I told him that's what you'd say."

She beamed. "But I'm right, aren't I?"

His chest tightened. "He *can't* be more than that."

"Why on earth not?" Grandma peered at Tom. "He's got two of everything he should have, right? And everything else… works, if you get my meaning."

Denny's mouth fell open.

"So what's the problem?"

If there was one person Denny couldn't lie to, it was Grandma.

"He… he's not into men." Except that didn't ring true, not after what they'd shared that morning.

That was just sex.

Grandma's eyebrows shot up. "He's into *you*, isn't he? He came here with you, didn't he?"

Denny sighed. "You say things like that, and you make it sound so simple." His pulse quickened. "But it isn't. I'm not going to explain, but… All you need to know is, I've been down this road before, and I… I can't do it again."

Even if everything in him told him his feet were already on that same path, leading him towards potential heartache.

Again.

A spasm contorted her face. "Did someone hurt you, sweetheart?"

Denny took her hand in his, aware of how cool her fingers were. "That's in the past, all right? All you need to know is, I'm happy." Another glance at Tom.

I could be even happier, but…

A cough snapped him back into the present.

Grandma twisted in her chair to peer at the patio doors

behind them. "Damn it. Boadicea wants me to go in for lunch."

Denny burst out laughing. "She's not that bad, is she?"

"You'd be surprised." Grandma's tone was grim. Then she smiled. "No, she's not that bad. But why don't you take that nice man of yours for lunch?"

It was useless to reiterate that Tom *wasn't* Denny's nice man. "We only got here two hours ago," he protested.

She nodded. "Thank you for those precious hours. But now you've got what's left of the weekend to show Tom some more of the island." She kissed his cheek. "You can visit me again when your studies are over." Her eyes lit up. "And you'd better invite me to whatever shindig they put on when you get your piece of paper." Her expression softened. "I missed your first graduation ceremony. I don't want to miss this one."

He returned her kiss. "I'll make sure you get an invitation."

At least someone from his family cared enough to be there.

He beckoned Tom to join them, and Grandma watched his approach. "If I were forty years younger, I might be tempted to steal him off you." Denny gaped at her, and she laughed. "Maybe not. I prefer blonds."

He was still laughing as they walked out onto the road.

Denny seemed brighter, and there was a spring in his step that had been missing before. They walked past the park, away from the town, and Tom was curious as to where they were headed, but he didn't want to intrude on Denny's thoughts.

"I'm glad you came," Denny said after a while.

"I like your grandma. You painted a very accurate picture of her, I have to say. All those not-so-subtle hints…"

Denny chuckled. "Yeah, I'm sorry about that. She did kinda lay it on thick with a trowel, didn't she?" He grinned. "See what I did there?"

Tom groaned. "Don't I suffer enough from Andy's bad builders' jokes? Now, how about you tell me where we're going?"

"I'm taking you somewhere nice for lunch."

"Oh. Someplace you've been before?"

"Many times. I used to go there every summer. There's a great beach with really soft fine sand, rocks to climb over, good food…"

Tom couldn't wait. Saturday was shaping up to be a wonderful day.

They came to a stop at the next corner, and Tom heard the dull thud of a ball striking a bat, followed by a smattering of applause. He followed the sounds, and saw a cricket pitch, a match in play. Then he saw the name of the narrow road.

"Love Lane?"

Denny chuckled. "I used to make sick noises every time I saw that as a kid." They turned left, walking beneath tall pines, their branches providing dappled shade. As they neared the end of the lane, Tom caught another sound.

"Is that the wind?"

Denny's smile was almost serene. "No, that's the sound of the sea." They reached three steps down, and then the path went in opposite directions.

Tom didn't move. He gazed down at a horseshoe-shaped cove, from which came children's squeals and loud cries. He could see people swimming, people out in kayaks or on body boards, boats sailing past, their spinnakers unfurled…

"Welcome to Steephill Cove."

Tom followed Denny down a very steep path, amused to see small green lizards darting in front of them. Then the path took a sharp left turn, and there was the sea ahead of them, with its sparkling waves and white foam that crashed on the shore.

Families queued for ice creams, and a couple headed up the hill toward them, a golden retriever tugging at its leash, the fur on its legs and underbelly damp and matted.

Denny stopped at the top of a short flight of concrete steps that led down to the beach. "Where's all the sand?"

Tom scanned their surroundings. In front of them was a small sandy stretch, separated from the main beach by a wall of huge boulders. "Okay, I might not have been to the seaside for many years, but that looks like sand to me."

Denny pointed to the left. "That used to be covered in sand." All Tom could see was orange-coloured shingle, strewn with seaweed. "I made sandcastles over there." He sighed, then turned to face the white painted wall to their right. He walked up to the low grey gate set into it and peered over it. "We might have to wait for a table."

A tall, slim young woman appeared, a clipboard in one hand. "For two of you?" When Denny nodded, she consulted the board, then opened the gate. "Go through to the end. You're on table eleven."

They walked through a covered passage, tables against the wall, before they emerged once more into bright sunshine. Denny pointed to a table in front of a high white wall that was decorated with a huge fishing net and colourful buoys. The tables were square, with metal-framed chairs tucked under them. Along the wall ran a wooden bench.

Denny sat on it and patted the space beside him. "We can both fit on here. That way, we're looking out to sea."

Tom joined him, and a young man appeared with a grey laminated menu card he laid on their table before walking off.

Denny perused it. "Do you like crab?"

Tom had to admit he'd never tried it.

Denny's eyes widened. "You're not allergic to shellfish, are you?"

"Not as far as I know."

"Then that's what we'll have. They've got crab soup, crab sandwiches, crab salad…"

The young woman carried two plates over to a table, and one glance was all it took to bring him to a decision. "Crab salad." Then she came over to them, and Denny ordered the food.

He glanced at Tom. "How about a glass of wine?"

Tom coughed. "Not sure about that. Strange things happen when I drink around you, and suddenly there are love bites everywhere."

The waitress blushed, and Denny grinned. "Two glasses of white wine, please."

Tom's face was on fire as she walked away from their table. "I can't believe I said that." He shook his head. "You're obviously a bad influence."

Denny leaned back against the wall, and Tom did likewise, its warmth radiating through his shirt. Right then he felt all was right with the world. The sun was shining, they were about to eat lunch, and he had the best company.

Not to mention he was sitting so close to said company that their thighs touched.

Tom wasn't about to move.

Denny's admission came to mind. "So what was so bad about love that it made you want to throw up?"

Denny laughed. "What little kid wants to think about love? Love back then meant soppy kisses, making Bambi eyes at someone. Thankfully, it's a phase we all grow out of."

"I don't think I ever grew into it," Tom murmured.

He regretted the words as soon as they slipped from his lips.

Denny turned his head slowly. "You were in love with Deb, weren't you?"

Now *that* was a good question.

"Was I? You know, I'm not so sure. At least, it wasn't the kind of earth-shattering, all-consuming love you see in films or read about in books." He frowned. "Don't get me wrong, I love Deb. But the way I love her now is pretty much how I loved her then." The confession saddened him, and that emotion had no place in his heart on such a gorgeous day.

He glanced at Denny. "What about you?"

"What *about* me?"

"Have you ever been in love?"

CHAPTER TWENTY-FOUR

Fuck.

Denny's heart hammered. His stomach hardened. His throat was so tight it hurt.

Tom sat still beside him, his eyes wide. "Did I just ask the wrong thing?"

Breathe. Breathe.

He straightened, not looking at Tom but gazing out to sea, listening to the waves crashing below them. "I *was* in love, once."

"Was it that boyfriend you told me about? The one you shot porn with?"

Despite the whirlpool of emotion that threatened to suck him down into its turbulent vortex at any minute, Denny laughed. "Jon? Oh God, no. That was lust, pure and simple." He paused. "His name was Adam, and once upon a time, he was the best thing that ever happened to me."

Tom's face contorted. "He... he didn't die, did he?"

Denny stared at him. "What? No. Nothing like that. We... It wasn't meant to be, okay?" He saw the waitress approaching and shivered. "I don't want to talk about it, all right?"

"Okay, okay." Tom's voice was soothing. "I'm sorry I asked."

"Hey, it's no big deal." The words came out calmer than he'd expected, and he was so fucking proud.

Except he'd lied to Tom. It *had* been a big deal. And if Denny wasn't careful, history would repeat itself.

Their crab salads arrived, and Tom shifted to give him a little more room. Denny ate slowly, savouring each mouthful as he pushed the conversation further and further back into his mind.

The chilled wine had a crisp edge to it, and it went perfectly with the meal. When he'd cleared his plate of every trace of salad, Denny leaned back once more. A man in a cowboy hat bustled around the tables, clearing plates, and chatting with the customers. Judging by the way he spoke to the staff, Denny figured he was the owner. When he came over to their table, Denny held up his hand.

"Can I ask you something?"

The man grinned. "You can ask."

"What happened to the sand? That used to be a great sandy beach when I was a kid."

The man shook his head. "It's been this way since Valentine's Day, 2014. We had an awful storm. I'd just finished getting this place ready to open for the season, and in one day, it was wrecked." He pointed to the cove. "There was debris past my knees all the way along there. And the sea took back the sand. It's returned a few times in recent years, but…" He shrugged. "This wasn't the only place that got damaged. Farther long the Undercliff, a road collapsed, and they've never been able to rebuild it. They had to bring in the Army to evacuate the homeowners."

"That sounds awful." Worse than that, it served as a reminder of just how long it had been since he'd visited the cove.

Another shrug. "Now it's a bridleway, and what was once a long winding road has become two cul-de-sacs. They keep making noises about building the road again, but then in the next breath they say that could cost two million, so I guess it's going to stay as it is." He glanced at their plates and grinned again. "You hated that. I can tell."

Denny couldn't help but return his grin. "Yeah, I had to force it down."

"Thanks. I made it."

He beamed. "Really?"

The man chuckled. "Stop, you'll have me blushing." He piled their plates and walked away, leaving their unfinished wine.

"What's next on the agenda?" Tom asked.

Denny had been thinking about that.

"How about a game of mini golf?"

Tom stared at the huge expanse of sky above the horizon, tinged with pink.

"A beautiful end to a great day," he murmured. They'd eaten at a nearby pub, seated on a deck. Tiny white lights covered the veranda, twisting around the wooden railings. A band played music, but thankfully, it wasn't as loud as the group at the Barley Mow. Pretty good though. The food had been delicious, but the view stole the show.

"So you're still talking to me?" Denny teased.

Tom gave him a mock glare. "You beat me, okay? But there was only one point in it. And if you hadn't coughed right when I was aiming for that last shot…"

"Oh, it's *my* fault you lost?" Denny's eyes sparkled. "Nothing to do with my superior golfing skills." He buffed his nails on his tee.

"Superior—" Tom gaped. "Whose ball went so high, it landed in the pterodactyl's nest? Hmm?" He stroked his beard. "Let me think. Oh yeah, it was you. And whose ball bounced so hard off one of the rock walls, it hit me on the leg?" He widened his eyes. "Hey, that was *you* again, wasn't it?"

"Are you always this sore a loser?" Denny demanded.

Tom grinned. "Wait till you see me play darts." He leaned back in his chair. "What do you have planned for tomorrow? And what time is the ferry?" Not that he was in a hurry to bring their weekend to an end, far from it. He needed to know how much time they had left to play with.

Denny got his phone out. "How early do you want to be back home?"

Tom snorted. "I'd be happy leaving on the last ferry, but I don't think that's feasible."

Denny scrolled and Tom waited. At last, he looked up. "Okay. The ferries run once an hour. There's one at quarter to six. That would get us to Portsmouth Harbour by just after six. Then there's a train at six-thirty, and that takes an hour. The next train for Ewell and Wimbledon leaves at eight-twenty." He put his phone down. "You'd be home before nine-fifteen. Although I could look at later trains, if you like."

Tom shook his head. "I think that sounds about right."

"And as for what I've got planned..." Denny's eyes glittered. "Want to go see some tigers?"

He blinked. "You're kidding."

"Nope. There's a wildlife sanctuary near Sandown. Used to be the zoo, but it's changed its act since I was last there, apparently." He smiled. "Grandma told me once she'd seen photos of the zoo owner walking two tigers on Yaverland Beach on leashes, years ago."

Tom gaped. "Oh my God. Imagine being a visitor to the island and coming across them."

Denny grinned. "Maybe it was a cheap way of feeding them. *You* know, the owner points to some little kid on the beach and says 'There you go, guys. Lunch.'" He burst into laughter when Tom's mouth fell open. "That was a joke, honest."

Tom kept a straight face. "I keep picturing a tiger with a chihuahua between its jaws."

Denny stared at him. "What have you got against chihuahuas? What did they ever do to you?"

"That's a serious question? Those yappy little things that bite at your ankles, and—"

The even harder stare Denny gave him was just short of murderous.

Tom sighed. "I'm pulling your leg, okay? I love all dogs." When Denny appeared mollified, he added, "Besides, I'd bet their little bones would get stuck in the tiger's teeth."

The look of horror on Denny's face cracked him up.

Tom was blissfully content. The combination of good food and a glass or two of wine relaxed him completely. The conversation was the icing on the cake.

And if that was so, Denny was the cherry on top.

Denny's hand was on the table, and Tom couldn't help himself. He reached across and took it, lacing their fingers.

Denny jerked his head to stare at their joined hands but didn't pull away. They sat like that until the sun dropped below the horizon, and both of them were yawning.

"I think another early night is called for," Tom announced. "Especially if we want to cram a lot into tomorrow."

"Are you going to set an alarm?" Denny smiled. "Or shall *I* wake you up?"

Fuck. Tom's dick reacted. "And there you go again, expecting me to make a decision." It was a lame response, but better than the alternative. Tom was finding it more and more difficult to keep a lid on his emotions, and he wasn't sure he could keep it up for much longer. At least he'd be busy for the next couple of weeks. No opportunity to see Denny.

This time there was no mistaking his reaction to that prospect.

The thought filled him with dismay.

Then Denny pulled free of his hand, severing their connection.

Tom knew what he wanted—another night with Denny in his arms, like the one they'd shared in Wimbledon—but shied away from voicing his desire. Waking up holding Denny when they'd clearly gravitated to each other in the depths of sleep was one thing.

Pulling Denny to him was something else.

The café at Sandown Pier was the perfect spot to grab a burger for lunch, followed by ice cream once they'd played on the amusements. Tom tried his hand at the grabber machine, cursing every time the steel claws let go of his prize. Denny didn't help, shouting out instructions while he pushed the button to move the claws into position, and Tom lost count of how many pound coins he'd fed into that hungry slot.

He reached into his pocket and found one more coin. He held it up. "This is the last one, okay?"

Denny rolled his eyes. "You said that five pounds ago."

"But it really is. The only option left would be changing a fiver, and I am *not* doing that. So that means I have five chances left. If I can't win one with them, I'll walk away."

Denny grinned. "I'll believe it when I see it."

That did it. Tom was *not* leaving there empty-handed.

He scanned the other machines, and one caught his eye. "Perfect." He walked over to it and selected his victim. He popped the coin in the slot and pushed the button.

"Why don't—"

Tom held his hand up for silence. His first attempt wasn't even close, and his second and third weren't much better.

"They make them this way," Denny told him. "It's really difficult for the claws to hold onto them."

He held his hand up once more, and studied the soft toys scattered around. There weren't many, but that was to be expected, given their size. He pushed the button, and the claws swung their way toward the rear of the track. He nudged them to the right and held his breath as they descended. The claws hit the toy and spread wide, then hooked themselves around it.

Tom didn't dare breathe as they carried the large toy toward the chute. He'd been at this point several times, only for the toy to fall at the last—

The toy fell down the chute.

Tom's heartbeat raced, and he couldn't contain his grin as he reached into the bottom of the chute and removed the toy tiger.

"Oh my God, you did it. And with one go left." Denny's face was flushed, his eyes bright. "And what an amazing prize." His jaw dropped when Tom placed it in his arms.

"It's for you. It was always going to be for you. I'm just sorry it took me so many tries to succeed." Warmth flooded him at the sight of Denny's parted lips and sparkling eyes. "Do you like it?"

"Like it? I fucking *love* it." Denny snuggled it. "And I know exactly what I'm going to call it." He beamed. "Tom."

Denny's glowing face and obvious joy put a shine on Tom's day that lingered for hours.

They sat in the café at the end of Ryde pier, two paper cups of coffee in front of them. The ferry was due in soon. Denny's tiger lay on the table, its front paws stretched out, and now and then Denny stroked it.

"I suppose I'd better find it some chihuahuas for dinner," he joked.

Tom chuckled. "I think all *I'll* need for dinner tonight is some toast. I haven't eaten this much since I was a teenager." He sighed heavily. "Oh well. Back to reality tomorrow." He didn't want to think about that. The day wasn't over yet.

"At least you have work," Denny reminded him.

"Yeah—working for someone else."

Denny cocked his head to one side. "How do you advertise? If you don't mind me asking."

Tom gave him a sheepish glance. "I don't." When Denny gave him an incredulous look, he shrugged. "I sort of rely on word of mouth. I did try my hand at making fliers once."

Denny gave him a confident smile. "Oh, I think we can do better than that."

"'We'?"

He counted off on his fingers. "Trade magazines, for one. Local billboards for another. Think about all those people who have second homes on the island, but who live on the mainland. You could buy advertising space on the FastCat. Remember all those ads we saw on the screen on the way over here? The digital displays out there in the terminal? How many people would get to see you if you did that?" He smiled. "If you want help with tech, I'm your man." Denny met his gaze, his shoulders back, chin high. "We're going to get your name out there."

In that moment Tom believed him wholeheartedly.

The train was almost into Ewell West, and the weekend was slipping through Tom's fingers. Beyond the dirty windows, the sky was already darkening. Denny sat beside him, quieter than he'd been all day, but then again, they'd got up early and crammed a lot in. The morning blow job or whatever else Denny had planned hadn't materialised, and what surprised Tom were the opposing emotions at war within him.

I don't know what I want anymore.

Except that was a lie. He wanted more.

More Denny.

More weekends like the one they'd just shared.

More mornings where he woke up to find his arms full of a warm, sexy man.

More evenings where they cooked for each other.

Spent time together.

Denny's soft murmur broke into his musings. "Thanks for coming along."

"Thanks for inviting me. I'm glad you got to see your grandma."

Denny's face brightened. "Me too."

The train began to slow down, and Tom's chest tightened. "This is my stop." He got to his feet, and Denny gazed up at him.

The one thought in Tom's mind was to bend down and kiss him goodbye, and it made his heart thump.

Instead, he smiled. "I'll be in touch."

"Will you?"

He nodded. "I'm meeting your landlord in a couple of weeks. I think he wants me to renovate your kitchen. So you'll see a lot of me."

"Good." Denny didn't break eye contact.

Tom glanced at the tiger across Denny's lap. "Don't go feeding him too many chihuahuas. He'll burst his seams."

Denny laughed. "He's going to live on my bed, and every night I'll cuddle him."

Tom couldn't stop the thought that flitted through his mind.

Lucky tiger.

Denny's gaze was still locked on Tom as the train shuddered to a halt.

"Well, bye for now." Tom hurried to the doors, pressed the illuminated button, and they slid open. He stepped down onto the platform and walked briskly toward the exit. As the train moved off, he resisted the urge to look back.

The weekend felt like a wonderful dream, only now he had to deal with real life. And that meant not falling for Denny.

Fuck, this was getting way too complicated.

CHAPTER TWENTY-FIVE

July

Denny came downstairs and paused at the door to the living room. Meena, Robin, and Chris were watching TV, and whatever was on sounded way too loud and violent for Denny's tastes. He went into the kitchen to make himself a mug of tea.

One week since their trip, and not a word from Tom.

I've got it bad, haven't I?

Logic told him Tom was busy.

He said he'd be in touch.

As Grandma used to say, fine words buttered no parsnips. Not that Denny was entirely sure what that meant, but it sounded good.

The front door opened, and a moment later, Lisa walked into the room. "Ooh, make us a cuppa, will you? I'm parched." She sat at the table and kicked off her shoes.

Denny grabbed another cup and a tea bag. "How was your day?"

"Long," she said with a groan. "How about yours?"

He smiled. "Guess who just finished his dissertation?"

Lisa's eyes lit up. "Oh brilliant."

"Well, I *say* finished. I have to meet with my tutor before I go through it one last time. Then I type it all up, hand it in, and..." He let out a sigh. "Can't believe I'm finally here."

"Are you happy with it?"

He nodded. He handed her the cup of tea, then joined her at the table.

Lisa said nothing for a moment. "Then what *aren't* you happy about?"

Denny frowned. "I don't know what you mean."

"I'd hazard a guess it has something to do with your love life." She leaned forward, her forearms on the table, hands around her mug. "What about this guy Chris was telling me about? The one who stayed the night while we were away that weekend last month?"

"What about him?"

"Well, he hasn't been around. Unless you're keeping him in your room and locking him in when you go out…" Warm brown eyes met his. "Did you break up or something?"

Denny huffed. "Nothing *to* break up."

"Oh, I see. Like that, is it?" Her tone was sympathetic.

He chuckled. "Trust me, it's *way* more complicated than whatever you're imagining."

"When isn't it?" Lisa sipped her tea. "Ken called last night, by the way. He said someone's coming in next week to work on the kitchen, and that we won't recognise it when it's done. I think it's the same guy who rebuilt the front wall." She widened her eyes. "That's it!"

"That's what?"

"We need to fix you up with the hunky builder. *He'd* put a smile on your face."

Denny took one look at her triumphant grin and burst out laughing.

"I didn't think it was *that* funny," she retorted.

He chuckled. "That 'hunky builder'?" He hooked his fingers in the air. "He's the guy who stayed over, the one Chris told you about."

Her mouth fell open. "Then what's—"

"And while I love the idea, there's one tiny little problem." Another shrug. "He's straight." *A straight guy who's okay with fucking another guy.* There were a few of those about. Denny had filmed with more than his fair share of them.

She frowned. "But then what was he doing—"

"I said it was complicated, didn't I?"

"So there's no hope he might… I don't know…"

"Deviate from his present course?" Denny suggested. "I don't know. Maybe? The point is, I'm not about to find out."

He had enough mental scars. He didn't want more.

"Are you positive he's not interested?"

Denny wasn't about to tell her the truth. He didn't want to run after Tom—he wanted to run away from his own feelings. He wanted to take his attraction to Tom and choke the life out of it, because it couldn't lead to any place Denny wanted to go.

But I miss him.

Lisa stood, picking up her mug. "I'm going to grab a shower and then change." She walked past him and ruffled his hair. "I'm sorry you feel it won't work out." Then she left him to his own thoughts.

Leaving it up to Tom hadn't worked, so Denny needed to think of another way to stay in touch. The problem was, he'd run out of ideas.

Did he even look *at the footage I sent him?* He hadn't mentioned it once, and Denny knew better than to push.

Speaking of which, Denny needed to log in to his account and see how he was doing. Messages awaited him, and he opened them, smiling at comments from his subscribers.

Then one caught his eye, from one of his subscribers, Naseem. Denny had to re-read it twice, just to make sure he'd got it right.

Okay, Tom needs to know about this.

He went into Contacts and scrolled to Tom's number. After four rings, he resigned himself to leaving a voicemail, but then Tom answered. "Hi."

"I'm not disturbing you, am I?"

"No, I'm just chilling on the couch. I'll be going to bed soon though."

Denny took the hint. "Then I'll be quick. Can you come

to my place tomorrow after you finish work?"

The silence that followed didn't fill him with hope.

At last Tom spoke. "What's this about? Because I'll be at your place in a week's time. Couldn't it wait until then?"

Denny was not going to broach this particular subject when any of his housemates were around. He knew from the calendar on the kitchen noticeboard that none of them would be home until past seven. "Not really. This... this is important. I suppose you could say it's about a job."

Well, it is, isn't it?

Sort of.

Another pause. "Okay. I can be there by four-thirty. Will that do?"

"Perfect. I'll have coffee waiting. And if you're *really* lucky, there could be one of Lisa's ginger biscuits left. That's if this lot haven't scoffed the lot."

"I'll see you tomorrow then."

Conversation over, it seemed.

Denny said goodbye and hung up. No sooner had he done so, than a light quiver started in his stomach.

This is wrong.

I shouldn't be doing this.

Naseem's message had provided a handy excuse to tug Tom back into his life. *And what if Tom agrees? Is this what I* really *want? Yet another encounter captured on video?*

Denny stared into his mug.

I'll take all I can get.

Tom switched off the engine and stared at the house. The driveway was empty, so he guessed the nurse wasn't home.

Maybe it's just Denny.

He wasn't sure how he felt about that. *Get the two of us alone, clothes magically disappear, and suddenly there's lube, and heat, and sweat...*

He couldn't think about *that*, not unless he was comfortable walking into the house with a hard-on.

The front door opened, and Denny stood there in sweats and a tank top, his feet bare as usual.

Does he always have to look so fucking hot?

It was time to see what this was all about.

He got out of the van and strolled up the path, making an effort to appear relaxed.

He was anything but.

Denny inclined his head toward the kitchen. "Coffee's on."

Tom glanced at his boots and dusty overalls. "We'd better keep this conversation out of the house."

"Then go through the garage. It's not locked. I'll meet you in the garden." He closed the front door.

Tom pulled up the rolling garage door and walked to the rear, his heart still pounding. By the time he stepped onto the patio, Denny was there, two steaming mugs on the table.

"It should be something cold on a day like this," Denny remarked.

Tom sat facing him. "So... what was so urgent?"

Denny arched his eyebrows. "Are you in a hurry or something? No 'How are you?' I mean, it's been a week."

Shit.

Denny hadn't meant to sound so petulant, but damn it, he'd *missed* him.

Tom's cheeks looked as if they were on fire. He crumpled a little into his chair, avoiding Denny's gaze. "I'm sorry. You're right. That was rude. I must be more tired than I thought."

"Long day?"

He huffed. "Long, hard, struggly kind of day."

Denny smiled. "'Struggly'?"

"Hey, it fits, all right?"

"Someone needs to add it to the Oxford English Dictionary. Good word." It was obvious Tom needed to go home and decompress. "Okay, the reason why I called you is…One of my OnlyFans subscribers messaged me. He *loved* that scene we did."

"The Hard Hats one?" Tom snorted. "I don't even know if that's out yet. I haven't gone looking for it, that's for sure."

"No—the OnlyFans one. He thought it was hot." Denny chuckled. "Actually, his exact words were, 'Holy shit, that was hot as fuck.' And the reason why he was messaging me? He wants us to shoot a scene just for him, not for the site. And he'll pay us… five thousand pounds."

Tom gaped. "For one video?"

"Uh-huh."

Tom narrowed his gaze. "What's the catch?"

"No catch. He's my biggest subscriber. What's more, he's good for it. And seeing as he wants to pay that kind of money, he was pretty specific about what he wants to see."

"Ah, *now* we have it. He wants something kinky, doesn't he? Does it involve animals?"

Denny stared at him. "Please, tell me you're kidding."

Tom rolled his eyes. "Do you have to ask? Tell me what this guy wants."

"He's after a private scene… with me fucking you."

Tom stilled. "Wait—what was that last part?"

"You heard me." Denny regarded him with arched eyebrows. "It's not as if you haven't taken a dick before."

Tom flushed. "Yeah, but that part didn't last more than five minutes. I imagine for five grand, he'll want a lot more than five minutes."

"And you'd be right. He'd want about fifty minutes to an hour."

Tom didn't appear to be falling over himself with enthusiasm to sign up for the scene, but then again, he'd needed a lot of reassurance to do the previous three.

What was one more scene?

Denny studied him. "So what do you think? We can try, can't we? If we're not happy with the result, then we'll turn him down. But still... two and a half grand each for a few hours' work? What do you say?"

Tom said nothing, and the hairs on the back of Denny's neck lifted. His scalp prickled. And the longer the silence continued, the more certain he became that he knew what the answer was going to be.

"You don't want to do it, do you?"

Tom shook his head. "No, I don't."

"Want to tell me why? I mean, you've already got three scenes under your belt. What's one more?"

Tom said nothing.

Then Denny saw the light. "Is it because you'd be the one getting fucked?"

Another shake of his head. "No, that's not it at all. Please, don't ask me to explain why I don't want to do this. Isn't the fact that I've said no enough of an answer?"

"You don't need the money? You're suddenly financially stable, is that it?"

"No, but..." Tom looked him in the eye. "I've done three scenes. I want to call it a day."

That was clearly all the explanation Denny was going to get.

At last, he gave a nod. "Fair enough."

Tom was still staring at him. "Would this guy still pay you that much for a scene if you did it with someone else?"

Denny shook his head. "You were part of the package."

He swallowed. "That means you're out of two-and-a-half thousand quid because of me."

Denny shrugged. "Don't worry about it. Ari's been texting me about doing some more scenes for him. I've got the time to do them, right?" When Tom frowned, he realised he'd left out an important piece of news. "Now that I've finished the dissertation," he added with a touch of pride.

Tom's eyes lit up. "Really? Congratulations." He beamed. "That's such good news."

His genuine elation went a long way to easing the constriction around Denny's chest.

Then Tom's face tightened. "Me not doing this scene isn't going to make things awkward next week when I'm working here, is it?"

There was no way Denny wanted Tom to feel uncomfortable around him.

"Not at all." Before he knew it, his mouth ran away with him, as usual. "Do you think once the kitchen is finished, we could... stay friends?"

Fuck, how needy do I sound?

Tom took a sip of coffee before answering. "Yeah, I think so." Denny breathed a little easier. "Not that we'll have that much time. I mean, you'll have some fancy high-flying job any day now, and I'll be up to my eyeballs in work, because I took all your advice from last week and acted on it."

Aw shit.

Denny wasn't stupid. He knew exactly what Tom's words had just done—paved the way for eventual disappointment.

At least he knew how the land lay.

Maybe this is for the best.

Fighting to keep Tom in his life was only going to end up torturing him.

Time to move on.

Denny leaned back and tilted his face toward the sun. "It's going to be a lovely evening."

It didn't feel lovely.

His heart was like a lump of lead in his chest.

He can't be what you want him to be because he doesn't want that. Isn't it obvious by now?

Unfortunately, it was.

Chapter Twenty-Six

Tom set his toolbox down on the kitchen floor and surveyed the room, making a mental note of what needed to be done first. The new cabinet doors and worktops were standing in the garage, together with the new carcasses, ready to be brought in through the back door. The tiles had to come off first, and Tom could see why. White was a much better way to go, rather than the old-fashioned tiles decorated with pots and pans, fruit, and vegetables.

"I think I saw these in my grandparents' house," he muttered.

"Delightful, aren't they?"

Tom jerked his head toward the door. Chris leaned against the frame.

"Hello again." He pointed to the strip of wall above the worktop. "We were going to ask you if you could manage to remove one in one piece. We were going to frame it and hang it on the wall, as a reminder."

Tom choked back his guffaw. "Seriously? Then I'll have to do everything in my power to make your weird dream come true."

Chris laughed. "Aw, thanks." He cocked his head. "So do you want us to stay out of your way? We've moved the microwave to the dining room, and we've got a spare kettle." He gestured to the one standing beside the hob. "We left that one for you. Denny says you drink a lot of tea and coffee, and we wanted you to feel at home."

Lisa pushed past him and came into the kitchen. "Chris, you're making the place look untidy. And don't annoy Tom on his first day." She went over to a cabinet, opened it, and removed a plastic box. "Denny asked me to make these for you." She handed it to him.

Tom popped the lid, and the delicious aroma of ginger met his nostrils. "Your biscuits. You shouldn't have."

"Are you kidding? You're about to make a silk purse from a sow's ear, and we're going to make sure you're happy while you do it."

"Hey, can I have one?" Chris batted his eyelashes and pouted.

Lisa smiled sweetly at him. "Of *course* you can't." She chuckled when he let out a strangled gasp.

"Are these two bugging you?"

Warmth coursed through him at the sound of Denny's voice. "No, they're fine. I haven't started yet." Denny wore his habitual sweats and tank top, and disconcertingly, Tom's attention was drawn to his nipples poking at the cotton. He averted his gaze.

"Hey, do you need a builder's mate?" Chris grinned. "I'm sure Denny would volunteer. After all, he's a man of leisure now."

Lisa glared at him. "Chris…"

He ignored her. "Yeah, I bet he could dress the part too… *You* know, with a pair of saggy jeans that show off his butt crack?"

Denny's eyes gleamed. "Chris, if you want to see my butt crack, you only have to ask."

Lisa burst out laughing.

Tom would never get started at this rate.

He cleared his throat. "Okay, here's how it's going to be. If you need something from the fridge, or water, that's fine, you get to come in here. Yes, moving operations to the dining room is a smart idea. Thank you for the use of the kettle, and the biscuits. And yes, I'd like you to stay out of my way while I'm working. I do *not* need distractions while I'm using a tile cutter, thank you very much." He fired a glance at Denny. "I'll be out of your hair by four o'clock each day, and it should take me a week to lick this kitchen into shape." He stared at the three of them.

"Any questions?"

Denny chuckled. "And you called *me* bossy."

"You heard the man. Scram." Lisa herded them out of the kitchen.

Tom unfolded his dust sheets to spread them over surfaces while he removed the tiles. There was no sense making too much mess.

"Hey."

He turned. Denny poked his head around the door. "You need something?" Tom was determined to keep things on a professional level, especially while the others were around.

"Yeah. Wanna have lunch with me in the garden?" Denny smiled. "Just us, I'm afraid."

He could do lunch. "Sure."

"By the way, I'll be having Meena's leftover macaroni cheese, and there's plenty if you want some too."

Tom pursed his lips. "Do I want some?"

Denny grinned. "I would. It's really good." Then he disappeared from view, and Tom caught the familiar *thud thud thud* of his bare feet on the stairs.

He gave himself a mental shake. *Get to work.*

Enough distractions.

Denny wiped cum from his stomach as Simon stood, grinning like a Cheshire cat. "Wow. That was… different."

Ari chuckled, coming out from behind the camera. "A good different, from what I could see. You gave Luke here quite a pounding."

Simon was still grinning.

Denny grabbed his clothes and headed for the shower, leaving Ari to talk. It was obvious the guy had a future in porn. He fucked like a machine, and judging by his performance, stamina wasn't an issue. Denny wasn't sure he believed the 'I'm a total anal virgin' line Simon had fed them—after shooting so many scenes, he trusted his instincts—but he knew the video would gain a lot of interest when it released.

He flipped on the jets and stood under the hot water, letting it sluice away the remnants of both their loads. He bowed his head, and the water pummelled his nape and shoulders. Denny closed his eyes, and what came to mind was Tom in the shower that Sunday morning at the Pink Beach Guest House. How Denny hadn't succumbed to giving him a blow job, he would never know. He'd tried to keep his hands off Tom's delectable body, but in the end the struggle proved too great to overcome. He'd poured body wash into his cupped palm, then proceeded to work up a lather on Tom's chest and stomach, sliding his hands over firm pecs and abs, while Tom stood there, eyes closed, his cock hard and inviting—

"Am I interrupting something?"

Ari's voice broke through his recollection. Denny jerked his head to stare at him—and realized his hand was wrapped around his dick. He let go hastily. "You nearly gave me a heart attack. I thought you were talking to Simon."

"I was, until he got dressed, said he wasn't bothered about having a shower, and walked out of there." Ari wrinkled his nose. "I mean, seriously? Who doesn't take a shower after a fuck?"

"Does that mean you won't want him back?"

Ari rolled his eyes. "I might be prissy, but I'm not an idiot. Did you *see* that arse? That cock? Of *course* I invited him back."

Denny turned the water off and reached for his towel. "Is there a point to this conversation, or did you just want to come in here and watch me get clean?"

Ari leaned against the tiled wall, his arms folded. "I wanted to tell you, I'm releasing the *Hard Hats* scene tomorrow. You know, the one you did with Jake and Tom?"

"Oh yeah. Sure." Denny rubbed himself dry.

"Tom hasn't taken me up on my invitation, by the way. You know, to shoot another scene." Ari cocked his head to one side. "Have you heard from him lately?"

Denny blinked. "Why should I have heard from him?"

"Oh, I don't know. No particular reason, I guess. Unless it's the fact that he asked you to hold his hand for that second scene." Ari's eyes gleamed. "Does that mean you haven't heard from him?"

Denny did *not* want to discuss that, especially with Ari, who had good instincts when it came to people. He saw a *lot*.

What did he see when Tom did his scenes?

Denny wasn't going to ask.

"All I was going to say was, should you chance to run into Tom again, be sure to put in a good word for me. I'd love to get him in front of my cameras again."

"Well, if I do see him, I'll be sure to tell him. But I'll be honest. I wouldn't hold my breath if I were you. I think his porn days are over."

Ari grinned. "And how would you happen to know that?" Before Denny could get another word out, Ari waved. "Good to see you again," he called out as he headed for the door. "Don't leave it too long before you do another scene for me. I've got a priest's outfit that would fit you perfectly. I think you'd look divine in it." He paused, his fingers on the door handle, and flashed white teeth. "Hey. See what I did there?"

And then he was gone.

Denny sat on the plastic bench that ran along the wall of the shower, leaned against the damp tiles covered in condensation, and closed his eyes.

Two days left, and then Tom would be finished.

No more lunches in the garden.

No more excuses to come over.

Then what am I doing sitting here, wasting valuable time that I could be spending at the house?

Denny had never got dressed so fast, but all the while he squirmed into his jeans, he did his best to ignore that quiet voice somewhere deep in his head.

The one that told him he shouldn't be holding onto Tom but letting him go.

Tom packed the last of his tools away and straightened. *What a transformation.* The house now had a bright, modern kitchen. Loomis had replaced the faulty induction hob, Tom had taken up every available inch of space with new cabinets, and pale quartz worktops reflected the pristine white tiles.

His phone buzzed in his pocket. It was Loomis.

"Tom, you got a minute?"

"Actually, your timing is perfect. I just this minute finished the job."

"I stopped by last night and saw your handiwork. You've done a cracking job."

Tom smiled. "If the customer is happy, then I'm happy."

"I've got a proposal for you. Not something I want to discuss over the phone. Would it be okay if we meet up in a couple of weeks' time? Not at the house—at my home. No rush."

"Sure. Now you've got me intrigued." If it was something as simple as another job, he'd have said, right?

"I'll text you the address. And thanks again." Loomis hung up.

What was that about?

He turned his head when someone rapped on the door frame. Lisa, Chris, and Meena poked their heads around, peering into the room.

Tom laughed. "You can have your kitchen back now."

Chris grinned as he came into the room. "Wow. Do you renovate bedrooms? Because if this is what you can do with a kitchen..."

Meena snorted. "Your room doesn't need renovating—it needs excavating."

"Tom, if you don't have plans for this evening, we'd like to invite you to eat dinner here with us," Lisa said with a smile. "Nothing fancy, just pizza, garlic bread, coleslaw, chicken wings..."

"Plus, there'll be beer, coke, juice," Chris added.

"Say yes, please?" Lisa met his gaze. "We want to say thank you for all your hard work."

Tom glanced at his overalls. "I'm not exactly dressed for dinner, even if it *is* pizza."

"We weren't planning on eating just yet, so you've got time if you want to go home and change," Meena told him.

"Denny said you don't live too far from us." Lisa wandered around the kitchen, touching the pale birch cabinet doors, and running her hand over the sleek quartz surfaces. "It's too nice to cook in here. I'm afraid to make anything in case I mess it up."

"Just let Chris loose in here to cook, and you'll soon forget how tidy it looks right now," Meena said with a grin.

"Will the others be joining us?" It felt better than asking specifically after Denny.

Lisa's eyes held a glint that made Tom think she saw right through him. "Denny will be here. He's been with his tutor today. And Robin should be home any minute."

"Then I'll say thanks for the invitation and go home to change."

One last night with Denny, then it really would be

goodbye. He doubted their paths would cross again, not once Denny found himself a job worthy of his talents.

And not once my business takes off again.

It had been an interesting episode in his life, one he would never forget. What made it memorable was the porn, of course, but more than that, it was Denny.

Tom didn't want to forget about him.

Does it have to be goodbye?

Why say farewell when you're attracted to him?

What if he's attracted to you?

Questions Tom didn't want to consider.

Denny had a bright future ahead of him, one that didn't feature Tom.

Denny opened the front door, and the enticing aroma of tomatoes, garlic, and pepperoni assaulted him. "Who ordered pizza?" His stomach rumbled.

"We're celebrating the kitchen being finished," Chris hollered. "Hurry up. We thought you'd be earlier than this. Lisa's put the food in the oven to keep warm."

Denny shucked off his shoes and left them by the door. "You didn't let Robin do the ordering, did you? He likes anchovies on his pizza."

He caught Robin's indignant huff. "Nothing wrong with anchovies."

"We let the guest of honour choose the toppings," Lisa called out.

"What guest of honour?" Denny went into the dining

room—and stopped dead at the sight of Tom's wide-eyed expression of surprise.

"You didn't know about this?" Tom frowned. "But I thought—"

"Not a clue." But he had an inkling about who'd come up with the idea. He glanced at Lisa, who was avoiding his gaze for some reason. Come to think of it, Chris was also doing a crap job of looking anywhere but at him.

Yeah, he knew all right.

Meena stood. "You sit, and we'll fetch the food." She and Lisa left the room.

Denny took the only remaining chair, which faced Tom's. "So... what did you order?" He wasn't concerned about pizza—he was too happy at the thought of one more evening with Tom, even if he did have to share him with the others.

Tom smiled. "Boring choices, I'm afraid. Pepperoni Passion, Chicken Feast, Hawaiian, and... Mighty Meaty."

Denny couldn't hold back his grin. *And your meat is pretty mighty.*

The twinkle in Tom's eyes made him think they'd shared the same thought.

"Plus, there are wedges, dough balls, garlic pizza bread, nachos, coleslaw, chicken dippers..."

Denny gaped at Robin. "We're feeding six, not sixty."

"And your point is? Leftover pizza for breakfast... yum."

Lisa and Meena returned, carrying four pizza boxes and a couple of brown paper bags that had to contain the sides.

Chris dove out of the room. "I'll get the drinks."

Dinner ended up being a mad free-for-all, hands grabbing slices, tipping wedges onto plates, sharing out tubs of dip, the air filled with the sound of nachos being crunched... It was also a time filled with laughter, and Denny couldn't remember enjoying a meal so much.

Except maybe that time he'd shared chicken parmesan

with homemade marinara sauce, green beans, and cauliflower mash, and mocha trifle with a certain builder.

Just the two of them.

Denny walked Tom to the door. The others were in the kitchen, loading the dishwasher and putting the bottles and boxes into the recycling bin.

He had the suspicion their absence was deliberate.

Lisa… Or Chris. Denny wouldn't put it past him either. Or the two of them could have teamed up.

He opened the door and peered out into the street. "I didn't see your van when I came home."

"I came by train." Tom smiled. "That way, I got to have a couple of beers. Good beer too." He inclined his head towards the kitchen. "Thank them again for me. This was a great idea."

"I agree. Just not sure why I wasn't included in the planning of it."

Lies. He knew why.

Tom stepped out onto the path. "Well, I guess this is goodbye."

Denny chuckled. "You think so?"

God, he hoped not.

Tom stared at him. "Do you know something I don't?"

"Nope. But every time we say goodbye—"

"You cry a little?" Tom grinned. "Sorry. I couldn't resist."

He had to smile at that. "Grandma used to sing that song to me at night when we stayed with her. It always sent me right off to sleep. And I was *going* to say, every time we say goodbye, something always happens to throw us together again."

Denny couldn't wait to see what it was going to be the next time.

"In that case... let's say goodbye... for now."

He smiled. "Goodbye for now." He wanted more than words. He wanted to step out of the house, move so close to Tom that he could feel the heat radiating off him, lean in, brush his lips against Tom's, and leave him a lingering kiss to remember.

Not a good idea.

Tom walked up the path to the pavement, turned right, and waved. Then he strolled out of sight.

Denny closed the door with a heavy heart.

It's wrong to want to see him again, especially when nothing can come of it.

Nothing *could* ever come of it.

That didn't stop him wanting it.

That line from a song Tom had mentioned, about saying goodbye... Denny recalled another that followed it. One that seemed apt, given his constricted chest and the lump in his throat.

It was something about dying a little.

I should have kissed him.

Tom walked slowly toward Raynes Park station, turning over and over again in his mind the look on Denny's face. *Did I miss something? Did he want to kiss me too?*

The more he pictured Denny's expression, the more convinced he became that what had stopped him leaning in to steal a kiss had been Denny's expression.

He isn't interested.

This situation bewildered the fuck out of him. There were times when he felt sure he was getting signals from Denny, but nothing happened. It was hard to get things straight in his head.

I want him.

But it wasn't just lust.

No, it was something deeper than that.

CHAPTER TWENTY-SEVEN

August

Tom hadn't stopped smiling since he'd left Loomis's house. *Ken. He said to call him Ken.* Given the new circumstances, Tom figured that was appropriate. He went into the kitchen and put the kettle on.

Well, what do you know about that? Things had finally, *finally* taken a turn for the better. He'd been wondering all week what was on Ken's mind, ever since he'd called to set up the meeting, but he hadn't expected this.

A permanent contract to take care of his properties. *All* of them.

When Ken had first told him he owned several properties, Tom had imagined a few houses like Denny's, suburban homes dotted around London. The real figure was so much larger, the properties more diverse than he could have suspected.

Oh my God. Ken must be worth a fortune. He owned a lot of houses, sure, but there were also apartment buildings, shops, a nightclub or two…

And he wants me *to maintain them.*

The proposal had been that Tom would carry out any repairs or renovations required, and if he needed to subcontract, he had free rein to do so—and a budget to do it with. Not only that, if he wanted to employ someone on a more permanent basis, he could do that too.

I need to pinch myself. This is a dream, right?

Ken had made it clear why he'd asked Tom. He liked Tom's work, sure, but what had impressed him was his reliability, his high standards, his work ethic…

And all of this because Denny gave him my name.

What was that quote about mighty oaks growing from little acorns?

Now Tom had a reason to call him. A good excuse, at any rate.

I miss him.

That thought was enough to wipe the smile from his face. The simple words couldn't do justice to the ache in his chest when he recollected the time he'd spent with Denny. He had somehow crawled under his skin and wound his way to Tom's heart. His voice filled Tom's head.

This is so fucked up.

It had been three weeks since he'd finished the kitchen. Three weeks of working with Craig, whose backlog of jobs had grown too great for him to deal with on his own. Tom hadn't minded. It had kept him busy.

It hadn't kept him from thinking about Denny.

A day didn't go by without him wondering what Denny was doing, now he'd finished his studies. It didn't take a genius to work out porn had to figure in there somewhere: Denny still had loans to pay off, right? And now that he had more time, that meant more scenes, more money to shrink his debt.

Tom didn't want to think about Denny having sex with other guys.

Guys who weren't him.

It wasn't jealousy. Okay, it *was*, but… He didn't resent Denny fucking men for money. To him it was a job. Tom got that.

What he resented was that Denny could do that and not get emotionally involved, when every intimate second Tom had spent with him served to lose a little piece of his heart to Denny, one bit at a time. Tom couldn't divorce his feelings.

Denny said he'd been in love once.

Tom was discovering how it felt to fall in love for the first time, because that was the only explanation for the way he was feeling.

He was falling for a man who viewed their physical connection as just sex.

Tom knew it was so much more than that for him.

He made himself coffee and went into his office. The bank statements were looking a lot healthier than a few months ago, now the door to financial stability had opened.

Another had closed, however, and he didn't know how to open it.

His phone rang, and he smiled when he saw it was Deb. "Hey. How are you?

"Wondering if you've died? You haven't called for a while."

He winced. "Yeah, I know. I'm sorry. I've just been snowed under with work."

"Really? Okay, now I don't mind so much. That's great. Work is always good. So my next question is… what are you doing Saturday afternoon? Three-ish?"

He chuckled. "Having a weekend off."

"Perfect. We're having a barbecue in our postage stamp of a back garden. You know, the one where you put down a patio for us? And built us that brick barbecue we rarely use because of the weather, thank you very much, British summertime."

Another wry chuckle. "It's not just the weather, it's all the trains that go rocketing past the bottom of your garden."

"Meh. We hardly notice them anymore."

"Except when they make the windows rattle. So, this barbecue… Is anyone else going to be there?"

"No, just the three of us."

Tom glanced at his desk and spied his cheque book. He grinned. "That sounds like a fantastic idea. Want me to bring anything?" Apart from a cheque that was bound to make Deb and Sharon smile.

"Yourself? A bottle of wine? We've got enough steak to

feed an army, not to mention everything else Sharon has stuffed into the fridge."

"Me? *I* wasn't the one throwing things into the shopping trolley," Sharon called out in the background.

Tom laughed. "Okay, I'll bring a bottle."

There was a pause, and he caught the sound of a door closing. "I have a question for you," Deb said in a low voice.

One she obviously didn't want Sharon to overhear. "What?"

"Whatever happened to Mr.-Snog-in-the-back-of-an-Uber?"

Oh shit.

"Can we forget about that conversation?" His gut went into spasm.

"That depends. Have you forgotten about *him*?"

Fuck no.

Tom pushed out a sigh. "Look, like they say on Facebook… It's complicated."

"Have you seen him since?"

"Kind of. He's… He's a friend, okay? That's all."

That's all he can be, because that's all he wants *to be.*

"Then I'm extending an invitation to him too. Bring him with you."

"What? You don't even know him." It felt as though someone had turned the thermostat right up. There was a tingling in his chest, and he couldn't draw enough air into his lungs. *Great. I'm having a panic attack.* And all because Deb wanted to meet Denny. *She doesn't even know his name.*

"Well, if you won't ask him, send me his number and *I* will."

"No!"

"I'm not taking no for an answer, so you might as well do as I ask. Does this friend have a name?"

There was no getting out of it. Deb had a stubborn streak

a mile wide.

"Denny. And I'll ask him, all right? But if he says no, that's an end to it."

"Fine—if he *does* say no."

Tom could always lie.

Yeah right. He wouldn't do that, and what was more, Deb knew it.

"I'll see you Saturday." Whether he went alone or not remained to be seen.

"I'll look forward to it." She chuckled. "Come by train? That way, if we decide to make cocktails, you won't have to drive home."

Cocktails?

Then he saw the light. "I don't have to ask what kind of cocktails, do I?"

The only response he got was Deb calling out to Sharon. "Love? Look up what goes into a porn star martini when you get a minute?" He caught Sharon's cackle.

Deb, you….

"Have I ever told you what a sneaky, conniving—"

"Many times, but you *know* you love me." She hung up.

Tom glanced at the calendar on the wall. Saturday was three days away. He could always leave off calling Denny until Friday night.

Except he wouldn't do that.

He scrolled through his contacts and clicked on Denny's number.

"Hey." The note of delight in Denny's voice warmed him. "How are you?"

"I'm fine. I'm not disturbing you, am I?"

Denny laughed. "Hardly. I'm putting all my books into boxes. What's up?"

Tom told him about Ken's business proposal. "And I have you to thank for that."

"Aw. All I did was pass on your details. *You* did all the work. But thanks. I'm glad it's turned out well."

Tom's heartbeat quickened.

"Tom? You've gone quiet on me. Was there something else?"

He took a deep breath. "Deb and Sharon are having a barbecue Saturday afternoon. And… you're invited."

"Me? They've never met me."

"That's true, but… I might have mentioned you a while back to Deb. I said you were a friend."

The pause that followed set his heartbeat racing.

"Denny?"

"A barbecue sounds like a great idea. Sure. Where do they live?"

"Epsom. I can meet you at the station, if you like. Then we can go there together."

But not *together.*

"That works. Text me what time train you'll be on, and I'll meet you there. Do I need to bring anything? Maybe some flowers?"

Despite his churning stomach and pounding heart, Tom smiled. "They'll like that."

"Okay. I'll see you Saturday." He sighed. "Back to my books."

Tom said goodbye and hung up. Ribbons of unease twisted in his belly, and he shivered.

It'll be fine.

It'll be fine.

He hoped.

By the time they'd eaten most of the steak, burgers, and hot dogs, Tom had to admit he'd been worrying over nothing. Denny, Deb, and Sharon were getting on like a house on fire. They sat on patio chairs, swapping funny stories. Tom discovered Denny had a thing for parrot jokes, each one funnier than the last. He hadn't seen Deb laugh that much in ages.

More importantly, she hadn't let on once that she knew about their drunken kiss, which puzzled him at first. Then he reasoned she didn't want to embarrass either of them, which relieved him no end. Denny appeared relaxed. He'd complimented them on the food, and Deb had loved the colourful bouquet he'd presented on arrival.

It really was going to be okay.

Then he remembered he had something in the back pocket of his jeans that he'd been saving for the right moment.

He couldn't wait to see their faces.

Deb glanced up and shivered. "Don't look now, but I think our barbecue is about to come to a soggy end."

Sure enough, dark, heavy clouds rolled across the sky, and thunder rumbled in the distance.

Sharon snorted. "It must be August." The two of them collected glasses and plates, and Tom and Denny helped. The first drops of rain hit the patio just as they closed the back door, the thunder louder.

"I'll make coffee," Deb announced while Sharon loaded the dishwasher.

"Can I do anything?" Denny asked.

Before either of them could reply, Tom cleared his throat. "Can you hold off on the coffee for a sec?" He reached into his pocket. "I've got something for you." He held out the small piece of folded paper to Deb.

She took it, frowning. "What's this?" she asked as she straightened it.

Sharon glanced at it. "Looks like a cheque, Deb. You know, those things no one uses anymore? Well, with the exception of Tom, appar—" Her mouth fell open.

Deb jerked her head up. "What's this for?"

"I thought you might have guessed." Tom smiled. "It's for your next round of IVF treatment. You *are* ready for round three, right?"

Deb gaped at him. "Yes, but… You can't afford this."

"I said I'd had a lot of work on recently, didn't I? So yes, I can." He followed them as they walked slowly into the dining room.

"Tom, I…" Sharon regarded him with wide eyes. "I don't know what to say."

He chuckled. "How about, 'Thank you, that will come in very handy'? Or 'We'll name our first boy after you.'"

Deb pressed her lips together. "I don't think we can accept this." She held it out to him.

He stilled. "What?"

Sharon blinked. "What?"

She gave Sharon a hard stare. "Well, are *you* going to ask him, or shall I? Because we need to know, right? I mean, it's not as if we weren't going to mention it anyway." Her hand was still outstretched.

Sharon bit her lip. "Oh. Yeah. I see your point. That does shed a different light on it, doesn't it?"

Tom gaped at them. "Will *one* of you tell me what on earth you're talking about? *What* sheds a different light on it?"

Deb handed Sharon the cheque, then went over to the coffee table and picked up her phone. She wiped her thumb over the screen, scrolling. "This work you were doing…. Would it have anything to do with *this*?" She turned the phone around and—

Fuck.

It was a screenshot of Denny deep in Tom's arse, his own

dick spearing into Jake's. Tom's face was clearly visible as he twisted to look back at Denny.

That cat was out of the fucking bag again.

"Oh shit," Denny whispered.

Tom gulped. "Where did you get that?"

"From Gavin." Sharon's eyebrows shot up. "You know, my gay brother who you meet here every Christmas? He recognized you immediately and sent this to me."

Deb glanced at Denny. "Well, at least I know now why the two of you were kissing in the back of an Uber."

Denny snapped his attention to Tom, but Tom couldn't deal with him right then. He had much bigger problems.

"Deb, can I talk to you in the kitchen? Alone?" His heart was thumping so hard, his chest ached.

He had to sort this mess out.

"Aren't I part of this too?" Denny's face was flushed.

"Yes, but... I just need to talk to Deb, all right?"

Denny swallowed. "Fine."

Deb walked into the kitchen, and Tom followed, pulling the door to after him. Before he could get a word out, she whirled around and gaped at him, her eyes huge.

"I can't believe you did gay porn to pay for my IVF."

"I didn't," he protested, his pulse rapid. "That money came from a building job, I swear." His stomach clenched. "Okay, I might have *initially* done it to earn the money, but then I—"

"But gay porn?" She stared at him. "You're not even gay." She glanced toward the door. "Bi-curious? Possibly. But to do that..."

"Does it matter so much how I made the money?"

Her eyebrows shot up. "You don't think I might feel a bit... awkward about the way the money was obtained?"

"I didn't *want* to do it, okay? I didn't know that was what it was going to be when I went there, all right? I was going to have sex with a woman."

"Oh, and that makes it okay?"

"Look, it just... sort of snowballed. They offered more money, and all I could think of was the bills. The second time, I—"

"'*Second* time'? How many videos have you made?" Her chest heaved. "You might as well tell me everything." She gave him a pointed stare. "How many, Tom?"

"Two. Three if you count the..." He clammed up.

She arched her eyebrows. "Count the what?"

His heart quaked. "The OnlyFans scene I shot with Denny."

Deb gave a slow nod. "I was going to ask how Denny figured in all this."

"That first time? When I thought I'd be doing a scene with a woman? Denny... he was part of the setup. They baited me with a wad of cash, and... I was desperate."

"So you took the bait. That doesn't explain why you went back. Unless you liked it."

"I didn't, okay?" His heart pounded to hear the lie fall from his lips. "And I only went back so I could get enough money to give to you and Sharon. But then a job turned up—a real job—and that's where this money came from, I promise."

Deb snorted. "I don't believe this. My ex-husband, the gay porn star."

"You make it sound as if this is something I'm still doing, but I'm not, and I won't ever do it again. I... I don't *want* to do it ever again. I didn't like it. I... I could never like something like that."

He knew his denial stemmed from sheer panic, and shame flushed through him.

Not just panic, though—bone-melting fear.

Then he realised Deb had gone quiet.

She gazed at him, her eyes wide. "I had no idea you could be so cruel."

He froze. "What... what do you mean?"

"How can you stand there and say such nasty things?" Her eyes glinted. "Because from where *I* was standing, it sure looked like you enjoyed it. One look at your face in that screenshot told me that." Her voice softened. "Tom, I just sat through a whole afternoon watching you light up like a Christmas tree every time Denny opened his mouth. And then you basically deny you have feelings for him."

Feelings? Fuck...

"I... I didn't say any of that to be cruel, all right? I was scared. Terrified, ashamed... I didn't want any of this to come out." Especially not like this.

She nodded. "And now we have it. Tom Ryder is afraid to come out. Afraid of people knowing he likes guys. You didn't think I'd understand that fear? Me, of all people?" She clenched her jaw. "Well, you know what? No one who cares for you will give a shit about that. They'll just be happy because *you* are. Except you're *not* happy, because you've let your fear get the better of you. Worse still, you've jeopardised whatever you have going on with Denny. So now you need to go out there and apologise to that sweet man for not telling us the truth." She raised her chin. "But it's not only us you've lied to—you've been lying to yourself."

The kitchen door slid open, and Sharon stood there, her face impassive. "Apologising to Denny might be a little difficult. He left."

Shock thrummed through him. "What do you mean, he left?"

She stared at him with wide eyes. "Did you really think closing the door would prevent us from hearing your conversation? We both heard every word. Then he went as white as a sheet, grabbed his jacket, and hightailed it out of here."

Fuck no.

"How long ago did he leave?"

"Right after you said you didn't like doing it—for the

second time, I might add."

"Don't just stand there—go after him." Deb gave him an impatient shove. "You can't lose him."

"It's not like that," he retorted.

Deb gaped at him. "Are you *kidding* me? It's *exactly* like that. So go after him and make it right. Or I'll never speak to you again."

Tom opened the front door and pelted out into the road. Rain hit the pavement and already huge puddles had started to form. He peered in the direction of the station.

There was no sign of him.

He ran to the end of the road, the rain soaking into his clothes, and turned the corner. The main road was full of people hurrying to get out of the rain as the wheels of the passing traffic sent waves of water breaking over their feet. Tom scanned the wet scene, oblivious to his own soaked state.

Where is he?

Then his heart thumped.

Denny was sheltering at a bus stop.

Oh thank God.

Tom ran toward him, and Denny jerked his head in his direction. His shirt was transparent, clinging to him like a second skin, his jeans almost black, they were so wet. His eyes bored into Tom.

"I don't want to talk to you right now."

CHAPTER TWENTY-EIGHT

The rain hitting the bus shelter roof was so loud it could have been hailstones. Tom blurted out the first thing that came into his head, raising his voice to be heard above the noise of rain and traffic.

"I didn't mean it." He was conscious of the people waiting under the shelter, obviously trying not to look in their direction, and failing miserably.

The last thing Tom wanted was an audience, but he'd take what he could get.

What did it matter who heard him, as long as Denny did?

Denny's eyes blazed. "Oh, so you didn't *mean* to apologise for fucking me?"

The words sliced through him, and the waiting bus passengers blinked and coughed, averting their gaze when Tom stared at them. He reached over to touch Denny's arm, to get him to lower his voice, to calm down, but Denny shrugged out of his reach.

"Don't you fucking touch me," he said through gritted teeth.

"You didn't hear all of it," Tom began, his stomach roiling.

Denny gaped. "Aw, did I miss the punchline? And what was that? Because I can guess. 'I'm not gay.' 'I don't like fags.' 'I was in it for the money.' You're not the first to come out with that crap. I've heard it all before." Another flash of his eyes. "You wanker. I *promised* myself I would *not* get into this mess again, and yet here I am, falling for yet another guy who only wants to stick his dick in a woman."

Falling? Oh my God.

Then the rest of Denny's words registered, and cold speared through his core. Tom wanted to yell that he'd never say such hurtful things, that he wasn't that kind of man, but at that point the bus trundled into view, and they fell silent as its doors opened and the passengers climbed aboard. Tom's heart hammered, the words colliding in his head.

Words he had to get out.

When the doors closed, Tom blurted out, "I didn't mean any of it."

"You said that already. Got anything else to say?"

Tom opened his mouth to tell him he wasn't the only one falling in love, but Denny cut him off.

"Fuck you, Tom." And with that, he ran out from under the shelter and kept on running, his trainers splashing through the puddles.

"Denny!" Tom yelled after him, charged after him, but Denny didn't stop, didn't look back once. Then he disappeared around the corner.

Tom stood in the pouring rain, water dripping from his beard, his shirt cold and damp against his skin.

Now what do I do?

He turned and walked back to Deb's, feeling sick, his throat tight, his hands clenched into fists. Deb opened the door, gazing past him into the street.

"Where is he?"

"No idea."

"Did you tell him how you felt? Did you at least apologise?"

He stepped into the house. "I didn't get the chance." His heart was like a solid lump of metal in his chest. Deb closed the door behind him, and whatever resolve had held him together until that point crumbled.

For the first time in his adult life, Tom Ryder wept.

I really fucked this up, didn't I?

Numbness pervaded him. His knees wanted to buckle, but he somehow managed not to sink to them. His shoulders slumped as pain lanced through his stomach.

Deb's arm went around him. "Sharon, make us some tea, would you?" Tom shivered, and she sighed. "You're soaked. You need to get out of these clothes. We'll throw them in the drier, and you can wear my dressing gown."

From the kitchen, Sharon snorted. "It's not his colour."

Deb glared in her direction. "A little sympathy wouldn't go amiss." She gave him a nudge in the direction of the bathroom. "My robe's hanging on the back of the door. Put it on, wash your face, just… take a minute to pull yourself together. We'll talk when you're ready."

Tom stumbled into the tiny bathroom, closed the door, and began the task of peeling off his wet clothes, that feeling of numbness still present.

There was a knock.

"Tom?" Sharon's voice was softer. "Wear mine. It's the pale blue one. You'll never get into Deb's."

"Thanks." He grabbed a towel and rubbed his hair and beard, then the rest of him. He put on Sharon's dressing gown, tied the belt around his waist, and stared at his reflection, his breathing returning to its normal rhythm.

He wouldn't even listen to me.

Not that Tom blamed him.

He gathered up his soggy clothing and opened the door.

"Give those to me." Sharon took them from him. "Go sit down." Her eyes twinkled. "By the way? You couldn't have found a better career, could you? I mean, talk about a name that's perfect for porn."

"That isn't helping," Deb yelled.

Sharon leaned in and kissed his cheek. "If we don't laugh, we cry. I know which one *I'd* rather do."

Tom didn't want to cry anymore.

Deb was waiting for him in the living room, three mugs of tea on the coffee table. She patted the seat cushion next to her on the couch. "Right. Let's see if we can fix this."

Tom joined her. He sat on the edge of the cushion, his head in his hands. "I know you mean well, but I think this situation calls for more than a box of chocolates and some flowers."

Sharon came into the room. "Never doubt the power of a determined lesbian. We are *not* going to let you give up on him."

Tom raised his chin. "You didn't see his face." There was a dull ache in his chest when he pictured Denny's set jaw, his blazing eyes.

She swallowed. "Oh yes I did. And if you have feelings for him, you'll find a way to make this right." Sharon bit her lip. "But no one is saying it'll be easy."

"Nothing worth doing is ever easy," Deb remarked.

Tom sagged into the couch. He couldn't leave things as they were.

Now all he had to do was get Denny to listen to him.

Denny fumbled for his key. His feet and back ached, and he needed a drink of water. As soon as he was inside the house, he kicked off his trainers and his waterlogged socks. The rain had made it to his socks ages ago. At least it had finally abated.

He glanced at the clock in the hall. *Two hours?* He'd walked for two fucking hours, most of it on autopilot, aware of nothing but the non-stop clamouring in his head.

The kitchen door opened, and Chris appeared. He frowned. "Aren't you supposed to be at a barbecue?" His eyes widened. "You look like a drowned rat."

"Thanks. I need to get out of these wet things." He trudged up the stairs, thankful he'd dried off a little on the long walk home. No dripping on the carpet.

He went into his room and stripped off. Then he opened a drawer, grabbed a clean pair of sweats and a tee, and got dressed.

There was a soft knock at the door. "Can I come in?"

Denny wasn't in the mood. "Can it wait?"

The door opened, and Chris walked in. "I don't think so." He blinked at the sight of the cameras and tripods, then held his hands up. "You know what? I'm not going to ask." He walked over to the foot of the bed and sat. "What happened?"

"Who says something happened?"

Chris snorted. "I may come across as an insensitive Jack the Lad whose only interest is having a good time, but there's another side to me. And *that* side notices when his housemate is in a right state. So take a pew, and tell me what the fuck is going on." He cocked his head. "Tom has something to do with it, doesn't he?"

Denny climbed onto the bed, shifting until his back reached the headboard. He shoved pillows behind him and sat cross-legged, hands clasped. "I overheard a conversation this afternoon."

"Must have been some conversation," Chris muttered.

Denny took a deep breath and it all spilled out: the scenes, the trip to the island, every word Tom had said in that tiny kitchen, what Denny had shouted under that bus shelter... Chris didn't interrupt once, for which Denny was grateful, and also a little surprised. When he was done, Denny rested his head against the rails.

"So now you know everything."

Chris didn't speak for a moment. He studied Denny's duvet cover, his brow furrowed. At last, he lifted his head and looked Denny in the eye.

"I think I understand why he came out with all that."

Denny stared at him. "Seriously? You're going to make excuses for him?"

"Not excuses, no, but… look at it from his perspective. He's been carrying around this big fucking secret, and suddenly it's out there." Chris shrugged. "He was scared. Afraid his ex would look at him differently. Maybe he didn't want her to know the truth."

"And what truth is that?"

Chris huffed. "That he likes doing it with guys, of course. Well, with you in particular."

"You're wrong." Denny's throat seized. "Tom doesn't want me."

"You don't know that."

Denny heaved a sigh. "Yeah, I do. I've been here before." He cleared his throat.

Chris got up. "Hang on a sec." He hurried out of the room and down the stairs.

Now what?

When Chris returned, he carried a bottle, a can of coke, and two glasses. Denny arched his eyebrows. "Rum?"

He shrugged. "It was all I could find. You need warming up. You don't look good."

"Nor would you if you'd walked from Epsom to Wimbledon in the middle of a storm."

Chris poured rum and coke into the glasses, then handed one to him. "Now. You've been *where* before, exactly?"

Denny took a sip, and the rum warmed his throat. "Tom asked me if I'd ever been in love. I told him I had, once, but it didn't work out." Another sip. "His name was Adam, I met him at uni, and he was my best friend—my *straight* best friend."

Chris winced. "Why do I get a bad feeling about this? What happened?" His breathing hitched. "Did he know you were in love with him?"

"I kept how I felt a secret for the longest time. What was

the point in telling him? It'd only ruin things, right?" He took a gulp of rum. "And then came the night when we both got a little drunk."

"You didn't make a move on him, did you?"

"Other way around." He could still hear Adam's voice.

What does it feel like to fuck a guy?'

Is it any different to fucking a girl?'

And then, that stunner of a question that had shocked Denny into silence.

Would you let me fuck you?'

Of course he would.

"He asked if we could have sex," he said simply. "And I wasn't about to refuse him. So... we did. Only... it wasn't just the once. He got a taste for it. And every time we fucked, I fell deeper and deeper. But that was where I made my first mistake."

"What was that?"

"I assumed he was falling too. He wasn't having sex with girls anymore—just with me. And we fucked pretty much every time he asked. So it stood to reason he had feelings for me, right? Especially after he..." The memories of their shared intimacy were still acute. An iron band constricted his chest. "Then I made my second mistake."

"You told him how you felt."

Denny nodded. "Imagine my surprise when I learned the truth. He didn't love me. It was just sex to him. And once he knew how I felt?" He shuddered. "He told me he could never feel anything like that for me." He took another drink. "He couldn't be around me after that. Hell, he went out of his way to avoid me. And when I tried to talk to him, it... it got ugly."

"All those lines you told Tom you'd heard before ... That's what Adam came out with, didn't he?"

Another nod. "So I made myself a promise. The only straight guys I would have anything to do with were the ones on set. I wasn't going to date one—and there were a couple of guys who wanted to, believe me." Pain lanced through his chest. "I wouldn't let another straight guy break my heart."

"And then you fell for Tom."

"Yeah. I thought this time was different—that *he* was different. And when he started getting too close, I backed off. I tried not to let him in, because I knew what his motivation was for doing porn—it was for the money. I could see what was happening, though. His emotions were all in a twist because of the sex, but it wasn't real." He locked gazes with Chris. "And I was right, wasn't I? Everything he said today confirms it. He was okay with fucking a guy, so long as no one close to him got to know about it."

Chris stilled. "Did you hear him say all those things? About not being gay, not liking fags?"

"No. I got out of there. I didn't hear how the conversation ended."

"Well, I may not have known him all that long, but he doesn't strike me as the kind of guy who'd say anything like that." He held his hands up. "Just trying to provide some neutral perspective here, that's all."

Denny swallowed. "I get that. And thanks for listening, but..." He inhaled deeply. "I think I need to put a little space between me and Tom. I don't want to think about him anymore, because it hurts when I do that."

"You're just going to forget him?"

Denny stared at him. "You think I can't?"

Chris gave him a sad smile. "I think you're deluding yourself, but if that's how you want to play it, fine. If he calls the house—"

"I'm not home."

"And if he comes over here?"

"I'm *still* not home."

Chris stood. "I think you need to be honest. You just said you tried not to let him in, but I think he managed it anyway. And getting rid of him might not be that easy." He patted Denny's shoulder. "Now you've calmed down a little, do *you* think Tom would have come out with ugly stuff like Adam did?"

No, he did not. His face tingled at the memory, and he cringed when he recollected Tom's shocked, hurt expression.

Not that it changed anything. It only strengthened his determination not to see Tom again. How could he face him anyway, after all that?

Chris walked out of the room, and Denny finished his drink.

None of it mattered. Tom wouldn't be back.

Denny missed him already.

I fucked it up the moment I kissed him in the back of that Uber. I shouldn't have done that. I should've learned my lesson.

Too late for that now.

CHAPTER TWENTY-NINE

Three weeks.

Three long weeks, and September was almost upon them.

Three *grindingly* long weeks, and no sign of Denny. It didn't matter how many times Tom called him, or sent him a text, or even an email. The result was always the same.

No reply.

Not that he was about to bare his soul in an email—he wanted to do that face to face—but getting the opportunity to do so seemed as likely as the next Pope being called Priscilla.

As a last resort, he'd driven to Denny's home, only to be met with gentle yet firm resistance from Chris, who'd stood at the front door, his arms folded, and before he'd even opened his mouth, Tom had known what was coming.

"Look mate, I'm not gonna say I understand all this, but... he's hurting, and he doesn't want to see you." His smile had been kind, though. "I suggest leaving it for a while."

And then he'd closed the door.

Tom had walked back to his van, turning quickly at the last second to see if Denny was at his window, watching.

Not so much as a curtain twitch.

It was maybe a week later that Tom discovered it hadn't been a last resort after all—he took out a subscription to Denny's OnlyFans account. At least that way, he got to see him. What surprised him was how few videos there were that featured Denny with other guys. All of the most recent ones were solos.

Then he found the one they'd made, and his finger paused over the touchpad, his heart hammering, his breath quickening.

I can't. I just… can't.

It took him a whole five minutes to decide he'd put it off long enough.

He *had* to see it.

Click.

He watched it all the way through, then watched it again.

I had no idea.

What shocked him into stillness wasn't the noises they made together, the sighs, the moans, the slick sound of his dick sliding into Denny's hole…

It wasn't the sight of his arse cheeks hollowing as he thrust deep into Denny or Denny's throat full of his shaft.

It was the expression in his own eyes as he made love to Denny.

It was what swam in *Denny's* eyes, the naked adoration as he clung to Tom, their cries growing louder the nearer they got to orgasm.

We were so close. We were one.

And he'd ruined that.

Why did I say no to that scene he wanted to shoot?

Except he knew why. Each time they'd touched, each time they'd kissed, Tom fell for Denny that little bit more. The time they'd spent together when they weren't having sex had only enhanced that intimacy. And the prospect of shooting a scene that would end up being an hour long?

It would have been impossible to hide what he felt.

And then it hit him.

But… I don't need *to hide it anymore.*

Quite the opposite.

He needs to see how deeply he affects me.

How much Tom loved him.

The thought knocked the breath right out of him.

I do love him. *I really* really *do.*

What other explanation was there for the fluttering in his

stomach when Denny kissed him? His racing pulse whenever Denny's fingers brushed his? Those electrical jolts he felt each time Denny's hand was on his neck, Denny looking deep into Tom's eyes? That feeling of joy when he knew he'd see Denny?

He could name a hundred things about Denny that affected him, in ways Deb *never* had. And with this newfound knowledge came a heartfelt desire.

Denny *had* to see how he made Tom feel.

Because if *Tom* could see love burning in his own eyes in a fucking *video*, then Denny had to see it too.

There had to be a way to bridge the chasm, to get close enough for Denny to see the truth.

Close enough to…

He was suddenly buoyant, his heartbeat racing, energy surging through him.

Holy fuck, there was one more last resort after all.

Tom grabbed his laptop, fired it up, and did a search for Ari's email—the original email with all Ari's contact details. When he found it, there was one moment of last-minute nerves, one brief spasm of hesitation, one panicked inner cry of *Can I do this?*

Then he found his courage.

Fuck it.

His hand trembled as he tapped in the number. It rang, once, twice, three times…

"Ari Metcalfe. What can I do for you?"

"Ari, this… this is Tom Ryder." Christ, his heart was pistoning like a steam engine.

"Hey, Tom. How's it hanging?"

He didn't have time to waste on small talk.

"I'm trying to get in contact with Denny Bailey."

There was a pause. "And? I'm not gonna give you his number."

"I've already got his number. He's not answering."

"Then I can't help you. Bye."

"Wait!"

There was no click. Ari was still there. "What?"

"You're the only one who can help."

"Help you? To do what?"

Tom had given this a lot of thought.

"You need to call Denny. Tell him you want him to do a scene for the site—a scene I'm going to film with him, only you can't tell him that part. He can't know I'm going to be there."

"Been there, done that. And by the way, that threesome is getting a hell of a lot of likes. Not to mention some hot as fuck comments. You're a hit—*Gavin*."

"Please. I need you to do this."

Silence.

"Ari? You still there?"

"Oh. My. God. I see where this is going. Who the fuck do you think I am—Cupid? Give me one good reason why I should."

Tom needed a carrot, a fucking big one. "Because it'll be the hottest video you'll ever film. Correction—the hottest *flip flop* video."

Another pause. "Okay, *now* I'm listening."

Denny loaded the dishwasher, straightened, and heaved a sigh.

"That sounded heavy," Lisa murmured as she poured coffee into five mugs. "Shouldn't you be dancing on air? It's your graduation next month." She widened her eyes. "Hey, do we get to call you Dr.?"

He managed a laugh. "No, Lisa, that comes with a PhD.

Getting a master's doesn't also get you a title. I'll still be plain old Denny Bailey, just with more letters after my name."

"Letters that'll look pretty fancy on a job application." She tilted her head. "And you will *never* be plain old Denny Bailey."

He gave her a hug. "You're sweet."

Lisa put the coffee pot back on its stand, crossed the room, and closed the kitchen door. "Can we talk?"

Here we go again.

"If it's to ask me if I'm all right—again—then no." He looked her in the eye. "I'm fine, honest. And I really don't need you and Chris clucking round me like a pair of mother hens."

Her lips twitched. "Wouldn't that make us lesbian hens? Because… no."

He pulled out a chair and sat. "I'm over him, okay?"

"Sure you are."

Denny gave her a mock glare. "No, I am, really."

"Whatever you say." Another twitch of her lips. "How does that saying go? Something about a lady protesting too much?"

"So now I'm a lady?"

Lisa handed him a mug. "I just think we've wrapped you up in cotton wool long enough. Something tells me you're going to run into him again—he only lives down the road, for God's sake—and you need to be prepared for that." She opened the door, picked up the rest of the mugs, and went out of the room.

Denny was surprised he hadn't bumped into Tom long before this, but then again, he'd hardly ventured out of the house. He hadn't been to Three Apes for weeks, because if there was one location where he might possibly see Tom, that was it.

The thought pissed him off a little. *Why should I miss out on my favourite coffee shop, just because I'm scared of running into Tom?*

Was it fear, though? And if so, fear of what?

Of realising how much I still think about him?

His phone buzzed in his pocket, and for a moment, he thought it was Tom calling again.

But he hasn't called for a while, has he? Tom's given up at last.

Cold trickled through him at the thought.

He pulled his phone out and expelled a breath when he saw Ari's number. "Hello there."

"Hey, it's been a while. All done studying?"

"Yup, all done."

"Great." He paused. "Listen, are you okay to come in and shoot a scene for me?"

"When?" Maybe that was what he needed.

"End of the week?"

"Sure. What kind of scene?"

"It's for the *Hard Hats* site."

His stomach clenched. "What's the deal?"

"Basically, you'll play a straight guy who gets seduced into sex with the builder who's working on your house."

His pulse quickened. "Who's my screen partner?"

Not Tom.

Not Tom.

Except there was a tiny part of him that wanted it to be him.

"I've got a couple of people still to call. There's this new guy I think you'll like. Built like a brick shithouse. Huge dick."

Despite his churning stomach, Denny chuckled. "Ari, according to you, they all have huge dicks."

"Hey, I'm supplying a service, meeting a need. If the subscribers want big dicks, then that's what they'll get. So... are you up for it?"

A new guy.

Not Tom.

Denny could cope with that.

"Yeah, that works."

"Great. Friday afternoon okay?" Denny told him that was fine. "I'll be shooting two scenes back-to-back, so make sure you're prepped."

Denny's dildo had seen a lot of action in recent weeks. "I can do that."

"Fantastic." Another pause. "You okay?"

Denny frowned. "Why do you ask?"

"Oh, nothing. Just something I thought I heard in your voice. Just checking, that's all."

"I'm fine. I'll see you Friday." And before Ari could ask another question, Denny hung up.

I need to get back into this. More scenes, more OnlyFans videos with hot guys, to chip away at his debts. He hadn't filmed for Ari since—

Since before the barbecue.

He hadn't filmed with anyone since then.

Lisa was right. Time to shove off the layers of cotton wool and rejoin the land of the living.

And if he saw Tom while he was out and about?

He'd deal with that when—if—the time came.

CHAPTER THIRTY

Denny perused the box full of underwear. "Are you kidding? I can't go commando?"

"No, you can't," Ari retorted. "You're supposed to be a straitlaced businessman."

He rummaged through the assorted boxers, briefs, jockstraps, and thongs, smiling when something caught his eye. "Ooh. I can picture our businessman in this." Denny held up a white lacy thong.

Ari rolled his eyes. "Will you be serious for a moment?" He strode to where the box sat on the table, peered into it, then yanked out a pair of white briefs. "Those. They'll fit." He dropped them onto the table.

"But they're boring."

Ari grinned. "That's because *he's* boring. Now put 'em on, then choose a suit."

"You don't expect me to wear a tie, do you?" Denny glanced at the wall rack. "Because frankly, your taste in ties is hideous." He gazed longingly at the lace briefs. "Could I borrow these?"

Ari arched his eyebrows. "Something you wanna tell me?"

"I like to jazz things up a bit now and then for the OnlyFans stuff."

Ari chuckled. "Well, they'd certainly do that." He pointed to the rack of suits. "Look the part, okay? Professional. Straight. You've never fucked a guy in your life, but all that is about to change when the builder comes onto you."

He laughed. "You know what I love about porn, Ari? How it's nothing like reality. The builder isn't even going to ask if this guy is gay, is he? There'll just be the assumption that they're going to fuck."

"Hey, this one has a plot," Ari remonstrated. "You're pissed with his work so far, and you make noises about ruining his rep. So he'll do anything to keep your mouth shut."

"Sure—like shove his cock in it." Denny held up his hands. "Not that I'm complaining." He was suddenly aware of the lump of silicone in his arse. "Oops. I'd better take the butt plug out."

"Bend over, I'll do it."

Denny batted his eyelashes. "Why, Ari… you sweet man."

Ari snorted, and Denny removed his towel. He put his hands on the seat of a chair, spread his legs a little, and Ari withdrew the plug with care, Denny trying to relax. He straightened, and Ari slapped it into his palm.

Denny dropped it into his bag. "So where's my screen partner?"

"He'll be here any second." Ari hesitated before continuing. "Look, Denny, about that…"

Denny frowned. "What's up?" He turned as the door opened, and—

"No fucking *way*." Denny couldn't breathe.

Tom stood there in jeans and a tight-fitting tee, his chest heaving. "Hi."

Denny gaped. "'Hi'? That's all you have to say?"

Before Tom could even open his mouth, Ari blurted, "I'll pay you an extra five hundred on top of your usual rate."

Denny folded his arms. "A grand." Ari could pay through the nose for pulling a stunt like this. Besides, he could afford it.

Ari swallowed. "Okay, a grand."

"Each."

Ari widened his eyes, then sighed. "Fine. Deal." Denny smiled, his heart still thumping. Ari cleared his throat. "And in case you're interested, I'm only paying both of you extra because it's a flip flop scene." He speared Denny with a searching glance. "You okay with that?"

Flip flop?

Denny's heartbeat slipped into a higher gear, his mouth open.

Ari smirked. "I'll take that as a yes. Now get your arse into a costume." His gaze flickered in Tom's direction. "I'll leave you two alone for a bit. I think you have some talking to do before we shoot." One last glance at Denny. "Give me a shout when you're ready." He walked out of the room.

Tom took a deep breath. "Are we going to talk?"

Denny stuck out his chin. "After." His heart was still racing. Fuck, this was so surreal. He was standing there, naked, his cock jerking.

Only, Tom's attention was nowhere near Denny's shaft—he was looking him in the eye.

"Why not now?"

"Because I'm getting into character." The words sounded lame and petulant. "I'm the client who's pissed at your shoddy workmanship—or didn't you read the brief? And you're supposed to win me over with your body." He met Tom's gaze. "Good luck with that."

He was doing his best to stay mad, but it was difficult when warmth radiated through him and adrenaline spiked through his system.

God, it's great to see him.

Even his dick was happy to see him.

Denny cleared his throat. "I know Ari probably thinks this is a good idea, but—"

"I fucked up, all right?" Tom's words reverberated around the small room.

He blinked. "What?" He picked up the towel from where he'd dropped it and wrapped it around his hips.

Tom pushed out a long breath. "I fucked up." His voice

was softer. "I shouldn't have said any of those things I did, but I was afraid, okay?"

"Of what?"

"Getting too close." Another exhale. "I... You remember I said I wasn't like you? How I couldn't keep my emotions divorced from sex, not the way you could. Only... it wasn't just the sex. The more time I spent with you, the more I realised I... I was falling for you. But I couldn't let myself do that, not when I knew you were only in it for the money. The last thing you needed was some straight guy losing his heart to you."

Oh my fucking God, the irony...

"I told Deb I didn't like having sex with you." Tom locked gazes with him. "That was a lie. I loved it, but... When you asked about doing another OnlyFans scene, all I could think of was that if I did, my secret would be out. I wouldn't be able to hide it. And then... I'd lose you."

"You weren't the only one who fucked up," Denny said, his heart racing. When Tom frowned, he shivered. "I shouldn't have kissed you that night. Our first kiss?" Tom nodded. "Because I had a secret too. That guy I was in love with years ago? The one I told you about? He was my straight best friend." He swallowed. "Except we were fucking too, and I thought that meant something—that *I* meant something to him. And then I made the mistake of telling him how I felt."

"He wasn't interested."

Another hard swallow. "Not at all."

Tom shuddered out a breath. "And he broke your heart."

He nodded. "So I made a decision. The only straight guys I fuck are the ones I'm doing a scene with. Strictly business." He stared at Tom. "And then you came along." He paused. "That day at the bus stop, when I said I was falling for you... why didn't you tell me how you felt?"

Tom's eyes widened. "You ran off, remember? And every time I called, texted, emailed, you wouldn't answer. How was I supposed to tell you how I felt when every time I tried, I hit a brick wall?" He gestured to their surroundings. "This was all I had left. I begged Ari to let me do this. I made him promise not to tell you, because I knew if you found out you were filming with me, you'd run a mile."

"*You* arranged this?"

Tom smiled. "Ari was my last shot." He cocked his head. "Do you... do you want to do this? Now you know it's with me?"

"Was it your idea to make it a flip flop scene?"

Tom nodded. He bit his lip. "A couple of days ago, I bought the longest dildo I could find. I've been playing with it ever since. I even bought a butt plug. I wanted to be ready for you." He took a step toward Denny, then another, until at last they were toe to toe. He leaned in, their foreheads meeting. "I've missed you so much," he whispered.

"Missed you too."

"There's something more I need to tell you."

Denny's pulse quickened. "What is it?"

"I know the truth now. I'm not straight—I'm bi. And I'm not going anywhere. And..."

Denny couldn't wait another second. He tilted his chin. Tom's lips were right there, and—

The knock at the door made them jump apart. "Is it safe to come in?"

Denny laughed. "Come right in, Ari. I think we're ready for you."

They'd worked out their dialogue, plus a rough outline of how the scene would go. The set was a living room, with a brick fireplace at one end. Lamps gave the impression it was night-time, and most of the floor space was taken up by a large three-seater Chesterfield sofa in oxblood red, its rolled back wide enough to lie on.

At least, Tom *hoped* it was, seeing as he'd be the one lying on it. Ari quipped that no one had fallen off it recently, which didn't help to quell his nerves, but he wasn't about to change his mind.

If this was to be his last shoot, he might as well go out with a bang.

Literally.

Besides, there was something else he needed to tell Denny, and he'd thought of the perfect opportunity to do it.

He agreed.

One obstacle crossed. One goal left.

"Nice couch, Ari," he commented. "Leather, though?"

Ari grinned. "Cum cleans right off it." He got behind the camera. "Get into your places."

Denny and Tom stood in front of the fireplace facing each other, Denny's arms folded, Tom's hands by his sides, his heartbeat racing.

"Ready?" Denny asked.

"As I'll ever be." He looked Denny up and down.

"What's wrong?"

"It's just that… I've never seen you in a suit before." Denny wore a white shirt open at the collar, beneath a dark blue jacket.

Denny grinned, his gaze dipping lower for a second. "I don't have to ask if you like it, do I?" He inched closer. "One evening we'll go out for dinner, and I promise to wear a suit."

"I'll hold you to that."

Denny's eyes gleamed. "You can hold me in it too—before

you get to take it off."

"When you two have quite finished with the banter…" Ari gave them a mock glare. "In case you missed it, there's a porno being filmed here. Now get back into your places."

"Yes sir." Denny grinned.

"And… Action."

Denny glared at Tom. "I'm not paying you. I refuse to pay for shoddy workmanship."

"I'll fix it," Tom promised.

"You think it's *that* easy? What would people say if they knew what kind of cowboy you are?"

"What?"

"You don't think this will get out? Word travels fast."

Tom frowned. "But… I could lose business if you do that."

"As if I care about that."

Shit, the dialogue was corny as hell, and Tom had no idea how Denny managed to deliver it with a straight face.

And Denny was staring at him, waiting for the next line.

"I'll do anything to keep my reputation."

Denny arched his eyebrows. "Like what?"

Here we go.

Tom took a step toward him, then another, and another, until they were only a hand's width apart. He stroked Denny's cheek with a single finger, down to his Adam's apple, pausing at the hollow at the base of Denny's neck before tracing a line all the way to Denny's waistband.

Denny's breathing hitched. "What are you doing?"

Fuck, he's good at this. Tom could really believe he was a straight guy.

He trailed his finger lower still until he met the outline of Denny's stiff cock pushing against the fabric of his trousers. He raised his head.

"Seeing if you're interested." He smiled. "You are." It was a heady sensation, knowing he was responsible for Denny's arousal.

"Take off your jacket."

Denny did so, taking his time. He placed it over one end of the sofa.

"Come here."

Denny walked back to him, and Tom took hold of his collar, tugging him closer. "Let's see." He unbuttoned Denny's shirt, baring his chest, then bent to flick Denny's nipple with his tongue.

A tremor rippled through Denny. "You... You need to stop that."

Tom cupped the bulge in Denny's trousers. "Why?" He gave it a gentle squeeze. "You're getting harder."

Denny shuddered. "If you think you're going to have your way with me, you can kiss my arse."

Tom grinned. "Funny. That was exactly what I had in mind." He mentally rolled his eyes.

Who writes this stuff?

He pulled Denny's shirt free of his waistband, then removed it. "Do I get to do that?"

Tom nodded, and Denny grasped the hem of his tee. Tom raised his arms, Denny yanked it over his head, and tossed it aside. They faced each other, naked from the waist up, and Tom moved in, cupping Denny's chin, tilted his face toward Tom's, closing the gap between them until their lips were almost touching.

"Don't," Denny murmured.

Tom paused. "Do you mean that?"

Denny's eyes met his, and for a moment there was silence. Finally, he shook his head.

"No."

A moment's hesitation, and then the dam burst. Denny's hands were on his neck, Tom cradled Denny's head, and they kissed, murmuring nonsensical words, soft moans of pleasure, Tom's tongue going deep. Denny opened for him, and Tom let go of all the fears and anxiety that had plagued him during the last few weeks, holding Denny steady while he claimed his lips over and over again.

Denny responded with a hunger Tom hadn't expected, his chest pressed to Tom's, his musky scent stirring something deep inside him.

"Oh, nice." Ari's whisper of approval made Tom feel as if he could walk on water.

Ari gave a signal, and Tom unbuttoned Denny's trousers, then his own. That was all it took to have both of them in motion, Tom reaching into Denny's tight white briefs to release his long, hard cock, Denny doing the same. They didn't stop kissing, Denny's finger in his crack, his in Denny's, his dick poking Denny's hip, pre-cum leaving a trail on his tanned skin.

Denny had said he was ready to go.

Tom's cock apparently had the same idea.

He spun Denny around. "Grab hold of the mantelpiece."

Denny did as instructed, arching his back, tilting his hips. Tom worked his own dick, rubbing the head through Denny's crease.

"Please," Denny begged. "Go slow."

Tom knelt behind him, tugged Denny's trousers and briefs down to his ankles, and spread his cheeks, revealing his glistening pucker.

"I believe you said something about kissing your arse?"

He buried his face in Denny's crack, licking over his hole, pushing at it, feeling it loosen, opening for him. Denny reached back and held him there, his hips rolling, his cock hard and pointing toward the fireplace.

"Don't stop."

Tom probed his hole, loving the moans pouring from Denny's lips, spurring him to delve deeper, to push Denny to his limits. Then he remembered. He rubbed his beard over Denny's hole, and the moan of pleasure bursting from him made Tom's heart sing. And when Denny twisted to stare back at him, his mouth open, eyes pleading, Tom knew he was ready.

Then Ari called a halt, and Tom cursed his timing.

Now I know why Denny prefers shooting his OnlyFans videos.

"Okay, lose the clothes."

He helped Denny out of his briefs and trousers, then stood. He spat into his palm before swiping it over the head of his dick. Ari threw Tom the bottle of lube as pre-arranged, and he slicked up his shaft. Once the bottle was out of sight, Ari went back to his camera, Denny bent his leg, exposing his hole, and Tom penetrated him slowly, catching his breath at the exquisite sensation of silken heat surrounding his cock.

"Fuck, you're tight," he groaned. He held onto Denny's waist, moving in and out of him at a leisurely pace, maintaining the illusion of claiming a virgin hole. Denny moaned, keeping still, bowing his head. It wasn't long before Tom picked up a little speed, anchoring himself to Denny's shoulders, hips pumping as he thrust faster, harder, punctuating each drive of his dick with kisses down Denny's back, Tom's jeans still wedged around his ankles.

"Stop!"

Tom pulled free of him, knowing what was coming.

Denny straightened and turned to face him, his face flushed, his chest too. "Can I fuck you?" He tugged on his rigid shaft.

Tom's chest heaved.

Sofa time.

"Yes. But you'll need to go slow too."

Denny smiled. "Don't worry. I'll take care of you."

Tom believed that with all his heart.

"Now remember," Ari said as he picked up the mobile camera. "Don't keep your noises to yourself. And dirty talk is okay."

"You edit out your instructions, don't you?" Tom inquired.

"Yeah, and other stuff." Ari grinned. "Like the times when my actors call each other by their real names." He shrugged. "It happens."

"It's not as if we have lines for this part," Denny added. "It's mostly a lot of 'fuck yeah.'"

Tom's heartbeat raced. He had one line to deliver, one Ari knew nothing about.

All he had to do was wait for the right moment.

CHAPTER THIRTY-ONE

Tom positioned himself on the back of the sofa. "This feels awfully precarious." His arse rested on the edge, his legs spread.

Denny moved to stand between them. "I won't let you fall, okay?" He drank in the sight: Tom's quivering belly, his firm thighs, his taut nipples, and his cock, rising into the air, so hard it made Denny's hole tighten. "I want that back inside me."

Tom grasped his shaft around the base, and their eyes met. "Later," he whispered.

Ari coughed. "Er, guys?"

Denny bent over, loving the strangled gasp that fell from Tom's lips as he swallowed his cock to the root, conscious of Ari zooming in for a close-up.

"Oh fuck." A full body shiver ricocheted through Tom, his breathing quickening as Denny bobbed his head, Tom's leg hooked over Denny's shoulder. A whimper fell from his lips when Denny flicked the head with his tongue before kissing and sucking on his balls.

Tom craned his neck to give Denny a beseeching stare. "Tease my hole."

Ari changed position, giving him the thumbs up. Denny licked a finger, and Ari focused on Tom's face while Denny applied edible lube. Then Ari was back, and Denny pushed into him, taking his time, bending over once more to take Tom's cock into his mouth, his thumb rubbing over Tom's taint.

Denny didn't want to be filming a scene. He wanted to be alone with Tom, no audience, free to do what they liked, with no time constraints or observation of camera angles.

And definitely no bubble-gum-flavoured lube.

He wanted to lose himself in it all: the whimpers and sighs Tom made while Denny rimmed him; the slick sound of Tom's hand working his own shaft; the breathless cry of "Fuck" when Denny insinuated his tongue deeper into Tom's hole; and the sight of pre-cum dripping from Tom's slit when Denny massaged his prostate.

And when he couldn't wait a second longer, Denny held his breath as he slid his dick into Tom. "So fucking tight," he murmured.

Ari changed position to focus on Denny's shaft as he penetrated Tom, until at last he was all the way inside him.

Tom's gaze met his. "Feels good," he whispered. He tugged on his dick, and Denny waited for the signal. Tom gave a nod. "You can move now."

Denny leaned over to kiss Tom, his hands on Tom's chest as he moved in and out of him, slow as you please, his hips undulating. Tom's foot was still on his shoulder, and Denny kissed it, licking his sole and creating multiple shivers.

He drove his cock home, and Tom gasped. "You're so big."

Denny had expected a break by that point, but Ari hadn't stopped them, shifting around the couch, capturing them from all angles.

That was fine by Denny, because he didn't want to stop.

"Put your arms around me," he told Tom, and Tom locked them around Denny's neck. Denny lifted him until he was almost sitting upright, then gripped his nape as he drove into him. Tom worked his cock, and they kissed, Denny fucking him with long strokes, Tom clinging to him. Their lips met once more, and Denny slowed, feeding off the moans of pleasure Tom couldn't contain. He buried his shaft to the hilt in Tom's body, and held him close, his fingers dragging over Tom's damp back.

"I need to be inside you again," Tom said with a gasp.

Denny wanted that too.

He pulled free of Tom, Ari stopped filming, and they each took a drink. Then Denny got onto the sofa on all fours, his cock pointing like the nose of a fucking English setter.

Ari chuckled. "Someone's eager."

Tom grabbed the bottle of lube and applied some to his fingers before joining Denny on the sofa, kneeling at his arse. He bent low, and Denny arched his back as Tom sucked his dick, unable to suppress a moan when Tom fingered him.

Denny rocked, lost in the twin sensations, pushing back hard on Tom's fingers, thrusting into his warm mouth. Ari called for them to stop, and Denny had never been more ready to be fucked.

Tom slicked up his cock, shuffled forward, and guided the head to Denny's hole. One firm push, and Tom slid all the way home. Denny groaned, arching his back still further, and worked Tom's dick with his body, riding it hard, hips snapping, his breathing laboured. Tom held onto his waist, Denny's arse cheeks slamming into him as he fucked himself on Tom's steel shaft.

Tom bent down and kissed between his shoulder blades. "I want you on your back." He pulled free, and Denny flipped over, drawing his knees higher. His chest heaved as Tom brought the blunt head once more to his pucker.

Tom rolled his hips and buried his cock all the way inside him.

"Fuck, yes, like that."

He leaned over, his hand on Denny's cheek. "Love how it feels inside you." Then he claimed Denny's lips in a heated kiss, hips pistoning. Denny grabbed his shoulders and held on, his body buffeted as Tom rocked in and out of him, their lips still locked.

Then Tom nudged his sweet spot, and Denny groaned. "Oh, right fucking *there*." Tom did it again, and again, until Denny couldn't control his shivers. "That's it, fuck me."

Tom slammed into him, Denny's cries in sync with each drive of his shaft. "Like that?"

"Fuck yeah." He dug his fingers into Tom's broad shoulders, holding on as Tom filled him over and over.

A flush rose up Tom's chest, spreading higher, until his cheeks were stained with it. "Feels too good."

And then Denny felt it, that throbbing deep inside him, and his heart soared.

Tom broke the kiss and looked him in the eye, trembling. "I love you," he whispered.

He froze, heart pounding, a wave of light-headedness washing over him, crashing into him. Warmth infused his body, and a tingling surge started in his chest, spreading outward. Sunbursts filled his vision, and he wanted to rise weightless into the air.

He stared at Tom, his lucidity returning. "You choose *now* to fucking tell me?" Tom's eyes locked on his, his Adam's apple bobbed, and Denny realised what lay behind that steady gaze. He cupped Tom's bearded jaw and drew him down into a long, fervent kiss. "I love you too," he murmured against Tom's lips, not missing the tremors coursing through him. Then he grinned. "Now get your cock out of my arse because I'm gonna fuck you so hard, your eyes will roll back."

Ari cackled. "Really feeling the love here, guys. And by the way, thanks for the shitload of editing I'll need to do on this one."

Tom pulled free of Denny's body, and Denny gave his own shaft a couple of tugs. "Sit on my dick."

Tom squeezed lube into his palm and swiped it the length of Denny's cock. He straddled Denny's hips and sat back on it, one foot on the sofa, the other on the floor, working his dick as he sank all the way down. Denny tilted his hips, thrusting up while Tom kept still. And then it was Tom's turn to ride him, bouncing on his cock, their shallow, harsh breaths filling the air as they moved together.

Tom's eyes widened. "Fuck." He came again, shooting his load onto Denny's chest, and that was all it took to push Denny over the edge. He pulled Tom down to him and kissed him, Denny's cock pulsing inside him, both of them shaking in each other's arms.

Tom eased out of him, and at last Ari spoke. "Well, at least I know which scene I'll be entering for the porn awards next year."

Denny was only half-listening. He was too busy kissing Tom, stroking his back, his face, his neck. "You mean it?"

Tom smiled. "Every word. I was going to tell you before we started shooting, but we got interrupted." He glanced at Ari who was fiddling with the cameras. Then Tom kissed him again. "And I'm sorry for not saying it sooner."

"You're sure about this? That this is what you want?"

Tom's smile lit up his face. "I want *you*, pure and simple." He sighed. "I figured this was the only way left to me to tell you how I really felt."

"Then I'm glad I said yes to the shoot. I haven't done a scene for ages." Denny huffed. "Do you know how much money I could've made the last few weeks? I turned down so many guys wanting to shoot content."

Tom chuckled. "You made up for it with a lot of wanking scenes. So many, I was sure your dick was about to drop off."

Denny blinked. "You were watching?"

"Not only watching—I was wanking along with you, wishing it was *my* hand on your cock, my dick in your arse instead of that dildo."

Denny smiled. "Funny. I was thinking of you while I was doing it."

Ari snorted. "Whatever happened to romance? Less talk of dildos and wanking, and more hearts and flowers."

Denny chuckled. "You've heard of saying it with flowers? Well, Tom just said it with cum."

"Oh, I think I can do better than that." Tom launched himself off the sofa and ran naked across the room and out of the door.

Denny stared after him. "Where's he going?" Then the breath caught in his throat when Tom returned, carrying a large bouquet of red roses.

Tom glanced at Ari. "Was this more what you had in mind?"

Ari beamed. "*Now* I feel like fucking Cupid."

Denny gaped. "For me?" He sat up.

"Well, they're not for Ari." Tom gave him a sheepish smile. "I left them out of sight… just in case."

"In case I said no?"

Tom managed a shrug and handed the flowers to him.

Denny loved the red velvet petals, their soft perfume. "No one ever bought me flowers before."

Tom's face glowed. "And when we've showered, I'll take you out to dinner."

Was this real?

"I'm only going with you if you say it again." Denny needed to hear the words, to reassure himself it wasn't all some fantastic dream he was about to wake up from.

Tom walked slowly toward him. Denny placed the bouquet on the sofa and rose to meet him. Tom took him in his arms, tilting Denny's chin with his fingertips. "I love you."

If it was a dream, it was the best dream ever.

Denny stroked Tom's beard. "Love you too." He grinned. "Now feed me. Sex always makes me hungry."

Tom laughed. "I know." He bit his lip. "I don't suppose Ari would let you borrow that suit?"

Denny laughed. "Not a chance."

Tom's eyes sparkled. "In that case…" He leaned in, his lips brushing Denny's ear, making him shiver. "I saw this lace thong in the costume room…"

Denny burst out laughing. "I think we might need to steal it." A delicious idea crept into his mind.

And maybe I'll steal a jockstrap for Tom. One that showed off his glorious arse.

Tom kissed him on the lips. "You think Chris might let me in the house now?"

"He'd better, because he's going to be seeing a lot of you." Denny glanced at the walls surrounding them. "I wonder if Ari's got any of these soundproofing panels left."

They might come in handy.

Chapter Thirty-Two

September

Tom thought his heart was going to burst with pride when Denny strode toward the Chancellor of Regent's University and shook his hand. He applauded until his hands burned, conscious of Denny's grandmother beside him, cheering loudly as Denny was handed his diploma. Then Denny walked down the aisle, resplendent in his black gown and mortarboard, and his green hood edged in gold. He searched for them in the assembled guests, grinning when he found them. Then he joined the rest of the graduates on the other side of the auditorium.

Tom wasn't listening to the speeches that followed—he was too busy wishing the minutes away until he could hold Denny in his arms and congratulate him properly.

Grandma wiped her eyes with a hankie. "I'm so proud of that boy," she said through her sniffles.

Tom put his arm around her and hugged her. "Me too, Grandma."

She turned her face toward his. "You think you might call me Susan? Because you calling me Grandma sounds weird," she said, keeping her voice low.

He laughed. "Okay—Susan."

"So what's the plan for after this shindig?"

"Denny hasn't told you?"

She snorted. "Since when does that boy tell me anything? Besides, he's been too busy making himself pretty for this. Did you see the suit he's wearing under that robe?"

"I bought that for him." It had been Tom's graduation gift to him.

Susan beamed. "A man with good taste. Denny's a lucky boy."

"And as for what's planned…" Tom removed an envelope from his jacket pocket, slid out the folded sheet, and handed it to her.

Susan opened it, and her mouth fell open. "We're having lunch at the *Ritz*? Did you two win the lottery and not tell me?"

He chuckled. "This is from Robin, one of Denny's housemates. It's his graduation gift." When he'd learned Denny had invited his grandma to the ceremony, he'd suggested taking her to lunch afterwards. Then he'd presented them with the booking, insisting that a special occasion required a very special venue.

"In that case, I'm glad I bought a new dress for my visit." She peered at him. "Will I do?"

He smiled. "You look wonderful."

Then it was all over, and the guests stood to file out.

"Let's go find him." Tom handed Susan the cane she'd laid on the floor and helped her to her feet. Once they were in the lobby, it didn't take long for Denny to find them. He hugged his grandma, then gazed at Tom with expectant eyes.

Tom didn't hesitate. He cupped Denny's cheek, leaned in, and kissed him on the lips. Around them, some of the graduates whistled and applauded, calling out Denny's name. Denny flushed.

"Is this your boyfriend?" one of them asked.

He beamed. "You'd better believe it."

There'd been days in the last few weeks when Tom didn't believe his luck. His weekends were taken up with a visit to the Isle of Wight, dinner with Deb and Sharon, and a party thrown by Denny's housemates to celebrate him getting his master's. During the day, he couldn't wait for evening to come so he could be with Denny. And when Sunday night came around, he hated the thought that they had to be apart.

Look at me. Well and truly smitten.

It was a good state to be in.

Grandma stared at the Seville Orange Soufflé the waitress placed in front of her. "Oh, look at that," she cooed.

Denny chuckled. "You're not supposed to look at it—you're supposed to eat it." The food had been sublime, from the salmon starter, to the duck main course, and now the beautifully presented dessert. Piano music played in the background, and he gazed at the chandeliers, the mirrored walls, the sparkling crystal, the snow-white napkins, and the gorgeous yellow chrysanthemums at the centre of their table. A bottle of champagne sat in its ice bucket, a napkin draped around the neck.

A perfect setting for a celebration. Robin had nailed it.

He glanced at Tom, who reached across the gap between them to take Denny's hand in his. "Have I told you today how much I love you?"

Denny smiled, his heart light as air. "Yes, but I could stand to hear it again." He caught his breath when Tom raised Denny's hand to his lips and kissed the back of it.

Love you, he mouthed.

Love you too.

Grandma cleared her throat. "Can I interrupt for a second?"

Denny blinked. "I'm sorry. Did you say something?"

"I want to talk to you both, and it's important."

That stopped him in his tracks. "You're okay, aren't you? There's nothing wrong, is there?"

She smiled. "I'm absolutely fine. I don't plan on popping

my clogs any time soon." She paused. "But what I want to discuss is what happens *after* that."

"This feels like a morbid kind of conversation to be having, especially today," Tom remarked.

Grandma huffed. "That's the problem. No one ever wants to talk about death, but it comes to us all." She leaned back in her chair. "I need to discuss the house."

Denny frowned. "But you don't have one anymore."

"Oh yes I do. I put it in the hands of a letting agency, but it's still mine. What do you think pays for the retirement home? But when I die…" She smiled at Denny. "I'm leaving it to you."

Denny gaped. "But… surely it has to go to Mum."

She frowned. "Says who?"

"Isn't she a direct descendant?"

"Yes, but you are too. I checked. And why would I want to leave my property to someone who cut themselves off from me?" She patted Denny's hand. "It's all perfectly legal. I've had my will drawn up and everything. They'll probably still make you pay tax on it, but who knows by then?"

Denny didn't know what to say.

"But you're not going to die for a long time," he said at last.

Grandma chuckled. "Does that mean you're okay with it?"

"Do I have a choice?"

She shrugged. "When I'm gone, you can sell it if you like." Her eyes gleamed. "Or… you could keep it and live in it. Think about that. You'd have a house on the island long before you're old enough to want to retire there." She picked up her spoon. "And now I think I've put off eating my dessert for long enough."

Tom chuckled. "She'd give Deb a run for her money in the stubborn streaks," he muttered.

Denny's phone buzzed. He turned it over and frowned. "It's Ari." He stood. "Excuse me a minute," he said to Grandma before walking over to the window. He clicked on Answer.

"Hello."

"Is this a good time to talk?"

Denny glanced at their table where Grandma and Tom were chatting. "Not really. What's up?"

"So it's official? You're qualified?"

"As of an hour or so ago, yes."

"Great. I've got a job for you to consider."

What the—

"I hate to tell you this, but I'm thinking of quitting the business." He'd already broached the subject with Tom.

"Why?"

"You *know* why. Because I need to get a proper job, and my future employer might not like the idea of me having that particular second career."

"Oh, I see. But it's not what you think. Could you meet me for lunch on Friday? Balans? I know you like that place."

There was a tingling at the base of Denny's neck. "Talk about intriguing."

Ari laughed. "All will be revealed. You can bring Tom too. He might want to hear this."

Now Denny really was curious.

He said goodbye and hung up.

"What was that all about?" Tom asked when he rejoined them.

"I won't know until Friday." He glanced at Grandma. "Let's discuss this later."

They had an afternoon of sightseeing planned before they took her to her hotel for the night.

Ari could wait.

Balans was heaving, and Denny scanned the tables, searching for Ari.

Max grinned as he walked toward them. "Hey. Your friend's already here. He's at the back." His gaze went to Tom, and he batted his eyelashes. "Well, hello again, handsome."

Denny swatted him on the backside. "Oy. He's mine."

Max widened his eyes. "No kidding." He gave Denny a hug. "Then no wonder I haven't seen you around." He smirked. "You've obviously been busy." He led them through to the rear of the restaurant, where Ari was perusing the menu card, a cocktail already in front of him. He stood as they neared the table.

"Congratulations!" He seized Denny in a hug, then held out his hand to Tom, and they shook. Ari gestured to the chairs facing him. "Take a seat."

"Do I have to ask what you're drinking?" Max inquired.

Denny beamed, but Tom gave him a warning glance. "Can we stick to a limit this time?"

He laughed. "No more than two, how about that?"

Ari leaned back. "Okay, let's get down to business. You know I have a few porn sites, right?"

Denny snorted. "I've lost count. You keep adding to them." When Tom gave him a puzzled glance, Denny explained. "He has a *lot* of sites. Hard Hats was just his latest venture."

Ari opened the manila folder on the table next to his glass and handed a stapled document to Denny. "Take a look."

Denny stared at the list. "You own all these?" He'd had no idea.

Ari nodded. "I had a goal—to be the owner of the largest group of gay porn sites in the UK. Maybe even the US." He tapped the sheet with his finger. "What makes these different is that they are *all* gay-owned and gay-run."

Denny sagged into his chair. "I thought you were doing well, but… this is incredible." He frowned. "So why am I here?"

"I'm launching all the sites under one new umbrella—and I want *you* to manage it."

Denny blinked. "Seriously?"

Ari nodded. "You'd be in charge of all the output, organising content, marketing, social media… And I've got loads of ideas I want to try out. I'm thinking of branching into erotic fiction." Ari looked him in the eye. "It'd be a full-time job, Denny, but you can do it. Plus, I'd have someone running things who knows the industry. And if you wanted to keep shooting content for OnlyFans, that'd be okay too." His eyes twinkled. "With one particular screen partner, I'd imagine."

Tom laughed. "I'm glad you added that last part."

Ari gave Tom a beaming smile. "Want to join us? You were a real draw."

Tom returned his smile. "No thanks." He took Denny's hand and squeezed it. "My business has taken off since Denny got his hands on it."

Denny's chest swelled.

Ari sighed. "Pity." Then he brightened. "I guess that only leaves one question. Do I get an invite?"

Denny stared at him, perplexed. "An invite to what?"

Ari gestured to their joined hands. "The wedding, of course."

The what?

Denny and Tom turned to face each other.

Tom swallowed. "You're not laughing at the idea."

"Neither are you."

And now Denny was thinking about it.

Ari snorted. "For fuck's sake. Go get a room and talk about it."

Denny found his voice. "I think it's a little too soon to be talking wedding bells." Another glance at Tom. "Don't you?"

Tom's brisk nod told him he found the idea as scary as Denny did.

We're not ready for that.

Yet.

"So? What about my proposal?" Ari demanded. "Do I have a new CEO?"

Denny looked at Tom, who laughed. "It sounds perfect for you."

He beamed. "Then yes, I'll do it."

Graduation and a new career, in the space of a few days.

And something else further off in the future, a huge something that made his heart thump and his pulse race.

CHAPTER THIRTY-THREE

Eight months later

Tom wiped his lips with his napkin. "That was delicious, as always. No wonder we keep coming back here." The Surrey Palace had to be his favourite Indian restaurant.

Denny snorted. "Are you sure it's the food, and not the fact that this place is about a four-minute walk from your house? And it *is* a nice place." He glanced at the restaurant's interior. "I love the purple lighting. Plus, the seats are comfortable." He cocked his head. "And speaking of comfortable... you got room for dessert?"

"If dessert means their lemon sorbet served in a scooped-out lemon, then yes." He peered at the plate that had contained his coconut rice. "That was a little odd though."

"What was?"

Denny's eyes were *way* too wide and innocent.

Tom narrowed his gaze. "Did *you* have something to do with my rice arriving in the shape of a heart?"

"Maybe?"

Tom chuckled. "They must have loved that in the kitchen."

"They were really nice about it when I called them to ask."

"But why a heart?"

"No special reason." Then Denny coughed, and Tom was instantly on the alert.

Have I missed something?

He racked his brains. First the heart-shaped rice—no, *before* that. Denny had been jumpy ever since Tom got home from work—then Denny's feigned innocence...

331

"This isn't just a Friday night date, is it?" It was a habit they'd gotten into, a chance to put work behind them, relax, enjoy a good meal—and then back to Tom's to reconnect in his bed.

Except it would soon be *their* bed. Denny had agreed to move in with him.

Bingo.

"Is this to celebrate your moving in with me?"

"Not exactly." Denny wiped his lips. "Do you know what today is?"

Aw shit. He *had* missed something. "No."

"We met a year ago today." Denny grinned. "On a couch."

Tom's chest tightened. "I'm sorry. I didn't know."

Denny waved a hand. "Hey, no need to apologise. I'd forgotten too. I know we count our first date as being after that scene last September, but then Ari sent me something today. It was a still from the shoot, and he'd written *Happy Anniversary.*"

Tom raised his glass. "Happy Anniversary, love."

Denny's face glowed. "You too." They drank a little of the chilled white wine.

"Oh. I knew there was something I'd forgotten to tell you." Tom put down his glass. "You know that new job I was starting today? Renovating some guy's bathroom? Well, when I got there, it turned out he was married—and I got to meet his husband."

Denny laughed. "This is beginning to sound like the plot for one of Ari's videos. Don't tell me—they wanted you to join them in a threesome."

Tom joined in with the laughter. "No, nothing like that." He stroked his beard. "Although they *were* hot." Denny's mouth fell open, and Tom chuckled. "I love pulling your leg."

Denny gave him a speculative glance. "We *have* talked about this, right? If you ever feel you want to…"

Tom nodded. "I know." Denny's porn career had given him a whole new perspective on sex. *Who knows? Maybe one day I'll want to… explore a little.* Denny had helped him understand it was okay to want to try new experiences. He didn't want Tom to have any hangups about sex.

Not that Denny was much of a porn star these days, not since Ari had taken over his life with the job. The only content he made was their OnlyFans stuff.

That brought him back into the moment.

"What I was *trying* to tell you was… they recognised me."

Denny gaped. "Where from?"

"OF. They're subscribers." Tom laughed. "And you're not gonna believe what happened next. One of them went to his laptop, pulled up one of our videos, did a screenshot, printed it out—and then asked me to sign it."

"No shit." Denny bit his lip. "Just how hot were they?"

Tom took Denny's hand across the table. "Not as hot as the man I see in front of me." He squeezed it. "The man I love."

Denny flushed. "Tom, I… I wanted tonight to be special."

"Does that mean you're going to wear the lace thong again?" Tom teased.

Denny grinned. "If you're going to wear that jock, then yes. But I—"

His phone pinged, and Tom's rang.

Tom rolled his eyes. "Hold that thought."

Denny turned his phone over and stilled. "It's a text from Lisa."

Tom jerked his head up. "Sharon's calling."

"Answer it!"

Tom put the phone to his ear. "Hi. Is—"

"You need to get to Epsom General."

"What?"

"Deb's had the baby."

"When?"

"An hour ago. Her labour lasted just under fifteen hours."

"Well, why didn't you tell us?"

"Deb wanted to wait until it was all over. And fifteen hours is normal for a first-time mum. We asked Lisa not to tell you either. She was wonderful, by the way."

"Tell me when we get there. We're on our way." He hung up and opened Uber.

Denny opened his text. "It says *Get over here now.*" He frowned. "Is Deb in labour?"

"She was, for about fifteen hours. She's already had the baby."

"Why didn't Sharon call? And why didn't Lisa tell us? She's their midwife."

"I'll tell you all about it in the Uber." He pushed out a breath. "There's a car on the way. It'll be here in two minutes."

"Great. You go outside and wait for it, I'll settle the bill."

Tom grabbed his jacket and ran for the door, his heart hammering. Fifteen hours of labour? Something in Sharon's voice told him it hadn't been an easy ride.

Epsom General Hospital, here we come.

Tom headed for Deb's private room, Denny behind him. It had only been twenty-five minutes since Sharon's call, and he'd asked their Uber driver to step on it.

Then he saw Sharon waiting at the door.

She was smiling.

Deb's okay. Thank God.

Tom came to a halt in front of her. "Well?"

"Well? Is it a boy or a girl?" Denny demanded.

Sharon grinned. "Yes."

It took him a moment to compute.

"Twins? It... it can't be. They'd have told you ages ago."

"They did." Her eyes sparkled. "Longest secret we ever kept. Twins run in my family."

Things slotted into place. "*Now* I know why you've never let us see the baby's new room."

"Uh-huh. It would've given the game away. Want to see the new mum?"

Tom wanted nothing more.

Sharon pushed open the door and they walked into the small room. Deb lay in a bed, red-faced with burst blood vessels around her eyes. Tom hurried over to her and kissed her on the cheek.

"Are you okay? You look exhausted."

Deb gave him a mock glare. "*You* try delivering two bowling balls and see how tired *you* feel." She smiled when Denny kissed her cheek.

"I think you look beautiful," he murmured.

She beamed. "*You* get to stay. Him? I'll think about it."

Two incubators sat on the other side of the bed. Tom went around and stood there, staring down at the two tiny figures, fast asleep.

"Are they okay?"

Deb hadn't been due for another three weeks.

Deb gazed at them, her eyes warm. "It got a little scary for a moment, but yeah, they're okay. They'll just need a lot of TLC for a while." She sagged back against the pillows and gave them a tired smile. "I'm glad you came."

"As if we'd stay away." Tom couldn't take his eyes off the babies. *So tiny.*

Sharon joined him. She sniffed. "Why do you smell of curry?"

He narrowed his gaze but said nothing.

Deb turned her head to stare at her new offspring. "I wanted you to meet your godson and goddaughter, Tommy and

Tricia."

"You picked names already?" Then he chuckled. "Of course you have. You knew you were having twins." Then Tom blinked. "You want me to be their godfather?" Warmth spread through him.

She nodded. "Both of you."

Denny beamed. "Aw, I'd love to."

She studied him with arched eyebrows. "When are you going to make an honest man of Tom?" Her lips twitched.

Denny rolled his eyes. "Well, if Sharon hadn't called to say you'd had the baby—sorry, *babies*—sending us over here in a mad rush, we'd probably be engaged by now."

Tom's heart stuttered. "What?" His pulse quickened, his breathing too.

Denny's eyes shone. "That's if you say yes, of course."

"If he doesn't, I'll kill him," Deb muttered.

Denny reached into his jacket pocket and pulled out a ring box. "I was just winding up to ask you." He opened it, and Tom swallowed at the sight of a wide gold engraved band. He removed it from its velvet bed and turned it. The engraving went all the way around, a dragon eating its own tail.

"Does this mean something?" Fuck, he was trembling.

"It's Ouroboros, one of the most ancient symbols, from Egypt—or was it Ancient Greece? I can't remember." Denny smiled. "All I know is, it means eternity, or something like it. And you haven't given me an answer."

Tom wanted to laugh and cry all at the same time. "Yes, of course."

Denny's smile widened. He took Tom's left hand in his and slipped the ring onto his finger. "Thank God. I chose the size based on your wedding ring that I found in a drawer. I was hoping your finger hadn't got fat since you last wore it." He looked Tom in the eye. "Love you."

Tom took Denny in his arms and kissed him, aware of Deb

and Sharon's mingled happy sighs.

Denny tilted his face toward Tom's, his eyes twinkling. "Now, aren't you glad you took the bait a year ago?"

Tom smiled. "*I* might have taken the bait, but *you're* the one who's proved to be quite a catch."

THANK YOU

As always, a huge thank you to my beta team.

Special thanks to Daniel Parry – it was so good to be plotting with you again!
Especially over a porn star martini in Balans…

Coming next from K.C. Wells

<u>In His Sights (Second Sight #1)</u>

Random letters belong on Scrabble tiles, not dead bodies. But when a demented serial killer targets Boston's gay population, leaving cryptic messages carved into his victims, lead detective Gary Mitchell has no choice but to play along.

As the body count rises, Gary gets desperate enough to push aside his skepticism and accept the help of a psychic. Dan Porter says he can offer new clues, and Gary needs all the insight into the killer's mind he can get.

Dan has lived with his gift–sometimes his curse–his entire life. He feels compelled to help, but only if he can keep his involvement secret. Experience has taught him to be cautious of the police and the press, but his growing connection to Gary distracts him from the real danger. As they edge closer to solving the puzzle, Dan finds himself in the killer's sights....

CONTACT KC

Website: www.kcwellswrites.com
Newsletter: http://eepurl.com/cNKHlT
I'd love to hear from you, so if you want to say hello or have any questions, please contact me and I'll get back to you:
Email: k.c.wells@btinternet.com

ALSO BY K.C. WELLS

Step by Step
Bromantically Yours
BFF

Collars & Cuffs
An Unlocked Heart
Trusting Thomas
Someone to Keep Me (K.C. Wells & Parker Williams)
A Dance with Domination
Damian's Discipline (K.C. Wells & Parker Williams)
Make Me Soar
Dom of Ages (K.C. Wells & Parker Williams)
Endings and Beginnings (K.C. Wells & Parker Williams)

Secrets – with Parker Williams
Before You Break
An Unlocked Mind
Threepeat
On the Same Page

Personal
Making it Personal
Personal Changes
More than Personal
Personal Secrets
Strictly Personal
Personal Challenges
Personal – The complete series

Confetti, Cake & Confessions
(FREE)

Christmas

Connections
Saving Jason
A Christmas Promise
The Law of Miracles
My Christmas Spirit
A Guy for Christmas
Dear Santa
Santa's Secrets

<u>Island Tales</u>
Waiting for a Prince
September's Tide
Submitting to the Darkness
Island Tales Vol 1 (Books #1 & #2)

<u>Lightning Tales</u>
Teach Me
Trust Me
See Me
Love Me

<u>A Material World</u>
Lace
Satin
Silk
Denim

<u>Southern Boys</u>
Truth & Betrayal
Pride & Protection
Desire & Denial
The Southern Boys Trilogy

<u>Maine Men</u>

Finn's Fantasy
Ben's Boss
Seb's Summer
Dylan's Dilemma
Shaun's Salvation
Aaron's Awakening
Levi's Love
Maine Men – the Complete Series

Salvation
Wrangled

Second Sight
In His Sights
In Plain Sight

CrossBow Protection
Broken Warrior

Standalones
Kel's Keeper
Here For You
Sexting The Boss
Gay on a Train
Sunshine & Shadows
Double or Nothing
Back from the Edge
Switching it up
Out for You (FREE)
State of Mind (FREE)
No More Waiting (FREE)
Watch and Learn
My Best Friend's Brother
Princely Submission

Bears in the Woods
Holy Hell – with Parker Williams
Teasing Tim
Str8 B8

Anthologies

<u>Fifty Gays of Shade</u>
Winning Will's Heart

<u>Come, Play</u>
Watch and Learn

<u>Writing as Tantalus</u>
Damon & Pete: Playing with Fire

ABOUT THE AUTHOR

K.C. Wells lives on an island off the south coast of the UK, surrounded by natural beauty. She writes about men who love men, and can't even contemplate a life that doesn't include writing.

The rainbow rose tattoo on her back with the words 'Love is Love' and 'Love Wins' is her way of hoisting a flag. She plans to be writing about men in love - be it sweet or slow, hot or kinky - for a long while to come.